Lisa,
Congratulate...
you enjoy.
Judith Erwin
11/2021

FAITH LOST

Shepherd & Associates Series — Book 2

JUDITH ERWIN

Emerald Cat Press

USA

Judith Erwin / Emerald Cat Press
Jacksonville, Florida
www.juditherwinofficialwebsite.com

Publisher's Note: This is a work of fiction. Names, characters, places, and incidents are a product of the author's imagination or used fictionally. Locales, entities, and public names are sometimes used for atmospheric purposes, but people and events are entirely fiction. Any resemblance to actual people, living or dead, or to businesses, companies, events, institutions, or locales is completely coincidental.

Book Layout © 2017 BookDesignTemplates.com

Cover Image: iStock.com/CHAINATP
Dog image (on Jake's card): Amelia Erwin
Cover Design: Marigrace Doran and Judith Erwin
Editor: John C. Boles

FAITH LOST / Judith Erwin. -- 1st ed.

ISBN" 978-0-9997056-4-3 - Trade Paperback
ISBN: 978-0-9997056-5-0   e-Book

Library of Congress Control Number: 2021920208

Dedicated to

The admirable men and women of law enforcement
who leave home daily, putting their lives at risk to
protect society, especially those of
The Jacksonville Sheriff's Office.

Novels by Judith Erwin

Shadow of Silence

Shadow of Doubt

Shadows from the Past

Shadow of Dance Series

The Ballroom

The Ballet

The Studio

Shepherd and Associates Series

Capitol Murder

ACKNOWLEDGEMENTS

As always, I am eternally grateful to those who provide input and support. First, a huge thank you to my brilliant editor and friend, John C. Boles, for his sharp eye and vigilant guidance. I could never have produced a book without him. Thanks to a fantastic author, Julie Delegal, for her unending support and valued suggestions.

Boundless gratitude goes to Marigrace Doran for her amazing expertise in technology and design, plus her phenomenal patience and infinite spiritual wisdom. She makes sure the finished product looks excellent inside and out. Also, a thank you to Katie Crain of Urban Sherpa marketing for keeping my online presence up to par.

With the creations of a book, no matter how much research is done online and in books, questions still arise requiring expert help. In Faith Lost, some of those questions were answered for me by Former State Attorney Angela Corey, Former Broward County Detective Paul Schad, Judith Bockel Poppell, Educator and Research Fellow, and all the Jacksonville Sheriff's Office presenters at the Citizen's Police Academy who gave of their time to share insight into the daily operations of a premier organization.

To my granddaughters, Mary Caroline and Amelia, I again express thanks for their outstanding photography. Also, a huge thank you to my daughter-in-law, Lynda, for her interest in my work and to my grandson, Judson, for his steadfast faith in me. Not to be overlooked, a big thank you to my magnificent grand dog, George, for playing the role of Jake's K-9, Kai.

Finally, words cannot express how grateful I am for the support and love of the rest of my family—Bill, Allison, Marshall, Keri, Sarah, John, Trevor, and Brooks. As I've said before, they are always there for me.

CHAPTER ONE

Neat stacks of sealed boxes stood in the center of Scarlett Kavanagh's Atlanta living room while furniture lined the walls, waiting for transfer to Virginia.

"This is a mistake," Grace Burton said as she handed her older sister a can of soda. "You could lose everything you've worked to build."

"As you've said more than a dozen times."

"What's really going on, Scarlett? You're leaving the family, friends, this beautiful condo, throwing away your law practice—your career? Is it him? Is there something between you and him you're not telling?"

"No. Nothing. Let it go. Please. I don't expect you to under—" A cell phone chirped before Scarlett could finish. "Mine or yours?" she said, setting her Coke down.

Grace pointed to the table. "Yours. Mine's in the car."

When she grabbed the device, a smile crept across Scarlett's face. "It's Jake." She held up an index finger. "Give me a minute."

Not waiting for a reply, Scarlett navigated a course between the boxes to exit the room.

"No problem," Grace said, unheard. "I need a break anyhow."

As soon as out of earshot, Scarlett turned her attention to the caller. "Jake, what's up? I didn't expect to hear from you."

"How soon can you be here?"

Scarlett tipped her head, a quizzical expression on her face. "What do you mean how soon? You know I'll be there next week. Grace is here, helping me pack."

"Need you yesterday. That is—*if* you want to work."

"Of course, I want to work. What's so urgent?"

2 • JUDITH ERWIN

"Critical case. Madison wants me on it. I'm swamped, plus this one needs a woman's finesse."

"And your finesse is in storage. Right? I thought you weren't going to let me work a case until I improved my skills."

"Do you want to debate or work, Harvard? I have a job for you. Coming? Or should I get Brenda?"

Wrinkling her brow, she held the phone out, staring at it for a second while shaking her head, and then brought it back to her ear. "Well, that's the Jake Shepherd we all know and love. Yes. Yes, I'll come. Of course. But I'll have to arrange for the cats and my car. And by the way, Shepherd, please don't trouble yourself with common courtesy."

"Sorry. Guess I was a little—"

"Abrupt? You think?"

"Said I was sorry. We'll cover the details from here: car, cats, and flight. Gotta go. See you tomorrow."

"Yeah. See you tomorrow." She slid the phone into her jeans pocket, took a deep breath, and returned to the living room.

"What did he want?" Grace said.

"Me—in DC—tomorrow."

"What? Why? Surely, you're not going. Does that man think he can snap a finger, and you run?"

"Why does he want me? Or why am I going?"

"You're going? I don't believe it. Have you completely lost your mind, Scarlett? I could understand, if there was something going on between the two of you—if this sexy PI had melted the ice queen, but you say it's strictly business. What if the job isn't what you think? You might hate it—or him. You hardly know him. Worse yet, he could fire you. You'll be stranded."

"Wow. Don't mince words. You're about as subtle as he is."

Grace dropped her chin and then glanced up with a contrite expression. "I guess that was pretty blunt. I apologize. But it's all crazy and totally out of character for the smart, sensible Kavanagh sister."

"You do realize you sound like Mom. I'm burned out, Grace. I want a change."

"Change is one thing but come on. Going from lawyer to detective seems to me like going from doctor to nurse. Are you sure you're not attracted to the guy?"

Scarlett gave Grace a dubious look.

"Don't give me that expression," Grace said. "He is a sexy guy—if you can get past his arrogance and rough edges."

"Cut it out. What you see is confidence, not arrogance. There's another side. And the answer to your question is I want to change careers—not seduce Jake Shepherd. You've got a beautiful marriage, but marriage isn't right for everyone. So, give up on the matchmaking—okay? We're friends, and I admire his skill. That's *all*."

"I'm not convinced." Grace rolled her eyes. "Did your *friend* tell you why you have to fly up there tomorrow?"

"He didn't have time. I'll find out when I get there. By the way, I'll need a favor. Can you oversee the movers for me at the end of the week? If you can't, I'll hire someone to do it."

"Of course, I will." Grace walked over and threw her arms around Scarlett. "I'm going to miss you, honey. I'm being selfish, but it's hard losing both of my sisters to the Capitol. At least when Scott was alive, Savannah still had a house here." She dug down in her pocket, took out a tissue, and wiped her eyes. "Don't be mad. I want you to be happy. I just hope you're not making a huge mistake."

As Grace released her, a tear inched down Scarlett's face. "I'll come back to Atlanta. I'm going to miss you guys. And any time you need me, call. As for making a mistake, the only permanent step I've taken is selling the law practice to Jennifer, and she said I have a job anytime I want it. You know I'm holding on to the condo and my license. I may even take the Virginia Bar Exam."

Grace shook her head, her eyes glassy.

Later that afternoon, Scarlett opened a text from Liz Glover, Jake's assistant.

All in place. Flight departs 6:35 a.m. Paperwork available on Delta website. MacGregors picking up cats and car keys tonight. Cats to travel on MacG plane Monday. Shipping service transporting car. Looking forward to having you back.

After replying with a thumbs-up emoji, Scarlett leaned back against the headboard and stroked the cat lying next to her. "No flight in cargo for you guys. You're flying private to our new home."

When Scarlett deplaned the next morning at Reagan International, Jake waited at the passenger boundary line, wearing his usual jeans, boots, and a leather jacket. As she approached him, her heart rhythm raged. *Think professional, professional, profess—*

When she reached Jake, his arms spread wide to welcome her with a hug. "Looking good, Harvard. How was the flight?"

Scarlett smiled, adjusting the shoulder strap of her purse. "Pretty smooth. How's DC? Have you been keeping it on track since I left?"

"Doin' my best. Do we need to go to baggage claim?"

"Nope. This is all I brought." She pointed to her rolling carry-on. "Everything else is scheduled to ship next week, including my wardrobe."

He leaned forward and grabbed the handle of her case. "I've got it."

"Did you think to book a hotel room for me?"

"No reason for that. Our prior arrangement worked fine."

"Jake!" She hit him on the shoulder with her fist. "You know that's not a good idea. We agreed. No more mixing business and personal. Me in your apartment? No—doesn't work."

"I beg to differ, counselor. I honor your boundaries—your rules. Will be a hell of a lot more convenient since your car won't arrive for a few days."

"Damn it, Jake. Who taught you to live on the edge? Yale or the FBI?"

He laughed. "DNA, which is probably responsible for this nutty idea of you working for me."

She blinked, shaking her head. "Okay, okay. You win, but—no cheating."

"I never cheat. Told you when you came up with your—*plan*." He slapped a hand down on her shoulder. "In all things business, I'm boss. All things personal, you are."

"We'll table that issue for now. So. Tell me. What's the case?"

"Let's get to the truck, and I'll lay it out for you."

When they reached his SUV, Jake loaded her bag in the back and then climbed into the driver's seat."

"So, bring me up to speed," Scarlett said, fastening her seatbelt.

"Child disappeared from school. Five-year-old girl. School says mom picked her up. Mom claims an impersonator signed her out. Authorities aren't buying it. She's their primary suspect."

"Oh my gosh. Are we working for the school?"

"Nope. The mom."

Her face registered surprise. "She's *your* client?"

"Our client, Harvard. Yep. She's the one, if I take the case. Haven't fully committed."

"Do you know what they have on her?"

"Apparently, a body of compelling evidence indicating the child was last seen with Mom, and she can't or won't give the whereabouts of the little girl."

Scarlett frowned, shaking her head. "What kind of evidence?"

"CCTV footage, signature in logbook, eyewitness."

"My gosh, Jake. Sounds open and shut. But you don't work for guilty people. Is that why you're letting me in on it?"

"Are you assuming she's guilty? What's wrong with you, Harvard? That Ivy League law degree didn't teach you to collect all the facts first?"

"Point taken. When do I meet her?"

"That's a bit complicated. She is being held in a psychiatric facility on an involuntary commitment order. If not found by the shrinks to fit the criteria for retention, Phil believes she will be charged with child neglect for openers and transferred to the local detention center."

"What is being done to locate the child?"

"All the usual, but Phil has the feeling they're not expecting a happy ending."

Scarlett winced.

He stopped to pay for parking but continued talking. "There's an AMBER Alert, and the Feds have been called in. But only because Phil threw a fit and insisted the locals notify the CARD team."

"CARD?"

"FBI team. Child Abduction Rapid Deployment."

"What does the mom say about the evidence?"

"That's the rub. She doesn't. She shut down after a maniacal show at the school where she screamed 'impersonator.'"

As Jake pulled out onto the main road, butterflies swarmed in Scarlett's stomach. "What about the father?"

"Single mom. No known father in the picture."

"Okay. Where do I start?"

"By treating the subject as you would in one of your domestic cases. Didn't you always begin with quizzing the client? Think you're up to an interview?"

She looked at him with squinting eyes. "You know I am."

A broad smile spread across his face. "That's my gal. You'll do the intake and front-run. I'll back you up and make the final decision on whether we sign on."

"So, you haven't met with her?"

"Nope. Right now, Phil is the only one who has seen her, and he got nowhere. Said all she did was cry last night."

Scarlett processed what Jake had said and then asked, "How did a single mom hire a high-priced lawyer like Phil?"

"She didn't. He's *pro bono*. Christine, Phil's wife, got a call from their church, which is where the woman works. Chris pressured Phil to help. He's covering us. But regardless of what is going on, time is of the essence. That's why I wanted you ASAP. If the mom has done something with or to the child, maybe you can get a bit of info from her. If she wasn't involved, maybe she knows something about who might have abducted the little girl."

"What if she did harm the child, maybe by accident? Are you still going to take the case?"

"Do the interview and brief me."

CHAPTER TWO

As Jake stopped the SUV in front of his office, he put it in park and turned to Scarlett. "I've got to meet with a client before lunch. Since time is critical in this case, Pete is sending someone over to drive you to Silver Spring for your interview."

"Silver Spring, Maryland?"

"Yep. That's where she lives and where the child was in school. Phil has you scheduled to talk to the school secretary at three, which should give you plenty of time with the client. If you don't need anything from your carry-on, you can leave it here in the truck."

"Sure. Do you anticipate my having any trouble at the facility with getting in to see the client?"

"You have your Georgia Bar Card, don't you?"

"Of course."

"That'll get you in. By law, she's entitled to consult privately with counsel during any reasonable hours."

"Even if I'm not technically representing her?"

"You're a lawyer, Harvard. She's a client. That's all they need to know."

As she reached down for her purse, she said, "Are there any suggestions you want to give me about the interview?"

He smiled. "Glad you asked. Don't expect to learn everything. You're dealing with a fragile client regardless of what transpired. Aim for determining whether she knows where the child is. If this is a third-party abduction, we've lost too much time. Unless we're already too late, the clock is ticking at warp speed."

"That gives me chills. Are you sure you trust me with this?"

He reached across the console and patted her leg. "You'll do fine. Think of it as a hybrid between a new client interview and the direct exam of a friendly witness. Be sure to lay out your predicate as you would in court and remember to pay careful attention to the body language and what is not said. Despite the urgency of locating the child, don't rush the interview. Work toward establishing a bond of trust with the client."

"Are you leaving it up to me to determine whether she's guilty?"

He looked directly into her eyes, tipped his chin, and said, "Knowing you as I do, it would be useless of me to think otherwise. Good luck, and I'll see you when you get back."

As Jake drove away, Scarlett proceeded to the office, pushed the doorbell, and Elizabeth Glover buzzed her in.

"Hey, gal," Liz, a retired FBI analyst and Jake's assistant, said as Scarlett entered. "Great to see you again. Jake says you're joining us."

Scarlett looked around the reception area and took a deep breath. *Nothing has changed in the six weeks since I left.* "That I am. Did he tell you he resisted the idea?"

"No, but of course he did. It wouldn't be Jake if he didn't. But I can tell you he likes it a lot more than he'll admit."

"All of a sudden, I'm nervous."

"You'll be fine. Personally, I think you're a perfect fit. I saw how committed you were with your sister's case and what strong skills you have. Plus, you're one of the few people Jake can't intimidate."

Scarlett laughed. "He is a challenge, but the satisfaction I experienced working with him on the investigation told me I wanted a change in my life. Do you know much about this new case he has me working?"

Liz reached into the file rack on her desk and took out a folder. "I've done a simple workup—not a lot of info, yet, but it may help you. I hate cases where children are involved. When Phil called yesterday, Jake was jammed up with a stalking case, plus a fraud for Washburn & Batson. Lila Stonebridge keeps him busy."

"I've heard you both mention her. What is the deal? I never asked but noticed an attitude when her name came up."

Liz hesitated, a skeptical expression on her face. "I don't want to speak out of turn, and much of what I know is speculation, but I'm pretty sure there *was* a little extracurricular action going on with Jake and Lila—nothing serious. More in the line of convenience, I think." She crooked an eyebrow.

"Was? As in past tense?"

"Definitely *was*. Jake began pulling away when he was working your brother-in-law's murder. I was a bit concerned we might lose the Washburn account, but apparently not. You know Jake. He says Lila is aware she can't get a better investigator. But listen, we should get you ready to go. Here's the file. I have a portfolio with a fresh legal pad, pens, and tape recorder ready for you. Is there anything else you need?"

"Sounds like you've got it covered," Scarlett said as she glanced through the manila folder.

"Brenda Lassiter should be here to pick you up any minute. You have met, haven't you?"

"We have. I got to know Brenda when she and her husband provided security for Savannah. Seems a little overkill to have a retired police officer drive me."

"Until you have driven in our traffic and know your way around, I think Jake wants to be sure you get there and back safely."

"Well, I could have ordered an Uber."

Liz shook her head. "He wouldn't have agreed to that."

By the time Scarlett arrived at the facility, she had reviewed Jessica Johnson's file and jotted down several notes on what to cover when she met the client. Brenda let her out at the front entrance with instructions to text when Scarlett was ready to leave. As she entered the facility, a sense of gloom came over her. *What demons torment the people here?*

The receptionist accepted Scarlett's credentials and led her to a small room sans windows. An attempt to create a homey ambiance in the area failed despite the bud vase containing a lonely sprig of fern and two daisies.

"Please make yourself comfortable, Ms. Kavanagh. An attendant will bring the patient to you shortly," the austere woman said.

Comfortable applied to this space is an oxymoron, Scarlett thought as she sat on one of the two chairs positioned at the table and placed her portfolio and file on the surface.

The seafoam walls seemed to shrink as Scarlett waited, wondering what Jessica Johnson would look like. *I wonder why Liz didn't include photos in the file. Surely, she Googled the client.* After ten minutes, restlessness set in and she stood, walked over to a side table, and picked up an old edition of *People.* As she was about to sit, a tap came on the door, and it opened. An orderly in white escorted a bewildered woman into the room.

"If you need me, press the button there on the wall," the man said and left without waiting for a response.

Scarlett nodded and then directed her attention to the client. "Jessica. I'm Scarlett Kavanagh. It's nice to meet you."

"The slender woman appeared to be in her early thirties, wore no makeup, and seemed confused.

"I'm an attorney but also an investigator. Phillip Madison has asked my firm to help you. I believe you met with Phil."

The woman stared at Scarlett with vacant eyes, under which dark circles contrasted with her pale complexion. She wore a nondescript pair of beige pajamas and robe that appeared two sizes too large. The robe had no belt, and she grasped it tightly together.

Is she sedated? Scarlett motioned toward the only other chair in the room. "Please. Have a seat, Jessica."

For several seconds, the woman remained standing but then eased onto the seat opposite Scarlett.

"Are they treating you well here?" Scarlett asked.

Jessica didn't move or change her expression.

"I know this is hard for you, but I can only help if you talk to me."

"You can't help," she said in a tone little more than a whisper.

Scarlett could barely hear what she said. "Did you say I can't help?"

Jessica's hands clung to the sides of her robe so tightly her knuckles were white. She looked down at the table and then back up, making eye contact with Scarlett. Barely moving her head, she nodded.

Stay calm. Don't rush her. "Maybe you're right, but maybe you aren't, and we won't know until we become better acquainted." Scarlett scooted her chair closer to the table and leaned forward. "Jessica, please believe me. I really want to help you. I understand your little girl is missing."

Jessica continued to stare at Scarlett.

"I've been told you believe she was abducted, but the authorities think you picked her up. Is that right?"

The client continued her silence as if her lips were glued together.

"Jessica, I read in your file Chris Madison said there was no way you could have harmed Faith. Faith is your daughter, right?"

A tear began to slide down Jessica's cheek.

"Chris said you adore that little girl, and you are a wonderful mother."

The tears multiplied, turning into a steady stream from both eyes.

Scarlett waited for a minute before continuing. "Phillip Madison is an excellent attorney and an important man. Having him on your side is huge. Do you know that?"

"They have to find her," Jessica whispered. "They have to."

Am I getting through? "That's absolutely true. There are a lot of people working on it—extremely capable people. Can you think of anything that would help them?"

As the client's chin dropped, tears pelted the table.

"Jessica, do you have any idea where Faith could be?" Scarlett made a concerted effort to maintain a sympathetic tone.

The distraught woman raised her wet face and stared at Scarlett.

"Tell me about Faith."

Jessica's eyes widened.

"Describe her for me."

The client released her grip on the robe, laced her fingers, and brought them up to cover her mouth.

"Is she blond, or is she brunette like you?" Scarlett detected a slight reaction from the otherwise stoic woman. "What color are her eyes?"

Although Jessica did not speak, Scarlett could see a relaxation taking place in her body and facial muscles. *She wants to talk to me.* "I would love to see a photo of Faith. Is there anywhere I can do that? Facebook? Instagram?"

Jessica shook her head. "I don't do social media. There's a school picture in my wallet, but they took my purse away."

She's talking. "I'm so sorry. Maybe I can get a copy of the photo at the school. Tell me, what are Faith's favorite toys? Dolls? Stuffed animals?"

A trace of a smile appeared on her face. "She loves her panda bears."

"She has more than one panda?"

"Five." An avalanche of tears burst forth. "I know she couldn't sleep without them. They've got to find her. I know she's so scared. She's never spent a night away from me."

Scarlett took a deep breath, fighting back tears. "Would you like something to drink? A Coke? Water? Tea?"

The only response was a negative motion of her head.

Turning a page of the legal paid, Scarlett said, "Can you tell me what happened yesterday?"

For several seconds, silence filled the space. And then like a clap of thunder, the subject said, "I'm not crazy. I did not pick her up. Someone has Faith, but no one believes me. Dear God, no one believes—" Her face fell onto her crossed arms on the table; her entire body trembled.

What hell this woman is going through if she's telling the truth. "Jessica. I understand your pain, but I can't help if you don't work with me. Can you look at me?"

Scarlett's plea went unacknowledged. After three long minutes, she decided to move in another direction. "Where is Faith's father? Could he have anything to do with what happened?" When she still refused to respond, Scarlett said, "Did you have a dispute over custody of Faith? Over child support? Please help me out."

As if calm had set in, Jessica lifted her face, once again making eye contact with Scarlett. "There is no child support. There is no custody dispute. Faith has no father. I'm all she has, and she's all I have."

"No father? Did you have artificial insemination?"

Jessica's head shook. "It was a mistake—a one-night stand with a stranger. I never knew his name, and he never knew I got pregnant. But it was the best mistake of my life."

Scarlett stared into Jessica's eyes. *I'm believing her. I can't jump to conclusions, but there's no sign of the dishonesty Jake described. I feel like I'm looking deep into her soul.* "Is there any way the man could know about Faith?"

"No. I never went back to the bar where we met, and I moved here from New York after she was born. We had a perfect life. I have a good job. Faith liked the school."

"Jessica, have there been any unusual things happening lately? Any strangers hanging around?"

"No. None I saw. There were a few phone calls—hang-ups. But I thought they were those sham calls everyone is getting."

"So, am I understanding you have absolutely no idea who might have posed as you and abducted Faith?"

Scarlett expected an immediate response, given the subject had begun to open up. Instead, another deafening silence pervaded the space.

"Jessica. Do you have any idea?"

Although she did not break eye contact with Scarlett, the woman's eyes went blank.

Either she knows something, or she's faking.

After several minutes of no response, the silence became awkward for Scarlett. *She wants to tell me something. What is your secret, Jessica Johnson?*

The combination of silence and the client's vacant stare caused Scarlett to lay down her pen and stand as she struggled to find the key words that would unlock the fragile woman's resistance. Although Jessica did not move, her eyes followed. With a deep breath, Scarlett sat back down and again engaged the client in eye contact.

"You can trust me, Jessica."

When the woman neither moved nor answered, Scarlett rephrased. "Are you afraid to trust me?"

"There wasn't a chapter for this." Jessica redirected her gaze over Scarlett's shoulder to the blank wall.

The muscles in Scarlett's face flexed, projecting confusion. "I don't understand. A chapter?"

Jessica's eyes reconnected with Scarlett's. "The books. The classes. There was no chapter on what to do if someone takes your baby."

Words failed Scarlett as she watched the pain oozing from the woman's eyes.

"Nothing matters without Faith." The tortured woman's words came forth in a murmur so low it was barely audible. Her head snapped up. "I do everything to make sure she has a happy childhood."

The edge in Jessica's voice, together with her choice of words, disturbed Scarlett. *Why would she say that?* She made a note and then said, "I'm sure you do, Jessica. I believe you, but you have to help us find her."

"I can't."

"You can't? Why can't you? Please, explain that for me." *What would Jake do now?* "I'm trying to be patient, but you're making it difficult. I can tell you know something. Are you going to sit there and refuse to talk when Faith could be suffering—dying?"

Even more color appeared to drain from the mother's face.

Scarlett lowered her voice. "Was it you who picked up Faith, and something happened—an accident?"

Jessica's jaw tightened, and her face contorted into an expression of bone-chilling hostility.

I went too far. "Jessica, listen to me. I don't want to scare you, but you've got to tell me everything you know. Surely, you're not trying to protect someone."

In response, the woman issued a frantic denial. "No. No. No. I'm not protecting anyone. You should go. I can't afford lawyers and investigators. I don't need you. I've never had help. I'll take care of it myself, like always."

"Are you out of your mind?" To her dismay, Scarlett's words escaped spontaneously. "Jessica, listen to me. Phil Madison is representing you *pro bono*. You don't need to pay him. He's paying for us to investigate. You need us all. You've got to believe me. This is serious on so many levels—most of all Faith's welfare."

Jessica sat back in her chair, a look of resignation blanketing her face. She said nothing, leaving the room, once again, encompassed in silence.

After waiting several minutes for a verbal response, Scarlett said, "I believe you are accustomed to taking care of yourself and Faith. It's obvious. As of right now, I'm going to assume you're telling the truth. However, I also believe you want help but are afraid to accept it. Before you dismiss me, think about how you will defend yourself without an attorney."

Jessica pondered Scarlett's question for a minute and then said, "I don't know."

"Right. It wouldn't be easy. So, let's go back. Tell me. What was your usual Monday routine? Did you always go straight home after picking up Faith?"

When she didn't respond, Scarlett took a deep breath and prepared for an objection. To her surprise, Jessica spoke.

"No. Some weeks, I took her grocery shopping with me. I had planned to take her this week."

"You don't work on Monday, right?"

"Right. I have Saturdays and Mondays off. I work a half-day on Sunday, counting the collection money, and preparing the deposits."

"Did you go anywhere before attempting to pick up Faith?"

"No. I was behind with laundry and cleaning the apartment. I take Faith"—her voice cracked—"to ballet class in the District on Saturdays. Afterward, we always get hamburgers at Wendy's. She loves their fries with ketchup." The tears returned, choking her for several seconds. "If there's a Disney movie playing, I take her." She put her head down in her hands. "How can I go on without her?"

"Don't say that. You've got to hold on to the belief you will have her back, hopefully, very soon. Jake said the FBI's Crimes Against Children team is working the case with the local police. They are good. But let's look at what we know. A woman took Faith. That's better than a man. There's a good chance the abductor is someone who wants a child and will be good to Faith. Did you ever have a babysitter, neighbor, or anyone who seemed unusually attached to her?"

Her head twisted in a silent no.

"Can you think of anyone who has a grudge against you?"

Jessica's eyes registered alarm, which Scarlett caught. The expression vanished as quickly as it appeared.

"No."

What caused that look? "Are you sure? Think hard. Sometimes what seems a minor attitude can be misleading. Has a neighbor ever complained you or Faith made too much noise? You parked in her parking place? Can you think of anyone who may have taken offense at something you said or did?"

"No." While the assertion came out with an adamant tone, Jessica looked away.

At least she's talking. "Let's go in another direction for a minute. Is there anyone else in your life? A family member? A boyfriend? A best friend?"

Jessica hesitated, her eyes looking around without moving her head. "No family. I have friends at the church—I work at the church in the District—but no one like a best friend."

Scarlett waited to see if she would say more, but she didn't. "Are you seeing anyone? A boyfriend?"

Silence.

"Jessica. Do you have a boyfriend?"

"Not really."

"Not really? What does that mean?"

"Nothing."

"Here we go again. I asked a simple yes or no question. You didn't give a yes or no answer. What is not really?"

"I don't have a boyfriend."

"But?" Scarlett raised her eyebrows, inviting an answer.

"There's a friend at church. He takes us out for lunch sometimes. It's not anything."

Scarlett shook her head. "Jessica, in a situation like this, everything is something. What is his name?"

"I don't want him brought into this."

"Jessica." Scarlett squinted one eye. "What is his name?"

"I'm not giving you his name. I know you're trying to help, but he can't tell you anything. I've been praying so hard, but I'm afraid, Ms. Kavanagh. No one believes me. I don't even think Mr. Madison believed me. Someone evil took my baby."

"I believe you. Trust me. Jake Shepherd is brilliant. He'll figure this—" A loud buzzer interrupted Scarlett.

Jessica flinched. "That's the lunch bell. I have to go." Without waiting for Scarlett to respond, she stood, walked across to the call button, and pressed.

"Jessica, before you go—"

She turned, clasping the sides of her robe, and stared at Scarlett.

"What is the name of the school where Faith takes ballet?"

As the orderly opened the door, she said, "Clariana Rassini Academy" and started into the hall.

"Jessica, I will be back. Don't give up."

"Are you coming out?" the orderly asked Scarlett as Jessica exited.

"In a second. Leave it open." With knots in her stomach, Scarlett made another note on her pad and then texted Brenda.

CHAPTER THREE

After lunch at a nearby café, Brenda drove Scarlett to Faith Johnson's elementary school. "Since you don't expect to be long, I'll park and wait in the car while you do your interview," she said as Scarlett gathered her purse and portfolio.

"I hate for you to sit in the car."

"No worry. It's what we do."

Scarlett smiled. "Well. If you don't mind, take some photos of the building and parking area. Couldn't hurt to put them in the file."

"Gotcha. Good idea."

Entering the school through double doors, after providing her ID to a faceless voice via a security camera, Scarlett stood for a moment, looking for a clue as to the office location. The hall bore the unique smell of every school she remembered—the undifferentiated combination of books, pencils, crayons, disinfectant cleansers, and children. A display case dominated the wall on the right while a gallery of photos, presumably faculty members, was on the left. Glancing up, she saw a sign indicating the main office was around the left corner.

As she entered the hub of reception, which included the principal's office and the school infirmary, she said to the only one present, "I'm Scarlett Kavanagh from Shepherd and Associates. Phillip Madison's office scheduled an appointment for me to meet with Ms. Howard regarding Faith and Jessica Johnson."

"That would be me," the woman said, rising from her desk and approaching the counter separating visitors from personnel.

"Is there a place with privacy where we can talk?" Scarlett said, glancing around the space.

"I doubt anyone will be coming in, but we can use the supply room." She circled the counter. "Right this way."

Bookshelves lined both sides and the back of the small room next to the office. In the center, a narrow table stood alone. Ms. Howard grabbed two folding chairs from near the door and set them up at the table.

After settling into her place, Scarlett opened her portfolio and took out a pen. "I'm sure you know why I'm here, and you've probably been asked a million questions by the police and the FBI."

"And the news media and the Children's Aid Society."

"I'm sorry to impose on you, but Mr. Madison represents Ms. Johnson and needs to have as much information as possible as to what happened on Monday. Were you in the office all day?"

"Except for my lunch break between eleven and eleven-thirty."

"So, you were in the office at both the time Faith was picked up and when Ms. Johnson came to pick her up?"

"Ms. Johnson came both times." The secretary's statement lacked attitude or judgment.

"I understand that is what you believe, but as you know, Ms. Johnson maintains she only came in once."

"Look, Ms. Kavanagh, I feel sorry for her. She's a nice lady, and I have no idea what is going on, but she came in right before I went to lunch and picked up Faith for a doctor's appointment. It's all there. Her signature in the logbook, her picture on the office surveillance camera. I can't explain it any further. Did she have a nervous break-down? An accident of some sort cause her to lose her memory? I don't know. I just pray Faith is okay. This is a nightmare for all of us."

"I'm sure it is, but if she's telling the truth, think of how Ms. Johnson feels. Her little girl is missing."

"You can't imagine how wild she was. It was crazy. She started screaming. It's all on video as well. I had no choice but to call the police. In fact, Ms. Underwood, our principal, and I talked the police into taking her to the Northview Behavioral Health Center for evaluation instead of arresting her right then. We've known her for over two years, and she's always been a sweet, thoughtful person and dedicated mom."

Scarlett stared directly into the woman's eyes for several seconds. *She seems sincere.* "Just so I have the full picture, Ms. Howard, did you actually talk to her—or whoever picked up Faith?"

"Not really. I was working on the daily attendance reports. I buzzed her in the front door, checking her ID, and looked up when she came in. I think I said something like, 'Hi. You here for Faith?' She nodded, signed the book, and I buzzed Mrs. Kilroy and told her to send Faith down to the office. Ms. Johnson walked to the door and waited with her back to me."

"Was there anything unusual about the way the woman acted that morning?"

"Yeah. A little." She squinted, her expression suggesting she was giving thought to the question. "She seemed preoccupied—not like her usual self."

"Did you happen to notice how Faith reacted to her?"

"No. I went back to what I was doing, and when I looked up again, they were gone."

"Can you describe for me what Faith's relationship with her mother appeared to be like?"

"Every time I saw them, it seemed above average. Faith would always light up at the sight of her mom. Ms. Johnson frequently came by on Monday for lunch with Faith and often brought treats for the class. She was one of our most active parents but never wanted to take a formal position."

"What was she wearing on Monday when she came in?"

"I didn't pay a lot of attention, but I've seen the videos from the front entrance and this office a dozen times. Both times yesterday, she wore the gray sweats she usually wears when she comes in on Mondays. I believe it's her day off."

"Was her hair the same or different than usual?"

"She had on a baseball cap the first time. That's about the only difference."

"Really? Was it her usual practice to wear a cap?"

"Not that I recall."

"Did it cover her face on all the film?"

"A little. Haven't you seen the film? I know Mr. Madison got a copy."

"No, I haven't. Wouldn't you have wanted a clear view of her face before releasing the front lock?"

"Not when I know the person. I know Ms. Johnson. I had no reason to be that suspicious." The woman began to appear agitated as if annoyed that Scarlett seemed to question her action.

Scarlett made a note on her legal pad. "Could I see the logbook?"

"Sure. Wait here, and I'll get it."

While the secretary was gone, Scarlett checked her text messages but found nothing.

As Ms. Howard re-entered the room, she said, "I brought the book, but I also brought a tablet with the video. Have you met, Ms. Johnson?"

"I met her this morning. How far back does the logbook cover?"

She opened the book for Scarlett and turned to the subject page. "We started it when school opened after summer vacation. It's almost full. See, there's her signature."

"To your recollection, did Ms. Johnson check Faith out early any other time this year?" Scarlett snapped a photo of the page as she spoke.

"I can think of several times. She had a dentist appointment and at least one other doctor's appointment."

"May I see those pages as well?"

"I suppose." She took the book from Scarlett and flipped through the pages, holding a finger between several. "Here. You can see the signatures match."

Scarlett again snapped photos of each. Each line in the book had six columns: Date, Parent or Guardian, Name of Child, Reason for Withdrawal, Time Out, and Time In. As she reviewed the entries, Scarlett noted while not exact, the signatures were sufficiently similar to suggest executed by the same person. However, one discrepancy caught her eye, but she said nothing.

"Here's the video," Howard said and turned the device around so the screen faced Scarlett.

Scarlett watched as a female, wearing a black baseball cap with an orange cartoon-type-bird logo, a gray sweatshirt, and matching pants, walked up to the counter. As she approached, her head tipped downward, denying a full-face view. The woman raised her hand to acknowledge the secretary, signed the book, turned, and walked out. Once facing away from the camera, she raised her head. "Do you know what the emblem is on her cap?" Scarlett asked.

"Yes. That's the logo for the Baltimore Orioles."

"The baseball team?"

"If you have to ask, you must not be from around here."

"I'm not. I also know little about baseball, but I assume they are pretty popular, and the hats easy to find."

"You bet. They're everywhere."

"Ms. Howard, think about what I'm going to ask before you answer. Is it at all possible the woman you saw could have been someone disguised to look like Ms. Johnson? Please, take your time."

Howard tipped her head forward, rubbed her temples, and remained silent for several seconds. Lifting her chin, she turned the tablet around and replayed the film, focusing her full attention on the screen. "Ms. Kavanagh, you've seen Ms. Johnson. That looks exactly like her. I know strange things happen, but I can't imagine anyone could make themselves look that much like her."

"But do you agree that, although unlikely, someone *might* have pulled that off? The hat hides part of her face from the camera."

"I did see her. As much as I wish I could say something else, I really believe it was Ms. Johnson—but I guess I could be wrong."

CHAPTER FOUR

By the time Brenda returned Scarlett to the office, it was after five, but Liz was still at her desk.

"Any word on the search for the child?" Scarlett asked as she entered the reception room.

"Nada. How did it go?" Liz asked.

Scarlett grimaced, shaking her head. "I was so hoping she might have been found. As for your question, I'm not sure I know how to answer. Probably good and not so good. Where is he?"

"Right here." Jake, followed by Kai, entered the reception area. "Can you define 'good and not so good' for me?"

"I got the client to talk—but she wouldn't answer certain questions, and I think she held back on others. But I believe she's innocent."

"Already came to that conclusion, huh. And what are you basing it on?"

"Demeanor. Attitude. Her history at the school. Even though the secretary believes it was the client who picked up the child, she gave glowing descriptions of what a good mother Jessica is."

"Nice, but I think we're going to have to pass on this one."

"What? Why? You haven't even met her."

"You said she refused to answer questions and held back on info."

"So? So did my sister, and you accepted her case. I didn't even believe Savannah half the time."

"It's a no, Harvard. Not going to get sucked in on this one. You're coming from emotion."

"Oh, that's a low, male chauvinist one even for you, Shepherd. I prefer to believe I'm going on intuition."

Liz sat at her desk, watching the tennis match played with words.

"Day one, and we're off to war. Exactly why I nixed making you my partner."

"If you don't take this case, Jake Shepherd, I'll take it on my own. I'll just have to set up my own shop. I saw a pitiful woman in more pain than I can imagine."

"That's a great idea. One day as an inexperienced PI and you're set to sail off on your own. Let me enlighten you, Harvard. You don't know who you saw."

"What's that supposed to mean?"

"Exactly what I said. The lady isn't who she says she is."

Scarlett looked around at Liz, a puzzled expression on her face. "Why do you say that?"

"Because I know it. She's not Jessica Johnson."

"Liz? What's he talking about?"

"I did a background on her, Scarlett. She doesn't exist before ten years ago. No birth record, no record on the social security card she's using. No nothing."

"Which means, Harvard, she's changed her identity and is likely an illegal immigrant, a protected witness, or a fugitive. I can pretty well guarantee she's not WITSEC because if she were, the Marshals would be swarming like a pack of angry bees, and there has been no such sighting. Did you notice anything to suggest she's foreign—anything in her language, appearance, accent?"

"No."

"There you go. Fugitive."

"You might want to factor innocent fugitive, such as domestic violence victim, into your little bag of assumptions. Damn it, Jake. You're not going to dismiss this woman without even talking to her."

"My, the lady gets riled when challenged," he said.

Liz spoke up. "Come on, Jake. You know you're going to check her out before you turn down Phil and Chris. Stop giving Scarlett a hard time on her first day here."

Scarlett whipped around to face him. "Is that what you're doing? Some kind of stupid test to see how I would react?"

"Easy does it, Harvard. You passed. As a matter of fact, we have a meeting with Phil and Chris tonight. We're invited for dinner. You can brief me on your interviews before we leave. I plan to do a follow-up visit with the client tomorrow morning."

"Do I get to go?"

"Yeah. You get to go. But be warned. There is a chance I won't take the case. I want to know who she is."

CHAPTER FIVE

When Jake and Scarlett arrived at the massive door of the Madison's Tudor home, a gracious, silver-haired woman welcomed them. "You must be Scarlett. Come in, my dear. You too, Jake. I'm so happy to meet you, Scarlett. Phil has told me you're to be working with this fellow." As the two entered, Christine Madison patted Jake on the back and then said to Scarlett, "I'm, of course, aware of your family's dreadful tragedy. I do hope your sister and her children are recovering from the unfortunate loss of her husband, the senator."

Scarlett smiled. "Thank you. Savannah's coping. She is resilient."

Phil Madison immediately appeared in their path. "Jake, my boy, come on in. Scarlett, you're as beautiful as I remember." He took her hand, leaned forward, and kissed her on the cheek. "What can I offer the two of you to drink?"

"One of those fancy, imported beers works for me," Jake said.

"And you, Scarlett? A glass of wine, a cocktail?"

"At the risk of embarrassing myself, considering how tired I am, I'll have a glass of white wine."

"Certainly. We have several to choose from. I'll show you," the lawyer said.

Jake put a hand on Scarlett's shoulder. "Allow Phil to choose, Harvard. He's a connoisseur. Whatever he suggests is sure to be excellent."

"Then I'd be foolish not to rely on your recommendation, Phil."

With a glance downward, the older man said, "I see you brought your briefcase, Jake. I suggest we table business until after dinner."

"No argument from me."

With a sweep of his hand, Phil said, "Right this way," and started across the large, marble-floored entry.

Trailing behind the group, Christine again put a hand on Jake's back. "Have you been behaving?"

He smiled, shook his head, and said, "You know me, Chris. I'd be off my game if I failed to piss off at least a dozen people a day."

"Well, I hope you've already met your quota for this day because I want no trouble from you."

"For you, I'll do my best to be civilized."

Christine turned to Scarlett. "Did he tell you he's like the son Phil and I never had?"

"No, he didn't."

With an affectionate gesture, Jake put an arm around the older woman's shoulders. "If you and Phil had me, you'd have put me up for adoption before I started school."

Christine gave his hand a pat, shaking her head. "You are incorrigible, but I love you."

After dinner, the party adjourned to a large, richly paneled entertainment room where the hosts relaxed with brandy while Jake and Scarlett had coffee.

"Much as I'm enjoying the evening," Jake said, "we'd better get down to business because I'm sure Scarlett is exhausted. Shall I spread out what we have on the Johnson case?"

Phil nodded as he pointed to a corner in the room. All stood with their beverages in hand and moved to a round game table.

"Scarlett interviewed Ms. Johnson at the mental health facility this morning and the school secretary afterward," Jake said, turning his face toward her. "You want to share your findings?"

Scarlett nodded. "To begin, I need to warn you; Jake is not as certain about Ms. Johnson's innocence as I am. But he has agreed to reserve judgment until he meets with her tomorrow."

Christine Madison gave Jake a scowl but said nothing.

"I admit she is troublesome in that she's withholding something, but the interview ended abruptly when a buzzer summoned her to lunch," Scarlett said.

"Scarlett accomplished what I hoped. She got the woman to talk, which is more than you managed, Phil."

The older man nodded. "Did you have an opportunity to review the video when you interviewed the school secretary?" Phil asked.

"I did. I also was able to review footage from outside cameras, showing the entrance and exit of both women—including a portion of the suspected abductor leaving with the little girl."

"Did the child appear distressed?" Phil asked.

"Nothing I could see suggested distress or reluctance. The school provided copies of those recordings to your office, Phil. While I admit, the two images appear to be the same woman, I think there is room for reasonable doubt, plus I found what I believe is another discrepancy."

"What's that, Harvard?" Jake said. "You didn't mention it earlier."

"That's because I didn't have time." Scarlett reached over to the manila folders and took out copies of pages from the school logbook, printed from images on her phone. "If you look at the signature on Monday's entry compared with Ms. Johnson's prior signatures in the book"—she pointed to places on several sheets—"the writing looks close enough to be the same person. But note the column titled 'Reason for Withdrawal.' Each time Ms. Johnson took Faith from the school, she wrote her reason in cursive. Plus, she didn't use the term 'doctor appointment.' She used the term 'medical appointment.' On the subject sheet, the signature is in cursive, but the reason is printed and called 'doctor appointment.' My guess is the woman who abducted Faith did not know that column would be there and had no frame of reference for how Ms. Johnson addressed it."

Jake stared intently at the documents. "Or had not practiced anything but the signature. Damn good catch, Harvard." Sliding the papers in front of Phil, he said to her, "I may keep you on the payroll."

She grinned. "Told you I could do it."

"I agree with Jake," Phil said. "Sharp eye, especially since you're new at investigative work."

Scarlett smiled. "You'd be surprised how much investigation a family law attorney does preparing a case. But this is certainly more intense as divorce rarely involves life and death situations. While we're talking about deviations, I learned from the secretary that Ms. Johnson never wears a baseball cap. Granted, she does wear the gray sweats on a regular basis, but anyone doing her homework could have known that."

"Good deduction," Phil said.

"Also, if you study the videos, not one time on Monday is there a full-face image of the woman picking up the child. What are the chances that both entering the building and entering the office, her face would be tipped downward? I think she knew there could be cameras and was avoiding identification. And isn't it strange there is no image of the abductor arriving in a vehicle or departing in one? She and Faith walked out of camera range without entering a vehicle."

"I promise you; the Bureau has recordings by now from all cameras in the area. If we take the case, can you work on getting copies, Phil? If they stonewall you, I'll reach out."

"Do you have a contact on the Crimes Against Children team?"

"It falls under Violent Crimes, my old department."

"Don't tell me. Jackie's husband?"

Jake grinned. "He comes under the umbrella but doesn't usually work these cases."

Jake's earlier comment brought Christine to life. "What do you mean, *if* we take the case, Jake? Phil is committed, and I thought you were as well. Scarlett has proved doubt as to the identity of the abductor."

"I know you're passionate about this, Chris. But think about it. Putting aside my policy of not working for a guilty party, if she's not as innocent as you and Scarlett believe, do you want me proving her guilt?"

The room remained silent for a minute before Christine responded.

"I think that's a chance I'm willing to take. It's not just Jessica's guilt or innocence; it's about saving that precious little girl. She's out there, Jake. God knows where or what is happening to her. Phil says most children are abducted for money or sex. That gives me cold chills. Jessica is not a likely target for ransom."

"The Bureau's top-flight team is working on it, Chris. They've got manpower, skill, and resources."

"You may not have manpower, but you have the skill, Jake Shepherd. Phil always says you can sniff out evidence better than a bloodhound and can work a suspect like a teenage girl works a horny boy."

"Gee, Phil. You say that?" Jake gave him a high-five.

"I might have, but don't let it go to your head. It's already big enough. But she's right, Jake. You have either a lot of luck or an uncanny knack for solving cases."

"So, is that horny boy thing from personal experience?" Jake grinned.

"Observation."

"Ahhh. Beth and Audra?" Jake said and then turned to Scarlett. "Chris and Phil have two gorgeous daughters. It's a wonder he ever allowed me to stay here during law school breaks."

"Don't worry. I kept a close eye on you and was hoping the girls would entice you to join the practice—but no, your relentless pursuit of justice lured you into becoming a prosecutor. You and Gray MacGregor were the smartest clerks ever to work for me. Lost you to the DOJ and Gray to his financial empire."

Jake turned back to Christine. "To answer your question, I haven't said I won't work the case, but it could turn on how Ms. Johnson comes across when I interview her. I know if I don't take it, there'll be hell to pay with you and Scarlett."

"You've got that right," Phil said and then turned to Scarlett. "So, what was your take on the school witness? Is she credible? Likely to hold up in court?"

"She likes the client, but she believes Faith left the school with Ms. Johnson—Jessica. While she saw the abductor, she didn't exchange conversation and wasn't paying close attention. I got her to admit she could be wrong."

"I can work with that. What about Jessica? In your lay opinion, is she psychotic?"

"I think she is out of her mind, but not crazy—just fear and grief."

"Were you able to get *anything* of interest out of her?"

"Very little, but I'm sure she has some sort of secret holding her hostage."

"Probably has something to do with who she is," Jake said.

"What do you mean 'who she is'?" Christine said.

"Honey, I forgot to mention, Jake called today and told me they ran a background on Jessica. It appears she changed her identity about ten years ago." Phil turned toward Scarlett. "Were you able to address that with her?"

"I didn't know at the time, but it may relate to her reluctance to talk. She doesn't seem to have close friends or family. I did get her to admit she has some sort of a relationship with a man she won't name. She said he attends your church."

Christine gave the table a slight slap. "Phil. I think I may know who he is."

All eyes turned to her.

"Ted McKay. You know him. He asked you for the name of a divorce lawyer about a year ago."

"If you say so."

"I've seen them talking. It caught my attention because I first thought it was Miranda, his wife, and wondered if a reconciliation might be in play. She and Jessica are similar types."

"Something only another woman would notice," Phil said, smiling.

"But it may be relevant," Jake said. "The client most likely didn't want to be the one to name him but wanted it out. Otherwise, she'd never have mentioned the church."

Phil nodded. "Sounds reasonable."

"Ted McKay. Know where I can contact Mr. McKay, Chris?"

"I don't remember where he works, but I'll call Susan at the church. She'll know."

"Text me the info. Was it a contentious divorce?"

"Contentious enough that he wanted a good lawyer," Christine said.

"Jake, have you considered Jessica could be in witness protection?" Phil asked. "That could explain the false identity and, God forbid, who might have abducted the child if her identity has been compromised."

Jake shook his head. "I told Scarlett I don't think she's WITSEC. There's been no sign of the Service rushing forth, but you're right. Pray it's not the case for the sake of the child."

"What are your chances of finding out?" Phil asked. "They won't talk to me without a court order."

"I do have a couple of contacts with the Service from my days at DOJ and my dad's role. I'll reach out but not likely to get anything more than a standard 'can't admit or deny.' However, if she's not one of theirs, I could get an unspoken hint."

Later, driving to Jake's apartment, Scarlett said, "Well, I guess today proves my point."

He frowned. "And what point might that be?"

"That business and personal relationships do not mix."

"It does? Explain that for me."

"Your obstinate attitude toward taking the case. If we were in a fully developed, personal relationship right now, you'd be sleeping on the couch."

He burst out laughing. "And what would make that different than my sleeping in another room under our current contract?"

"Kindly stop being obtuse, Shepherd. You know exactly what I mean."

CHAPTER SIX

"Good morning, Jessica. I'm Jake Shepherd. You know Ms. Kavanagh, I believe." He tipped his head toward Scarlett as the orderly who delivered Jessica to the tiny room brought in a third chair. When the door closed behind the man, Jake continued.

"I'm sure you've been told I work for your attorney, Phillip Madison. For openers, I'm not Ms. Kavanagh—Scarlett. I won't offer you tea and sympathy. You may not like me, and I'm fine with that. I'm not a contestant in a popularity contest. What I am is an investigator and a damn good one. What I will do is solve your case—but only if you cooperate, are honest, and forthcoming."

Jessica stared at Jake. Her face moved slightly to the right as though she wanted to look away but couldn't.

"What do you want, Jessica?"

She blinked and then opened her eyes wide. "How can you ask me that? You know I want my baby. Have they found her? No one tells me anything in here."

Surprised at the spunk shown by the client, Scarlett leaned forward, studying her overall appearance. *Same shabby clothing, no makeup, but her hair is combed.*

"Not yet. There's a massive search continuing. Once the doctors clear you, I'm sure the FBI will want an interview. Unless your child is found, we alibi you out, or otherwise clear you, there's a distinct possibility you will be arrested and charged. I don't see you going home soon."

Typical Shepherd style. Never sugarcoat the facts.

"What will they charge me with? I can't kidnap my own child."

"I think it will be along the lines of child neglect, based on your being reported as the last one seen with your daughter, and you can't or won't produce her."

"That's not fair. All I want is my baby safe and back with me. I haven't done anything wrong, Mr. Shepherd."

"Well, I need to know how badly you want her. Because I could be your best shot at getting her back."

She shook her head. "Why? Why are—" Her voice cracked, but her back straightened as though coming to attention. "Why are you my best shot?"

"Because I'm exceptionally good at what I do. I solve cases. My record speaks for itself. If you trust me and give me your full cooperation, I will find who took your child. Finding the abductor is key to finding the victim. Do you want me to do that?"

Jessica started to shake, her eyes remaining fixed on Jake.

"What makes you good?"

The query impressed Scarlett. *Good question.*

He smiled. "Since you ask. Probably a combination of genes, law school, and my FBI training. My father and grandfather were U.S. Marshals. You might say law enforcement is in my DNA."

The client stared at Jake, unmoving.

"Jessica, look me in the eye."

She complied.

"Did you pick up your daughter?"

"No." Not a muscle moved. She neither blinked nor looked away.

"If you had anything to do with what happened to . . . Faith? That is her name, right? If you had anything to do with it, you don't want me on the case. Just say the word, and I'll walk away and forget we ever met."

Scarlett winced. *Damn, Jake. You don't have to be that mean to start.*

Her head twisted in a silent no as she broke eye contact and turned to Scarlett. "I want to talk to her."

Jake glanced at Scarlett and nodded. Returning his focus to the distraught mother, he said, "I'll leave you alone"—he looked at his watch—"until nine-fifteen. But keep in mind"— he pointed toward Scarlett—"she works for me." He stood, pushed the call button on the wall, and exited when the door opened. Before leaving, he leaned over and said to Scarlett, "I don't have to warn you against coaching, do I?"

She gave him a dirty look and then turned toward Jessica.

No one spoke until the door closed behind Jake. "Is he telling me the truth?" The pupils of her blue eyes enlarged. "Are they going to arrest me?"

"It may happen, Jessica. He is brutally honest—sometimes it comes across as mean-spirited, but it's not. If that happens, you need him. But he won't lie or spin the facts to either tell you what you want to hear or obtain a false result. If he works your case, you have to be open and honest. Unless you committed a serious crime, Jake is on your side regardless of how blunt or gruff he appears. And he's even more concerned about Faith. He has a daughter he loves."

"A daughter? That's good." She looked down at the table and then lifting her chin, said, "I've been thinking a lot about what you said yesterday. I do believe I can trust you, Ms. Kavanagh, but he and Mr. Madison scare me."

"Call me Scarlett. Phil is a nice person, and you'll get used to Jake. Just tell yourself he's excellent at what he does. If I were in trouble, Jessica, if my life were stake, or if the life of someone I love was in jeopardy, I would pray to have Jake Shepherd on my side."

"Have you seen him solve a case?"

"I have. I've seen him in a lot of scenarios, including a dangerous hostage situation."

"Some problems can't be fixed." The distraught mother's gaze wandered like the day before.

"You need to let him be the judge of that. He will be honest. Nothing you say to either of us can ever be used against you. Our investigation is protected by a legal doctrine called work product. Are you familiar with that?"

Jessica shook her head.

"All the information your attorneys, or people they hire to work under their direction, collect to prepare your case is confidential unless the lawyer chooses to release it. And an attorney is not allowed to take any action detrimental to his client. Do you understand? It's like the attorney-client privilege."

"I think so. You seem to know a lot."

"Jake and I are both lawyers."

"Oh. And he was an FBI agent?"

"He was."

"That's why he's so good."

Scarlett nodded. "Ready to talk to him again?"

Jessica took a deep breath and mouthed a "yes."

When Jake re-entered the room, he glanced Scarlett's way. A slight blink of her eyes conveyed to him the meeting with Jessica went well. With a statement-making flourish, he slid onto the chair directly across from the petite woman and said, "Ready to talk to me?"

"I think I need you. Faith needs you." She looked down to her lap and then back up to Jake, her eyes projecting a desperate plea. "Will you help us?"

"Let's talk for a few minutes and see how it goes." He tipped his chin, simultaneously raising his eyebrows. "As I see it, there are two objectives here—finding Faith and identifying who took her. Am I right?"

"Yes. But, Mr. Shepherd, finding her is the most important."

"Very well, it should be, but discovering who took her is the best road to finding her. Scarlett believes you know something you're holding back. I need to know what it is and who you are."

Jessica's pupils dilated, her breathing accelerated, and her hands tightened into knuckle-whitening fists.

"Jessica?"

Despite tensing every muscle in her body, the distraught woman began trembling. "What do you mean?"

"You know exactly what I mean. Let's cut to the chase. You're not Jessica Johnson. There is an abundance of them, but you're not one. If you want my help—and trust me—you need it, I have to know who you are and why you changed your identity ten years ago."

Tears flooded Jessica's face. "I can't tell you."

Jake raised an eyebrow. "I'm taking that to mean you acknowledge your name is not Jessica Johnson."

The tears continued, though Jessica squeezed her eyes closed. She rocked slightly, which might have been interpreted as an assent, but no words came forth.

"You're going to need to do better than that. Who are you?"

She opened her eyes and stared at Jake. "I can't. I really can't. I want to, but I'm afraid."

"Can't or won't?"

"Can't. I would if I could. You've got to help me."

"Have you ever killed anyone, Jessica?"

His statement caused Scarlett to grimace and Jessica to flinch. But the frightened mother didn't break eye contact.

"I repeat. Have you ever killed someone? Accidentally? Intentionally?"

"No. No." She stood, grabbing the edge of the table to maintain her balance.

"Sit down." Jake's tone left no room for debate as she exhaled and then slowly sank back on the chair, covering her eyes with a hand.

"Look at me, Jessica."

She moved the hand away to face him, a trace of rebellion in her eyes.

Unaffected, he said to her, "If you haven't killed anyone, most anything else can be worked out. You've got one of the best lawyers in the country on your side. But none of us can help you if we're functioning in the dark."

"I haven't killed anyone. I haven't done anything wrong except run away, but if I tell you why, they'll take Faith away from me." She burst into another round of tears. "Either way, I'll lose her. I can't take the chance."

Jake sat quietly for a minute and then with a quizzical frown said, "Jessica, is Faith your biological child?"

Choking on her emotions, she struggled to respond. "Ye . . . yes. What are you thinking?"

"I'm not thinking; I'm probing. You gave birth to Faith, right?"

"Yes."

"And I can find records to prove that?"

Scarlett's face contorted in a scowl. *Is he thinking Faith was adopted—or maybe a kidnapped, black-market baby?*

"Yes." The response came with more force than previously displayed. "I gave birth to her in New York-Presbyterian Queens. I have her birth certificate."

He made a note of her answer. "And there's no known father, right?"

She nodded.

"Does Faith have a cell phone?"

"No. Should she? I didn't think a five-year-old would need one."

"I'm not inferring she should have one. Just asking if she does. It could be traced."

"Oh, my gosh. I should have gotten her one. Oh, no. I try to be a good mother. I try to give her everything she needs and most of what—" Suddenly, her expression turned from defiance to self-reproach. "I should have let her have the kitten. Why didn't I?"

Jake watched as Jessica grew more agitated.

"She wanted that kitten so much. Why did I say no? I could have let her have it. Now, I may never see her again, and I didn't let her have something she wanted with all her heart. *Why?*" She put her head down on the table, burying her face in her arms. "If I ever get her back, I'll get her a kitten."

Tears formed in Scarlett's eyes.

Jake gave Jessica time to compose herself and then took three sheets of paper from his portfolio. Fanning them out on the table, he pointed to a line on one sheet as she lifted her face. "Pull yourself together. We need to move forward, Jessica. I'm sure you recognize these as copies of pages in the school logbook. Please look at the signature on the line I'm pointing to and identify it."

Without hesitation, she said, "It's mine."

"You signed that page. Correct?"

"Correct."

"And what about this one?" He pointed to the bottom of the second sheet.

Jessica nodded. "Yes. But that was three months ago." She pointed to the top of the sheet. "See the date?"

"I do. Now look at this one."

Staring down at the third piece of paper, she pulled back from the table, shaking her head. "That's not me. I didn't sign that."

"Look at them side by side. Aren't the signatures alike?"

She refused to answer.

"They're alike, aren't they, Jessica?"

"It's not me. I didn't sign the book on Monday. Faith was gone when I got there. And it was after school hours. You don't have to sign a child out after school."

As he pulled the sheets back to his side of the table, he said, "Did you touch the book?"

"No—at least I don't remember touching it."

"Did you pick up the pen?"

She shook her head. "No."

"So, your fingerprints and DNA won't show up on a pen in that office?"

"No."

After making a note on each log sheet, he tucked them back into his portfolio and said, "Walk me through from the beginning—when you got to the school on Monday afternoon."

"I drove to the student pick-up area and waited in the line of cars. When I reached the spot where the children stand with the teachers, she wasn't there. Faith's teacher wasn't on duty. So, when I asked about Faith, the woman told me to check at the office. I drove around to the front, parked, and went inside." She paused to take a breath, the tears having dried on her cheeks. "I asked the school secretary if she knew where Faith might be. I thought she could be in the infirmary. That's when she said, 'You picked her up before lunch.' For a second, I stood there, trying to understand what I heard."

"And you said?"

"I thought she had us mixed up with another family. So, I said something like you have us mixed up with someone else. Faith is here. I haven't been back since I brought her this morning."

"What happened next?"

"She came over to the counter, ran her finger down the logbook, and said, 'There's your signature, Ms. Johnson. Don't you remember?' My heart stopped. I thought I was going to pass out. My knees went weak, I broke out in a sweat, and I think I started screaming. She called the police."

"Did you threaten anyone or engage in any type of physical violence against a person or property?"

"I just remember screaming. I didn't hit anyone—maybe the counter. I was so upset; I'm not sure what I did."

"What exactly did you scream?"

"I don't remember. I know I screamed, 'You can't have let someone take my baby—not Faith.'"

Jake maintained a constant stare as he said, "When the police arrived, did you resist them in any way?"

"All I remember was crying and begging them to go find Faith."

"Jessica, did you threaten to harm anyone, including yourself?"

The room went quiet again. With her elbows on the table, Jessica dropped her face into her hands.

"What did you say?" Jake looked at Scarlett and then back to Jessica. "This is not an option. You have to tell me, Jessica. What did you say?"

Without lifting her head, she said, "I think I said if I lost Faith . . ." Her focus drifted off, away from both Jake and Scarlett.

"If you lost Faith, what?"

"If I lost Faith, I would . . . I would kill myself."

Jake dropped his pen and leaned back in his chair. "There you have it. That's all they needed for involuntary commitment." He put his hands on the table, palms down. "That's when they took you into custody and transported you to the hospital, right?"

She nodded, new tears flooding her face.

Lowering his voice, he said, "Try to pull yourself together. I need you to look at something else." Jake leaned forward and rubbed his forehead with the heel of his hand and then sat back, watching Jessica.

Scarlett stood and walked to a small bookcase where there was a box of tissues, pulled several out, and returned, handing them to Jessica.

After several minutes, Jake withdrew an image from his portfolio and slid it across the table to Jessica. "Look at this screen shot, taken from the surveillance camera in the school office. Do you recognize the figure in the baseball cap?"

She stared at the picture for about thirty seconds and then turned her head away.

"Who is it, Jessica?"

"I don't know."

"Is it you?"

"No. No, it's not me."

"Looks like you, doesn't it?"

"I don't know."

"Don't start that again. I told you, if you want my help, you have to cooperate."

"I can't. It's not me."

Scarlett reached over and touched Jake's arm.

He turned toward her. "Yeah?"

"May I ask a question?"

He gestured toward Jessica. "Be my guest."

"Jessica, look at me."

As the two made eye contact, Scarlett said, "Are you a twin?"

The jerk in Jessica's body was clear as she looked away. But before she could respond, a heavy knock came at the door and then it opened. The orderly appeared with two uniformed police officers standing beside him.

"Jessica Johnson?" The stocky officer said. "Are you Jessica Johnson?"

Jessica sat frozen while Jake and Scarlett stood.

"What's going on?" Jake said.

"Who are you?" the stocky one said.

Jake reached for his wallet, exposing an empty waist holster.

The cops immediately drew weapons.

"Where's the gun?" the first cop said.

"In my vehicle. I'm reaching for my ID. I'm Jake Shepherd, attorney, here to consult with my client."

The first cop moved closer to Jake and said, "Why are you wearing a holster if you're not armed, and why is a lawyer carrying?"

Jake extended his hands in the air. "I'm an attorney and a private investigator. I work cases of a nature that require being armed during and after."

"Pat him down, Buzz. He might have another concealed."

Scarlett stood frozen; her sight glued on the cops. When the second one started to frisk Jake, her protective instinct sprang into action, getting in the way of her judgement. "Is that really necessary? He's got credentials."

"Stay out of it, Scarlett. They're just doing their job. I would do the same thing."

Finding nothing, cop number two stepped back and holstered his weapon.

Once the stocky officer reviewed Jake's ID, including his business card and Bar card, he said, "You're a lawyer, private dick, and a former Fed? Which agency?"

Lowering his hands, Jake said, "FBI. I'm assuming you have a warrant. Show it to me."

The second cop pulled a folded document from the pocket of his uniform and handed it to Jake.

Scarlett's heart was pounding almost as fast as Jessica's. *Thank God, Jake's here. I'm not ready to address something like this on my own.*

"Looks in order. Child neglect, resisting arrest, and disturbing the peace. Your bosses had to dig pretty deep in the books for these charges. Can you guys let me have a couple of minutes alone with my client before you take her?"

"I don't kn—"

"Come on"—he leaned forward, squinting, to read the cop's nametag—"Officer . . . Smith. Those charges are misdemeanors, there's no escape window in this room, and you'll be standing outside the only door—fully armed. What's the harm?"

"You can talk to her downtown, after she's been processed," the other cop said.

"Give me a break. Try to remember if your people have it wrong, you're transporting a victim not a criminal."

"I guess we can give him a minute or two, Charlie. He seems on the up and up."

Jessica's expression displayed a degree of fear exceeding her control as her glassy gaze bounced from the police officers to Jake.

Hang in there, Jessica, Scarlett thought, her eyes cutting back and forth between all present.

The first officer returned Jake's credentials and backed out of the room, saying as he went, "Five minutes."

When the door closed, Jake turned to Jessica, his eyes wide. "Listen up. You say *nothing* until Phil is present. Don't say anything to these guys, to any detectives you may see at the center, or to anyone you share a cell with. If they press you, the script is, 'My attorney instructed me not to answer questions unless he is present.' Phil will be on it and will get you released as soon as possible. Do you have personal items here—a purse? Keys to your apartment?"

She nodded. "The people here have my purse."

"I'm going to take possession of it. You won't need them at the detention center. Just to let you know, I'm going to search your apartment, so I need the key. You signed authorizations with Phil, right?"

"I think so. Why do you have to search my home?"

"Because there may be something that can give me a lead as to what happened. I promise you; the FBI team executed a search warrant within hours of coming onboard."

"How could they do that?"

"When a child of tender years goes missing, they can do just about anything in the course of searching for him or her. They probably have your computer. Is your phone in your purse?"

She nodded.

"Good. I'm sure the investigators will be looking for it soon. Now, hang in there. You're not alone. I'll notify Phil you've been arrested. We'll see you again at the detention center."

"You're taking my case?"

"Yes, Jessica. I'm taking your case. But I expect full cooperation. That means you give me all the information I ask for—plus a lot more."

A large grin spread across Scarlett's face.

....

CHAPTER SEVEN

As the police left the room with Jessica in handcuffs, Scarlett's gaze followed the trio until out of sight while her stomach churned. "What do we do? We can't just let them lock her up."

"Your emotional side is showing, Harvard. You know there's nothing we can do. Phil will be on it. That's his department. Want to meet me at the car? I'm going to the desk to retrieve Jessica's property."

"I'm going with you."

Swooping up his documents, a grin softened his expression. "Now, how did I know you would say that?"

After retrieving his weapon from the safe in the back of the SUV, Jake holstered it, climbed into the driver's seat, and cranked the Lexus.

"Are we going to the police station to finish the interview?"

"Nope. Not our priority. We're headed to Jessica's apartment." With one hand on the wheel, he used his free one to mount his cell phone in the holder and then gave Siri a verbal command. When a subject answered, he said, "Millie, Jake Shepherd. Can you put me through to Phil?"

Upon picking up, Phil Madison said, "Jake. What's up?"

"The Silver Spring boys interrupted my meeting with the client and took her into custody. You need to do your thing."

"Damn, that was faster than I expected. I assume they had a warrant?"

"Without one, they wouldn't have cuffed her with me there."

"And the charge?"

Jake chuckled. "You're going to love this. Misdemeanor child neglect, disturbing the peace, and resisting. How the hell do you get a charge of resisting when they take you to a mental facility? You should have no trouble working your voodoo to get her out."

"I take it you're on the case?"

Jake brought the vehicle to stop for a red light. "We all knew I would be." He turned to Scarlett and winked. "I didn't make it through my interview but got far enough to believe she's not involved in the disappearance. Scarlett and I are headed to the client's apartment. I suspect the Feds have her computer. I'll have Liz contact the cloud services. If she finds the right one, she'll have Jessica's files downloaded to one of my computers. When you meet with Jessica, get her passwords and don't take no for an answer. I have her cell."

"I'll make some calls, have lunch, and head to the pretrial detention center. It'll take them that long to process her. Chris is texting you the contact info on the guy—McKay, right?"

"Yeah. Good. He's next on my list. We need the client out ASAP, Phil. There's a little girl out there who needs to be found. Jessica's the only connection we've got at the moment."

"I'll work on an emergency hearing. Keep me posted on what you find."

"Ten-four." Jake clicked off the call as he drove forward. "So, Harvard. What have we got?"

"A frightened client and a missing child."

"Come on. You can do better. Who are our suspects?"

"I assume Jessica's off the table."

He nodded and gave her knee a pat.

"You tell me, Sherlock. You're the ace."

"You struck a chord. I was impressed."

"I did?" Scarlett made a face.

"The twin thing. What made you think of it?"

"Oh. I don't know why at that moment, but wouldn't it make sense? Only, why? What could cause a sister to do anything so awful? And if she did, what has she done with the child?"

"Never had evil thoughts about Savannah after she danced away with your fiancé?"

"Not that evil."

"Probably a good thing. With your relentless determination, you would be sure to inflict mortal wounds."

"Very funny. For your information, that's the trademark of a Capricorn, but I would never kidnap my sister's child." Scarlett took her cell phone out of her purse and checked for messages.

"All the same, it's worth exploring the idea of a twin, or even a non-twin sister. But I'm also interested in looking into the ex-wife of the boyfriend. Interviewing him is next up after we cover the apartment."

Scarlett dropped the phone into her purse, a puzzled look on her face. "Jake. What if Faith is not Jessica's child? What if she's the sister's child? I know she said she gave birth to her, but twins have been known to switch identities. What if the child is her sister's, Jessica took her for some reason, and never gave her back? I know it sounds crazy."

Jake turned the vehicle into a shopping center lot. "Stranger things have happened. No theory should be discounted at the onset of an investigation. Write it down. I would welcome that situation. It would provide hope for the child's well-being." He pulled into a parking place.

"What are we doing?"

"I want a coffee, how about you?"

"Sure."

Forty-five minutes later, Jake and Scarlett arrived at Jessica Johnson's apartment, located in a four-story brick building in a quiet neighborhood. Although most likely built in the late 1940s or early '50s, the structure and grounds were well maintained.

"Third floor, right?" Jake said as they walked up the steps to the entry.

"Right. I thought there might be crime-scene tape around the area."

"The scene would have been processed by now, but the fact no sign tape was here suggests the forensic team found no evidence of foul play. They would need it to designate this a crime scene since the child was last seen at school. Looks like there's no elevator. While we're here, we'll knock on a few doors. See if anyone in the complex has any information. I'm sure most have been talked to by one of the agencies."

When they reached the apartment, Jake used Jessica's key to unlock the door. It opened to reveal a serenely decorated living room with ample sunlight streaming through a set of French doors leading to a small balcony. A medium-size TV hung on the long wall, opposite a sofa and a pair of occasional chairs. Tall, narrow bookcases flanked the screen. The room was immaculate with the exception of a slight disarray of books.

"Jessica's a neat housekeeper," Scarlett said. "Except for the books."

"Oh, she's a neat housekeeper. The out-of-place books are the handiwork of the search team."

"They don't put things back in order?"

"Are you kidding? It's not uncommon for them to trash a place and leave it. No rule says they have to clean up. This is pretty neat for a tossed apartment. They probably saw our gal was not the average suspect. The majority of warrants are served on drug houses that are not by nature showplaces."

"Aside from the obvious search for signs of the child, what would they have been looking for? What are we looking for?"

"First, signs of foul play, a struggle, blood, weapons. Second, records that might lead to associates, things going on in the life of the client. Financials. Plus, anything that doesn't look right. I'm sure they dusted for prints to see who has been in the apartment. Any signs of things that would have DNA, like empty drink cans, cigarette butts, eating utensils."

Scarlett picked up a couple of the books and started to reshelve them. "Jessica has good taste in literature—Joyce Carol Oates, Margaret Atwood, Jane Austen."

"No Stephen King or James Patterson?"

"Nope. But there's quite a few Nora Roberts. No doubt her guilty pleasures. And a lot of these books are Faith's. She has *Grimm's Fairy Tales,* Disney books, *Charlotte's Web.* I'm impressed with Jessica."

"Give a quick look under the seat cushions, under the furniture. Doubt you'll find anything. If there was something, my former colleagues probably took it. I'm going to check the kitchen."

When Scarlett finished the living room, she called out to Jake. "I'm going to check a bedroom."

"I'm right behind you."

Scarlett entered Jessica's bedroom first, with Jake following. "What a cheerful décor," she said. I love her quilt." The covering was a patchwork amalgamation of gingham and florals in sunshine colors. The pillows were slightly askew. "It looks like the cops made an attempt to straighten their intrusion."

"Yeah. They definitely gave her a little respect."

"Look, Jake." Scarlett pointed to a large, framed collage hanging over a simple desk. "It must be Faith's dance recital. Look at her. She's precious."

Jake turned and took a step closer. "I was there."

"What do you mean, you were there?"

"I was there. That's Sabrina's dance school. I recognize the program."

"You're kidding."

He shook his head. "I'm not. I've written enough checks to the place. It's supposed to be the best."

"Do you remember Jessica?"

"Hell, no. I don't remember anyone but my child. But I want you to talk to the teacher. Ask if she noticed any strangers around when Faith was present."

"I already have it on my list."

Jake slapped the top of the desk. "If Jessica had a computer, my guess is it would be right here. Of course, it's gone." He glanced around. "I'll take this room; you check Faith's."

She nodded and turned to leave as he pulled open the top desk drawer.

Faith's door was open. As Scarlett looked around, tears fought to be released. "It's perfect," she whispered. "A cross between a ballerina and a princess." Dolls, stuffed animals, a miniature kitchen, complete with pots and pans and a china tea set, dominated the area. It took Scarlett a few minutes before she began opening drawers and checking the closet. All of Faith's clothes were arranged neatly on the rack. A bookcase held puzzles, coloring books, art supplies, and a DVD player. Before she finished, Jake appeared at the door.

"Look at this room, Jake. Jessica's love for this child is obvious. She could never hurt her. There's everything a little girl could want, except a kitten."

"Got to you, didn't she?"

"Yeah. Yeah, it did. I'll own it." Scarlett gave him a reprimanding look. "It got to you, too. You're just too stubborn to admit it."

He smiled. "I assume you haven't found anything."

"No. Have you?"

"Nada. I'm going to give the bathroom a once over, and then we'll knock on some doors."

"I'll straighten up the books in the living room while you do that. Under the circumstances, I'd hate for her to come home to a messed-up apartment."

He patted her on the shoulder. "Do your thing."

Jake wasn't in the small bathroom five minutes when he called out, "I may have struck gold, Harvard."

Scarlett shelved the two books she held and went to the bathroom. "What? You found something in here?"

"Look." He held up a prescription bottle. The cylinder-shaped, amber plastic container with a white cap was approximately two and a half inches tall.

"What's so special about that? Looks like an antibiotic prescription."

"Open it."

Scarlett took the container and removed the cap, a puzzled look on her face. "Oh!"

"Yeah. Some strange antibiotic—right?"

"Why would she keep a key in her medicine cabinet?"

"Take out the slip of paper coiled inside."

Removing it, Scarlett studied it for a couple of seconds. "A storage facility?"

"Looks like it. Big overlook by the search team."

"You think this is important?"

"If it weren't, why would she go to the trouble to disguise it, Harvard? We're skipping the canvas for now and heading to this unit. If my hunch is right, we're going to find a clue as who Ms. Jessica Johnson really is."

Her voice shaky, Scarlett said, "Jake, you don't think we're going to find something bad—something horrible—do you?"

"Don't speculate. We'll know soon enough."

As Jake drove through the town, Scarlett detected an unusual pattern to his driving. "Are all these turns necessary?"

"Cautionary."

"Why?"

"Just in case the apartment was under surveillance. I didn't see anyone, but that doesn't mean they weren't there. I don't want to lead them to our location until I know what the client has stashed away."

Scarlett turned, craning her head to look out the window. "You think someone could be following us?"

"Never know, but they'll have trouble keeping up with me."

The address Jake found in Jessica's medicine cabinet led them to a low-rent storage facility. There was no screening of visitors, only a sign indicating the gate would be locked at six p.m. and unlocked at six a.m. A green panel truck, bearing locksmith signage, occupied a parking spot next to the entrance.

"Joey beat us here, I see," Jake said.

"Joey?"

"Forgotten already? Joey helped out with the safe and locks in your sister's house. Remember?"

"Oh. Yeah. Why do you need him? You have the key."

Jake raised an eyebrow. "We don't know what lock the key fits. It may be the entry, or it may be something inside the unit. Often people secure these units with combination locks. The key could be for a drawer, lockbox, or something else. I texted Liz and had her send him to save time."

Jake pulled onto the property and then stopped, jumped out, leaving the door open, and approached the truck. The driver met him, raising a hand for a high-five.

"Yo, Shepherd. Liz said for me to get my stuff over here ASAP. Whatcha got going?"

"Might need you to get me into a unit here—maybe the contents."

"Not going to find a dead body, are we?"

"Would I do that to you? But grab your gear and get in my truck. I wouldn't want to cause a commotion with the caretakers or other tenants by bringing a locksmith onto the property."

Joey glanced around the premises. "This doesn't look like the type of place where anyone would notice, but sure."

As Joey got into the bucket seat, behind Scarlett, Jake said, "You remember Ms. Kavanagh from several months ago at the Georgetown house of Senator Kingsley, don't you?"

Scarlett craned her head around and nodded to the locksmith.

"Sorta. It was dark. Is this something to do with the senator's murder? Thought that was all tied up."

"It is. Scarlett is now working with me."

"No, sh—" Joey caught himself. "Sorry. No kidding. Jake Shepherd's taking on a partner?"

Scarlett gave Jake a smug look.

"Not exactly a partner. More like an employee."

"Damn, Jake. You must be raking it in if you can afford to hire a senator's sister-in-law."

Scarlett grinned.

"She's interning. What's the unit number, Harvard?"

Scarlett took a small leather notebook from her purse, opened it, and read the number. "G-Eleven."

He circled the first set of buildings and then turned down another row. "There we are," Jake said, stopping the Lexus. "I was right." He pointed to the building. "That's a combination lock. If you have trouble cracking it, Joey, cut it off and leave us a new one. We don't have time to fool around with it."

The words were barely out of Jake's mouth when Joey got out and went to the roll up door with Jake close behind and Scarlett trailing. "No need for the cutters. Cheap lock," the locksmith said. "I could do this one in my sleep." He spun the dial, listening to the tumblers, and within a minute or two, the lock opened. "I hate to charge you for this one, Jake, ole boy. My kid could have opened it."

Jake patted him on the shoulder. "This one's on Madison. But hang around until we see what's inside. Might need you to open something else." Jake raised the door of the small unit.

The chamber contained only a two-drawer file cabinet standing against the back wall, with a plastic storage box on top. "I think we've found the mate to our key, Harvard." He took the pill bottle from the pocket of his jacket, removed the key, and slid it into the lock at the upper corner of the cabinet. The mechanism immediately popped out. "Smooth as silk." He yanked open the top drawer, which held a number of hanging file folders. After a quick flip through, he closed the drawer and opened the lower. Again, there were hanging folders.

"Jake, could the FBI have found the key and address, come here already, and taken other contents?" Scarlett asked.

"Nope."

"What makes you sure?"

"Didn't you notice the lock, Harvard? The accumulation of dirt indicates it hasn't been touched in weeks, maybe longer."

"Jeez. Why would anyone pay rent to store no more than that?" Joey asked.

"It's not the space being paid for. It's the privacy."

"This a federal case?" Joey asked.

"Pretty much, but at this point, the less you know the better."

Joey gave Jake a dubious look. "We're not breaking any laws, are we?"

"Come on, bro. You know me better than that. We've got the usual power of attorney signed by the client-slash-owner of this stuff. Let me make sure there's no locked strongbox, and then I'll run you back to your truck." As he crouched down, flipping through the bottom drawer, he said, "Harvard, check the plastic container for anything needing Joey's expertise."

Scarlett removed the top and propped it against the concrete wall. Inside the black box were cards, photos, and other papers. "Nothing with a lock in here."

"All clear in this drawer as well. Be right back." He motioned to Joey to follow and the two left.

Scarlett began looking through what appeared to be Jessica's stash of memorabilia. Placing the lid back on top of the cabinet, she sorted the items, looking for names as she placed each item.

Within five minutes, Jake returned. "Whatcha got, Harvard?"

"All kinds of personal notes, greeting cards, a few photos."

"Any clues as to who Jessica really is?"

Scarlett shook her head. "Nothing so far. It's almost like she made certain to discard envelopes. Wait. Here's a photo with two little girls—twins—and a shabby, unkempt woman."

"Let me see." He took the photo, stared for a few seconds, and then turned it over. "'Mama, me and Zee.' Looks like you nailed it. This is likely Jessica, her twin, and her mother. Any others?"

Scarlett scrambled through the contents, extracting every photo. "I don't see any others of the twins. There's a couple of school photos of what could be Jessica, a couple of photos of a teenage boy."

"Names?"

Scarlett flipped each image over. "Only first names. Wait, here's one of what has to be Jessica or her twin with a guy. They're on a beach. The back says, 'Keith and me. Perfect day.'"

"Most likely Jessica. Not much to ID it with. Unfortunately, oceans seldom have signatures. Too bad there isn't more of the coastline in the shot. It could be anywhere," Jake said.

"Several of these mushy cards are signed, 'K forever' or 'Keith.' Must have been a relationship."

"How old would you estimate she would have been in the photos?"

Scarlett held the photo closer to her face to scrutinize it. "Probably a senior or just out of high school—maybe nineteen, twenty at most."

"Then, it's unlikely Keith is Faith's dad. Jessica claimed on Phil's intake paperwork to be thirty-two. Probably not her exact age, but close. That would have put her in the neighborhood of twenty-seven when Faith was born."

"Jake, here's a school report."

"Name, date, location?"

"All blacked out. But it's definitely high school subjects—AP Chemistry, AP Calculus, AP Computer Science, and she had straight A's in every one."

"Our Jessica is a smart lady."

"Not the type to derail. Makes me think that what she was running from wasn't her fault. What do you think?"

"She reads well on my radar, Harvard, or we wouldn't be on the case. Is there a parent's signature on the report?"

"No. No signature."

"Go ahead and put all the stuff back in the container. We'll take it with us." As he talked, he flipped through the bottom drawer of the file cabinet. "I need a box to keep the files together. Guess I can stack them on the floor between the—" He stopped mid-sentence, pulled a file out, and said, "What do we have here?"

"What?" Scarlett dropped what she was doing and peered over his shoulder.

Jake's chin bobbed up and down as he perused a newspaper clipping from the file. "Well, well, well. And look. There's a notebook computer and a cell at the back of the drawer. Wonder what we'll find on those."

Scarlett turned to the items left in the box, intending to put back those she had removed. But something caught her eye. Pulling out a piece of notebook paper, she found a poem written in a child's handwriting. The paper bore the signs of age with fold marks and a small rip.

> *She is alone.*
> *She is scared.*
> *The lade said don't lose faith.*
> *She is me.*

A red circle enclosed the word lade and lady had been written in the margin. The letter A appeared near the top, also in red.

A school paper. The simple words struck a chord with Scarlett as she reread it twice, and once again, her eyes misted. "I think Jessica had a rough childhood, Jake."

"Dial back on the emotion, Harvard."

"Come on, Jake." She dropped the poem in the box. "You are not as damn hard as you pretend."

"PI lesson one-o-one, Harvard." His fingers reinforced the numbers in sign language. "Emotions distort reality. If you're going to do this job, you'll have to compartmentalize. Sentiment skews perception."

She wanted to refute his theory but resisted.

"Check this out, Harvard." He carefully handed her a newspaper clipping from the file.

No date or identifying source appeared on the short piece. The headline read,

DEFENDANT RECEIVES 10 YEARS
ON FELONY MURDER CONVICTION

"Wow. That's interesting. It has to mean something to Jessica for it to be in this file cabinet—even to have a folder, but what good is it, Jake? The name of the defendant is blacked out, and there's not even a city listed."

"Trust me. Liz will put her voodoo on it and track it down," he said, standing and clearing room on the cabinet top for the files he removed from the drawer. "Get packed up. I want to take this stuff to the office and interview the boyfriend today. What's his name?"

"Ted McKay." Scarlett's face pinched in a frown as she carefully layered items in the box. "Why do you do that?"

"Do what?"

"Act like you don't remember a name. You've got a mind like a steel trap."

He chuckled, patting her on the shoulder. "Just like to see if you're paying attention."

CHAPTER EIGHT

Forty-five minutes later, after dropping the files and notebook computer with Liz, they were on their way to Ted McKay's office.

"I thought you might leave me with Liz," Scarlett said as the GPS voice announced, "Turn left at the light."

"You did? Why?"

"You rarely let me be in on interviews with Savannah's case."

"I had my reasons. But your family law experience should play well in this interview. I'll do the questioning. You assess him for lying-husband-syndrome." He turned left as directed and then pointed to a building on the right. "There. Looks like we're here."

"Nice," Scarlett said. "Mr. McKay looks successful." Not far from the White House, McKay's office address was a sleek, eight-story, modern building with a great deal of glass reflecting the sun.

Within a few minutes of parking in the underground garage, Jake and Scarlett rode an elevator to the top floor. As the silent car whooshed upward, Scarlett took in the brass trim, mahogany wood, and spotless mirrors. *This is a high-rent building. McKay must be wealthy.*

When the doors parted, they faced a double-glass entry showcasing a string of names topped by Theodore A. McKay, PE in black and gold lettering. "Does he know we're coming?" Scarlett asked.

"Yeah. Liz set it up." Jake held a door open for Scarlett and then proceeded to the reception desk.

It took less than three minutes for a tall, gray-haired man, who appeared to be in his early fifties, to appear. He walked toward Jake with a hand outstretched. "Mr. Shepherd, I'm Ted McKay." He motioned to the receptionist, "Hold my calls, Sherry." Turning back to Jake, he nodded to Scarlett and said, "Come on back to my office where we can talk."

As they walked to McKay's corner office, Scarlett continued to absorb the tasteful richness of the premises. *Does Jessica know who this guy is?*

"Mr. McKay, this is my associate, Scarlett Kavanagh. As I'm sure my assistant told you, we've been retained on behalf of Jessica Johnson in the disappearance of her daughter."

He nodded, extending a hand to Scarlett. "Pleased to meet you." Turning his attention to Jake, with an urgent expression on his face, he said, "Has there been any word?"

Jake shook his head. "Not yet."

"Dear, God. This is awful. Pray Faith is not being—I can't even go there." He inhaled, blinked, and shook his head. "Please have a seat. Can I offer you something to drink?"

"Not for me."

Scarlett shook her head. "I'm fine, thank you."

"How is Jessica? Have you seen her?" McKay said as he sat in the chair behind his massive desk.

Scarlett glanced around the room. At the far end stood a drafting table in front of built-in bookcases atop cabinets. Behind McKay, the glass wall revealed a picturesque view of the area.

"She's pretty worked up as you can imagine," Jake said. "You are aware the authorities arrested her?"

"I heard. Is there anything I can do to help? There is absolutely no way Jessica Johnson neglected or harmed her daughter. That child is the center of her universe."

"Right now, you can help by telling me everything you know about Jessica. I'm looking for clues as to who might have had a motive to abduct the child."

"I'd be happy to tell you what I know, but Jessica is a private person. When I think about it, I know very little about her."

"Assuming you've seen her with her daughter, how would you describe Jessica's interaction with Faith?"

"Attentive. Loving. Gentle." His demeanor changed. "Don't tell me you have any thoughts Jessica could have done something to her child?"

"Did I say that?"

"No. But you may have implied it."

"That wasn't intended. Tell me about *your* relationship with Jessica."

"I'm not sure you can call it a relationship, Mr. Shepherd. As a member of our church vestry, I met Jessica when she was initially hired—about four years ago—but only knew her in passing. When I served as the chairman of a major building fund, she sat in on all the committee meetings, usually remaining quiet. One Sunday afternoon, there was a heated discussion. I don't recall what it was about, but Jessica surprised me. She spoke up on behalf of my position. After the meeting, I thanked her for her support and invited her to dinner." He stopped talking and tipped his head as though thinking.

When close to a minute passed, Jake said, "So, you took her to dinner."

McKay raised his head. "No. She declined."

"But you eventually began dating."

"It took several months. I didn't want to pressure her, but I had come to admire her."

"How long ago was that?"

"About a year. My divorce had just gone through."

"During any of your dinner dates, did she ever talk to you about her past? Her family? Siblings? Where she grew up?"

He shook his head. "Only thing she said about her past is it was complicated, and she didn't like to talk about it."

"Did she ever mention having a problem with anyone? Anyone making her nervous?"

"No. I'm very fond of Jessica, Mr. Shepherd. Could even find myself becoming serious, but she won't let the relationship move forward. She pulls back if our conversation becomes personal. I've learned to tiptoe. We have Sunday lunch after services and dinner once or twice a month. She's only allowed me to take her to dinner at my private club once."

"When was that?"

"About ten days ago."

Jake made a note and then said, "Do you and your ex-wife have mutual friends who are members of that club?"

McKay gave him a puzzled look. "Yes. Is that important?"

"Could be. Was Faith included in any of your dates with Jessica?"

The man nodded. "Several. Always our Sunday lunches. As a matter of fact, we took Faith with us to the club. Jessica does not like leaving her with sitters. Like I said, she is a devoted mother."

"Where else have you been seen together with the child?"

McKay thought for a minute or two. "I did attend Faith's dance recital a couple of months ago. She's a great kid. Quiet like her mom, well-behaved with nice manners—better than my kids at her age."

Jake smiled. "How many children do you have?"

"Two adult sons, but I don't see them much. One is in grad school at Stanford; the other is in training to be a pilot in the air force."

"How are they with your dating Jessica?"

He shrugged. "I'm not sure they even know. My relationship with Jessica is so superficial. I've never talked to the boys about it, and they've never met her."

"What about your ex? How is she with you keeping company with another woman?"

He groaned. "Not thrilled." He leaned back in his chair. "Miranda is a strong-willed woman with a short fuse."

"If you don't mind, tell me about your ex-wife. Describe for me how negative her attitude toward Jessica is?"

McKay's jaw tightened, and a frown blanketed his face. "My ex-wife has problems. She's not happy with anything."

"I'll take that to mean she's pretty pissed off about it."

"I'd be lying if I tried to deny it."

"I'm going to ask you a hard question, Mr. McKay." Jake put his pen down. "Do you believe your wife could have been involved in Faith's disappearance?"

McKay's brow wrinkled, and his head slowly shook. "It has not occurred to me. I can't give you an answer. Miranda is not the woman I married. Could she do anything so atrocious as to abduct a child? It would be hard for me to believe, but I won't say impossible."

"What happened to your marriage, if you'll forgive me for asking?"

"It's no secret. In a word. Hydrocodone—Lortabs. My ex is an addict. Three stints in rehab with three failures, and I gave up."

"I'm sorry to hear that."

"Me, too. She was in an auto accident, had to have surgery on her back, and never got off the damn things. I'm probably a sorry son of a bitch for not sticking it out, but I couldn't let her choices destroy my life. Thank God, our children were grown before it all exploded."

"So, you believe your ex is jealous of Jessica?"

"Probably. She's not rational much of the time. Who am I kidding? She is extremely jealous. She confronted Jessica and me at a restaurant and made a scene. Fortunately, Faith wasn't with us. It was humiliating, and Jess refused to go out with me for several weeks afterward."

"Must have been hard on both of you. I heard your ex is of similar description to Jessica. Do you have a photo of her?"

"Not readily available, but I can get one for you. I gave what few photos I had to the boys, but I'll contact my mother. She's got some, I'm sure."

"What about an address for your wife? Do you mind giving it to me?"

"Not at all. She still lives in the marital home." He reached into his top drawer, took out a pad of Post-it Notes, jotted down the address, and handed it to Jake.

Jake tucked the note into a pocket of his portfolio. "Thanks." Looking the engineer squarely in the eye, he said, "I'd appreciate your discretion, Mr. McKay. I would prefer Ms. McKay does not prepare for my visit or attempt to avoid it."

"I understand. Believe me, Mr. Shepherd, my concerns are for Faith and Jessica. I'll do whatever to help. Just name it. I understand Phillip Madison is representing Jessica. Will he be able to get her released? If she needs bond money, I'm here."

"I'll pass that along." Jake rose. "If you think of anything further that might be of interest, please give us a call, and don't forget the photo of Ms. McKay." Jake took out a card and wrote additional contact information on the back. "Feel free to give my assistant, Liz, any updates you have if you don't reach me."

Little was said on the walk back to the parking garage, but once in the vehicle, Jake turned to Scarlett. "So, Harvard. Did McKay pass the sniff test?"

She nodded. "He did. Do you agree?"

"So far. He seems like a decent sort and quite smitten with our client. But keep in mind. With his thing for Jessica, he could consider Faith an obstacle."

"Oh, my god."

"Relax. That's a long shot. I like the ex-wife better at this point."

"You think she could have taken Faith?"

Jake cranked the SUV and started to back out of the parking space. "That remains to be seen." He handed Scarlett his phone. "Check my messages and email for anything from Phil or Liz."

As the phone came on, Scarlett said, "You've got a text from Liz."

"Read it."

"'Found lead on client's ID.'"

CHAPTER NINE

Kai greeted Jake and Scarlett at the office door. "Whatcha got for me?" Jake asked Liz as he scratched behind the shepherd's ears.

"I think you're going to like it. I tracked the newspaper clipping to Jacksonville, Florida. The defendant's name is Xenia Crystal Arnold. She participated in the armed robbery of a convenience store in which law enforcement shot and killed her male partner during the getaway attempt. Her rap sheet includes petty drug dealing and prostitution in addition to the big one for felony murder. She served eight and a half years of the sentence. Released fifteen months ago."

"Wow!" Scarlett said, her eyes widening with interest. "Jake, Xenia makes sense for the photo with the two little girls. Remember, it said on the back, 'Mama, me, and Zee.'"

"Looks like we may have a match. Good work, ace." He gave Liz a high-five. "If she served eight and a half and been out about a year, give or take, she should still be on parole."

"Nope," Liz said. "Florida abolished parole in 1983. Her early release was based on gain time."

"Bad break for us. It means no one is tracking her. Anything more in your research to tie her to our client?"

"As a matter of fact, it gets better. I pulled up her DOC records." She reached into a manila folder on her desk and pulled out a sheet of paper. "Take a look at this."

"Damn." After looking at the inmate image on the sheet, he turned to Scarlett and handed it to her. "Take a look, Harvard. Looks like you nailed it indeed."

"Oh my gosh. That could be Jessica if the hair color were different."

"It's got to be the sister—likely twin," Jake said. "Find any mention of a sister, Liz?"

"Nothing in the news or court records, but I did find a Nyx Sierra Arnold listed in certain records as a member of the same family and the same age as Xenia Crystal Arnold. Don't ask how I got them." She gave him a dubious look.

"I never question your sources. So, Jessica may very well be Nyx Arnold."

"Nyx? Is that like short for Nicole?" Scarlett asked.

"It's spelled N-Y-X."

"That is unusual but kind of goes with Xenia."

"Comes from Greek mythology," Jake said. "Nyx was the Goddess of Night. Xenia comes from Greek for hospitality. All fits."

Liz and Scarlett stared at him.

"I wouldn't have taken you for a student of Greek mythology," Scarlett said.

"I wasn't. Took it in college to impress a girl. Did you find Nyx Arnold in any other data?"

Liz suppressed a laugh begun when he mentioned the girl in college. "No. Nothing. The father's name is Frank Milton Arnold, and the mother is Arlene Bascom Arnold. Father has a longer rap sheet than my granddaughter's Christmas list. Doing life in a West Florida prison—Santa Rosa."

"Were you able to match birth dates for the two Arnolds?" Jake asked.

"Not yet. But, if I can get a date of birth for Nyx from the DMV in Florida, I can compare it with the one DOC has for Xenia."

"Be sure to consider the day before and day after," Scarlett said. "Twins can be born on different days if the first one came close to midnight. My sister and I actually have different birthdays." She reached down and rubbed Kai as he sniffed her purse. "Sorry, ole boy. No gun in there today. Don't have a permit yet." She looked back toward Liz. "What about the mom? Where is she?"

"Her trail has gone cold, but she came up in charges against him for aggravated domestic battery and two civil actions seeking injunctions for protection against domestic violence. Mom has a sheet of her own—bad checks, shoplifting, drug charges."

"Oh my gosh. I was right. Jessica had a terrible childhood. No wonder she left and changed her name." Scarlett picked up several documents from the open file on Liz's desk. "Jake, she could be in WITSEC."

He shook his head. "Not buying it, but there's more to her behavior than wanting to erase a miserable past," Jake said. "The woman is terrified of her real identity being discovered to the extent she went to jail rather than offer a potential explanation. I've got to ask. Is she running from someone or from the law?" He turned to Liz. "Have we heard from Phil? Do we know if he got her released?"

"No word. I'll give his office a call. Maybe Joyce knows something. By the way, Lila called. She's got a slip and fall she wants you to handle. Looks like a career plaintiff."

Jake grimaced. "Slip and fall? Can't be that big a number on the table unless the claimant is an NFL quarterback."

"I think she just wants you in the loop. And don't you dare tell *me* to call her with your excuses. Lila Stonebridge is your—your whatever."

"Yeah. Well, she's also at least a paycheck a month for both of us. Don't give me that reprimanding look. I'll call her. Convince her Pete and Sonny can get the case started."

Scarlett's eyes cut back and forth between Liz and Jake.

"Right now, I'm going to touch base with the Bureau and find out what is happening with the search." He looked at Liz. "Yes, I'm going to call Lila. While I'm making my calls, you can find out if Jessica has been released. I think I'll postpone canvassing Jessica's neighbors until tomorrow. By the time we could get back to the complex, it would be getting dark, and people would really resist talking to strangers without badges."

"Is there anything I can do?" Scarlett asked.

"Check out the room across the hall from the work room. We cleared it out for your office. You can get an idea of what furniture you want."

A smile broke on Scarlett's face. "Really? Thank you. I didn't expect a private office."

He returned her smile. "You'll need a place to work, do interviews and intakes. I can give you a small budget to work with."

"Don't worry about that. I sold my practice and most of the furniture. I will buy my own furnishings. But thank you for the offer."

He nodded. "I should have known. That said, the only thing I have left on my list for the day is to take Kai over to the school and see if he can track the location where Faith and her abductor ended their stroll to disappearance. I'm sure the Bureau has used their dogs, but all dogs aren't created equal."

"Jake," Liz said, "I'll stay late and work on the notebook computer you found in the storage unit. See what's there."

"Appreciate it, but don't stay past eight. I don't want you here alone any later."

It took Jake twenty minutes to complete his calls. When he finished, Scarlett stood in her new office space, making notes and measuring sections of the room. As he walked in, she said, "Any news on Faith?"

He shook his head. "Unfortunately, nothing." Without an explanation, he took a nylon zip tie out of his pocket and threaded the free end through the ratchet to form a loop. He then took the pad and pen from her hand, laying them on a small, empty bookcase, the sole piece of furniture in the room.

Scarlett watched, wondering what he was doing.

Taking her hands, he looped the tie over them, and then pulled it tight.

"What are you doing, Shepherd? Take that off."

"Nope."

"What do you mean, nope? That's not funny." Every muscle in her face tensed, those in her body following suit.

"Not meant to be funny."

"Get it off, Jake. I don't like it." Her eyes developed a near wild expression.

"Calm down. You look more agitated than when you had a gun to your head."

"Yeah. Well, I knew you were going to take care of that, but this I don't understand or like. It's not funny. I have a phobia. I can't stand being bound."

"As I said, it's not meant to be funny. So, I guess that means hand-cuffs in the bedroom are off limits."

She glared at him. "Damn it. What the hell are you up to?"

"That *was* meant to be funny."

"Stop being . . . being whatever you're being. Cut me free."

He shook his head. "Nope. You're going to figure it out."

"Figure it out?" She glared at him for a minute and then called for help. "Liz. Come here and tell Sherlock he's going too far."

Jake watched her, grinning. "You want to be a detective? You have to be prepared to find yourself in some tough spots. Figure out how to get out of the binding."

"I can't. No one can. It's not possible unless you're Houdini. Cut me free." She pounded on him with her bound fists.

He laughed, backing up, and again shook his head. "It is possible."

Liz appeared in the doorway. "Jake, what are you doing?"

"Scarlett wants to be an investigator. She needs to know self-defense."

"Tell him to cut me free, or you do it," Scarlett said, thrusting her bound hands toward Liz.

With a reprimanding glint in her eye, Liz turned toward Jake. "Either show her how, or cut her free. Stop torturing her."

He whipped another tie out of his pocket, made the loop, inserted his hands, and pulled it tight with his teeth.

Taking a deep breath, Scarlett watched his every move, some of her tension relaxing for the first time since he stripped her of autonomy.

Raising his hands above and slightly behind his head, with a rapid motion, he thrust his arms down, elbows skirting his waist. The tie popped.

With an impish grin, he said, "See? No sweat."

"That's because you're strong as a rhinoceros."

"No. It's simple physics. Try it."

"No." She shook her head. "I can't."

"*That* is your first mistake. Never say can't. If you're in an untenable position, you have to say to yourself, 'I can do this. I can figure this out.' If you don't. You're dead." He pulled a third zip tie from his pocket. "Here. Liz can show you." He made the loop and put it around Liz's hands. "Show her."

Liz worked the ratchet to the center, between her two hands, pulled it tight with her teeth, and mimicked Jake's action. As in his case, the nylon broke.

"See. Now you do it. It's the only way you're getting out of it."

"You've got a cruel streak, Shepherd. Did they give you that at Yale?"

"Nope. HRT training—actually, before. My dad first taught me, but it was also on the menu at Quantico. You were warned. Told you I am a terrible teacher."

"You're really going to leave me tied up?"

"I really am. Now do it. Sabrina's been able to do it since elementary school."

"Damn you, Shepherd. If I break my wrist, it's on you." She took a deep breath, raised her hands, and jerked down with the full force of her ability. The tie snapped, and Scarlett jumped—shocked. "I did it."

"Of course, you did it. Once you knew you had to. If I had let you whine and whimper your way to release, you'd never learn."

"I hate to interrupt, Jake, but if you're done with self-defense lessons, Joyce said the client has not been released. The judge went rogue—set bond at one hundred thousand."

With a look of shock and disbelief, Jake struck a nearby desk with the side of his fist. "Damn. You've got to be kidding. On child neglect and disturbing the peace? Did Phil phone it in?" He shook his head. "Call her back. Phil needs to contact Ted McKay. He'll cover it." He glanced down at his watch. "But it's not happening today. Clerk's office will be closing shortly."

Scarlett's eyebrows came together in a frown. "Poor Jessica— she'll have to sleep in a cell tonight on top of worrying about her baby."

Traces of twilight remained when Jake, Scarlett, and Kai arrived at Faith's school. Pole lights, sprinkled around the property, began coming on, producing ample illumination. Since Jake's self-defense lesson, Scarlett had little to say but watched intently as he put Kai through the tracking paces while she made a rough diagram of the trail.

Beginning at the door identified on the surveillance video as the exit Faith and her abductor passed through, Jake took a pajama top he had removed from a zippered, stuffed bear on Faith's bed. After holding it for Kai to sniff, Jake issued the tracking command in German.

"Can he find a trail after all the traffic that surely passed through this door since the abduction?" Scarlett asked.

"You'd be amazed what shepherds can detect. It's been said they have as many as two hundred million scent receptors."

It took him a few minutes, but the dog began to pull at the lead, suggesting he found his target. Following him, the trail led off the property, out of camera range, and up a side street where it ended. "Let's see what you've got," Jake said to Scarlett, and she held out the pad.

"Looks good. I'll get with the investigation team and compare with what they have. Should be a start on tracking the means of exit transportation." He surveyed the area. "Doubt if there's a camera within range. Let's grab dinner and head home. We'll do the neighbor canvas at Jessica's complex around eleven tomorrow."

"Won't people be at work?"

"We're looking for those who would have been home after Faith left the school with her abductor and before Jessica appeared in the office."

"That makes sense."

"I'm sure a complete canvass has been done without success. If either the Silver Spring PD or the Response Team obtained info suggesting Jessica was seen with the child, they would have used it at the first appearance, and Phil would have mentioned it. We're just covering every base."

After stopping for dinner at a small Italian restaurant with outside tables where Kai's presence was permitted, the trio returned to Jake's apartment. He unlocked the door and held it for Scarlett. As she passed, he said, "Still mad about the zip tie?"

She snapped her head around to face him. "Why would you ask that?"

"Maybe because you hardly talked at the restaurant, and you've only spoken when you had to the rest of the time."

"Well, you could have handled the situation with a little more consideration of my feelings."

He closed the door and then put both hands on her shoulders. "If I didn't care what happened to you, I wouldn't have been quite so hard. But admit it. You are headstrong and independent. I like it. But I can't let you put yourself in unnecessary jeopardy. Like it or not, your safety is in my hands."

"What kind of cases do you handle that would be that dangerous?"

"Let me feed Kai, get us something to drink, and then we'll talk about it."

She nodded and went into the bedroom to change her shoes and freshen up. When she returned to the living room, he was sitting on the couch with two glasses of wine on the coffee table.

As he handed her one of the wine glasses, he said, "Here. This is pretty good."

She took it and sat at the opposite end. After taking a sip, she said, "You're right. It is good. Now talk."

"Harvard, you're accustomed to investigators who make a good living tracking cheating spouses, doing surveillance on plaintiffs milking personal injury claims, or trying to prove or disprove liability in accidents. That's not what I typically do. Not to say I never work some of those, but my rate is usually over the budget."

"What do you do?"

He laughed. "Amazing how sure you were that you wanted to join but didn't really know what you were getting into. I do a lot of high-end insurance fraud, arson, wrongful death of the intentional kind, blackmail, stalking—but big ticket. The bigger the bounty or higher the stakes, the greater the risk. You have to be prepared. Are you sure you still want to do this? I could put you with Pete. He does the security and the simple cases."

She stared at him for more than a minute before answering. "Are you trying to scare me off?"

"No, and that's the truth. I like having you around, Harvard, but I won't let you blunder in and get yourself hurt or worse. I know you said family law was dangerous, and I believe it can be. But there's a larger helping of jeopardy in this line of work. I've been trained to sense the danger and to handle it. You haven't. Today was just a sample. You're smart, have good instincts; you're a thorough investigator and know the law—but you're not a cop."

"I can learn. Tell me what classes to take."

He smiled again. "Okay. We'll try it. But right now, let's get some sleep. Probably have a long day tomorrow." He patted her on the shoulder, took her empty glass, and went to his room, dropping the stemware in the kitchen on the way.

A few minutes past two a.m., Jake, wearing only boxer briefs, came out of Sabrina's room where he slept when Scarlett stayed in his apartment. Light from inside the bedroom provided dim illumination. As he headed toward the kitchen, he noticed Scarlett curled up on the couch with a legal pad and clip-on book light in her lap. "What are you doing up at this hour?"

"Pink, Shepherd? You wear pink underwear?"

"Didn't expect to run into anyone at this hour."

She gave him a once over, tilting her head slightly to the side. "I couldn't get Jessica out of my head. Her sleeping in a jail cell with who knows what kind of people. So, I decided to study my notes." She shook her head. "But I can't believe Rambo wears pink briefs."

He laughed. "I'm color blind. Have no idea what color they are. But if they bother you, I'll be happy to take them off." He snapped the elastic waistband that read "Calvin Klein."

"I bet you would. You obviously didn't dress for company."

He chuckled. "I guess it depends on who the company is. But you look quite prim and proper in your silky robe." He moved closer to the sofa.

With a flirtatious glint in her eyes, she said, "Yeah, but it's warm in here. I could take it off."

He grinned. "You could." He leaned over, took the pad from her lap, and put it on the side table. "In fact, as your host, I should help with that."

....

CHAPTER TEN

Whether it was the aroma of bacon or the pair of dark-brown eyes staring at her that woke Scarlett at seven-fifteen Thursday morning, she wasn't sure.

"Kai?"

The shepherd stood, frozen in place. Not even an ear twitched.

"We're still friends, aren't we?" Groggy, she glanced at the clock, the empty side of the bed, and back at the dog. "Jake!"

Within seconds, he appeared at the door. "Good afternoon. Welcome to the world."

"Oh, you're cute. Why is he staring at me like I just murdered one of his puppies?"

Jake laughed. "I told him to find you. Don't you think it's about time you got up?"

She reached down, grabbed her robe, and slid her arms into it. "What do you mean about time? I've only had four hours sleep."

"A detective's life is never easy, Harvard. Hustle. We've got work waiting."

"I think I hate you."

He laughed again. "I'm used to it. As a matter of fact, a night with you is like an affair with a praying mantis. You never know the next morning if you're going to be kissed or killed."

She grinned sarcastically, wrinkling her nose, and then shook an index finger at him as she began to climb out of bed. "We're not having an affair—and pink underwear, Shepherd?"

"Well, enlighten me. What do they call it at Harvard? As for my boxer briefs, it's what happens when you mix red and white in the washer. What would you have me do? Throw them away? If you like, I'll give them to you as a trophy."

Squinting, she glared at him. "At Harvard, it's called a lapse. You know. Like laying a line of cocaine in front of a junkie. What can you expect? Told you I should stay in a hotel."

"Oh. Is that what it is—an addiction lapse? Interesting. Well, since I'm not your lover, as your boss, I'm saying get your chassis ready to go. We're on the road in"—he looked at his watch—"twenty minutes."

"Twenty minutes? Give me a break, Shepherd."

"Okay, thirty. Breakfast is on the bar. I'll be tending to Romeo."

"Where is he?"

"Who the hell knows, but he'll show when he hears me rattle the bag of rabbit food."

At eight forty-five, Jake and Scarlett reached the office. As they walked in, Liz said, "I was beginning to worry. Not here by eight. Not like you, Jake."

He grinned. "Scarlett can explain."

"Never mind. It sounds like none of my business."

Scarlett rolled her eyes.

"Update me," Jake said. "Anything new?"

"Not yet. I'm having trouble hacking into the notebook, and the battery is dead on the cell. I have the Carbonite download of Jessica's primary computer but so far only routine info. I'll keep working on all three." She closed the pen in her hand with a click. "Are you in or out of the office today?"

"Out this morning. Not sure about the afternoon. Depends on when Phil gets the client released." He turned to Scarlett. "We've got time for another self-defense lesson, and then we'll head over to Miranda McKay's house."

"Thanks for the heads-up on the lesson."

He patted her shoulder, chuckling. "No more ambushes. You have my word.

CHAPTER ELEVEN

An hour later, as Jake drove toward the McKay woman's house, he adjusted the air conditioning. "By the way, you look sharp today in your blue and green blouse."

She looked at him, pinching her eyebrows together. "Thank you, but I thought you said you were color blind."

"Did I say that?"

"You did."

"Guess I lied." He laughed. "I think we're here. Nice house." The sleek, two-story house in modern-styled architecture spread across the width of the property with a predominately paved front area.

"Very nice house."

"Let's take a shot at the former Mrs. McKay," Jake said as he stopped the SUV.

Miranda McKay took her time answering the doorbell, leaving Jake and Scarlett standing at the door. In thirty-second intervals, he pushed the button until she finally responded. A voice came over a speaker in the surveillance camera. "What is it you want? I don't buy from door-to-door solicitors, and I'm not interested in a religious spiel."

Jake looked at Scarlett and back toward the door. "That's excellent since we have none of the above to offer. Mrs. McKay, I take it?"

"Who's asking?"

"Jake Shepherd, private investigator. I'm working the disappearance of Faith Johnson and understand you knew her mother."

"I'm not talking to you."

"That's your choice. But if you don't, I'll have to turn what I know so far over to my former colleagues at the FBI, and they usually don't take no for an answer. The way I look at it, you can have a short chat with me or risk an interrogation by them. What is your preference?"

Scarlett gazed at Jake. *He is good. Qualifies every statement but gets the power words in.*

"Who did you say you were again? Did my ex-husband send you?"

"I'm Jake Shepherd, and my colleague, Scarlett Kavanagh, is here with me. Your ex did not send me, but he did give me your address."

"How do I know you're not a robber or a rapist?"

"That's a good question. I'm glad you asked. Your cameras have sent a clear image of me to the Cloud. If I were to commit a crime against you, I'm reasonably sure I would serve time. Now, why would I risk that?"

The intercom went silent for several seconds. "Show me ID."

Jake removed his DC investigator's license, business card, and driver's license from his wallet and positioned all three toward the doorbell camera.

"Do you swear my ex didn't send you?"

Jake chuckled. "I swear."

She said nothing else but took her time opening the door. When she did, her gaunt face, disheveled hair, and shabby clothing shocked Scarlett. *She doesn't fit with the house.*

Miranda McKay wore a faded and paint-stained, navy-blue warmup suit and fuzzy, black bedroom slides. Despite the dim light in the entry hall, the pupils of her eyes appeared constricted, failing to dilate.

As Scarlett observed the woman, she made a mental comparison. *At a distance, she might pass as Jessica.*

"Thank you for allowing us in," Jake said. "Is there somewhere we can sit for a few minutes?"

Miranda motioned toward the large living room, furnished in an austere, contemporary style. Neutral colors dominated, accented with impressionist art. The room appeared unused.

"Lovely home," Jake said.

"It's not a home. It's a house," the woman said as the three took seats—Miranda on a white leather couch, Jake and Scarlett on gray-and-white striped chairs facing her. Between them stood a glass-topped cocktail table with out-of-date, French magazines fanned out on top beside an abstract, black-marble sculpture. "Homes have families. I live here alone."

Jake let the remark pass. "I won't take too much of your time. Just a few questions. You are aware of the child's disappearance, aren't you?"

"What child?"

The response startled Scarlett, but Jake took it in stride.

"Faith Johnson. Jessica Johnson's little girl," he said.

"Jessica Johnson is a whore."

Scarlett flinched.

"That's a strong comment, Mrs. McKay. Could you elaborate for me? What do you base it on?"

"I will not. It's none of your business."

With uncharacteristic patience, he said, "I understand. So, is it fair for me to believe there's no love lost between you and Jessica Johnson?"

"Believe whatever . . . whatever you like. She's a whore. Homewrecking whore."

Jake adjusted his position on the chair. "Using the term homewrecking, should I take that to mean she broke up your marriage?"

"You're an investigator. Figure it out for yourself."

Jake continued to ignore her attitude. "So, it's safe to say you don't like Jessica Johnson."

The woman glared at him. "Whore."

"I got it. Making a note." He wrote "WHORE" on the legal pad in his portfolio and turned it for her to see. "Do you know the child?"

"What child?"

How long before he loses it with this nut job? Scarlett cut her eyes back and forth between the pair.

"Jessica's daughter, Faith."

"I've seen her. Poor kid. Slut for a mother." She gazed around the room and up at the ceiling.

"When did you last see Fa—"

Miranda McKay stood up and walked out of the room without a word.

Jake glanced over at Scarlett, a tight grin fighting to erupt on his face. Scarlett rolled her eyes and said, "Now what?"

"Now, we wait."

Scarlett shook her head and, in a hushed tone, said, "What if she doesn't come back? Do we go look for her, leave, what?"

"One thing at a time, Harvard. We'll give it a few minutes."

After nearly fifteen minutes of Scarlett and Jake gazing around the room, checking messages on their phones, and exchanging facial expressions, Miranda McKay waltzed in as nonchalantly as she left.

"You're still here? What was your name again?"

"Jake. Jake Shepherd and Scarlett Kavanagh. Of course, we're still here. You didn't get to finish your last answer."

"What answer?"

Is this woman for real or playing Jake?

"Tell you what," he said. "Instead of going back to that. Why don't you tell me a little about yourself? This is a beautiful house. Do you take care of it or have help?"

"I take care of it. I'm between housekeepers. It's hard to find the right person."

"I understand. I have the same problem. You have two sons. Tell me about them."

Her demeanor changed as a hint of sparkle flickered in her eyes. So absorbed in responding, she did not question why he would ask. "They are wonderful. Clint is in . . . in what's that big state on the other side of the country?"

"California," Jake said.

She smiled. "Of course. How could I forget? He's in college."

"And your other son is in the Air Force, right?"

Her brow furrowed. "How did you know? Oh, Ted told you."

"He did. You must miss your sons."

A veil of sadness dropped over her eyes as her focus appeared to slip. After a pause, she said, "You can't imagine."

"Do you work outside the house?"

"No. My home is my career."

Now, it's her home.

"Well, how do you fill your time?" Jake's tone conveyed sincerity as he guided the dialogue toward his goal.

She frowned. "This and that—I don't know."

"Do you have plans for today?" Jake asked.

"I don't remember."

Does he believe her? I can't tell if she is a crazy loon or sly as a fox.

Scarlett expected him to press the woman, but instead, he glanced around the room.

"You have excellent taste, Mrs. McKay. Did you do the interior decorating?"

A big smile broke across her face. "We had a designer, but I chose all the major pieces. He just tweaked things and made suggestions on accessories."

"Who chose the painting over the fireplace?"

"You like it?"

"I do. It's beautiful."

Miranda McKay's attitude shifted like crystal beads in a kaleidoscope.

"It's a—" She leaned forward and whispered, "It's an Edmund Graecen original. Don't tell anyone. Ted says someone might break into the house to steal it."

Scarlett looked up at the pastel landscape by the American Impressionist, having not previously noticed it. *Oh, my god. It's gor-*

geous, but I would have expected more contemporary art with this decor.

Acting as though he knew the value of the painting, Jake said, "Impressive."

"I designed the room around it. Ted freaked when I bought it. But he didn't go to the auction with me, and I wasn't going to miss the opportunity."

Jake smiled. "You certainly strike me as a woman of discriminating taste who knows what she wants and doesn't give up until she gets it."

Miranda McKay tucked her chin, a tight smile on her face. "I listen to motivational tapes. My father said Vince Lombardi was right when he said, 'Winners never quit, and quitters never win.'"

"And you want a reconciliation with your former husband, right?"

She glared at him with a trace of contempt. "Of course, I do. Marriage is sacred."

"I understand. Felt the same, myself."

"You're divorced?"

"Unfortunately, I am. My ex found someone she liked better."

The contempt vanished as she tipped her right ear slightly toward her shoulder with a sympathetic expression on her face.

There you go, Jake. Getting her to identify with you. Wish I could have seen you in court. Bet you had witnesses eating out of your hand.

"It's usually the man who cheats," Miranda said.

"So, I've heard. But I didn't. Tell me about your week—what you did yesterday."

"Yesterday?" Her eyes cut around the room as she appeared to comb her memory. "I was home. I read a book."

Jake nodded, making a note. "And the day before?"

A frown began to form on Miranda's face. "I can't remember." She cut her eyes at him again, with a look of confusion, bordering on anger. "Wait. I went to the gym and baked a cake."

"At the gym?"

Oh, come on, Jake. You knew what she meant. What are you doing? Playing her dumb game and raising her one?

"No. In my kitchen. I felt like chocolate."

"Of course. My bad. How about Mon—" His phone pinged, but he ignored it. "How about Monday?"

Miranda's back stiffened as she sat back on the sofa. The muscles in her face tensed, and her brow came together. "You ask a lot of questions."

"I do. I apologize." Jake's phone pinged again. He took it out of his pocket and glanced at the screen. "It just goes with the territory. Excuse me a second." Reading the text messages, he maintained an inscrutable expression and then slipped the phone back into his pocket. "Where were we? Oh, yes. Where were you on Monday?"

Miranda's breathing grew rapid; her eyes shot daggers. "Who are you working for?" The edge in her voice sliced through the room.

He shook his head. "Again. I apologize, but that's confidential."

"How do I know you're not an undercover police officer?"

That one caught you off guard, didn't it? Scarlett focused on Jake, waiting for his reply.

"Because I told you who I am. Go look me up on your computer."

"Show me your ID again." She squirmed in place.

"No problem." He reached into the breast pocket and pulled out his wallet. Handing her the three cards he had held up to her surveillance camera, he said, "I'm not a cop." Balancing his portfolio on his knees, he opened his jacket. "See. No badge. No weapon."

Miranda studied the cards, turning each over. "Anyone can make fake IDs on the computer. My sons did it all the time."

"I hope they didn't make fake government issue—not cool."

"Who is she?" Miranda pointed to Scarlett.

"Ms. Kavanagh just joined my firm. She's in training and hasn't obtained her local credentials."

"I can show you my Georgia driver's license," Scarlett said, "and my Georgia Bar ID."

"Bar?"

"In Georgia, I'm a lawyer, but I'm learning to be a private detective."

Miranda turned to Jake. "There's a JD after your name. That means lawyer, doesn't it? My attorney has that after his name."

"I am a lawyer, but I'm not here in that capacity."

"Why are you here?"

"I told you. I'm helping with the search for Faith Johnson. You're welcome to check out my website—shepherdandassociates.com—it's on my card."

She rose and thrust his cards at him. "You need to go."

To Scarlett's surprise, Jake took them, closed his portfolio, and stood. "You're right. We need to go. Thank you for your time." Drawing his business card from the group, he laid it on a nearby table, he said, "Keep this one—just in case you think of something I should know."

Once the two were back in Jake's SUV, Scarlett said, "I thought you might push her harder about Monday."

"No point. She was done."

"Well. What do you think? Is she a suspect?"

"Everyone's a suspect until they're not," he said, attaching his phone to the magnetic mount on the dash.

"But do you think she could have taken Faith?"

"It depends. Was that an act? Or is she a psycho?"

"You don't have an opinion?" Scarlett buckled her seatbelt.

He started the engine. "Only a preliminary. I think she was faking most of it."

"What the devil did she do when she just walked out of the room? That was bizarre."

"My guess? Either she went to her computer and looked me up or got a fix of her drug of choice. Maybe both. She wears all the signs of opioid addiction—constricted pupils, nervous, a little wacky, questionable hygiene, too thin. She couldn't think fast enough to fabricate a story. Therefore, she chose to refuse to answer. Probably smart of her. What we do know is she hates Jessica, and she's all alone in a *large* house."

"Are you thinking she has Faith in that house?"

"I'm not thinking. I'm noting the possibility. However, the texts I received while we were talking were from Liz. Mrs. McKay seems to have herself a record."

"What?"

"Criminal assault and an injunction for protection." He hit messages on his cell. "Take a look. Liz sent a photo of the arrest report. It appears our scorned lady has a propensity for violence."

Scarlett leaned forward, looking at the screen. "Good grief. It looks like she went berserk on a friend at the gym."

"For starters, that throws suspicion on her claim of having gone to the gym this week. Good chance she's barred." As he stopped for a red light, he said. "I'm going head over to the client's apartment. We'll canvas the neighbors. Maybe Jessica will be released and home by the time we finish."

CHAPTER TWELVE

After parking the SUV in front of Jessica's building, Jake picked up his phone as Scarlett reached for the door handle to exit. "Hold up, Harvard. I want to check in with the Bureau to see if there's any progress on the search for the child."

Scarlett released the lever and settled back in the seat.

"Marge, it's Shepherd here. Can you put me through to someone on the CARD team working the Faith Johnson case?" Upon hearing the response, he shook his head. "You've got to be kidding. How the hell, and when, was he put in charge?" His eyebrows pinched together in a frown. "Anyone from my old team working with him?"

Scarlett stared at Jake.

"That helps. I've got Deke's cell number. I'll make the call." He clicked off, turned to Scarlett, and said, "Kirby's been made On-Scene Commander for the case. Seems CARD is covering several other abductions and had a couple of agents go off the clock for emergencies, leaving them short-handed."

"So, how does having your ex's husband work on this case affect us?"

"A little good—a little not good. Kirby will work with me, but he'll make it as difficult as he can. At least Deke Weston is on board. Deke worked on the CARD team before he came into our unit. You met him."

"I remember."

He scrolled through his contacts and then hit Weston's number, clicking the connection to speaker mode. "Weston, Shepherd here. What's up with the Johnson case? Any leads on the search?"

"Thought I'd be getting a ring from you. Heard you and Madison are working for the mom. Nothing to report so far. Kirby and I are just getting up to speed. Have you got anything for us?"

"I'm weeding out. What's your official position?"

"Operations. The brass moved both the On-Scene and the Operations guys to an Iowa call. You know it looks bad for your client, don't you? Cameras don't lie, Shepherd—eyewitnesses, maybe, but recordings—nope."

"Things are not always as they appear."

"Yeah, yeah. I hear ya. Kirby said you'd stand by your gal."

"That's because Kirby knows I wouldn't be on the case if I thought she was guilty. I think you know that too." He winked at Scarlett.

"Why don't you give us a crack at her? You know she's our best shot at a lead—if she's not guilty of foul play. And where is her phone? Do you have it?"

"Yeah. I have the phone. But an interrogation, that's Madison's call. When she's released, we'll continue our interviews with her and give you anything relevant to help with the search."

"She's out. Sprung this morning. Are you going to give up the phone?"

Jake made a face, and Scarlett shrugged, her eyes widening.

"Hadn't gotten the word. Thanks for that. As for the phone, I'm fairly sure Madison will surrender it, especially if you produce a warrant. I'll check back with you later."

Weston chuckled. "I'll take that to mean you guys found nothing on it."

Jake smiled. "You know the danger in assumptions. Talk with you later." With that, he terminated the call and turned to Scarlett. "So, our gal *is* out. I wonder if Phil knows. I'll check my messages." He looked down at his phone and then flipped the messages app open. "Yep. Here's a message from Liz. 'Client bailed out at nine a.m. No word from her.'" He glanced at his watch and frowned. "It's almost eleven. She should be home, but this is the best time to do our neighbor queries. Bring your pad and question list. We'll touch base with Jessica and arrange to meet up with her later and then go on with the canvas."

When they reached the Johnson apartment, Jake knocked on the door.

"Sounds pretty quiet," Scarlett said.

He knocked again.

"Maybe she's taking a nap, Jake. I'll bet she didn't sleep at the jail."

They waited a couple of minutes, and then Jake took a deep breath, shaking his head. "Let's get on with the canvas. Are you comfortable asking questions on your own?"

"I can read. Do I ask all of these?" She held up a sheet of paper, turning it around. Questions spread over both sides.

"Use your discretion. If you think one is irrelevant, skip it, but try to cover most of them."

"Where did this list come from?"

"Official issue of the DOJ slash FBI abduction of child response guide."

She nodded. "Got it."

"Then you take apartments on the even floors; I'll take the odd." Pointing toward the opposite side of the hall, he said, "If someone's home over there, I'll take it, and you can observe on the first one. For safety's sake, do not go into an apartment alone. If someone invites you in, wait for me. These are strangers, and while unlikely, anyone could have been involved in this abduction."

"Oh, my gosh. I never thought about that."

He grinned. "That's why you're not ready to be on your own. You're going to have to become more cynical, Harvard."

It took nearly three hours for Jake and Scarlett to cover the neighbors. When done, they agreed most people either didn't know Jessica or only knew her in passing. All who admitted knowing her thought she was a pleasant person. "I did have a woman in 4-B of Jessica's building say she had noticed an unknown woman hanging around once or twice but couldn't describe her," Scarlett said.

"Flag that sheet. We'll probably want to come back to her with photos at some point. Now, let's wake our client."

They returned to Jessica's door, and once again, Jake knocked.

They waited but no response came. After nearly five minutes, Jake called Phil Madison.

"Phil, I hear the client's out."

"Yeah. McKay sprung for the bail and picked her up at the detention center."

"Have any idea where he took her? Scarlett and I are at the apartment and getting no response." Jake shifted his weight from one leg to the other.

"I assumed he would take her home. Her car is still in impound. When he called, I told him I wasn't certain when it would be released. I'm sure they're combing it for traces of blood or other evidence. McKay said he would take her for a rental, but that should not have taken long. Have you guys learned anything of relevance?"

"The McKay woman isn't crossed off the list, but not much here at the apartment. Scarlett talked to a neighbor who noticed a strange woman in the area but nothing concrete. I'm getting a bad vibe."

"What do you mean?"

Scarlett's attention perked up with Jake's last remark.

"Can't explain—maybe the spirits of my Cherokee ancestors sending me a message, but I'm not thinking Jessica's status is good. I'm going to call McKay for a chat. Catch up with you later."

As he pulled out his wallet to retrieve Ted McKay's business card, Scarlett said, "What are you thinking, Jake? Do you think something has happened to Jessica?"

Without looking up, he said as he tapped in the phone number, "If your daughter were missing, and you have been in custody since she disappeared, would you be out of touch with those who are working to help you? A nap I could buy, but no devoted mother would sleep the day away. Call Liz and have her check at the church where Jessica works while I talk to McKay."

"I'm getting knots in my stomach."

CHAPTER THIRTEEN

Scarlett completed her call to Liz before Jake reached Ted McKay. He was about to hang up when McKay finally answered.

"Jake Shepherd here. I'm at Jessica's apartment and not getting an answer. I understand you picked her up at the pretrial detention center. Any idea where she is?" Noticing Scarlett's interest, he switched the call to speaker.

"I'm five minutes from the apartment. I dropped her there after a couple of errands and told her I would come back after lunch to take her for a rental car."

"Well, she doesn't seem to be here. I tried to get her to the door at approximately eleven this morning and again now." Jake looked at Scarlett with a raised eyebrow.

"She said she was going to rest. I can tell you; she looked beat. Maybe she's asleep. If you'll hold on, I'll be there shortly."

"Ten-four. We'll wait."

Scarlett shook her head. "Maybe she was so exhausted that she's out cold and hasn't heard us. She might have earplugs."

Jake squinted one eye, giving a slight tip of his head. "Maybe."

"But you don't think so. Do we dare go in? You've still got her key, don't you?"

He nodded. "I'll run it by Phil. I think we can justify it on the basis of a welfare check—even exigent circumstances—but to cover our bases, I think we'll wait for McKay."

Before Jake was off the phone with Phil Madison, Ted McKay came bounding up the stairs, two at a time."

"Still no answer?" he said, his breathing labored from the sprint.

Jake shook his head. "You remember my associate, Scarlett Kavanagh."

"I do," McKay said.

Scarlett nodded, a serious look on her face.

"What exactly went down when you picked Jessica up this morning?" Jake asked, taking a small notepad and pen out of his pocket.

"She wanted to stop at the bank and Walmart for a phone. She said you have her purse with phone, wallet, keys, etcetera."

"I do."

"I took her to the Walmart in Germantown, bought the phone for her, and then took her to her bank. She knew the teller, so she had no trouble making a withdrawal."

"How did you pay for the phone?"

"Credit card. Does that matter?"

"It could. Do you know how much cash she withdrew?"

He shook his head. "I made it a point not to eavesdrop. I felt it was none of my business, and I knew she needed cash since you had her ID. I could tell by the expression on the teller's face she was offering her concern over Faith's disappearance. Jess tried to pay me back for the phone, but I refused."

"And then you brought her here?"

"Right. She's got to be here. With no car, I don't see her leaving."

"She might have taken an Uber to rent a car," Scarlett said.

"She wouldn't have done that," McKay said. "We talked about her lack of her ID. Without it, she could not rent a vehicle. I planned to put it in my name."

"Do you recall what time it was when you dropped her here?"

"I do. I was in a hurry and looked at the clock on my dash. It was ten-fifteen."

"And you didn't come in with her?"

McKay stared for a second and then said, "No. As I said, I was in a hurry. I had a hearing before the DC zoning board this morning at eleven and a lunch date at twelve-thirty with a Deputy Commanding

General of the Corps of Engineers. I told her I would come back at two-thirty, and we would go pick up the rental."

Jake glanced down at his watch. "And you're right on time. How was she going to get into the apartment since I had her keys?"

"She said she keeps a key hidden. Has there been any word on Faith?"

Jake flicked his head. "None that I know. Let's do this. I'll knock again. If she doesn't answer, we'll enter. If she's not in plain sight, Scarlett, you try her bedroom. I'll be right behind you in the hall. Call out to give her a chance to respond. Don't enter the room until you either see Jessica or see that it's empty."

She nodded.

Although Jake could tell Scarlett was nervous, he liked her commitment. *She's green, but I can work with it.*

"McKay, you stay in the living room," Jake said as he pounded on the door. When no response came, he unlocked it, slid the key in his pocket, and drew his weapon.

The sight of the Glock brought a startled expression to McKay's face, and Scarlett flinched as Jake grabbed the knob with his free hand. Glancing back toward them, he recognized their unasked question. "We don't know what is going on inside. We go in prepared for anything."

The apartment was dead still as Jake entered, followed by Scarlett and Ted McKay. Jake raised a hand, signaling them to hold their positions while he checked out the kitchen. Finding no sign of Jessica, he returned to the living room, giving Scarlett a nod. He could see her take a deep breath.

As they proceeded down the hall, Jake tapped Scarlett on the shoulder. She glanced back, and he signaled her to pause and then stepped into Faith's room, gun aimed forward, and looked around like a tiger on the prowl. After checking the closet, he crossed over to the hall bathroom, checked it out, and then signaled Scarlett to proceed.

Jessica's bedroom door was open, just as they had left it the day before. When Scarlett reached the opening, she knocked on the doorframe.

"Jessica. It's Scarlett Kavanagh. Are you here?"

No response. She leaned to the left to get a better angle with which to see into the room. Turning back to Jake, Scarlett shrugged. "There's no one in there."

"Okay, go to the bathroom door, stand to the side, and call her." With his gun still in firing position, he entered the bedroom.

Ignoring Jake's instructions, McKay moved into the hall but remained a few feet from the bedroom.

After Scarlett called out for Jessica without receiving a response, Jake motioned her away and moved to the bathroom door. With a swift flourish, he kicked it open, brandishing his weapon. The room was empty. Backing out while holstering the gun, he said, "It's clear."

Drained of color, Scarlett's face formed an expression of concern as she took a deep breath.

McKay appeared at the bedroom door, his face flushed. "You don't . . . you don't think there's been foul play?"

Jake holstered his weapon. "No sign, yet."

"Maybe we should call the police and report Jessica missing."

Jake shook his head; his eyebrows pinched in a frown. "Can't do that. Voluntarily leaving the jurisdiction violates the terms of her release. Unless we have evidence of an abduction, we don't want to alert the authorities to her absence."

"Surely she wouldn't do that. Something must have happened. Maybe Faith's abductors grabbed her."

Jake glanced toward Scarlett and back toward McKay. "Maybe, but I don't think so. We only know of one abductor so far. Where *exactly* was she when you last had eyes on her?"

"Entering the hall downstairs. As she passed through the front door, I pulled away. She definitely came inside the building."

Jake shook his head. "The building, not the apartment. I see no sign she came in here. Do you, Harvard?"

Scarlett looked around for a second. "No. Not really."

"Tell me, again, everything she said this morning. Did she give you any clue as to what she might be planning?" Jake said to McKay.

"Other than getting some rest, no. She wanted a phone and some cash. I thought she might need some groceries. I offered to give her money, but she refused. She said I had done enough."

"What was her overall demeanor?"

"What do you mean?"

"Was she relaxed, happy, depressed, angry?"

"Quiet, as always. A little sad, but mostly exhausted. How could she not be? Her child is missing. She's been in jail. What are you going to do, Mr. Shepherd?"

"Try to find Jessica and her child."

"How?"

"Sorry. I know you're concerned, but at this point in my investigation, I don't share."

McKay grimaced. "That's pretty paranoid of you, isn't it?" He looked around toward Scarlett, who remained stoic.

"Maybe, but that's the way it is. Go back to your office, and if you should hear from Jessica, let me know immediately. You've got my cell number. Let me caution you. Do not take any action without passing it by me or Phil. You could unintentionally cause Jessica more trouble."

McKay nodded. "What if we offer a reward for information about Faith? I'm willing to put up twenty-five—fifty thousand."

Scarlett's expression lit up as she turned toward Jake.

"Not yet."

A frown creased Scarlett's brow, and McKay's jaw tightened.

"I don't understand, Shepherd. Money talks. Someone's got to do something to find that child."

"Let's get something straight. You're an engineer; I'm a detective. I've worked in the criminal cesspool a long time. You want to get that child killed?"

"How could offering a reward get Faith killed? I'm trying to help."

Scarlett stared at Jake, curling her lips as if contemplating how the dialogue might go.

"I appreciate your gesture, but until we have a handle on who abducted Faith and why, it is too risky. An unsub, unidentified suspect, hearing there's a price on his or her head can panic—dispose of the victim. Keep your bounty on hold. It's good to know it's there if we need it. But let us handle the tactics. And for the sake of Jessica and Faith, *don't* talk to the media. The experts will release information as needed."

Scarlett took a deep breath and exhaled, while the muscles in McKay's face relaxed and he said, "You're right. What was I thinking? You are the expert."

"Right. Hang on to my card. Call if anything comes up. If you can't get in touch on my cell, call my office. My assistant always knows how to reach me. I ask that you stay available as well, and don't mention to anyone that Jessica is MIA."

"Certainly." He turned and started for the door. "I don't mind telling you, Mr. Shepherd, I don't like any of this. You're right. I'm an engineer. My biggest worries fall under the category of meeting deadlines and staying under budget. The closest I come to criminal activity is vandalism on a job. Please keep me up to date on what you can share. You can see I'm very fond of Jessica and Faith."

"Right."

As the door closed, Scarlett said, "He seems like a nice guy."

"I've got no trouble with him so far," Jake said as he took out his cell and punched a number. "Millie, Jake here. Is he available?" Within a few seconds, Phil Madison answered. "We've got a problem, Phil. Client's MIA. I'm thinking my best course is to take a trip to Jacksonville, Florida. See what I can dig up. Since we're operating on your tab, are you good with that?" He smiled. "Great. Also, I'll need to put surveillance on her apartment." Jake glanced up at Scarlett and nodded as he signed off on the call.

"You're going to Florida?" she said.

"We're going to Florida."

"But Jessica's missing from here. Don't we need to look for her?"

"That's what we're going to do. We've got a gal on the run, Harvard. One who knows the ropes. My job is to understand everything I can about her to figure out where she would run to. I need to check with Liz to see if she's found out anything of use on social media."

"Our Jessica's not on social media," Scarlett said, "although a lot of other Jessica Johnsons are. At least she's not on Facebook, Instagram, or Twitter. I also ran Nyx Arnold and Xenia Arnold. Nothing there either."

"I'm impressed. Good work." He punched in another number on his phone. "Liz. We'll be at the office in about thirty minutes, depending on traffic. In the meantime, I need two plane reservations ASAP to Jacksonville, Florida—tonight if possible." He paused, listening. "We can be at the airport by"—he looked at his watch—"by six. We'll need hotel reservations near the airport." He grinned at Scarlett. "Yes, two rooms. I'm not sure for how long. Better make it for four nights." After listening to Liz for a second, he said, "Can you cover Kai and Romeo and put together the Johnson file for me to take?"

Scarlett's eyes lit up. "My cats, Jake. They're due to come to DC on Monday."

"We should be back, but if not, we'll get it covered, Harvard. MacGregor told me he flies up here all the time, and I know Fury has no problem taking care of the guys for you. I know you miss them, but—"

"Don't say it. I know. We've got work to do. I'll call Fury."

CHAPTER FOURTEEN

As Jake drove to the office, he put his phone on speaker and made another call to Pete Cooper, who ran the security agency Cooper and Jake owned. "Coop, Jake here. I need surveillance on a Silver Spring apartment. Need our best—maybe Sonny, plus an alternate. I need it twenty-four-seven for the next two days. Who else do we have who can follow the subject if necessary and be trusted to not fall asleep on the clock?"

"We're booked pretty tight. How do you feel about the new guy?"

"The one I sent you?"

"Yeah. He has a good record with the Capitol boys."

"Don't think he'd have any problem with the surveillance but quiz him on experience tailing a suspect. If you think he can handle it, use him. Liz will email you the details. I want someone on the job ASAP."

When he terminated the call, Scarlett said, "The new guy isn't Randy Cummings by any chance?"

"It is."

"You didn't tell me you hired him."

"Technically, I didn't. Coop did. I just sent him over for an interview. After all the media coverage of the Kingsley murder, including the exposure of his relationship with your sister, he couldn't stay on the Capitol force, and like me, he didn't want to leave the DC area because of his kids. Kinda related to the guy."

"Really? Jake Shepherd has a compassionate side?" Scarlett rolled her eyes. "Savannah has a knack for bringing chaos to everything she touches."

"Takes two to tango, Harvard. Cummings is an alright guy. Don't know if he and Savannah can make it for the long haul, but you might cut them some slack. I think she has paid her dues."

When they reached the office, Kai greeted them. Jake quickly filled Liz in on the events of the day and then gave her instructions while massaging the dog's shoulders.

"I need everything you can dig up on Xenia Arnold—where she is, where she was incarcerated, her known associates, the works. And see what you can find out about our client's life in Jacksonville— where she went to school, who her friends were, where she lived? You know the drill. Before I forget, I need Sonny Lassiter to do a second interview with a witness Scarlett talked to at the client's apartment building. Put together a packet of photos, including Miranda McKay and the stills lifted from the video of the woman picking up Faith. Get them over to Coop and have him pass them to Sonny. Scarlett can fill you in on the details. I want Sonny to see if the witness can identify who she saw lurking around the building."

"Got it," Liz said, as Scarlett tore a page out of her notes and laid it on the desk.

"And warn Sonny some of Kirby's crew could be on site as well. I didn't see any Feds when we were there but probably because notice of her release hadn't worked its way up the chain."

"Anything else?"

"Just a couple more. Get Phil's office to run down how much cash Jessica withdrew from her account. Could give us a clue as to her plans. He's got releases from her. I'm betting you'll see the name of her bank in the computer records downloaded from Carbonite. Also, get in touch with McKay, and ask him to track down the phone number of the disposable phone he bought Jessica. Should be possible since he paid with his credit card. He can give them the excuse that he misplaced the phone and needs the number to call it."

"Will do. Now, I have something to share with you I think you're going to like. Although the battery was dead on the disposable you found in the storage unit, I was able to charge it with a universal charger. When I ran through the history, the only incoming and outgoing number on the device belongs to a Ronald Gibson in Jacksonville, Florida."

"Good work, ace." He gave her a high-five. "Pure gold. Were you able to find out anything about Ronald Gibson?"

"The number is a landline to a residence. Gibson is married, and his wife's name is Hannah. Since it's a shared line, no way to tell who Jessica talked to."

"Million-dollar question—but I'm betting it's the wife. No man on the prowl uses his home phone to further his affairs. Did you—"

"I know what you're gonna ask. Yes, I have an address, and I'm working on developing the connection. Haven't narrowed it down yet."

"But you will. I have faith in you."

Liz grinned. "Remember that when you're writing my paycheck."

"Signing your paycheck is my greatest pleasure. It reminds me how I couldn't run this place without you. By the way, when was the last call made or received on that phone?"

"There aren't many calls, and the majority originate from Jessica up until recently. The last outgoing was over six months ago, but there have been a number of missed incomings from the Gibson phone in the past three months up to about a month ago, plus text messages simply saying, 'Call me.' It looks like the caller was trying hard to get in touch with Jessica."

"Now, that's interesting," Jake said.

"Jake, you said the storage unit hadn't been opened in quite a while," Scarlett said.

"True. It looks like we may be getting somewhere." He looked at his watch and then toward Liz. "Time to take off for the airport. What time is our flight?"

She held up eight fingers.

He nodded and turned to Scarlett. "How long will it take you to pack what you need?"

"Twenty minutes—thirty tops."

He smiled. "You're getting the hang of it." He looked back at Liz. "Refresh my memory. Do I need to carry a Florida license, and do I have one?"

Liz handed Jake a briefcase containing the Johnson documents and their travel arrangements. "No, Detective Shepherd. You do not need one. Like Georgia, Florida has a reciprocity agreement with Virginia."

"She's a gem, isn't she? We'd better rock and roll if we're going to have time for dinner before the flight." As they started for the door, Jake patted Kai on his shoulder and said to Liz. "Appreciate your taking care of my partner and the rabbit. I'll touch base later."

CHAPTER FIFTEEN

"Liz booked us at the Crown Plaza," Jake said as their flight took off. "It's about two miles from the airport. With the layover in Atlanta, we won't land until midnight. . . . . Scarlett."

"Huh? I'm sorry. What did you say?"

"What planet were you visiting?"

She shook her head. "I can't get Faith out of my mind. It's been nearly four days without any sign of what has happened to her. What must she be thinking? How frightened she must be."

"Not good."

"Don't they say the first twenty-four to forty-eight hours are critical to saving a child in an abduction?"

"Something like that. But it all depends on the abductor's intent. We don't know the objective in Faith's case. But yes. Time is of the essence."

"I'm scared for her, Jake. Tell me the truth. Do you think she's still alive?"

"Don't make me speculate on something like that."

"You think she's dead."

"I didn't say that." He reached over and took Scarlett's hand. "I think there's a good chance she's still alive, Harvard. We know a woman took her. That's better than a man. Makes sexual motives less likely—not a guarantee, but less likely. Jessica is not wealthy, doesn't work in a sensitive job, and doesn't have state secrets. That's good. It wasn't for extortion or ransom. Our prime suspects at the moment would most likely have jealousy or revenge as a motive. It is unlikely the revenge would extend to cold-blooded murder unless the unsub is spooked. But if it is revenge, what is the end game? Finally, there's possibility X."

"X? What's X?"

"X equals unknown. Some barren woman wants a little girl? Someone needs a kid as a cover? Some deranged mother of another kid wants to knock out the competition? The possibilities are wide open."

Scarlett sat quietly for several minutes and then said, "Jake. You're not known for patience with uncooperating clients. Where are you with the idea Jessica may have run away?"

Another grin crossed his face. "You know me too well, Harvard. You're right. I don't like it. Not one little bit. It was a dumbass move, distracting us from the primary objective. But Jessica is a damaged woman, haunted by trouble and living by her wits for a long time. I'll give her a pass on this one, but when we find her, I'm going to lay it on the line—no more screwups. Also, walking away from Jessica at this point is walking away from Faith, which would be unacceptable."

The corners of Scarlett's mouth gave way to a bare upward curve as she studied Jake for a minute before being distracted by the flight attendant giving her spiel.

By the time they reached the hotel, it was nearly one a.m. Scarlett opened the door to her room and held it for Jake to bring in her luggage. Looking around, she thought, *cookie-cutter*. A king-size bed, an easy chair with a matching ottoman, a large desk, and a chest with a flat-screen TV positioned on top completed the décor. The overall appearance projected a clean, fresh, no-frills, but comfortable atmosphere.

"Get some sleep, Harvard. You look beat."

"My plan. What time do we get started tomorrow?"

He opened the folding luggage rack, swung her carry-on in place, and then stacked her briefcase and cosmetic case on top. "That'll depend on where we start. Let me check messages and emails for updates from Liz."

With his phone in hand, he scanned down the screen. "Ah-ha! Liz says Xenia Arnold was incarcerated at Levell Correctional Facility, a women's prison. She says it's roughly eighty-five miles away. Think we'll head over there first. I'll text her to set up an appointment with the warden for early tomorrow if possible. Rather not risk the warden being off on the weekend."

"Think you'll have any trouble getting cooperation?"

He shook his head. "We'll find out. This is when a badge would come in handy, but the phrase 'abducted child' should open some doors. I'll have Liz stress that when she makes the call. Been thinking about McKay's offer. Here is where his money might come in handy. But I'll have to tread carefully." He tapped on a door between the chair and the TV. "Keep this locked. Can't be too sure about your neighbor."

"Doesn't that connect to your room?"

"Exactly. Keep it locked." He grinned.

Scarlett chuckled, nodding. "Good idea. I hear the neighbor has a reputation for roaming around at night in pink underwear."

He patted her shoulder as he moved toward the door. "Better than having a record. Back to your question. Let's aim to leave here by eight."

....

CHAPTER SIXTEEN

A little over halfway to the prison Friday morning, Jake's cell pinged. "Want to catch that, Harvard?"

Picking up the cell phone, Scarlett said, "It's a text from Liz."

"You know my password. Read it."

"'All clear for meeting with warden. Janice Croswell. She sounds cooperative.'"

"Nice," he said and glanced at the clock. "With luck, we should be at the prison by ten or a little after. Hard to know how long we'll be there. Giving a half-hour to lay out our purpose to the warden, two to three for interviews, and two hours back to Jacksonville, I doubt we will make it much before close of business."

As they pulled up to the visitors' parking lot, a loud alarm siren blasted through the air.

"Oh, my gosh. You think it's a prison break?"

Jake grinned. "Not likely. They blow those to signal a headcount or end of mealtime. Never been to a prison, have you?"

"Nooo." She gave him an are-you-crazy look. "I've been to the jails in my area when a client was arrested but never a prison. Have you?"

"Several. Let's go meet Warden Croswell, shall we?"

As Scarlett exited the vehicle, she looked around at the twelve-foot, razor-wire fence, topped with triple concertina wire. "I'm depressed already."

"Then brace yourself. It doesn't get prettier."

Proceeding through security checkpoints, they provided identification and submitted to electronic body scans before reaching the warden's office.

"I didn't expect warm and cozy with fresh flowers, but this is as bleak as it gets," Scarlett said as the last barred, metal door clanged shut behind them. Every sound made in the concrete and metal structure reverberated through empty corridors.

An armed corrections officer stood beside the door. Jake handed him both his and Scarlett's identification and waited while the guard reviewed the cards and then announced their arrival through his shoulder-mounted communications radio. At the sound of an electronic device releasing the lock, the guard returned the ID cards, reached forward, and opened the door for the two to enter.

Inside the anteroom, a secretary sat behind a desk. As they entered, she barely looked up. Almost immediately, a stately woman in a navy-blue suit entered, approaching Jake from the opposite side of the room.

"Mr. Shepherd, I'm Warden Croswell. Welcome to Levell. Follow me."

Jake nodded and complied, allowing Scarlett to enter the inner office first.

"I understand you've come from Virginia. I'm not sure what this is all about, but your secretary said it involved the kidnapping of a child in Maryland."

"That's right. I'm a private investigator, and this is my associate, Scarlett Kavanagh. She's working the case with me."

"How can our lowly institution be of help? Wouldn't the FBI or local law enforcement be working a case like that?"

"May we sit?" Jake said. When the warden made the appropriate motion for the two of them to be seated, he said, "You're right about the Bureau and state police. Let me fill you in. On Monday, a five-year-old child, female, was picked up at her school by a woman posing as her mother. The FBI's Rapid Response Team is pursuing all leads but no progress so far."

"Forgive me, Mr. Shepherd, but I'm still not seeing how a Florida correctional facility plays into that scenario."

"I'll be candid. We represent the mother, who, because of questionable evidence, is being considered the prime suspect."

The warden appeared to pull back, the expression on her face changing from interest to apprehension.

"I'm not here to clear a guilty party, Warden. I'm here to learn all I can about another suspect—our client's twin sister. Finding the child is the primary objective. Her safety is our priority. Since I know my client is not responsible for her disappearance, the rest will fall into place when the little girl is found. I'm hoping you'll be willing to help with that."

"Of course, I'm certainly willing to help locate a missing child, but I'm still lost. You mentioned a twin. Am I safe to assume the twin has something to do with this conversation?"

"Bingo."

"What is the twin's name? Is she currently in our custody?"

"No. She was released about a year ago. Her name is Xenia Arnold."

"Zee?" The woman sat back in the chair behind her desk.

"You know her?"

"I know her, but I was not aware she had a sister, let alone a twin."

As Jake and the warden talked, Scarlett glanced around the office. Several bowling trophies and appreciation plaques occupied places on a three-shelf bookcase. Above it hung a college diploma and several framed award certificates. On the warden's desk, photos of two children and one of a German shepherd caught Scarlett's eye. *She's got children. She'll help.*

"When I arrived at Levell, Zee Arnold was pregnant, which is why I remember she had no relatives listed in her file."

As the warden spoke, Scarlett's eyes grew wide, focusing on the woman.

"I was immediately confronted with her demands to keep her baby. She refused to name the father. Since she had no outside male visitors during the relevant time, I could only assume it had been one of the staff. It's a problem we confront too often. Zee wouldn't name him, and he never stepped forward—probably because he was married and would lose his wife and his job. She named no family to take the child but desperately wanted to keep the baby. She even tried to get media attention, which brought it to my desk."

"When was that?" Jake asked.

"I have been at Levell six years, six months. She delivered about four months after I arrived and created quite a scene when the Department of Children and Families took the child away at the time of her discharge from the hospital."

Scarlett took in a deep breath. *Six years and two months.*

"I'm assuming that was standard protocol," Jake said.

"It was. When an inmate becomes pregnant, she is required to complete a Child Placement Plan and arrange for a caregiver to come for the baby simultaneously with the inmate leaving the hospital. Zee Arnold never completed a plan. She claimed she had no one to serve as a caregiver. With multiple years remaining on her sentence at the time, there was no choice but for DCF to file to terminate her parental rights. According to the statutes, a child should not remain in foster care for that extended a period. I was new at this job, and I'll admit, Mr. Shepherd, it got to me."

"Was her child male or female?" Jake asked, his expression steady.

"A girl."

Scarlett stifled a gasp and said, "And termination of parental rights with no known father made the baby eligible for adoption, right?"

"I believe so."

"Do you know what happened to the child?" Jake asked.

"No, I don't. Once DCF took her away, that was the end of it for us. Zee went into depression, was hostile for a while, and then seemed to simmer down."

Scarlett's mind raced, but she decided to keep her thoughts to herself until she and Jake were alone.

"There's nothing else I can tell you, Mr. Shepherd. I doubt this information is of any help in finding the missing child—the sister's."

"Actually, you have helped more than you know. But I still have a favor. We need to find Xenia Arnold—ask her some questions about her whereabouts on Monday."

"I'm sorry. I can't help you with that. Once time is served, we never hear about inmates unless they become repeat offenders."

"I understand, but I would like to find out all I can about Ms. Arnold from people who knew her here, exercising discretion, of course."

"Mr. Shepherd, your assistant told me you are a former FBI agent; therefore, you know the inmate mindset. You won't get anyone to talk."

"I've got some ideas on that. But I need your cooperation. I'd like to start with guards who might have been familiar with the subject and work out from there. I am prepared to offer financial incentives."

"Our staff cannot accept compensation."

"But your inmates could accept a reward if the information provided leads to discovery of the child."

"Are you thinking Zee Arnold kidnapped her niece?"

"I'm thinking it's possible. Who else could better impersonate the mother? What I'm looking for here at Levell is if she had motive, opportunity, who were her friends, and did she have outside contacts. However, I don't want my inquiries spread around for obvious reasons."

"You're probably safe on that. If you get anyone to talk, they will not want it known in the dorms. The women have as strong a code on ratting on one another as the men."

"I'm sure you have secure attorney-client conference rooms. Scarlett and I are both lawyers. The inmate could tell others she met with attorneys who might be able to help her. Not really a lie, just a slight deception. Someone in your population knows something about Xenia Arnold. Telling me Xenia failed to admit having a sister, even in the face of permanently losing her child, says a lot. Why? Just how deep does that go? If she took Faith Johnson, we need to find her."

"Give me an hour. I'll see what I can come up with."

"Scarlett and I will drive into town and grab an early lunch. We'll be back," he looked at his watch, "before noon."

CHAPTER SEVENTEEN

As Jake and Scarlett settled into the gray Toyota Highlander, she said, "I feel like I need a long shower. What a creepy place."

"And we didn't even go on the actual cell blocks. Maybe a field trip to one of these places should be incorporated into school curriculum. Might make young people think before they mess up their lives."

"Yeah, but a lot of people would think it was wrong to expose them. Jake, are you thinking what I'm thinking about how close in age Xenia's baby is to Faith?"

"Hard to miss that."

"You don't suppose? I mean, there's no way Jessica could have gotten Xenia's baby. Is there?"

"Are you thinking Jessica had custody of her sister's child"—he cranked the SUV—"and now the sister has stolen her back? The warden said they never knew about a sister, and Jessica was in do-it-yourself WITSEC. That would be a long shot. Even if, what did she call it here? Department of—"

"Children and Families."

"Even if the Department discovered the connection, how would they have found Jessica? She did a damn good job of covering her trail. Tell you what. Text Phil, and tell him we need Jessica's medical records from that hospital in New York. You have the name in your notes, don't you?"

"I do."

When Jake and Scarlett returned to the prison, the Florida sun was bearing down on the campus. Sparks seemed to fly off the Concertina wire atop the fencing while the sound of voices echoed from behind a building Scarlett speculated to be a recreational yard.

At the entrance, the guard apparently remembered them from earlier and gave scant attention to the IDs. However, a new guard stood at the door to Warden Croswell's office.

"What did you say your business is with the warden?"

"If you'll announce us, I'm sure this can run smoother. We are returning from an earlier visit."

This guard is obviously full of his authority, Scarlett thought as she watched for Jake's reaction. After taking enough time to read every line on the cards, the CO radioed in and was given immediate authority to admit Jake and Scarlett. However, he did not open the door as the earlier man had done.

"Come in, Mr. Shepherd, Ms. Kavanagh," the warden said. "I have Lieutenant Baker in my office waiting to answer your questions. I believe he is the best person for you to interview."

Upon their entry, Baker stood up and shook Jake's hand and nodded to Scarlett.

"Lieutenant Baker served on Xenia Arnold's dorm block for most of her time here at Levell. He remembers her well. I explained a little about what you are looking for, but I'll let you fill him in with the details. If you don't mind, I'll leave you alone while I grab a bite of lunch. Is there anything more you need from me before I leave?"

"I think we're good," Jake said. "Thank you."

An extra chair had been added to the office since Jake and Scarlett left earlier. As soon as all were settled, Jake turned to the CO. "Worked here long?"

"Almost twenty years—six at Santa Rosa—the rest here. About ready to hang it up and go fishing. I hear you're former FBI."

"For what it's worth."

"How long?"

"Something like twelve years."

"Guess you have stories to tell. I shoulda done something like that but got married and started having kids. Never got around to it."

"I'm sure you served the community. But let's get started. You knew Xenia Arnold?"

"Yeah. She was okay. A little on the radical side, but Zee didn't cause me any trouble. She wasn't exactly a sucker ducker."

Scarlett's eyebrows pinched at the CO's reference, which caught his eye.

"That's jail talk for an inmate that stays away from troublemakers," Baker said.

Scarlett smiled, nodding.

He continued, "But I always thought Zee had personal demons and was on a private mission."

"So, she kept to herself?"

Baker nodded. "Always figured there was another side, but she kept it outta sight."

"How long was she one of your charges?"

"Not sure exactly, but at least six, maybe seven years. I got my promotion and moved out about six months before she was released."

"Let's get the elephant out of the room," Jake said. "Were you the father of her child?"

"What? Hell, no."

"Sorry. I had to ask. Do you have any idea who was?"

"Look, Mr. Shepherd, the best way to get along in a place like this is to not know too much about too many things. Just keep putting one foot in front of the other, and don't look too far in either direction."

"I get it. I know that no one in the prison knows officially what happened to Xenia's child, but were there any rumors?"

He shook his head. "No one wanted to bring up the subject. Zee took it hard. Everyone danced around it to avoid setting her off. She didn't seem the motherly type, but she wanted that kid."

"Did she develop a friendship with any of her confederates here in Levell?"

"As I recall, only one. A gal named Sherlene Thomas. Had a brother that took a shine to Zee. He was a badass biker-gang dog."

Jake flinched but kept his expression steady.

"Bastard was just out of Raiford—big prison south of here. Started coming to visit Zee. Can't remember his name. The warden can pull the visitor logbooks and should find it."

"Is the sister still here?"

"Nope. She went on paper 'bout half a year before Zee."

Scarlett shifted in her chair. *On paper? Must mean released.*

"That's the story, Detective. I don't know anything else. Understand you've got a missing kid. I hope you find her."

"Thanks. You've been very helpful. Only one more question. If I were to interview any of the prisoners about Arnold, who would you recommend?"

Baker squinted, apparently giving the question thought, while Jake sat back in his chair, waiting.

"Best shot. I'd say Marlene, Marlene Smith. Maybe Denise. Can't think of her last name, but her cell was directly across from Zee's. Warden can get that one too. They're both in for all day. The Warden said something about a reward. I think either one of those ladies would bite."

Jake stood. "I appreciate your candor, Lieutenant. You've given me several things to look into." Jake extended his hand as the CO stood.

"I wish you luck. Missing child—that's the worst."

When the door closed behind the guard, Scarlett stood and shook out her arms. "Wow! He dropped some bombs. What did he mean by the two women are here all day?"

"Lifers. We'll have to get you a dictionary of prison slang."

"Obviously, you know the language."

As usual, Jake grinned. "It's not my first time in the game, Harvard."

After perusing his notes from the interview and making a list of the high points, while Scarlett watched, he took out his cell, opened the browser, and typed in "Raiford."

"What are you searching?" Scarlett asked.

"To see how far it is to the prison the CO mentioned. Looks like the formal name is Florida State Prison, and it's about fifty miles from here. We should be able to make it today."

Within ten minutes of the CO leaving the office, the warden re-entered.

"I hope Lieutenant Baker was of help," Croswell said.

"He gave us a couple of names of inmates I would like to interview." Jake gave her a quick rundown of his interview of Baker and the list he made, including the request for identification of Xenia Arnold's male visitor. "To cover several bases, I would like a shot at all the inmates who associated with Arnold, but particularly the two Baker named. As a matter of strategy, can you scramble them up so it's not obvious who my targets are?"

"Certainly." Scanning the list, she said, "I'll get to work on this. My secretary will show you to one of the private meeting rooms attorneys use. I can tell you right off, Denise Packard is the inmate Baker had in mind. She's one of the tougher gals, so I can't guarantee she'll tell you anything."

She doesn't know Jake, Scarlett thought.

"I understand," he said.

"Is there anything else I can help you with?"

"There is. Can you grease the wheels at the men's prison where the boyfriend served time when you get his name? Baker thought it was Raiford. A call from one warden to another will carry more sway than one from my office—less explaining and convincing."

"I can do that. He's a reasonable guy. And good luck finding that little girl, Mr. Shepherd. I'm a parent."

CHAPTER EIGHTEEN

When Jake and Scarlett walked into the designated room, she said, "Looks like the attorney-client interview rooms I've been in." Windowless, like most of the prison, the ten-by-ten-foot, austere room held a metal table, one end against the left wall. A chair on either side provided a respective seat for Jake and a subject. In an askew position in the right rear corner, an observer's chair afforded a place for Scarlett.

The first two inmates Jake interviewed were polar opposites. A gray-haired woman in her late fifties came in first. A long-time occupant, she possessed a typical prison mentality. Give up nothing. However, she admitted that Xenia Arnold kept to herself. The second appeared to be in her early twenties, absent the rode-hard-and-put-away-wet look of the first one. Jake wasted no time with either woman.

Watching him in action, Scarlett admired the way he seemed able to extract what information each possessed and move on quickly.

The third woman to enter the conference room was Denise Packard. She sauntered in, her pelvis thrust forward, with her thumbs stuck in the waist of her prison-issue pants.

Jake stood, swept a hand around to indicate the woman should sit as he took his chair. She looked at him with disdain and remained standing.

"What the fuck am I here for?" she said.

"I'll be happy to get to that, but first, I'd like to know who you are. I'm Jake Shepherd, and this"—he pointed to Scarlett—"is my associate, Scarlett Kavanagh."

"That don't tell me nothin'."

Jake studied the woman's face for several seconds and then handed her his business card.

"What's the dog for?" she said, referring to the image of Kai on Jake's card.

She can't read, and Jake knows it, Scarlett thought, watching how the woman looked at the card.

"Okay, you're some fucking guy with a mutt." She tossed the card on the table. "Whadda you want from me?"

"Your name for starters, and maybe you'd like to take a seat."

"You don't need for me to tell you my name. The guard out there will tell you who I am."

"If it makes you happy, that's how we'll play it." He turned to Scarlett. "Do you mind checking with the guard for this person's name?"

Interesting that he didn't say woman, lady, inmate. He's got a reason. "No problem." As Scarlett stood and walked around the table to the door, she gave Packard a quick smile, but the woman looked away, avoiding eye contact.

Within a couple of seconds, Scarlett re-entered. Jake looked up as she said, "Jake, this is Denise Packard."

"Okay. Nice to meet you, Ms. Packard, or may I call you Denise?"

"Don't matter." Without taking her eyes off Jake, she swung the chair around and sat straddle style.

"Let me explain, Denise. I'm here to gather information about Xenia Arnold. The warden thought you could help."

"You mean Zero Arnold."

Although the response may have taken Jake by surprise, he didn't miss a beat. "So, her nickname was Zero?"

"For me, it was. Uppity little bitch. Thought she was too good for the rest of us. What are you? Some kind of cop? Whatcha trying to hang on the bitch?"

"Not a cop." He pointed to his card. "Private investigator."

"Humph. Private dick. You working for Zero?"

"I'm working to locate a missing five-year-old child, who is believed to be related to her. I'm hoping that in learning about Xenia Arnold, I can locate her, and then she can help us find the child."

"Whose kid? Zero's?"

"Her sister's."

"That don't make sense. Never heard of any sister. But it's no sweat to me. I don't know nothin'."

"Probably doesn't make sense. But before you dismiss me, you might want to know a reward is being assembled to give to anyone who provides information leading to the discovery of the child or the arrest and conviction of a possible abductor. So, are you sure you have nothing to tell me about her?"

Packard sat silent for a couple of minutes, apparently digesting the information. "I already did. Uppity bitch. When she came in here, she was strung out—a coke withdraw. I offered to let her catch a ride. I had a source at the time. She was good to go, but then she moved on—became a trick. Tried to help the bitch, but she turned on me. I cut her loose."

"But you continued to be on her block of the dorm, right?"

"Yeah. But she was on her own. Stayed in her cage most of the time. Finally, hooked up with a loser whose brother rode with the Rattlers."

Jake flinched. "The Rebel Rattlers out of Mississippi?"

"The one."

"Pretty tough pack."

"Yeah. Zero liked that. She had some vendetta cookin'. When the guy got out, he started coming 'round. Think she was getting some action, but her real mission was to use his connections."

"What do you know about the vendetta?"

"Nothin'. Just that she said, 'It ain't over til it's over.' After she had the kid, and they took it away, she doubled down. Poured over books in the library, looking for who knows what?"

"I've got to ask. Do you have any idea where she planned to go when released?"

She shook her head. "Not a friggin' clue. Like I said. She's not in my crew. We done?"

"I think we are," Jake said, laying down his pen.

"Let me know about that reward. I might think of somethin' else."

Jake nodded.

Following the interview with Packard, three more prisoners came and went, failing to produce useful information. As the last one exited, Scarlett wanted to ask Jake a question, but entry of another inmate stopped her. The new woman appeared younger than the rest, and despite the lack of makeup and hairstyle, her piercing blue eyes, long lashes, and fair complexion generated an attractive image.

"Hello, I'm Jake Shepherd, private investigator, and this is my associate, Scarlett Kavanagh. And you would be?"

She hesitated, looking from Jake to Scarlett and back. "Marlene. Marlene Smith. Why am I here?"

"Please relax, Ms. Smith. I'll be happy to explain. We're working on a case involving a little girl who was abducted from her school in Maryland. We have reason to think that a former inmate here at Levell is a relative. Warden Croswell believes you knew the woman. Do you mind answering a few questions?"

Again, the woman looked at Scarlett and then back toward Jake. "I guess not."

"Good. Please have a seat." Jake stood. "I'm going to turn the questioning over to my associate."

The statement took Scarlett by surprise. *Thanks for the warning.* She stood, suppressing her shock with a forced smile. Clenching her portfolio, she took the chair directly across from the inmate, taking a deep breath as she sat.

After she opened the leather case holding the legal pad she had been taking notes on, Scarlett made eye contact with Smith. "As he told you, I'm Scarlett Kavanagh, and we're trying to find Faith Johnson, a five-year-old girl who we believe is the niece of a Xenia Arnold. Did you know Xenia?"

Smith focused on Scarlett for a minute. Without warning, a siren blare blasted the institution, causing Scarlett to jump.

Without flinching, the inmate grinned. "Scared you, didn't it? That's just for an inmate headcount."

"Are you required to report?"

"They know where I am. When out to meet with a visitor, we're not required to show up to the count."

Scarlett shook her head as if to shake off the offending noise. "That's good."

"So, you say Zee is the kid's aunt?"

"Yes. What do you remember about her?"

"Not a lot. Her house was across from mine. Saw her every day, but we weren't what you would call best friends. If you really want to know about Zee, you need to talk to Sherlene. Don't know her last name. She was Zee's buddy."

"We heard, but she's no longer here, right?"

"Yeah, right. She finished her time."

"Can we talk about what you know about Xenia?"

"I guess. This won't get me in any trouble, will it?"

"Trouble? With whom?"

"You know. The population. I don't want to be labeled a snitch."

"No one needs to know you told us anything. And by the way, there is going to be a financial reward for information that leads to finding the child."

"No shit. How much?"

"It's being decided, but there is someone willing to put up a substantial amount. I don't know if that would make a difference to you."

"Of course, it would. I've got two kids. I'm never going to get out to be with them, but I could help make their life better with some money. They live with my mom, and she struggles."

"Then let's talk about Xenia. Did she ever tell you about any of her plans for after release?"

"Nothing about her plan, but she was hot about something. She never would say exactly what. In this place, you don't ask questions. Not good for your health. One thing she said was she was going to get her kid back—that it was wrong to take a mother's child."

"Really." Scarlett's interest soared. "Did she indicate she knew who had the child?"

Smith shook her head.

"I understand she had a boyfriend. What can you tell me about him? Did she talk about him?"

"You mean the Rebel Rattler?"

"That's the one. Do you know his name?"

"Uh-uh. She always called him K.B. Said it stood for Killer Boy. Probably his gang name."

"Did she ever mention anything else about him? Where he was from? Names of any of his friends?"

She shook her head. "Not that I recall. But he was a mountain of a man, probably six three or four—all tatted up, long hair, beard, ear-ring—the works. Fairly good bod. Sherlene's his sister. That's how they hooked up."

"Can you remember any comments Xenia made about him? What he did for a living?"

"That last one's easy. He steals for a living. Either that or he deals. That guy has never done an honest day's work in his life. But I'm sorry, Ms. . . . What did he say your name is?"

"Kavanagh."

"All I know is Xenia was really into the guy. Whether it was the sex or the connections, I couldn't tell you. But when he came around, the sun shone on her day." She paused, taking a deep breath. "I wish I could help you more, Ms. Kavanagh, but people in here don't always tell their story, and if they do, it's not always the real story."

"I appreciate what you have shared. Did Xenia ever talk about where she planned to go when she was released?"

"Far as I know—Jacksonville. That's where she's from. She never talked about any other place. But she said it was a crap town for her. That all she ever got there was grief. So, what's new? I'm pretty sure she had a juvie record. Can't put my finger on it, but it just comes to me. She had drug history. Got off of them when she was pregnant. I felt sorry for her about the kid. I don't know what I would do if mine were put in the system. I'm lucky I have a mom. But Zee was real determined to get the kid back, no matter what."

"Did she know who had her child or where she was?"

Smith shrugged. "I don't think so, but I don't know. She said K.B. would help her."

Scarlett finished making a note and then turned around to Jake. "Do you have any additional questions for Marlene?"

He stood. "I think we're done. Thank you for your candor. If you think of anything that might be relevant, please let the warden know. She has my contact information. And be assured, anything you've told us will be kept confidential."

Seconds after the inmate left the room, Janice Croswell walked in. "I hope you've gotten some helpful information, Mr. Shepherd. Here is the name of Xenia's visitor from our records, and I've spoken to the warden over at Raiford. I don't think you'll have a problem there."

Jake looked down at the slip of paper. "So Killer Boy is Jeb Mayfield Thomas."

"Killer Boy?" Croswell said.

"That's apparently his gang moniker."

She rolled her eyes.

Jake smiled, nodding. "I appreciate the cooperation you've given us."

"Happy I could help. I'll keep an eye on the news about your case, but it might not make our media. If you think of it, let me know how it plays out."

Scarlett gave a slight nod as Jake said, "We will, and if any of these ladies remembers something else, here is a couple of my cards."

As soon as they were in the vacant corridor leading to the exit, Scarlett said, "Nice of you to warn me I would be questioning that woman."

He put a hand on her shoulder. "Got to always be on your toes, Harvard. You did fine."

"I am a litigator, or did you forget? What am I thinking? You don't forget anything."

He grinned.

CHAPTER NINETEEN

When they settled into the vehicle, Jake took out his phone and checked for messages before starting the motor. "Better check in with Liz." With the phone on speaker, he mounted it on the dash and then started the engine.

"What's up?" he said when Liz answered.

"A couple of things. Phil wants you to call ASAP."

"Any idea what's going on with him?"

"No. I was out to lunch when he called. But his voice mail sounded fairly urgent."

"And what else?"

"Sonny showed the client's neighbor the photos, and she recognized one."

"Sweet. Which one?"

"Miranda McKay."

Scarlett's head snapped around toward Jake, her eyes wide.

"Really? She identified McKay's ex as the woman hanging around the apartment building?"

"She did. Sonny said it was a positive ID."

"Damn. Just when I was about ready to eliminate her from the suspect pool. Tell Sonny, good work. We're on our way to the other prison to see what we can find out about a boyfriend of Jessica's twin. How did you do with the prosecutor on Xenia's case?"

"Good and bad. She's still with the office but can't meet with you until Monday morning. I made the appointment for eight a.m. That should give you time to catch a midday flight back."

"It is what it is."

He hit the off button as he pulled out of the prison parking lot. "See why I don't draw conclusions too early? You never know until all the chips fall into place."

"I can see that. I had come to the conclusion Xenia was the primary suspect, and now, I'm not as sure."

"Do me a favor and hit Madison on my call list. Better find out what he wants."

"Speaker?"

He nodded.

Phil Madison answered on the first ring. "Jake. Where are you?"

"Between prisons in Florida. What's up?"

"We got a problem."

"Yeah, what?"

"Your buddies at the Bureau know Jessica isn't Jessica. They've been all over the church and Ted McKay. It's only a matter of time before they find out about Florida and the sister—maybe that Jessica is MIA. Jake, you know they'll get her bond revoked."

"And what are they doing to find the child?"

"Although no one has said it, they think Jessica killed Faith and therefore aren't pressing too hard to find her. They believe they're looking for remains."

"As soon as I tie up all the leads I've found, I'll lay it out to Kirby. But not before we find Jessica and have a better set of breadcrumbs to give him. Were you able to get the medical records from that New York hospital?"

"Not yet. They're having computer issues and said it might take a few days. Are you working on finding Jessica?"

"I've got a hunch. But I'd rather not say until I do a couple more interviews," Jake said as he turned into a convenience store property and parked.

Scarlett gave him a quizzical look.

"How long are you going to be in Florida?" Madison asked.

"I'd say 'til Monday night or early Tuesday."

Scarlett flinched, and her eyebrows pinched tight for a moment.

"Good luck," Madison said, "If the Feds put anything in motion, I'll do my best to stall. Keep me posted."

"Likewise." As Jake terminated the call, he said to Scarlett, "I caught that look. What's the deal?"

She shook her head. "If we're not going to be back in Virginia by Sunday night, I'll need to tell Fury not to put the cats on Gray's plane Monday."

He studied her face for several seconds. "You're missing them, aren't you?"

"I'd be lying if I said no, but I understand. We have to finish up here."

"Tell you what. Let MacGregor transport them as planned. I'm sure Liz won't mind looking after them for a day. We'll just have to arrange for her to get into your apartment. Probably not a good idea to spring them on Kai and Romeo."

Scarlett smiled. "You are the epitome of contradiction, Shepherd. On the surface, you're hard as marble, but underneath, there's—"

"Shh. That's classified info."

By the time they reached the prison, the sun was dropping to the right of the vehicle. As Scarlett positioned the visor to the side, she said, "My gosh, this is one of several prisons in this area."

"Prison city. But we're headed to the kingpin. It houses the men on death row."

"How depressing. But they are all so bleak. No trees, no-frills architecture, and fences with barbed wire."

"You left out the guns in the towers."

"The accent pieces. We will be out of here before dark, I hope."

Jake grinned. "You don't want to stay for dinner?"

"Don't think so. But first, I want to get back to our hotel and take a long hot shower."

"Sounds like a plan. Need any help with that?"

She winced. "Keep your mind on the job, Shepherd."

"Just checking the temperature of our—*association.*"

Her look of disgust quickly morphed into a twinkle in her eyes and a sly grin. "Well, I'd hate to sue you for harassment. But I could point out that if I were a partner in the business, it wouldn't stick."

"Why am I getting the idea I'm being set up?"

"Just saying."

After clearing the security checkpoints, Jake and Scarlett were escorted to the administrative office, where a middle-aged man in shirtsleeves greeted them.

"Welcome to Raiford, Mr. Shepherd . . . Ms. Kavanagh. I'm Bill Cutler."

Jake shook his hand. "I appreciate your seeing us on short notice and late on Friday. We'll try to keep it short."

After leading them into his private office, the warden took a seat behind his desk as Scarlett and Jake sat. "Janice Croswell told me you're working a missing child case—the ones we all hate the most. She said you have reason to believe a guy who served time here might have information."

"True. The little girl's mother has a twin sister who I've been told has or had a pretty tight thing going with a Jeb Mayfield Thomas. Know him?"

"I have some recollection. He came in here on a twenty-year ticket for second-degree murder. Got it tossed when a lawyer he shouldn't have been able to afford got the guys in Tallahassee to overturn it on a technicality—illegal search. Here's a copy of some of his records I had my staff pull."

"Rumor has it he's gang-affiliated."

"Absolutely—the RRs. That's how he got the suit to represent him. With no honest income or visible means of support—what do you think?"

"Rebel Rattlers are a violent crew. I didn't know that club had a presence in Florida."

"Thomas set it up. He's the president of the state chapter, as I understand it. You're looking at a mean son of a bitch, Shepherd. But kidnapping doesn't fit unless he's moved into trafficking. How old is the kid?"

"Five."

"That makes her just right for the eight-is-too-late clientele."

"Let's hope it's not the case. Did the State attempt to retry him?"

"I had my assistant check that out. No. Of course, on murder, they still can refile, but with the search voided, they lost the knife—fruit of the poisonous tree, which I'm sure you understand. I hear you're a former Fed."

Jake nodded.

"Thomas carved the guy up pretty bad, and he bled out. Without the murder weapon, all the State had was circumstantial evidence. It was a gang fight, and Thomas had associates swearing he was nowhere near the scene at the time, and the other side swearing it was him. Neither had credibility. I think the prosecutor jumped the gun—relied on the mindset of the community to convict, which would've worked if Thomas had not dug up the backing to appeal."

"I'm assuming you have no info on where he might have gone when he left here?"

"Nada. If you had time to hang around, my money is on seeing him back here, unless he's left the state or someone takes him out. He's a career criminal. Check with FDLE. They may have a handle on where the gang is anchored."

"Is there anyone here who might give me information on the guy?"

"You're a pro. You know these guys don't talk. But I don't think anyone would know. We don't have any other members of that gang in our facility."

Jake rose. "Thank you for your time." He glanced down at the manila folder the warden provided. "And thanks for putting together the dossier."

####

"Dinner was very good last night," Scarlett said as the waitress in the hotel restaurant walked away with their breakfast orders.

Jake nodded. "Sometimes, the reviews get it right. Since we're going to be in the heart of town today, I've made a dinner reservation for Ruth's Chris Steak House."

"Nice. What is first on today's schedule?"

"I'm about to make the call to the Gibson house."

"What if he or she won't see us?"

"I can't let that happen. Worst case scenario, I'll ask for help from the prosecutor on Monday, but hopefully, that won't be necessary because it will waste two precious—" His cell phone rang. After looking at it, he held it up for Scarlett to read the caller ID.

"Kirby?" she said, little above a whisper. "What do you think he wants?"

"Probably not to tell me what Sabrina is doing today."

Jake let it ring without answering, but it no sooner stopped than it rang again. "Whatcha need, Kirby?" He hit the speaker button.

"Who the hell is your client, Shepherd?"

Jake grinned at Scarlett, cocked his head, and raised an eyebrow. "Which client would you be referring to?"

"Don't fuck with me, Shepherd. Who is Jessica Johnson?"

"Do you have some reason to believe she is anyone other than Jessica Johnson?"

"Cut it out. You know exactly what I mean."

"Whether I do or whether I don't, I don't think I'll be discussing it with you at this time." He tipped his head toward Scarlett, who was stifling a chuckle.

"You gonna hide behind attorney-client privilege?"

"Something like that."

"You realize you are playing with a child's life?"

"Put your horses back in the barn, Kirby. I know what's at stake. It's probably even more important to me than it is to you."

"Then give me the information."

"I'm assuming you've already tried to browbeat it out of Madison." Jake absentmindedly twirled his knife around on the table like a whirligig as he spoke.

"You're a former agent, Shepherd. I don't expect a lawyer to cooperate with us. But I would think you would have enough fucking sense to play it straight, and by the way, your daughter is pretty upset that you let her down again this weekend."

"If you'll climb down from your damned self-importance, I'll give you something."

For several seconds, the only sound coming through the phone was heavy breathing. "Give."

"First, you need to dial back on your theory Jessica had anything to do with her daughter's disappearance. Second, I'm working a lead. As soon as it's ripe, I'm going to give you chapter and verse. But like it or not, you're going to have to trust me and dig some patience out of your bag of infinite resources."

"I swear to God, if you still worked for me, I'd fire you."

Jake laughed. "That's why I don't work for you. Now, go play nine holes at your club and leave the real work to me."

"Damn—"

Jake terminated the call.

"You sure push his buttons."

"Don't I?" He took a gulp of coffee and then said. "Here goes." Taking a small leather notebook out of his pocket, he opened it to a phone number and then dialed. When a female voice answered, Jake said, "Mrs. Gibson. My name is Jake Shepherd. I'm a lawyer-investigator working for Jessica Johnson, alias Nyx Arnold. I know someone at this number has been talking to her by phone."

The phone remained silent for nearly a minute.

"Please don't hang up, Mrs. Gibson. This is important."

"How do I know who you are?"

"You don't. And I respect that. If you use the Internet, go to Shepherd, spelled S-h-e-p-h-e-r-d, and associates—one word—dot com. You'll find a phone number. Call that number and give the woman who answers, her name is Elizabeth Glover, this number. She'll verify who I am."

There was another silent pause.

"Why are you calling me? Has something happened to Nicky?"

"Mrs. Gibson, I would really like to talk to you in person."

"I don't know if I can do that."

"I understand. My associate, Scarlett Kavanagh, and I can meet you anytime and anywhere you would feel comfortable."

"How do I know you're really working for Nicky and not someone else?"

"You don't, and I understand your apprehension."

"I'm going to get my husband."

"That's fine."

Jake and Scarlett exchanged looks as he waited.

"This is Ron Gibson. What's this about?"

"As I told your wife, my name is Jake Shepherd. My associate, Scarlett Kavanagh, and I are working for a woman you, or your wife, may know as Nyx Arnold; and I'd like to talk to you. It's imperative. If you have access to a cell phone, I'll text you my photo. Your wife has my website address. You can verify who I am from there. If you still have any doubts, call attorney Phillip Madison in Washington, DC. He'll vouch for me and confirm we are all working for Nyx Arnold. Google us both. I can't stress enough how important this is. Once you are satisfied as to my identity, text me a time and location where you and your wife are willing to meet with us. I understand you'll want a public place."

Gibson gave Jake a number. After receiving it, Jake took a selfie and a photo of his business card and sent them to the number.

By the time a message came back from Ron Gibson, Jake and Scarlett had finished breakfast and were about to leave the restaurant. "It's a go. He says they'll meet us at ten-thirty at the snack area of Target on San Jose Boulevard." Jake looked down at his watch as Scarlett expressed relief. "He says he'll know me from the photo. We'd better start that way."

It took Jake and Scarlett forty minutes to make the drive, but they arrived ten minutes early, went in, and walked to the small refreshment area at the front of the store. The Gibsons were there but mulling around in the nearby ladies' accessory department. They immediately approached Jake and Scarlett.

"Mr. Shepherd, I'm Ron Gibson, and this is my wife, Hannah."

Hannah Gibson offered a weak smile, appearing to be nervous.

Scarlett took the initiative and extended her hand to the woman, "I'm Scarlett Kavanagh. Thank you for coming."

Jake handed the husband one of his business cards and produced his Virginia Investigator's license. "We can talk here, or if you're comfortable, we can go somewhere with a little more privacy."

Gibson looked down at his wife. "I think they're okay, honey. What do you think?"

"What is it you want from us?" she said, directing her focus toward Jake.

"We're hoping you can help us learn more about Nyx. Right now, she's missing."

Hannah Gibson's face erupted in shock. "Oh, no. I knew something was wrong. Don't tell me they found her."

Jake's brow pinched. "They? Who are they?"

Hannah took a deep breath. "You don't know?"

CHAPTER TWENTY

"Know what?" Jake asked as Scarlett's brow creased with puzzlement.

Hannah Gibson looked over her shoulder as if she didn't want anyone to overhear what she might say.

"Maybe not here, honey," Ron Gibson said to his wife, who appeared to be trembling. He turned to Jake. "I looked you up, Mr. Shepherd. You're pretty impressive."

Scarlett looked at Jake, wondering what the man had read.

"You were an FBI agent on some major events, according to several news articles I found. I believe we can trust you."

"Then I suggest we get out of here," Jake said.

"Hannah, I'm comfortable with these people coming to the house. Are you?"

She started to speak but moved her chin up and down instead.

Gibson glanced down at Jake's portfolio, lying on a table next to where he stood. "We're only about five minutes away. If you can give me a piece of paper, I'll write our address down for you."

"That's not necessary. I have it. We'll meet you there," Jake said.

Jake hesitated before leaving the Target parking lot. "I'm going to give them a chance to settle in before we arrive," he said to Scarlett as he adjusted the vent on the air conditioning.

"I wonder what she was talking about when she said we don't know."

"We're going to find out." He cranked the engine and backed out as she buckled up.

When they reached the one-story, peach stucco house, Ron Gibson answered the door. "Hannah will be right out. Understand this is unnerving for her. She needs to get herself together."

"Is there anyone else in the house?" Jake asked, glancing around the living room. "Children?"

"No. Our kids are with my mother-in-law. Please have a seat." He pointed to an ivory leather couch with a pair of matching chairs, which, along with a black marble-topped cocktail table in the center, formed a grouping. A thick Oriental rug in shades of burgundy, ivory, and black covered most of the hardwood flooring.

Jake and Scarlett claimed the chairs while Gibson settled down on the couch. The pristine room had the look of a decorator's showroom. Scarlett stared at a large, charcoal sketch of a couple sitting on a garden bench beneath a trellis. The entrance of Hannah Gibson broke her concentration.

"I'm sorry. I'm just so nervous." Hannah Gibson took a seat next to her husband. He immediately took her hand. "You said Nicky is missing. I've tried to reach her for weeks. What are you thinking has happened to her?"

"That's complicated. Short answer is there are problems—serious problems," Jake said, opening his portfolio.

"What kind of problems?" Hannah asked.

"Or better yet," Ron said, interrupting the flow of Hannah and Jake's exchange. "Why don't you start with why you're here?"

"Right. Scarlett and I are currently working for Nicky, who we know as Jessica Johnson."

Hannah frowned but focused intently on Jake.

"On Monday of this week, her five-year-old daughter Faith was taken from the school she attends by a woman impersonating Ms. Johnson."

Hannah Gibson gasped.

"Unfortunately, the unsub—unidentified suspect—was so good at the ruse the authorities believe Jessica picked up the child and may have done her harm."

"No," Hannah said. "No way would Nicky harm her baby." Alarm written on her face, she looked toward her husband, clasping his hand tighter.

"Scarlett and I agree."

Refocusing on Jake, Hannah said, "Nicky has a twin. Could it have been Zee?"

"That's what we're trying to figure out. What makes her come to mind for you?"

"Zee has been angry with Nicky for years."

"And you know that how?"

"Nicky and Colleen have told me several times."

Jake studied the woman's face for a second. "Colleen? Who is Colleen?"

"Nicky's mother—her adopted mother."

He immediately made a note on his legal pad. "So, Nicky was adopted. What about the sister? Was she adopted?"

"No. As far as I know, she was in foster care until she turned eighteen."

"Where do Colleen and her husband live? She is married, I presume."

Hannah turned to her husband.

"That's what Hannah was referring to at Target," Ron said. "Colleen's husband was murdered, violently, a few months ago during a home invasion."

Scarlett's face tensed at the revelation.

"Was the killer or killers caught?" Jake asked.

"No," Ron said. "Not that we are aware, and Hannah talks to Colleen regularly."

Jake turned to Hannah. "Are there any suspects?"

Hannah shrugged. "Not that I've heard. Colleen and I tried to tell Nicky, but she never communicated back when I left messages. I doubt she knows."

"Was Colleen—what's the last name?"

"Powell," Ron Gibson said.

"Was Colleen Powell home at the time?"

Hannah did not respond for several seconds. Her body appeared tense. Blinking, she said, "Jerry was alone. Colleen was in the hospital for gall bladder surgery. She had been trying to call Jerry but got no answer. She called a neighbor to check on him. When he didn't answer the door, the neighbor called the police." A tear crept down Hannah's face. "The police went to Colleen's hospital room to inform her."

Scarlett reached into her purse, took out a small package of tissue, and handed it to Hannah.

"Thank you." She wiped her eyes and then faced Jake. "I'm sorry. I'm a crybaby. I cry at happy movies."

Scarlett gave her a sympathetic smile.

"Had to be brutal," Jake said. "Do you have any details about the break-in?"

When Hannah didn't respond, Ron said, "Only that it appeared Jerry let the attacker or attackers in. The police told Colleen there was no visible sign of forced entry. A van was seen in the drive—"

Hannah interrupted. "There were two strange vehicles seen at the house during the day by neighbors."

"She's right," Ron said. "But one was a handyman the Powells used for maintenance. I think they pretty much cleared him. But no one saw the occupants of the other van." He stopped for a moment and put an arm around Hannah's shoulders.

"The cops identified the other vehicle, from surveillance footage caught on neighbors' cameras, as a late-model Dodge Ram—granite color. Unfortunately, none captured the license plate."

"A van model with limited window exposure. Probably stolen," Jake said. "Chosen for its anonymity—not likely an amateur. So, what time of day did this happen?"

"The van was seen about two o'clock."

Jake nodded. "Best time of day for people to be away from their homes, but at least it was daylight. Did anyone hear anything?"

"No. The closest neighbors were at work."

"Was anything taken?"

"That wasn't mentioned on the news, but Colleen told Hannah a stash of emergency cash they kept hidden in the house is gone."

"Nothing else?"

"Not as we've heard. Colleen believes the thieves knew they had the money."

"How much are we talking?"

"Several thousand. Colleen said Jerry always wanted to have enough if we had to evacuate for a hurricane."

Scarlett glanced over at Hannah, noticing the color had drained from her face. "I don't mean to interrupt, but I would love a cup of tea if you have it."

Jake cut his attention to her, thought for a second, and then said, "I *could* use a caffeine fix if it's not too much trouble—instant is fine."

Hannah exhaled, seeming to relax. "No trouble. I'll get it."

Rising, Scarlett said, "I'll help."

In the kitchen, Hannah retrieved a package of tea bags from her pantry.

"Where are your mugs or cups?" Scarlett asked.

"Right side of the sink. We don't have instant coffee. We use Keurig pods."

"Do you have expresso?"

"Mr. Shepherd likes it strong?"

"That's an understatement."

Hannah smiled. "I'm fairly sure I have some Death Wish K cups left. Ron drinks it during tax season. He's an accountant." She reopened the pantry and took out the coffee.

"Sounds perfect. How many mugs should I take down?"

"Four, I guess. I'm sure Ron will have a cup, too."

Scarlett watched Hannah as she filled two cups with water, added tea bags, and covered them with folded paper towels before placing them in the microwave.

"What aren't you telling us, Hannah?"

The petite blonde snapped her head around as she put the coffee maker into action.

"I can tell you're scared."

"I don't know what you mean."

"I think you do. We're trying to help Nicky, and we can't do that if we don't have all the information."

Hannah closed her eyes for a second, taking a deep breath. "I, I'm just not sure."

"Trust me, Hannah. Whatever it is, Jake can help."

"I could be wrong."

"That's okay. We can figure it out."

"How long have you been an investigator?"

Scarlett smiled. "About a week, but don't judge us by that. I am a lawyer, like Jake. Believe me. Jake wasn't just an FBI agent. He was an assistant U.S. attorney with the Department of Justice and a member of the most elite unit of the FBI. His instincts, training, and intelligence are top of the line. However, his patience and social skills—not so good. There are a lot of balls in play and little time to sort them all out. Faith has been missing for a week."

"What about Nicky?"

"Nicky went missing on Thursday when she was released from jail in Silver Spring, Maryland. She had been charged with child neglect, resisting arrest, and disturbing the peace. Jake says they were bogus charges—just to get her in custody, take fingerprints, DNA, etcetera.

Two things are going on. First is Faith's safety, for sure. But also, clearing Jes—Nicky."

"You need to talk to Colleen."

"I agree." Scarlett nodded. "Can you call her and set it up—please?"

"I'm not sure." The microwave beeped and cut off, causing Hannah to flinch. She reached into a cabinet and took out a sugar bowl.

"Please try. What do you know about Xenia? Were you ever around her?"

"No. We never met. She was only at the Powells' for about three weeks, and I was in Gainesville. All I know is what I've heard from Nicky and Colleen. The sisters were separated when DCF, that's the Department of Children and Families, took them away from their mother because of her drug addiction. I think they were about ten. She ultimately died of an overdose. The father was in prison, so the girls went into foster care. Nicky went to live with the Powells, first as a foster child, and then they adopted her. She never knew where Zee was."

"So, Nicky hasn't seen her sister since they were children?"

"Not until she was in college. The idea of finding Zee started gnawing away at Nicky our sophomore year. I guess it was the genetics thing—wanting to have contact with your birth family. Ron and I were at the University of Florida. We were high school sweethearts. Nicky planned to go to law school and was here in Jacksonville at Florida State College. But tracking down Zee ruined her life."

"Exactly how did that ruin Nicky's life?"

"Zee was dancing in a girlie bar on Emerson. She had been in trouble and was on probation. She was a mess—using drugs. I think she was also working as a—you know."

"Hooker?"

"Yeah. Nicky wanted to help her. So, she asked the Powells to let Zee stay with them until she could find a decent job. Being the sweet people they are, they agreed. But it all blew up when Zee asked Nicky to give her a ride to the store to buy feminine supplies."

"I'm guessing that was about ten years ago."

"Yeah." She gave Scarlett a how-did-you-know look.

"What happened?"

Without answering Scarlett's question, Hannah changed the subject. "Nicky and I have been close friends since we were thirteen, but I haven't seen her in over ten years."

"That would coincide with the time Nyx became Jessica. Am I right?" Scarlett said.

Hannah nodded. "She's never done anything wrong. I can't believe someone kidnapped Faith. Oh, my god. If that happened to one of my kids, I'd . . ."

"So, what happened when Nicky took Zee to the store?"

Hannah cleared her throat. "I'm not sure I should be telling this."

"Hannah, the more Jake knows, the better his chances of helping Nicky."

"Zee tricked Nicky. She wasn't going to the store to buy anything. She was going to meet her boyfriend and rob the place."

"And Nicky was there?"

"She was in her car. Apparently, the guy had a gun. When Nicky heard a shot and a woman ran out of the store, her gut told her what Zee had done. She drove off and then left town a few hours later, afraid the police would never believe she wasn't part of what Zee planned. I don't blame her. According to the news, the cops spotted the couple making a getaway on foot. There was a chase and a shootout. The boyfriend was killed. Zee went to prison for murder even though it was the cops who killed the guy."

"Felony murder. And you never met Zee?"

"No. I just saw her pictures in the newspaper clippings my mother sent me. Colleen says Zee blames Nicky for everything—the boyfriend's death and her going to prison."

"Can you call Colleen now?"

Without answering, Hannah went over to a cordless landline on her kitchen desk and dialed a number. After a minute, she said, "Colleen, this is Hannah. Please call me as soon as you get this message. It's important." She hung up and turned to Scarlett. "She wasn't home."

"I got that. Were you calling a cell or a landline?"

"Landline."

"Does she have a cell?"

Nodding, Hannah picked up the phone and dialed again. "Colleen. Where are you?" She stood listening for several seconds. "I'm sorry to bother you, but when are you coming home? There are private investigators here about Nicky." She began shaking her head. "No, no. Ron and I are sure it's okay. I can't explain it all, but they need to talk to you. When can you do that?"

After hanging up, Hannah turned to Scarlett. "She's in Alabama at her sister's. She'll be back Monday morning and will meet with you Monday afternoon. She wants me to be there."

"No problem. Thank you."

As Jake and Scarlett drove north on I-95, toward their hotel, after she had briefed him on her conversation with Hannah, he said, "I'm impressed, Harvard. I like your initiative. You picked right up on Gibson's anxiety. Good instincts. Might make a decent investigator of you after all."

"And you doubted me? Thought you were smarter than that. I'm *going* to be your partner."

"God have mercy on me if that ever happens. But you're light-years away. You don't know what you don't know."

"So, what do we do tomorrow?"

"Since we can't do any interviews, we'll review what we've gathered and then do something for pleasure." He gave her a quick look with a wink.

"Sounds nice as long as it doesn't involve zip-tie escaping or karaoke."

"Come on, Harvard. You were good on stage. We made a great team."

She looked down and smiled. "Yeah. We were pretty good."

....

CHAPTER TWENTY-ONE

At barely past six Sunday morning, a loud knock on the door between Scarlett's room and Jake's jolted her to a conscious state. Blinking, she climbed out of bed and staggered over to open it.

"Did I wake you?"

Scarlett pinched her eyebrows together in a frown. "You know damn well you woke me, Shepherd. Where's the fire?"

He laughed. "My, my, we're testy this morning." He put a hand on her shoulder. "You're on the Shepherd and Associates clock now, Harvard."

"So?"

"So, reset to Shepherd time." He tilted his head slightly to the right and gave her an eye. "Do what you do to go public while I take a shower and then meet me downstairs for breakfast." After patting her shoulder, he started to turn away.

"I have a better idea. I'll get in a little more sleep and skip breakfast."

He turned back. "Negative. You're a trainee, and I'm the instructor. See you"—he glanced down at his watch—"at six-thirty. Gives you plenty of time."

Scarlett groaned. "You're—"

"An f-ing son of a bitch." He snickered. "That's well established. Now get ready."

It was five past seven by the time Scarlett made it to the hotel restaurant. Jake looked up from a corner table by a window and then checked his watch. As she approached, he stood, shaking his head. "They didn't teach punctuality at Cambridge?"

"I guess not, but they did teach courtesy and consideration, which Yale obviously skipped."

He smiled and pulled a chair out for her, sliding it back as she sat. "I asked the server to bring a pot of tea when you arrived."

"Thanks." She looked down at his open portfolio. "I didn't bring my notes. I thought we would go over everything upstairs."

"We will. I brought mine down to plug any holes." He closed it and slid it onto one of the empty chairs at their table. "Shouldn't take us more than an hour to review everything and then close up shop. What is your pleasure for the rest of the day?"

"I have a choice?"

"I'll ignore that. According to my weather app, the forecast is seventy degrees and sunny. Google says we're about an hour's drive from St. Augustine—oldest city in the U.S."

She unwrapped her utensils and spread the napkin across her lap. "I knew that. Ponce de Leon thought he found the Fountain of Youth there," she said as a waitress set a pot of hot water and a chest of assorted tea bags on the table.

"Yeah. Seems there are quite a few tourist attractions and good restaurants. You game?"

Scarlett chose a packet of Darjeeling, smiled at the server, and then looked at Jake. "Absolutely. Thanks."

"Thanks? For what?"

"For giving this depressing week a modicum of fresh air."

Later in Jake's hotel room, as each opened their respective notes from the two days before, Scarlett said, "I dread meeting with Colleen Powell, considering what happened to her husband."

"Anytime you work a violent crime case, Harvard, there will be unpleasant moments. You'll toughen up but never become totally desensitized. You'll be conducting the interview."

She did a double take. "That comes as a surprise."

"Don't know why it should. She's a fragile subject. Much better to have a feminine touch. You're good at interviewing. I'll give you a few key questions I want you to ask."

"Nice to hear you think I'm good at something."

He laughed. "Give me a break. You wouldn't be here if I didn't think you have potential. Just don't try to get ahead of yourself."

"Not likely with you around. I'm kinda glad the meeting is at her brother's house. The thought of what happened at hers might be morbidly distracting. If I were her, I don't think I could ever live in that house again." Scarlett shuddered.

Jake began flipping through the pages of his legal pad. "My guess is she'll never go back there to live. However, I want to look through the house—not that there's likely any evidence left, but it never hurts to put another pair of eyes on the crime scene. With that in mind, I'm glad it has remained vacant."

"You don't think there's any connection between the murder and Faith's abduction?" She stopped as though a revelation dawned. "Oh, my god, Jake, if there is—they're killers. Faith and Jessica could be dead."

"Slow down. At this point, that's a reach. No one has come forward with information as to how many were involved in the Powell home invasion, whether male, female, or both, no descriptions. Nothing to tie the incident to Jessica's sister. Although we can't rule it out, I'll admit what we've learned shows Xenia had a strong revenge motive, which places her high on my suspect list for the abduction. But as well as Jessica covered her tracks, there's a big question as to how Xenia could have found her. And don't forget; Miranda McKay is still in the race."

"That's right. She was stalking Jessica."

"Never underestimate the actions of a woman scorned, especially one whose computer is missing a chip."

"Good point. By the way, where's the Shepherd Glock? I thought you never left home without it."

He reached down, pulled up the right leg of his jeans, revealing a Sig P365 nestled inside his boot. "A little less obvious."

Their sightseeing began at the old Spanish Fort, Castillo de San Marcos, built in the late 1600s. The collection and demonstrations of arms and armament of the era intrigued Jake. Afterward, they toured major sites in an open-air trolley, strolled down St. George Street in the Historic District, and enjoyed lunch at the Café Alcazar, located in what had been the indoor swimming pool of the Golden Age Alcazar Hotel. Built in 1888 and closed in 1931, the decaying hotel was refurbished and transformed into the Lightner Museum in 1947. In the modern era, the museum hosted traveling exhibits as well as possessing an impressive permanent collection of art and antiques. By five-thirty, they were headed back to Jacksonville.

As she settled into the passenger seat of their rental, Scarlett reached both hands over her head and stretched. "Nice day, Shepherd. Thanks for indulging me at the museum."

"Glad you enjoyed it. I think a dip in our hotel's pool would bring it to a relaxing close. Interested?"

"Might be a little awkward since I don't have a swimsuit with me, and I doubt the hotel encourages skinny dipping."

He glanced at her with a sly smile. "That's an interesting idea. If you want to play it safe, there's a discount mall we passed coming into town. You can grab a suit there."

"What about you?"

"I keep one in my gym bag for use when I work out in a facility with a pool."

"I should have known, the always-prepared Boy Scout you are. I hope it's not pink."

He gouged her ribcage playfully. "No, Harvard. It's not pink. As I recall, it's black."

The sun had dropped below the horizon when they made it to the pool. Scarlett waded in while Jake dove into the deep end. The warm water provided a soothing sensation to Scarlett's body and mind. As the eve of the usual influx of Monday business travelers, the hotel stood relatively quiet. Only two guests were in the pool when the couple arrived, and both left soon after. While Jake swam laps, Scarlett floated on her back, basking in the soothing tranquility of dusk. As darkness fell over the area and artificial lights came alive, Jake approached her.

"Ready to call it a night?"

She opened her eyes, pushing her feet to the floor to stand in the neck-deep water. He grabbed her hands for balance.

"Probably a good idea. By the time I dry my hair and have a snack it'll be time to—" Taking a step forward, she had stepped on something in the pool, stumbled, and fell against him. Jake steadied her, their bodies making brief contact. For an extended moment, their eyes connected, each knowing how the day was going to end.

####

To Scarlett's surprise, on Monday morning, she woke before Jake left for the gym. Although the room was dark, she could see the outline of his physique as he rose from her bed and headed toward his room. She started to speak but changed her mind.

So much for resolutions. Score one for chemistry—zero for good judgment.

As soon as she heard the hall door of his room close, she climbed out of bed, determined to be ready for breakfast before he returned, which included organizing her things for a possible return to Virginia later.

When Jake returned from his workout, Scarlett sat at the small desk in her room, dressed in lawyerly attire—her makeup and hair flawless. She was reading through her notes and making a list of matters to cover when meeting with Colleen Powell. All of her things were stowed in her luggage in preparation for a trip home. Although not formally made, the bed linen was smoothed over neatly, hiding evidence of activity the night before. The open drapes admitted the first light of day.

As he appeared in the open doorway between their rooms, he glanced at his watch and said, "Six-ten and all decked out for court? Who are you? And what have you done with Sleeping Beauty, AKA Scarlett Kavanagh?"

"Have to keep you on your toes. As I recall, there's an eight o'clock meeting with the prosecutor. You'd better hustle if we're to have time for breakfast." Closing her portfolio, she stood. "I'll meet you downstairs"—she took her phone out of a pocket and read the time—"at six-thirty. Don't be late, Shepherd."

Shaking his head, Jake said, "To what do I owe credit for this burst of early morning efficiency? Making up for yesterday or"—he grinned—"morning-after satisfa—"

"Don't say it. Don't even think it. Nothing happened."

"Oh, okay. We're back to that, are we?"

She stood, walked over to the door, and punched him in the chest with her index finger. "Get your shower, Shepherd, and try to dress like a grownup today instead of a cowboy."

"Damn, you're getting bossy."

CHAPTER TWENTY-TWO

As they waited for their breakfast orders, Jake glanced up from his phone. "From the map, it looks like the State Attorney's office is close to the local courthouse. To save time, you go to the clerk's office and pull copies of the contents of Xenia Arnold's case on the chance the prosecutor's office has purged or stored their copy. Also, dig into the parents. See what you can find. I'll do the consult with the prosecutor and meet you back at the courthouse."

After dropping Scarlett off at the front of the Duval County Courthouse, Jake parked the vehicle and proceeded to the State Attorney's Office on Monroe Street. Traffic in the area moved with Monday morning aspirations for the week ahead. Briskly walking toward his destination, a flash of history crossed his mind—not of his time as a DOJ prosecutor but of the Federal Courthouse in Oklahoma where his father's killers were tried and convicted. *Where did that thought come from?*

When he reached the office of the assistant State Attorney who handled Xenia's case, Maria Caballero, she invited him to sit.

"This is an old case, Mr. Shepherd. I'm surprised it had not been pulled. However, since the defendant accepted a plea, there's not a whole lot in the file."

"Do you remember her?"

"Spotty. Looking over the file when I arrived this morning, I see she had a record for street crimes—possession, prostitution. The boyfriend was clean, but I think it was a matter of never being caught."

"Would you have any problem giving me a copy of your file?"

She shook her head. "None at all. Case is long closed. The defendant is out—I checked this morning." She buzzed her secretary. "Doris, would you make a copy of the Arnold file for Mr. Shepherd before he leaves?"

Jake nodded his approval and then said, "Were any accomplices named in the course of the investigation?"

She flipped through the file. "No. Not that I see or remember. I was told you're here because of a child abduction in Maryland. What's the connection to this case?"

"The mother of the missing child is the twin sister of Xenia Arnold. By impersonating the mother, someone picked up the child at school."

"And who better than a twin to pull that off. But why?"

"Still working on that one. Is the PD still around who defended her?"

She flipped through the file again. "She had a private attorney."

"Really?" *How did a gal living on the edge have money for a lawyer?*

"Now that I think about it, I wondered at the time where the money to hire Bart Masters came—" The secretary came in, and Caballero closed the file and handed it to her. Returning her attention to Jake, she said, "He's one of the best defense lawyers in Duval County. But he was probably cheaper back then."

"He's still in practice?"

"Oh, yes." She turned to the laptop on a table adjacent to her desk. After scrolling through, she took a pen, wrote a number on a Post-it, handed it to Jake, and then picked up her telephone. "I'll give him a call. His staff might blow you off, but I usually get through."

Wasting no words, the savvy prosecutor arranged for Jake to meet with Bart Masters at ten o'clock.

As Jake started to leave, he said, "Are you familiar with the Jerome Powell murder?"

"It's not my case, but I am familiar with it. So far, there are no leads. Why do you ask?"

"I have reason to believe he was the grandfather of the missing child."

"Now that's interesting."

"Right. What's the policy here on releasing crime scene photos?"

"Next of kin, government agencies. Sol would probably let you look at them, given your background and a possible relationship to your case, but I'm fairly sure he's in trial right now."

Jake paused for a second before responding and then said, "I need to finish up here in Florida, so I can't hang around. I'll ask the widow to arrange for me to have copies."

Catching up with Scarlett at the Courthouse, Jake filled her in on his meeting and then inquired as to what she found.

"The juvenile dependency cases are confidential, which is pretty common, but I found the criminal cases on both parents and the domestic violence cases. Mom was a habitual drug addict with mostly possession charges, but Dad was an Olympic-level bad actor. They were a dysfunctional family for sure. I ran an inmate search and found the father is a lifer in the Santa Rosa Correctional Institution. He raped and beat a seventeen-year-old and left her to die. Fortunately, she lived and testified against him."

Jake shook his head. "So, where are you in the process?"

"The files are being copied. The clerk said it would take at least thirty to forty-five minutes."

Jake looked down at his watch. "Does this place have a snack bar or any place we can kill time? Maybe get a coffee. If the copies are ready by nine-thirty, you can go with me to the defense attorney's office."

"Yeah. There's a restaurant on the second floor. We can take the escalator. I passed it when I went to the library to look up Florida law on the statute of limitations for a case falling under the felony murder rule."

"Well, aren't you the smart one? What did you find?"

"No limitation if the crime is a capital or life crime, which felony murder is. However, I think Jessica has a good defense."

"I doubt there's any public interest to be served in pursuing Jessica on the felony murder or the unlawful flight to avoid prosecution. But if a hardass prosecutor wanted to flex his or her muscles, they'll have to deal with Phil." As they walked toward the tall escalator, Jake scanned the building with its central atrium rising seven stories to the roof, porcelain tile floors, and richly stained wood. "Impressive building."

"It is. How wrong do you think Jessica was to run?"

"Hard to say. However, she did use illegal means to establish a new identity, but that seems to be a victimless crime. I'll let Phil sort it out when this is over."

"If we find her—and Faith."

CHAPTER TWENTY-THREE

Jake and Scarlett walked into the defense attorney's office in the Blackstone Building on Bay Street at ten-fifty. The receptionist informed them that the lawyer was at the courthouse for first appearances but should return shortly. She offered refreshments, which they declined. Within minutes, the short, heavy-set attorney breezed in, scarcely noticing Jake and Scarlett.

As he snatched telephone messages from a spindle on the woman's desk, she tipped her head in the direction of the pair.

"I'm sorry. I'm Bart Masters, and you're Mr. Shepherd. Am I right?"

Jake shook hands with the bearded man, handed him a business card, and said, "You're correct. This is my assistant, Scarlett Kavanagh."

"Come on back to my office." He turned back to the receptionist. "Hold my calls, Sue."

The well-appointed office screamed success with brass lighting fixtures, Oriental rugs, and tasteful artwork. Grass cloth covered the walls above milled wainscotting with walnut paneling below. Completing the ambiance, classical music played softly in the background. To Scarlett, it meant a five-figure retainer, possibly six. *This guy doesn't represent the corner pot dealer.*

If the rich reception area and halls impressed, Masters' private office overwhelmed.

Jake glanced around. "And they told me crime doesn't pay. Looks like you made it work."

Masters chuckled as he removed his jacket and hung it on a rack in the corner of his office. "Alcohol bought sixty percent of what you see here—spoiled teenagers the other forty. You might be surprised what the financially successful are willing to pay for a good DUI defense or getting junior off on a petty charge, so he doesn't get rejected from an Ivy League college."

"So, how did you come to represent a client like Xenia Arnold?" Jake asked.

"That was a long time ago. I was just out of the PD office and taking everything that came through the door to keep the lights on. Please, have a seat." Masters sat behind his desk.

Jake sat. "I was a bit surprised to hear she had a private attorney. It's my understanding she was giving the drunks a thrill in a girlie bar."

"I hardly remember her. My secretary pulled the file from our archives." He picked up a manila folder from his desk. "I haven't had a chance to look at this, but from what I remember, it was one and done. She knew her benefactor could not pay for protracted litigation. With the possibility of a life sentence looming, she snapped at ten years. Negotiations only went two rounds. They offered fifteen and a five-year probation. We countered with five years and no probation, and we settled on ten. I hear she's out."

"Yeah. Have you heard from her?"

"No. No reason. We didn't become best friends. What's your angle?"

"I represent Ms. Arnold's sister whose young daughter was kidnapped last week. I'm trying to locate Xenia Arnold and hoped you might be able to help."

"Wow! That's heavy. No. I don't have any idea where she is. I didn't even know she had a sister."

"That's interesting. She never mentioned the sister?"

"Not as I recall, although I wasn't requesting pedigrees back then."

"Who paid your bill?"

He glanced through the file on his desk. "I'm not at liberty to say other than it wasn't a relative. As I recall, Xenia said they were friends of a relative. If the check cleared, I didn't probe. In this business, it doesn't pay to know too much. Her case was in and out. I hardly knew the woman—only that the guy she was hanging with tried to knock over a convenience store but got free room and board at the morgue." He glanced down at Jake's card. "You're a lawyer?"

Jake tipped his head in Scarlett's direction. "We both are when needed to be, but we're primarily investigators."

"That's unusual." He glanced toward Scarlett and smiled. "I wish I could help you. Nothing worse than a missing child. I will say this, as I recall, Ms. Arnold was a tough gal. She had circled the block more than once. She wasn't mouthy. More the silent snake in the bush— you know—the type that has a switchblade in her pocket, waiting for you to turn around. I had a gut feeling there was something I didn't know. That's all I can tell you."

Jake stood. "Thanks for your time. If you think of anything that might help, or if you hear from Ms. Arnold, you have my card. I'd appreciate a call."

CHAPTER TWENTY-FOUR

After stopping in the San Marco Square section of town for lunch, Jake and Scarlett headed to the home of Colleen Powell's brother a few blocks away. When they arrived at the two-story frame house, Louise O'Sullivan, Colleen Powell's sister-in-law, escorted them into the living room where a somber, frail woman in her mid-sixties sat in the corner of a sofa. Hannah Gibson sat at the opposite end.

Jake took a seat across from the subject, leaned forward, and said, "Mrs. Powell, I'm Jake Shepherd, and this is my assistant, Scarlett Kavanagh." Scarlett smiled and sat on an adjacent chair.

"I believe Mrs. Gibson"—he gestured toward Hannah—"explained to you on the phone the purpose of our visit."

She acknowledged him by nodding.

"First, I want to express my sincere condolences on the loss of your husband and to thank you for allowing us to come talk to you."

"How is Nyx? Where is she?" The woman's pale-blue eyes expressed urgency.

"Right now, we don't know. I'm hoping you can give us information that can help with locating her."

"What has happened to Faith?" She twisted a linen handkerchief she held in her hands.

"That's what we're trying to find out. I'm going to let you talk to Scarlett. Is that okay?"

Before she could respond, the front door opened, and a tall man entered. Jake stood.

"Michael O'Sullivan," he said, extending his hand to shake Jake's. "You're a private investigator?"

"That's right. I'm assuming you're Mrs. Powell's brother?"

"Right. I wish she had never taken that girl in." The muscles in his face appeared tense as he focused on Jake with hostility emanating from his eyes.

"Michael," Colleen said, a frown crushing the fear in her eyes.

He looked over at Colleen and then toward his wife, who was giving him a dubious look. "I'm sorry, Colleen. I just hate to see you put through more anguish. What is it you want, Mr.—"

"Shepherd. Why don't we go in another room, and I'll bring you up to speed while your sister and my assistant talk."

Looking toward the frail woman, Michael O'Sullivan said, "I think I should be with Colleen." Turning back toward Jake, his eyes flashed. "Do you have any idea what she's been through?"

"Actually, I do. But it's your choice," Jake said.

Scarlett cut her eyes around the room, assessing each person.

"It's okay, Michael. I want to talk to these people. They are working for Nyx. If I can help in any—" She broke into tears.

"Okay, okay. Okay, Mr. Shepherd. We'll go in the den. If you need me, Colleen, call."

She nodded again, wiped her eyes with the handkerchief, and said, "I'm fine. Hannah and Louise are right here."

"Would anyone like something to drink?" Louise asked.

"I'm fine," Scarlett said as she moved into the chair Jake vacated. The other two women concurred.

"Like Jake, I'm also so sorry for your loss, Mrs. Powell, and I'm also sorry we need to discuss painful subjects. Please feel free to ask me for a break any time. Do you mind if I record our conversation?" She held up her smartphone and pointed to the Record icon. "It will keep me from having to take the time to make a lot of notes."

"That's fine. I'll do my best to answer your questions. I want to help Nyx. She doesn't know about Jerry, but she must be crazy with Faith missing. I'm devastated."

"She is, wherever she is right now. I've got to ask you if you've heard from her in the past few days."

"No. I haven't had any contact with her since before Jerry died—maybe six months. She's been afraid to have a lot of communication. You know, I haven't seen her in at least ten years."

"I know you care a lot about her, but you would not be doing her a favor by lying to us. I realize that's a concept you may be having trouble with, but we are on her side and probably know all the secrets she's harbored for years. Are you sure you haven't heard from her?"

"No. That's the truth."

Scarlett engaged Collen Powell in eye contact. "How much do you know about where Nyx has been living and the name she uses?"

Hardly anything—only that she is in a large city, works as an office manager, and uses the name Jessica."

"Do you know the surname she is using?"

"No. She didn't even tell me she was going by Jessica until about two years ago."

"You haven't seen her since she left Jacksonville?"

"No."

"When did Nyx tell you she was pregnant with Faith?"

Colleen's brow pinched, her head moving slightly in a negative manner. "She didn't tell me about Faith until after she was born. Nyx said she was superstitious and afraid to jinx the pregnancy."

"Did she ever tell you anything about Faith's father?"

"No. I didn't want to pry." Colleen stopped speaking to cough for a minute.

"Do you need a glass of water?" Scarlett asked.

Colleen took a deep breath. "No. I'm fine. I didn't ask about Faith's father. I was afraid if I said anything to upset her, she wouldn't communicate with me anymore. I did ask her if she planned to get married. She said absolutely not."

"How did Mr. Powell feel about Nyx?"

The woman teared up again. "I'm sorry. Give me a minute."

"Of course. Take your time."

"Let me get you a cup of tea or a glass of water, Colleen," her sister-in-law said.

"No. I'm okay." She turned toward Scarlett. "What was your question again?"

"I asked how Mr. Powell felt about Nyx. Did he share your devotion?"

A slight smile forced its way onto her face despite the stream of tears inching their way to her chin. "Jerry loved Nyx. He wanted to send her money to help, but she wouldn't give me an address. Poor thing had to do everything all by herself."

Scarlett waited a few seconds, giving the woman a break. "Going back to when Nyx was still in Jacksonville, I understand Xenia stayed in your home for a while before everything went crazy. What can you tell me about her?"

"Hard. So different from Nyx." Colleen stared down at her clasped hands. "She didn't mix with Jerry and me very much. Mostly stayed in the bedroom, but she wasn't with us but about two weeks, maybe three, before that horrible incident." She looked Scarlett in the eye. "For Nyx's sake, I tried to like Xenia, but I didn't trust her."

"Have you heard from Xenia recently?"

She flinched. "Once since she was released from prison."

Hannah Gibson's face registered surprise. "Colleen, you didn't tell me you heard from Xenia. When?"

"A few months ago, before—" She covered her face with her hands for several seconds. "She called and wanted to know where Nyx was living." She paused, staring at a cardinal that landed on the outside sill of a nearby window. Blinking, as if to clear her eyes, Colleen continued. "I told her I didn't know. It made her angry. She said I was lying, so I hung up and didn't answer the phone when she called back. I wasn't going to listen to her if she couldn't be polite. I guess that's the schoolteacher in me."

Scarlett smiled. "I don't blame you, Mrs. Powell. Was the call you received about six months or seven months ago your only interaction since the convenience store robbery?"

Colleen didn't speak for close to a minute, appearing as if she was debating a personal decision. "Not exactly. Xenia contacted us from the jail two days after her arrest. She demanded we get her a lawyer if we wanted to keep Nyx out of it."

"Did you?"

She nodded. "I'm not sure I should be talking about this."

Scarlett tipped her chin with a trace of a nod. "Please remember, Jake and I are here to help Nyx and Faith. You can't make a mistake telling me all you know. Please trust us."

As Colleen heaved a heavy breath, she squeezed the handkerchief tighter. "Jerry contacted an attorney he had read about in the newspaper. We were never wealthy, but we wanted to protect Nyx. She didn't do anything wrong. She was tricked."

"I believe you," Scarlett said.

"Jerry told the lawyer we could pay five thousand dollars, but that was all we had." Colleen wiped her face with the handkerchief, let it fall on her lap, and began twisting her wedding ring.

Watching the woman's gesture, Scarlett said, "And that would have been Masters?"

"Yes. That's his name."

"Looking back at the home invasion, which I know is hard for you, have you been back to your house to check for anything the assailant or assailants took?"

Colleen shook her head. "I can't."

"So, you don't know if anything is missing?"

"Michael went with a police officer to check, pack things I needed, and to bring our cat here. The emergency money we kept in Jerry's desk, Jerry's wallet, cell phone, keys, and our computer were gone. But Michael wouldn't know if anything else was taken. I told him to check for the money. He said the house was a mess with drawers and doors left open, clothes—"

Jake and the brother walked into the living room, interrupting Colleen.

"The house had been ransacked," Michael said. "As a precaution, I had the house locks changed and new ignition lock cylinders installed in the cars."

"Was that the only time you went back to the house?" Jake asked.

"I went back the day the locks were changed and when a crew came to clean—" He glanced over at his sister, who grew visibly agitated, and said no more.

Colleen put her face in her hands and began crying hysterically. Louise moved over to comfort her.

"I think we've asked enough," Jake said, "Scarlett?"

She nodded.

"With Mrs. Powell's permission, I would like to take a look at the house."

Without lifting her head, the distraught woman nodded.

"You can follow me," Michael O'Sullivan said.

Pulling herself together, Colleen said, "Michael, please bring me the photo of Nyx and Faith that's on my nightstand."

"What time do you usually arrive home from work, Mrs. Powell?" Jake asked.

"I have not worked since the robbery, but when I do, I am usually home by four-thirty, if I don't stop for errands."

Scarlett looked at Jake, wondering why he asked, and then looked at her watch, which read three-fifteen.

It took less than fifteen minutes to reach the Powell home. On the way, Scarlett filled Jake in on her interview of Colleen Powell. She barely finished before he received a text from Liz, telling him Phil Madison received hospital records, confirming Jessica's gave birth to Faith.

When Michael O'Sullivan pulled onto the Powell driveway, Jake followed and then parked beside O'Sullivan's car in front of the double garage doors.

As Scarlett started to open her car door, she watched the gray-haired man approach the house and insert the key into the lock, fumbling for a second. *He's uncomfortable. Who wouldn't be? I am.*

Trailing O'Sullivan, Jake and Scarlett entered the house. With drapes drawn, it was dark until O'Sullivan opened the window coverings. The muggy room smelled musty with traces of disinfectant and the lack of fresh air.

"I apologize for the odor. The house has been closed up for months. I turned the thermostat to eighty-five to save on electricity."

There was no sign of where a body might have been, and the floors had been cleared of debris. Papers, books, clothing were stacked neatly on chairs. *Cleaners must have put them there, not knowing where they belonged.* Scarlett anticipated a spooky feeling would pervade the house but was surprised to find it only seemed sad. One corner of the living room was conspicuously empty.

"Where was the victim found?" Jake asked.

O'Sullivan pointed to the empty corner. "The chair he was in was hopelessly stained. Regardless, Colleen would not have wanted it. In fact, she may never want anything in this house."

"She wants a photo from her bedroom," Scarlett said.

"Right." He turned and walked toward the master bedroom of the one-story bungalow.

Scarlett followed O'Sullivan while Jake wandered around the main room, looking closely for any clues.

"No photo in here," O'Sullivan said. "Either she moved it, or some of the cleaning crew did."

"Why would the cleaning crew move a photo in this room? Weren't they here to clean up the murder scene?"

"True. Maybe the police took it."

"Took what?" Jake said as he entered the room.

"The photo of Jessica and Faith that Colleen asked her brother to pick up."

"Give her a call," Jake said. "Confirm it was on the table. If so, have her check the inventory list of items the cops removed, if she has a copy."

"Why? It's not that important. She hasn't mentioned it in six months."

"Actually, it could be very important, Mr. O'Sullivan," Jake said. "I'd appreciate your doing as I ask. And while you're at it. Ask how she got the photo."

Scarlett looked at Jake. *I think I know what you're thinking. Who but Xenia Arnold would want that photo?*

O'Sullivan gave a look of disgust but followed Jake's directions. After hanging up, he turned back toward Jake. "Colleen says it was definitely on the table because she considered taking it to the hospital but decided it wasn't a good idea. It's not on the list of items the cops took. Nyx emailed her a few photos, and Colleen printed that one out to frame."

Jake looked at Scarlett with an I-knew-it expression.

"What are you thinking, Mr. Shepherd? You're not thinking the killer took a photograph?"

"At this point, all I'm prepared to say is the whereabouts of that photo is important." With that, Jake turned and left the room.

"Is he always that damned rude?" O'Sullivan said to Scarlett.

She nodded, smiling. "Trust me. He knows what he is doing."

"He's an arrogant—" O'Sullivan caught himself before completing the sentence.

"Yeah. He is. But what would you rather have, Emily Post or competence?"

After about twenty minutes of checking drawers, cabinets, windows, doorways, and the garage, Jake called Scarlett into the home office of Jerry Powell. O'Sullivan had gone outside to smoke a cigarette.

"Did you find something?" she asked.

"It's what I did not find."

"Okay. What did you not find?"

He pointed to a four-drawer file cabinet and then opened the second drawer from the top. Separating two hanging folders with his fingers, he said, "No phone bills."

"So?"

"All other household bills are neatly filed, but this folder is empty. Someone took the phone bills."

"What are you thinking, now? Wait. If Xenia broke into this house, she was probably looking for information on finding Jessica."

Jake nodded.

"And what better than to track phone records. But Jessica only communicated with Colleen and Hannah with disposable phones."

"Xenia is smart. What she lacks in morals, she makes up for in street smarts fueled by anger and hatred. Disposables have area codes."

The kitchen door opened, and Michael O'Sullivan came back inside.

"But Jake. Even if Xenia had the area code, how could she ever find Jessica?"

"She may have gotten the first name from Mr. Powell. We don't know. Thomas's gang is big, Scarlett. Members all over the country. Gives him resources to tap." Jake glanced down at his watch. "Hmmm. Four-forty."

"What time is the last flight out tonight?" Scarlett asked.

Before he could answer, the doorbell rang. As Jake emerged from the office, O'Sullivan headed for the door. "Allow me," Jake said and stepped ahead of the man with Scarlett close behind.

Both Scarlett and O'Sullivan looked at Jake with quizzical expressions as he opened the door.

"Come in. I've been expecting you," Jake said.

At the sight of Jake, unequivocal shock transformed the face of Jessica Johnson.

"Come in, Jessica. Or should I call you Nyx?"

Scarlett's expression mirrored the surprise on Jessica's.

Catching her breath, Jessica said, "How? What are you doing here?"

"If you'll come in, we'll discuss that."

Michael O'Sullivan's face bore an expression blending surprise with hostility. "What the fuck?" he said.

Raising his hand in the traditional halt gesture, Jake turned to O'Sullivan. "Take it easy. I'll handle this." Turning back toward Jessica, he said, "Come in unless you want to go public with your story."

Her body tensed; her chin quivered.

"I know what you're doing, Jessica. You think you can find your sister and your child on your own. It ain't gonna happen, kiddo. Now come on in, and let's sort a few things out."

"Jessica. Where have you been?" Scarlett said.

"I can answer that," Jake said. "She's been zigzagging her way down here. Probably arrived a day or so ago and found no one home. Right, Jessica?"

Still stunned, Jessica walked into the living room without saying a word.

"Sit down," Jake said in a tone that left no room for debate. Speechless, Scarlett stared at the pale woman, who appeared terrified.

O'Sullivan shook his head with disgust, turned, and took steps back toward the kitchen. He then reversed his direction like a pacing lion.

"You're angry with me," Jessica said, still standing.

"You *might* say that," Jake said. "It was a dumbass move on your part—made my job that much harder, but true to your MO. You cost us precious time and a measure of worry, but we're going to get back on track now. No more games. We know all your secrets and then some. And there are a few things you don't know."

She collapsed into tears. "I have to find Faith. You don't understand."

"The hell I don't. But finding your daughter is my job, and you'd better leave it to me, or you're going to screw everything up."

Conflicted, Scarlett wanted to reach out and comfort Jessica but also wanted to chew her out.

"I couldn't tell anyone. I could be arrested for what my sister did, and Faith would be put in foster care. No one can know I'm here."

"Relax. There is no warrant for your arrest lurking out there."

"You don't know."

"*Au contraire.* I've met with the prosecutor on the case, reviewed the file, and did not find your name. If anything should arise, Phil Madison will shut it down before you can blink. But right now, there's something we have to tell you. Now sit."

She complied.

He glanced around at Scarlett. "Maybe it would be best coming from you."

Scarlett's stomach did a flip, but happy to apply compassion to mitigate Jake's attitude, she stepped forward and sat down across from their client. "Jessica, this is not easy."

"They haven't found Faith's body—no—"

"No, no. It's not that. There's no word on Faith. It's your adopted father."

"Jerry? What's wrong?" She looked around the room. "Where is Jerry? Where's Colleen?"

"There's no easy way to say this." Genuine sympathy emanated from Scarlett's eyes as she took a deep breath and said, "Jerry Powell died several months ago."

"Oh, no!" Jessica covered her face for several seconds. "How? Heart attack? Oh, poor Colleen. Where is she?"

The two men stood silent, watching Jessica crumble further into emotional turmoil.

"It was bad. I'm so sorry, Jessica. He died during a home invasion."

Jessica's face froze again in shock—all color vanishing. "You mean . . . you mean. I can't say it."

Scarlett looked toward Jake, who just shook his head slightly while blinking his eyes.

Scarlett reached over and took one of Jessica's hands. "I don't think we need to talk about details right now. I'm so sorry for your loss."

"Scarlett's right, Jessica." Jake softened his tone. "We've got to return to DC tonight—all three of us."

"I can't go back. I need to see Colleen. And what if Xenia has Faith here in Florida?"

"First of all, it's not certain your sister took Faith," Jake said. "Second, you've still got charges pending in Maryland to deal with. Coming down here doesn't make that easier. I know you've been on your own and handling everything in your life independently, but the time has come for you to turn things over to pros. Regardless of who took Faith, but especially if your sister is the unsub, this is way over your paygrade."

"What do you mean?"

Jake stood. "You're going to have to trust me. If you can't do that." He stopped, gave her an admonishing look, and turned to Scarlett. "We've got a plane to catch." Turning back to Jessica, he said, "Coming or not? Your call."

Amidst a torrent of tears, Jessica nodded.

Jake turned to Michael O'Sullivan. "A word in private."

O'Sullivan pointed to the kitchen.

"At the risk of scaring you, I'm going to say if the twin abducted the child and had anything to do with what happened here, your sister could be in jeopardy. I don't know if the locals will offer any protection, but I recommend you either hire private security or get Mrs. Powell out of Dodge until this is resolved."

"It's overwhelming. I thought the murder was—how do I go about what you're suggesting?"

"If you can't afford security and have no safe place for her to go, get her to DC. I'll be making arrangements for a safe house for Jessica."

"Aren't you overdramatizing?"

"Do I look like someone who overdramatizes?"

O'Sullivan stared at Jake for a minute. "Do you plan to go after the child by yourself?"

A grin relaxed the scowl on Jake's face. "I'm damn good, but I'm not Superman. I'll be meeting with the FBI team tonight or tomorrow. I expect they'll coordinate with the local detectives on the case. Contrary to what you see in movies and on TV, the agencies do work together."

"Do you think that woman has done anything to the child?"

"I suggest you pray that *whoever* took her hasn't harmed her."

CHAPTER TWENTY-FIVE

Scarlett rode in the back with Jessica to the airport, while Jake drove. The cheap, beat-up car Jessica had bought with cash remained at the Powell house to be disposed of by Michael O'Sullivan. For most of the trip, the young woman remained quiet, her skin tone almost as gray as her warmup suit. It was the same clothing she wore the week before when she went to pick up Faith. As they passed the Dunn Avenue exit, a few miles south of Jacksonville International, Jessica said, "He won't trust me now, will he?"

Scarlett frowned, debating for a second how to answer. "You'll have to ask him."

"You're both mad with me, aren't you?"

Carefully choosing her words, Scarlett said, "I'm not angry, Jessica." She squinted one eye. "Maybe a bit disappointed, but I understand you're desperate. I don't have children; however, I can imagine how scared you are."

"Mr. Shepherd is really mad." Speaking as though Jake was not in the car, she said, "Is he going to quit working on my case?"

"Jake?" Scarlett shook her head. "He's angry, but he'll get over it; and if he planned to fire you as a client, he would have made it clear at the Powell home. She tipped her chin and raised her eyebrows. "But you can't screw up again. Until Faith is found, do what he says, and don't do anything on your own without checking with him. No more secrets or excursions. Okay?"

"I promise."

"I believe you. I told you when we first met; Jake is your best shot for getting Faith back. You're lucky to have him, Jessica."

"I know. So, what does he plan to do when we get back to DC?"

"I don't know everything—only that he wants to meet with the FBI team investigating the abduction as soon as possible."

Jessica flinched. "Why would he do that? They think I did something to Faith."

Scarlett glanced at a sign providing lane directions to the airport. "I suspect Jake will convince them they're wrong."

"How?"

Before answering, she took her cell from her purse and checked the time. "He plans to share the information we've gathered that shows at least two other people had motives and looked enough like you to impersonate you."

"Why should they believe him?"

"Because they know him. Jake, do you need to change lanes?"

"I do. My mind wandered for a minute."

Scarlett took a breath and adjusted her position. "Don't worry. The FBI people know how good he is and can't ignore him. He worked with a lot of them—actually the supervisor in charge of the investigation."

Jessica glanced over at Scarlett, who gave a nod of affirmation.

After turning in the rental car in the parking garage of the airport, the trio made their way into the terminal. Jake took care of boarding passes, leaving his and Scarlett's carry-on luggage with her to monitor. Since Jessica left Maryland without luggage, she carried only a cheap tote bag containing the one change of clothing she purchased on her way to Jacksonville.

As Jessica stood inside the terminal, shifting from foot to foot and watching Jake at the ticket counter, she said, "I dread going back to my apartment. I don't believe I can bear to be there without Faith. The few minutes I was there last week were brutal."

Scarlett stared at the distraught mother, thinking how hard her life must have been. *Amazing she's done so well, considering the cards dealt to her.* "You may not be going back to the apartment. I'm not sure, but I believe Jake is coordinating with Phil Madison to place you in a safe house."

"You mean he wants me where he can be sure I won't run away. I know he has no reason to believe me, but I won't run. I see how stupid I was."

Scarlett smiled. "It's not because he's afraid you'll bolt." Shifting her purse from one shoulder to the other, she said, "He wants to protect you in case your sister and her boyfriend *are* involved. You have good people working for you, Jessica—Jake, the Madisons, Ted McKay—trust them."

Jessica bowed her head, giving it a slight shake. "Ted must think I'm horrible. I wouldn't blame him if he never spoke to me again." She looked up, making eye contact with Scarlett. "I was going to come back before I had to appear in court. I would never have caused him to forfeit the bail money, but I had to try to find Xenia."

"I think Mr. McKay will understand. He seems to be a sensitive, compassionate man and gives me the impression that he cares about you."

"I don't know how to handle that. I like him. Like him a lot, but he doesn't know who I am—what kind of family I'm from." She blinked a tear. "I believe my sister did this, Ms. Kavanagh. Does Mr. Shepherd?" She glanced toward Jake, who was talking on his cell phone.

Scarlett adjusted the air vent, contemplating how to respond. "She's high on his suspect list. But he hasn't ruled out the possibility of someone else. What worries him is the man Xenia is involved with. The guy is a member of a violent gang, which causes Jake concern that if Xenia is responsible for abducting Faith, the two of them are dangerous."

"Dangerous like she might have—"

"Don't go there. He hasn't said that. Do you have any idea *why* Xenia would have abducted Faith?"

Jessica gazed around the area as if not hearing the question. After squeezing her eyes shut for a moment, she forged a determined attitude. "She hates me. Hates me for driving away—leaving her at the convenience store that day." Curling her lips as though fighting to maintain composure, she took a deep breath and then said, "She tricked me into driving her there. She didn't care if she ruined my life, but she resented me even before that, Ms. Kavanagh." Jessica paused, staring at her feet while Scarlett remained silent. "I was lucky—I was. The state placed me with Colleen and Jerry. From what Xenia told me during the time she stayed with us, DCF placed her in miserable homes. She claimed she had been abused sexually and physically. I don't know if it's true. Telling the truth was never a priority for her—even when we were kids."

Before the conversation could go further, Jake put his phone in his pocket and walked over to them, holding their boarding passes. Noticing tension in his facial muscles, Scarlett concluded his phone conversation revealed alarming information.

"Something wrong?"

"No. Just thinking logistics. Sonny is meeting us at Ronald Reagan. He'll take Jessica to a safe house Phil is arranging and stay with her." With a furrowed brow, he glanced down at his watch. "I'm trying to decide whether to strong-arm Kirby into meeting with me tonight or early tomorrow. We won't be landing until after ten, which means it could be midnight before I can connect with him." Looking up, he said, "We've got more than an hour before takeoff. Let's grab a quick bite to eat where I can go over a few things with Jessica."

"Won't Kirby object to meeting that late?"

"He'll growl, but it's his job."

"Isn't Sonny doing surveillance on Jessica's apartment along with Randy Cummings?"

"I pulled them off on the way here. Sonny and Pete have set up a camera in a parked car across the street from the apartment to record the traffic in and out now that we have Jessica with us. Either Kirby or the locals have a team on-site, according to Sonny. But apparently, she gave them the slip as well." He glanced toward Jessica with a look of disapproval.

"Do you think the authorities know she isn't in the apartment?"

"No. If they did, fairly sure Phil would have heard. For their benefit, Sonny had Phil and Chris pay a fake visit to the apartment, carrying grocery bags."

"Am I going to be able to get some things from the apartment?" Jessica asked, her eyes wide with interest.

"Make a list. I'll have someone bring whatever you need."

"You said this man, Sonny, will pick me up. Am I going to be staying in the house with him—a strange man?" Her voice quivered slightly.

Jake laughed. "You are, but your virtue is safe. Right, Harvard?"

"You'll be fine, Jessica. Sonny is a retired FBI agent." She turned to Jake. "Is Brenda going to work with him?"

"They'll split the shift."

"Brenda is Sonny's wife and a retired police officer. You'll like them."

Upon hearing the explanation, Jessica seemed to relax.

"I need to caution you," Jake said. "You aren't to contact anyone. Anything you need, one of us will handle. No guests."

"Not even Ted?"

"Not even Ted. He could be followed."

"So could you."

Jake grinned. "Don't underestimate me."

Scarlett spoke up. "Jake knows how to spot someone following him and how to lose them." She cut her eyes toward him. "In fact, I think it's his favorite sport." With an alarmed expression, she said to Jake. "How is Jessica going to board the plane with no ID?"

"I called Liz and had her send a copy of Jessica's driver's license to the airline. I have the copy in my pocket."

While waiting for their food orders in a semi-quiet airport lounge, Jake probed Jessica about her pregnancy, Faith's birth, and her knowledge of Xenia's pregnancy. She once again told him about giving birth in New York and denied any knowledge of Xenia's baby.

"I never had contact with her. I did check the Internet for her release, but that's all. How could she have found me?"

Jake stared at Jessica for a minute or longer, locking her in eye contact. She didn't move.

"We don't yet know whether she found you. I understand you provided one or more photos of you and Faith to Colleen Powell, correct?"

Jessica nodded.

"By email?"

She nodded again.

"Am I correct to assume you used the computer you kept hidden in your storage unit?"

Alarm arose on Jessica's face. "How did you know about my storage unit?"

"My question was *did* you use that computer to send the photos?"

Jessica recoiled from the sharpness of his tone. "Yes."

"Where were the photos taken?"

"Different places. Mostly at the apartment."

"Where else?"

"Why?"

"Just answer my question."

She stared at her glass of tea for several seconds and then took a swallow. "I know I sent Colleen one taken of us both at the church, one at the school when the four-year-old class did a little Christmas play"—her chin started to quiver—"and one from each of Faith's dance recitals."

Jake ignored the emotion welling up in Jessica. "Who took the photos?"

Blinking hard to hold back her tears, Jessica said, "Me—all but the one of the two of us."

"And who took that one?"

"Ted. It was Mother's Day, and he took us to lunch after church. I thought the photo turned out well."

"What kind of camera was used for each of the photos?"

"I don't have a camera. I used my phone."

"And the one McKay took. What did he use?"

"His phone."

"And he forwarded it to your phone?"

She nodded. "Why? What does it matter what kind of camera took the pictures?"

"It matters," he said as the waitress arrived with their food.

CHAPTER TWENTY-SIX

At eleven-thirty, Jake and Scarlett entered his apartment.

"Do you mind getting me a bottle of water while I call Kirby?" Jake asked as he dropped his carry-on into Sabrina's room.

"Not at all."

While rolling Scarlett's bag to the other bedroom, he made the call, using the number for Hal Kirby's work mobile.

"Yeah. This better be good," Kirby said as he answered, clearing his throat.

"Need to meet with you before daybreak. I'll be at your office by five-thirty. Have your team ready—field agents and analysts."

"What the—? Who the hell do you think you are, Shepherd? I've got to change this number."

"You won't. And I'm the SOB who's going to solve your case. Be there." Without waiting for a response, Jake hit the red icon, terminating the call. As Scarlett handed him a water, he tapped the number at the top of his favorites list.

"Hi, buddy. Sorry to call so late, but we've got work to do ASAP. Can you make it to the office by four-thirty? Need you to pull photos from email sent by Jessica to her adopted mother. Extract the EXIF data and make prints. Got a five-thirty with Kirby."

"Thank her for taking care of my cats," Scarlett whispered, assuming he was talking to Liz Glover.

Jake smiled. "And Scarlett says thank you for taking care of her cats. She made me stop at her apartment before we made it up here."

When he terminated the call, Scarlett said, "Did I hear you say four-thirty?"

180 · JUDITH ERWIN

"You did. You can sleep in unless you want to go with me to the Bureau."

Her brow wrinkled. "Of course, I want to go. Are you planning to work out first?"

He laughed. "Don't think so, and we'd better turn in if we're to get any kip as the Brits say."

At four a.m. Tuesday, Jake and Scarlett left to meet with the FBI team, stopping by the office on the way. As soon as she settled into the passenger seat, she said, "You amaze me. How do you get Hal Kirby to do what you want? I'm sure he wasn't happy about meeting this early."

"If I told you that, I'd have to kill you." He grinned.

"Very funny. But that line doesn't work on me any longer."

"Okay. It's simple. I have something he wants, plus he knew I might show up at his door at two a.m. if he didn't agree to an early meeting."

"I was thinking it was more like he has something you want."

He swung the vehicle around in a sharp left turn, jolting Scarlett. "Yep. He does. They call it reciprocity—*quid pro quo*. Ever heard of it?"

"Oh, you're cute."

"Joking aside, right now, he's got nothing. His people overlooked the medicine cabinet at Jessica's apartment and lost their best opportunity. He knows I'm on to something, and, although he'll never admit it, he knows I'm right."

Scarlett frowned. "You're not going to tell him his team screwed up?"

"I might because I like to rattle his chain, but the truth is they didn't. Their warrant probably named records of Jessica's activities and contacts such as calendars, address books, electronics, plus evidence of foul play—blood, signs of struggle, etcetera. Doubt a small, non-narcotic prescription bottle would have been within the scope."

The lights were on when Scarlett, Jake, and Kai reached the office at four-twenty.

"My gosh. Liz is already here," Scarlett said.

"Working for the Bureau as long as she did, she's used to a twenty-four-hour clock. Unlike divorce, crime work doesn't function within business hours, Harvard."

When they entered, Liz was in the workroom, putting a file together.

"You found the photos?" Jake said.

"I did. I figured you'd be taking a file to Hal, so I've made copies of the relevant evidence we have on Xenia Arnold, Jeb Thomas, and Miranda McKay. Flip through it and see if I included everything you want or if there's anything you want to extract."

"My guess is you've got it sewn up tight."

After passing through security at the FBI building and having their permission to enter confirmed, Jake and Scarlett got on an elevator. She said, "What if he's not here?"

"He's here and itching to know what I've got. We wouldn't have gotten in otherwise. Don't be fooled by Kirby's shallow attempts to put me down. He knows I've found solid info, but it galls him to admit it. Kirby likes to bark, but he's too smart to bite."

When they reached the designated floor, silence filled the empty space until Deke Weston appeared. "Come on back to the conference room, Shepherd. Kirby's waiting."

Jake turned to Scarlett, raising his eyebrows in an I-told-you expression. "Deke, you remember Ms. Kavanagh, I'm sure."

"Of course, I do. I heard you're working with Shepherd now. Good luck putting up with him." The agent grinned as he spoke while shaking hands with Jake. "If he gives you any trouble, call me."

Scarlett chuckled, glancing at Jake. "I'll keep that in mind."

Hal Kirby stood when Jake, Scarlett, and Weston entered the room and immediately approached the pair as Jake hoisted his briefcase onto the table.

Nodding to Scarlett, Kirby said, "You didn't mention Ms. Kavanagh would accompany you. Nice to see you again."

Scarlett tipped her head.

"She's working for me and needs to get to know the ropes."

Kirby gave a nod of acknowledgment. "Well, take a seat, and let's get down to what you're here for. You know Weston and Fran Silverstein, but I don't think you know Jarrod Bush. He's filling in with Deke while Sylvia is out on maternity leave."

The younger agent stood and extended a hand to Jake and then to Scarlett, after which Jake turned to Scarlett and said, "Fran took over Liz's job when she retired and came to work with me."

"So, what have you got that's so urgent you got us all out of bed at an ungodly hour?"

Yep, Jake thought. *Scarlett's presence is causing you to dial back on your language and sarcasm.* He opened his case and removed multiple folders, fanning them out on the table. "Just a few things for you to check into."

Kirby's eyes latched onto the manilla folders. "Quite a stack there. Can you give us the *Reader's Digest* version?"

"You bet. I've uncovered two persons of interest and a collateral in the abduction of Faith Johnson."

"And I'm guessing none are your client."

"Bullseye. My primary is her twin sister."

Expressions on the faces of all the Feds registered surprise.

"And my secondary is the ex of a man my client was seeing."

"Theodore McKay, right?" Kirby said.

"Correct. Miranda McKay is the classic jealous woman, compounded by a drug habit. She has been seen stalking Jessica. While my interview demonstrated to me that she is not playing with the full deck of fifty-two, her propensity to violence is on a lower scale. Also,

I don't see a gain for her in kidnapping the child, unless she has no ability to think logically. If she acted, I would see it play in the form of physical harm to Jessica."

"We've been looking at her but don't see anything more than petty rivalry," Kirby said.

"The Montgomery County surveillance team caught her hanging around the apartment a few times, but nothing else to tie her to the case," said Deke Weston. "We figured she was on a hunt for the ex."

"So, what's with a twin sister, and how did you uncover her—your client? We're still running down the woman's background, right, Fran?" Kirby said.

The analyst nodded. "We hit a dead end in her history about nine years back, but we're still on it."

"I don't have to remind *you*, Shepherd, people with untraceable history usually have legal issues. Your client is still flying number one on our suspect list."

"After you see what I've dug up, you are going to change your mind."

Kirby turned to Weston. "Don't you love the way he knows what we will think?"

Weston snickered. "Yeah. And he's usually right. She's really got a twin, Jake?"

Jake whipped out an eight-by-ten copy of Xenia's mug shot from one of the files and slid it across the table to Weston. "Need I say more?"

"Sure that's not your client in a former life?" Kirby said, straining to see the image.

"Since this lady was released from the Levell Women's Prison in Florida, a year or so ago, after serving eight plus eight of a ten-year sentence on a felony murder charge, I doubt it."

Deke Weston picked up the photo, shaking his head. "Damn sure is the spitting image." He passed it on to Kirby.

Staring at the image, Kirby shook his head. "Xenia Arnold. Even if this is a twin sister, it proves nothing. Why wouldn't your client be screaming 'twin, twin, twin,' if she thought it was the sister? Or maybe your client changed her identity because she was involved in the same crime this one went to prison for? Do you know your client's real name?"

Jake took another folder from the group and slid it vigorously down the table to Kirby. "This is the prosecutor's file on the case. I challenge you to find my client's name in it, which, by the way, is Nyx Arnold—same date of birth." He turned to Fran Silverstein. "Run a background on that name."

"Why would the sister abduct her niece?" Weston asked.

"Bad blood. Don't you watch TV? Investigation Discovery has a couple of series dedicated to siblings. The Arnold women came from dysfunction at the Olympic Gold level. Both ended up in foster care. My client drew the better straw, and sis resented it. It got worse, but that's not important. Just know Xenia Arnold could be harboring enough anger to be playing with a king-size deck of vengeance."

"Did the sisters stay in contact?"

"No."

"So, how did the twin find Johnson when the FBI hasn't been able to run down her true identity?"

"I'll get to my theory on that, but first, you need to know Scarlett and I met with the inmates, a correction officer, and the warden of Levell. There we learned Xenia was connected to a Jeb Mayfield Thomas—a name that may ring a bell with your Violent Gang Unit."

Both agents sat straighter in their chairs.

"Which gang are we talking about?" Kirby said.

"Rebel Rattlers." Jake took still another folder and slid it across the table. "Mr. Thomas is said to be the president of the Florida chapter and a graduate of one of Florida's toughest prisons. And this story goes deeper. Shortly after the time Xenia Arnold was released, there was a violent home invasion of the residence of Colleen and Jerome

Powell—the couple who fostered and adopted Jessica, alias Nyx. During the course of the invasion, Jerome Powell was murdered."

"And that ties to our current case how?"

"It's not certain. But during the invasion, in addition to the standard money and electronics, a photograph of Jessica and Faith Johnson was stolen. There's also evidence of phone records being taken." Jake looked around at the four Feds with a dubious expression as if to say, "Do the math." *Got your attention, haven't I?*

"I think I hear a question as to what robber would want a photograph of a woman and child?" Kirby said, while Weston, Bush, and Silverstein stared wide-eyed at Jake.

"Exactly."

"Do you have any forensic evidence implicating the twin and Thomas in the invasion, evidence they have been in this area," Kirby said as he flipped through Jake's file on Jeb Thomas, "or evidence the twin located Ms. Johnson—or whatever her name is?"

"No forensics on the invasion unless the Jacksonville detectives found some." Jake pulled a fourth file from the array and removed four photographs, laying them one by one on the table, turned in a manner for the others to review. "But here is my circumstantial evidence. All of these were shot on smartphones. All were emailed to the murder victim's wife and likely stored on the stolen computer. *And*—all bear full metadata, including GPS coordinates that would provide a clear map to where Jessica and Faith Johnson live, where Faith attends school, and where Jessica works."

"Damn, Shepherd. You really do have something," Weston said.

Kirby didn't speak, just studied Jake's face intently for at least a full minute. "So, what do you want? Knowing you, there's a price tag somewhere."

"There is. Use your phenomenal resources to find Arnold and Thomas and hopefully the child. Go public in a big way with an announcement that Jessica is no longer a suspect. Convince Montgomery County to drop the bogus charges against her so Madison doesn't have to make them look incompetent for arresting her in the first place. And finally, contact the Jacksonville PD for their evidence in the murder case and perhaps gain their cooperation."

"How about a new car and a vacation on the Riviera?"

"Very funny. You must keep my ex-wife and daughter in stitches."

Kirby flashed an evil eye at Jake while Weston and Silverstein stifled smiles. The new agent's face registered confusion.

Without hesitation, Jake continued, "I've given you enough to crack this case, hopefully bring a little girl home to her mother, and maybe save her life. You need to work with me. Dismissing Jessica as a suspect may bring the sister out of hiding. My guess is Arnold wants to inflict as much misery as possible and will not like her sister being exonerated."

"And if I were to agree, what do we get from you?"

"Complete cooperation. Perhaps access to Jessica if Phil agrees. Access to information I can provide."

"Maryland may not agree about the exoneration. I'm not sure I agree."

"Jake, may I say something?" Scarlett said.

He gave her a nod. "Be my guest." He leaned back in his chair, watching her.

"Agent Kirby, all of you." She glanced around the room. "You don't know me, and all of you have a great deal of training and experience in criminal investigation I don't have. But don't discount me. I do have ten years of practice as a family law attorney. In that role, I interviewed and evaluated hundreds of clients, witnesses, and opposing parties. I've spent time with Jessica. I've viewed her apartment, met her adopted mother, talked with her personal and business associates. Combining all that, I can emphatically state she did not harm her child."

As she spoke, Scarlett's tone strengthened, and sparks shot from her eyes. Kirby and his team sat motionless, staring at her.

"What Jessica has gone through since the abduction has exceeded the realm of torture. She's faced a mother's worst nightmare with the disappearance of her precious little girl, who is her life. Add to that her involuntarily commitment to a mental facility, her arrest in handcuffs, the brutal murder of someone she loved and respected, and her current fear for her daughter's life and her own. If all that isn't enough, the police and the FBI suspect her of harming her child and may not be looking for the real abductor. *You* need to listen to Jake. I believe everyone in this room is exceptionally intelligent, and everyone wants the same result—the fastest rescue of little Faith Johnson. Have any of you got better ideas as to how to make that happen? I repeat, listen to Jake. Relieve Jessica of one aspect of her agony. To do otherwise would be egregious, criminal, and a perversion of justice in my eyes."

Damn. Glad I brought you, Harvard. Jake grinned. *Lay it on him.*

"That's a very compelling argument, Ms. Kavanagh," Kirby said. "I'm sure you are an excellent attorney."

"Harvard Law, for the record," Jake said.

"Fran, can you explain why we didn't turn up the twin on CODIS? Twins have the same DNA, right?" Kirby said.

"Most. But it's not absolute. There can be minor deviations." Silverstein flipped through the files on her tablet. "Here it is. We ran the report." She scrolled down the screen. "Yes, they found a close match, but the lab thought there was a mix-up since our suspect has been in this area for nearly five years. The DNA in CODIS belonged to an incarcerated individual, released only months ago. Our techs did a double check and found no error on this end, so they requested Florida recheck." She turned the screen around for Kirby to see. "The reply said their sample was the only one available, and the subject was no longer in custody."

Hal Kirby scanned the screen, squinting, and then stood. "Jake. My office."

Jake didn't move. Kirby's order struck a dissonant chord, igniting resentment. "No problem as long as we both remember you're no longer my supervisor, and I'm not subject to your command."

"Noted."

As they left the room, Fran Silverstein raised her eyebrows and rolled her eyes in an apparent reaction to the exchange between the two men. She then stood. "I'll get back to my station. If Hal needs me, Deke, buzz."

"Gotcha."

As Silverstein exited, a staff member entered. "Jarrod, there's a call for you. Should I take a message?"

"Go ahead," Weston said to his young partner. "If we need you later, I'll let you know."

With only Scarlett and Weston remaining at the table, she said, "I may have overstepped?"

He chuckled. "Hell no. You couldn't have handled it better. Hal would much rather yield to your demands than to Jake's."

"I was a bit presumptuous. Jake may be annoyed. I've only been on the job a week."

"Are you kidding? Jake loved it. I saw the look on his face. If you ask me, you're a perfect fit for him—strong enough to keep him in his place and polished enough to smooth some of his rough edges."

"It's good Jake and the ASAC are able to work together as well as they do, considering."

Weston chuckled. "That pissing contest predates the Jackie affair."

Scarlett made a face. "Really?"

"Jake was offered Hal's job first and turned it down. Being second choice festers inside of Hal."

"Why did Jake turn it down? Do you know?"

"When you've been with him a little longer, you'll see issuing orders from behind a desk doesn't fit. Jake's a cowboy and thrives on being in the saddle, chasing the rustlers. He's smart, intuitive, and unbelievably accurate, but he doesn't have any use for being challenged or doubted. Doesn't want anyone telling him what to do. I know he misses having a badge, but otherwise, Jake is probably where he belongs—wearing jeans and closing cases."

"You sound like you know him pretty well."

"Guess I do. One of the best partners I've ever worked with. I hated to see him leave the Bureau."

"Do you have any idea what this private meeting"—she tipped her head in the direction of the door—"is about?"

"Kirby wants to know how Jake got information we don't have, which I'm betting Jake won't tell him—at least not until this case is closed. Hal's primary motive is he wants to close any holes in our process, plus he doesn't want our team to appear incompetent."

CHAPTER TWENTY-SEVEN

Once the door closed inside Kirby's office, the ASAC said, "How the hell did you find out Johnson's identity, if she didn't tell you? And how does a church bookkeeper afford you and Phil Madison? That looks pretty dicey to me."

"Relax. Your people didn't fuck up, and you would have tracked it down in time. As for the financing, Madison is *pro bono* and picking up my tab."

"That's interesting. Has he got something going with Ms. Johnson?"

"Switch tracks, Kirby. For the record, Phil's wife asked him to take the case."

"His wife, huh. You haven't answered my first question."

"You know, you're right. I haven't, and I'm not going to—at least not at this point. Your search wouldn't have allowed a look at what I found that led me to the answer. When your warrant specifies elephants, you can't search a birdhouse. That's all I'm going to say. So back off. Your team would have found it. I just got there first. When the case is closed, you'll get all the credit, and I'll get paid. Works out for both of us. But we're wasting time. Are you or aren't you going to go along with me?"

"When did I ever have a choice? Let's go back and map out the details with Deke and your new partner."

"She's not my partner. She's my associate."

"I stand corrected." He gave Jake a smug look. "Have to say, I'm impressed."

"You want the rookie back?" Weston asked Kirby as he and Jake re-entered the conference room.

"Yeah. He can learn something."

While Weston left to summon Jarrod Bush, Jake arranged photos on the table to map his theory of the case.

As the two agents returned, Jake began to walk the Feds through his investigation.

"I admit there are holes to plug, but as I see it, Arnold has a documented history of bitterness toward my client. There's evidence suggesting she spent her time in prison planning revenge." He tapped the image of Xenia Arnold. "She had no contact with my client after the robbery; therefore, it follows she would look to someone she believed would have that information. I suspect she and Thomas"—Jake pointed to Jeb Thomas's mugshot—"forced their way into the Powell residence and found Jerome Powell home alone, his wife hospitalized. When he didn't give Arnold what she wanted, things got rough. At some point, she saw the photo of Jessica and Faith, which pulled a trigger." Jake reached over for the print of Jessica and Faith Liz pulled from Jessica's secret computer and held it up for the Feds.

"Her twin had everything Arnold didn't, including a daughter about the same age as hers would be. Fueled by anger and resentment, sight of the photo finished off her unstable psyche, catapulting her into a cataclysmic rage. Thomas, being an old hand in the game of torture and kill, joined the affray. Flip a coin for who fired the shot that took the man's life." He held up a newspaper clipping with the headline "Southside Man Murdered During Home Invasion."

As he laid the item in front of Kirby, Jake continued. "Arnold knew the Powell family kept a stash of emergency cash from the time she spent in their home—taking that was a given and probably a big incentive for Thomas. She's smart enough to know the Powell computer could hold clues as to Jessica's location, so that went into her shopping bag. As for the missing phone records, she probably thought they would provide clues as to Jessica's whereabouts. But the metadata on the photograph and the others stored on the computer was gold." He spread the multiple images of Faith across the table.

"Where did you get all those?" Kirby asked.

"In due time. Just be glad I have them."

Kirby scowled and muttered under his breath.

"I have to ask, Jake. Why do you think she knew about that data? I didn't know phones recorded that information," Scarlett said.

"I admit it's speculative, but certainly offers the most plausible explanation for how she found Jessica and knew the school Faith attended. Cellblock sisters said she spent significant time in the library. She might have stumbled on the information there. Prison offers a master's degree in criminal skills taught by seasoned comrades talking about what got them caught. Others listen and learn."

"But we haven't seen her on any CCTV footage scouting out any of the relevant locations. I'm sure we would have marked it up, even if we believed it to be Johnson," Weston said.

"Of course, you haven't. She's far too smart to be seen there. If she checked it out, she wore a disguise. But more than likely, Thomas or some of his crew covered the surveillance for her. But speaking of surveillance footage, Kai tracked the path taken by the abductor and child to a side street, the address is in my synopsis. If you reexamine all the recordings you have that lead into or out of that street on the day of the crime, you'll find the vehicle that took the little girl away. Probably stolen. Send out a BOLO to all law enforcement for any stolen vehicles matching the description. I'd also put a flag on the DNA profiles of the two suspects in CODIS. You never know when or where a match might turn up."

"You made your points," Kirby said. "I'll notify our people in the gang unit to drill down on undercovers and CIs to locate the boyfriend. And I'll touch base with the detectives in Jacksonville. It looks like if we find"—he looked down at his notes—"Thomas, we find the twin."

"Exactly," Jake said. "And, with any luck, the child." He began scooping up the photos and documents. "Can I count on you to move forward on the press release and dismissal of charges against Jessica?"

"Yeah. Yeah. Deke, set up a press conference." Kirby turned toward Jake. "We'll make sure to time the announcement to hit the evening news where it'll have the most viewers. I'll do my best with the State Prosecutor. Both of you"—he gave a nod to Scarlett—"understand I cannot force him to dismiss."

"A word of caution," Jake said. "Avoid mentioning you have a suspect to the press. If Arnold thinks you're on to her, she and Thomas might decide the child is a liability."

"Give me some credit. I agree."

"As for the local prosecutor, if you convince him of your belief in Jessica's innocence, it's got to have sway. By the way, since you're clearing her, we'd like whatever you removed from her apartment returned. I know you have her computer."

"It'll be arranged. Are you and your buddy Madison going to let us interview Ms. Johnson—allow her to actually answer questions?"

"Can't speak for Phil, but as soon as you give your statement to the media, I expect Phil will look favorably on an interview. One more thing, Kirby."

"Just one?"

Jake ignored the remark. "You will keep me in this loop, right? If you locate Thomas and Arnold, I want to be there."

"I knew it was a mistake to think you might turn the investigation over to us. When are you going to remember, Shepherd, you're not part of this team?"

"That's not an answer to my question."

Deke Weston glanced from Kirby to Jake and back, a smug look on his face. The expression on Jarrod Bush's face registered total confusion.

Kirby snorted. "I'll include you, but don't try to take over, or I'll cut you out faster than you can draw your weapon."

As Jake and Scarlett entered the elevator to leave the building, she said, "If I overstepped in there, I apologize."

Jake chuckled. "Hell no. You were spot on—a tiger putting the hunter on the run. I hear the Harvard gods cheering." Holding the elevator door for her to exit, he said, "Let's get some breakfast before we head back to the office."

"Okay, but what do we do next?"

"Notify Madison of what's happening, comb through the evidence we've gathered to be sure we haven't missed anything, and wait for Kirby to follow through. After he does the press conference, Phil will probably let him talk to Jessica. Why don't I drop you off at the safe house on my way to Phil's office? You can bring Jessica up to date with the news?"

Scarlett smiled. "Love it. What are the odds Kirby will be able to locate Xenia and her boyfriend?"

"Thomas in the picture makes it easier. The Bureau's gang unit has a finger on the pulse of all the major tribes. They should be able to put out a call for a lead. Unfortunately, it might take a few days. That's why I wanted to get in early this morning. The undercovers don't check in every day, and the informants sometimes take a day or two to locate."

"There's not enough evidence to arrest them, is there?"

"Not yet. But enough to bring them in for questioning and obtain search warrants."

"Whoops, I've got a text." She took out her phone and read the screen. "My furniture's here. Should I tell them to hold it for a few days?"

"It's up to you. Keep in mind; we could be called to travel anytime. Unless you want to stay here if the suspects are located."

Scarlett bristled. "Absolutely not. I'll put the delivery on hold."

After breakfast, Jake and Scarlett headed to the safe house. "Here, take my phone and text Brenda to let her know we're coming. Add that we'll send a second text when we reach the house before coming to the door," Jake said to Scarlett as he cranked the Lexus.

"Are you coming in?"

"No. I'll be back around four-thirty or five."

Brenda Lassiter answered the door at the safe house. "Good to see you again."

"Likewise," Scarlett said, smiling as she entered the living room of the small bungalow.

"How is it working with Jake?"

Scarlett smiled. "So far, it's good."

"And your sister. How's she doing?"

"Savannah? I guess she's okay. I haven't seen her since returning. Other than DNA, we don't have a lot in common."

Brenda chuckled. "I got that impression when we were in North Carolina."

Scarlett glanced around the modest area. "How's the client?"

"She's quiet. Cooperative but nervous. Any news on the child?"

Scarlett shook her head. "No. Where is Jessica?"

"Taking a shower. Want a cup of coffee?"

"Thanks, but no."

"That's right. You like tea. I don't think we have any."

"I'm fine." Glancing into the dining room of the small bungalow, Scarlett said, "Who's working the jigsaw puzzle?"

"We've both been working on it. Helps pass the time. It seems to calm the client."

Scarlett surveyed the room. "There's no TV?"

"Nope, but I've got my tablet. Probably just as well. Too much inside noise can mask any sound of someone fooling around outside."

The bedroom door opened, and Jessica joined the two women. "Ms. Kavanagh, I thought I heard your voice. Is there any news about Faith?"

"Not yet, Jessica. I'm sorry. But I do have news I think you'll like."

The grief-stricken woman's face seemed to light up.

"Jake and I met with the FBI this morning, and they are ruling you out as a suspect in Faith's abduction. The Assistant Special Agent in Charge agreed to make a public announcement saying you've been cleared. He's also going to speak to the Maryland State Attorney about dropping all charges."

A smile broke out on her face but quickly faded. "But he doesn't know about me driving Zee to the robbery."

"He has the Florida file on Xenia's case. It does not have your name anywhere."

A tear appeared on Jessica's cheek. "If only someone would find Faith."

"I know," Scarlett said, "but the FBI is now working with Jake. They're trying to locate Jeb Thomas. Jake is confident they will find him and your sister." She reached into her purse and took out a new TracFone. "Jake said to give you this. You can make a call to Ted McKay. Let him know you're okay, but don't tell him where you are."

"But he'll think I'm still on the run."

"You can tell him you're in a safe location Jake arranged—don't tell him you're back in the DC area."

Jessica lowered her gaze to the floor. "A month ago, I thought—" Raising her chin, she stared at a lamp near the drawn blinds of the window facing the street. "I was beginning to hope—"

Scarlett and Brenda Lassiter stood silent for a minute, and then Scarlett walked over to Jessica and put an arm around her shoulders. "This nightmare will end, and you can have your life back—better than before."

"Not without Faith." Jessica looked into Scarlett's eyes. "Do they believe Faith is still alive?"

"Everyone has hope that Faith will be found soon. Why would your sister dare harm a little girl?"

"To hurt me. Mr. Shepherd thinks she and her boyfriend killed Jerry. If she could do that, she could—" Jessica burst into tears.

Scarlett tightened her grip and led Jessica to the couch. "We're not going to think that."

Brenda left the room briefly and returned with a box of tissues.

Taking one and wiping her face, Jessica said, "I'm sorry. You're right. I have to keep praying that God is protecting Faith."

"Let's talk about something else," Scarlett said. "Tell me. How did you manage to leave Jacksonville without leaving a trace? I know that Jake's assistant," she nodded to Brenda. "You know Liz, don't you?"

"I do. Very smart lady. Sonny worked with her when he was with the Bureau."

"Jake's assistant, Liz, tried to track your background, and the FBI has as well. The only way Jake was able to track you was through the secret computer in your storage unit."

Jessica wiped her eyes once more. "I went to the bank and took out the savings I had accumulated for law school in cash. I knew I had to leave in case someone knew I drove Zee to that convenience store. Our birth father was an abusive man. I stayed out of his way, but he beat Zee and our mother. She would take Zee and me and run away to a women's shelter—sometimes in Jacksonville and sometimes in Orange Park or St. Augustine. She never gave our real names. So, I did the same. I just went from shelter to shelter, telling them I was running from an abusive boyfriend. When I got to New Jersey, I asked for help with changing my identity because I was afraid he would kill me if he ever found me. At the last shelter, I used the computer to search for the most common names to make it even harder to find me." She looked from Scarlett to Brenda and back. "You know, I came to believe I *was* Jessica Johnson—like Nyx Arnold never existed."

CHAPTER TWENTY-EIGHT

True to his word, Kirby, together with a PR specialist from the Bureau, made the anticipated announcement on Tuesday afternoon. When asked by reporters if authorities had another suspect, Kirby indicated his agents were working several leads but nothing concrete to report. The rest of the week dragged along. Jake addressed minor cases while Scarlett observed. On Thursday, Brenda called Jake, asking for help.

"Jessica is having a meltdown, Jake." I'm a cop, not a therapist.

"I don't know what to tell you, Brenda. I'm the last person you want for tea and sympathy advice."

After terminating the call, he turned to Scarlett, "Our gal is apparently losing it. Are you up for some handholding?"

"I'm a family law attorney. That's what we do. Fifty percent law, fifty percent psychology. I know she must be going crazy. With Faith gone ten days, no word from the FBI, and stuck in that little house. Can I take an Uber? I know you're tied up."

"I'll take you. I need to run by the insurance company and go over a couple of things with Lila. We can grab some sandwiches on the way. Give Brenda a call and ask what kind of barbeque they would like from Smokecraft."

"Do you ever get tired of barbeque?"

"I'm an Oklahoma cowboy. Of course not."

When they reached the safe house, Brenda met them at the door. "She's in the bedroom with the door locked. She won't answer."

Scarlett looked at Jake. "You or me?"

"You try. You know I have the bedside manner of Attila the Hun."

"Yeah. I know."

Scarlett crossed the room and tapped on the door. "Jessica. It's Scarlett. I want to talk to you. Can you unlock the door?"

There was no answer.

"Jessica, you're making me nervous. Jake is here. If you don't let me in, I'm going to have him break down the door to be sure you're okay. I don't think you want that."

Brenda looked over at Jake, who shrugged.

Scarlett held her breath, waiting for a response. When over a minute passed, she was about to issue one final ultimatum when the sound of a lock turning came through, but the door remained closed. Easing it open, she found Jessica was already in the one chair in the room, curled in the fetal position, crying.

Standing in the doorway for several seconds, contemplating what to do, Scarlett turned and waved Jake out. Taking a deep breath, she approached Jessica. When she reached her, she said, "Jessica, I want to help. I know—"

"I can't stand it any longer. I'm sorry, but I can't. Nothing is happening. My baby…"

Scarlett extended her arms. "Come here. You can't give up now. We're going to hear something soon. I know it."

Jessica stood and let Scarlett wrap her arms around her in a compassionate hug. She could feel the devastated mother trembling. "They are going to find Faith. You've got to hang on. She's going to need you. Brenda says you haven't eaten since you've been here."

"I can't. I choke when I try to swallow. What if she's—"

"No. No. Don't say it. Don't think it. They are going to find her. You are going to get her back. Jessica, the FBI is huge. They can do it since they know who to look for."

"She's scared. I know she is. She's never been away from me."

"That's why you must stay strong for her, Jessica. When they find Faith, she's going to need her mommy more than ever. You don't want to collapse and be in the hospital when that happens. Come on out. Jake and I brought a lot of food—barbeque pork, beef, and turkey. If you don't feel like eating anything solid, we stopped at a super-market, and I bought some soup. You have to eat." Scarlett brushed loose strands of hair off Jessica's forehead.

Sniffling, Jessica pulled back, her face soaked in tears. "I'll try. I'm sorry."

As they emerged from the room, Jake motioned to Scarlett. "A word at the car."

Apparently taking her cue, Brenda said, "Jessica, come on in the kitchen and look at what we've got for lunch."

At the car, Jake said. "Just got a text from Liz."

Scarlett nodded. "And—"

"An email came in on Jessica's little secret computer we have at the office."

Scarlett's face registered alarm. "Who was it from?"

"Unsigned and unknown sender. Have a look."

Taking Jake's phone, Scarlett read the screen. "Oh, no." She looked up at him, alarm expanding her pupils. "Oh my god, Jake. You're not going to show this to Jessica."

"Nothing to be gained by that. This was what I hoped would come out of Kirby eliminating Jessica as a suspect."

"But the message says Jessica will never see Faith again. That could mean Faith is dead."

"Yes, it sounds that way, but that's what the sender wants. I think it's meant to torture Jessica. What it gives us is a footprint. With any luck, Kirby's people can get an idea as to what part of the country this was sent from. Probably not where the suspect is now, but a starting point. By the way, good job in there with the client."

She curled her lips inward and blinked, a somber expression blan-keting her face. "She's tearing my heart out. They've got to find that little girl."

"I think we may have something soon." He glanced down at his watch. "I'd better get moving."

"You're not going to eat?"

"I kept a sandwich out. I'll eat on my way. Phil wants me to show up to a conference with the Maryland prosecutor after I meet with Lila Stonebridge. He and Kirby, or someone from Kirby's team, are going to pitch for a dismissal of the charges against Jessica. Phil believes I can better convey the significance of what we found in Florida."

"I'll say a prayer you succeed. Jessica needs some good news."

"Will give it my best." He slid the phone into his pocket and put a hand on her shoulder. "Try to keep the waters smooth in there. Lassiter looks frazzled."

CHAPTER TWENTY-NINE

Later, as Jake drove away from the high-rise headquarters of Washburn and Batson Insurance, headed to the Montgomery County State Attorney's Office in Rockville, his mind wandered. Despite an awkward start, the meeting with Lila Stonebridge went well. The relationship between the insurance executive and the PI took a sharp hit when Scarlett Kavanagh entered the picture; however, he left Lila's office with three new cases. Although neither Jake nor Lila ever considered developing a long-term relationship, both had enjoyed physically fulfilling encounters. But with the entry of Scarlett, Lila's frosty, professional tone had gathered icicles distinctly heard during telephone connections. The meeting was their first face-to-face in months. While seated in Lila's office, Jake felt a warning circle his chair. *If she could find another PI as good as I am, I would be history. But Lila's too ambitious to risk hiring a mediocre investigator.*

As he drove over the line dividing the District of Columbia and Maryland, images of Scarlett and Lila sprang into his head. He exhaled a huff, thinking to himself, *Two similar women, both sharp, independent, ambitious, and attractive—but not alike.* He glanced at the speedometer and back to the road. *Ruthless! That's the distinction. Lila would sell her firstborn for a ticket to the CEO office. What the hell am I thinking?*

When Jake reached the State Attorney's office, a receptionist escorted him to a conference room where Phil Madison, Deke Weston, Jarrod Bush, and two others sat around a long table.

"Sorry I'm late. Traffic this time of day—"

"Oh, my god. Madison didn't tell me you were his investigator," Assistant State Attorney Javier Pereira said as he stood to greet Jake.

"You two know one another?" Madison asked.

"I should say we do," Pereira said. "Back in the day, we worked together at the DOJ. Two pups, with the ink still wet on our bar cards, out to rid the world of crime and corruption." Turning to Jake, he said, "When did you leave the Bureau?"

"Several years back. But what are you doing on the State tab? Thought you were a Fed through and through."

"I finally woke to the realization that I wasn't on track to be the AG, so when this offer came across my desk, I jumped. Planning on running for the top spot next election."

Jake nodded. "Impressive. So why are you prosecuting misdemeanors?"

"High profile. Missing child saturates the media, and it's expected to turn into a major felony."

With a snap of his head, Jake frowned. "I get it. A bevy of sound bites and photo ops—politics. Never been good at that." Jake looked down the table at a man in uniform he didn't recognize.

Glancing around the table, pointing to those seated, Pereira said, "You probably know Special Agents Weston and Bush."

"Just slightly," Jake said, smiling as Deke Weston stood, shook his hand, and patted him on the arm.

"Any news?" Jake asked.

"Not yet," Weston said. "We've got the pedal to the floor."

"I guess you do know one another," Pereira said and pointed to the stranger. "Jake, this is Chief Bill Sandler of our local police department. His team is working this missing child case along with the FBI. I asked him to be here."

"After acknowledging the officer, Jake moved to the end of the table, took a seat across from Madison, and opened his briefcase. As he placed each item of evidence in order, Deke Weston spoke.

"For the record, we vetted all the evidence Shepherd has there and found it to be credible. As a matter of course, our behavioral analysis people worked up a profile on an unsub, which coincides with his conclusions. Based on all the data, the Bureau removed Ms. Johnson from the suspect list, which I'm sure you heard through the televised announcement of ASAC Hal Kirby earlier this week."

"Yeah. We heard, but we don't have any evidentiary basis for dropping our charges."

"At the risk of coming across as an effing a-hole, what have you got?" Madison said. "I think Jake's body of evidence, which the FBI"—he pointed to Weston—"acknowledged, clearly shows Ms. Johnson did not pick up her daughter. The lady took her child to school, came back, and walked into a mother's worst nightmare. An unknown imposter had taken her little girl. Your charge of neglect is down the toilet."

"That remains to be shown to me, but regardless, we've still got the matter of disturbing the peace and resisting arrest."

"Bullshit. Come on, Pereira. To begin, she didn't resist. Jake and his assistant were present at her arrest. As for the scene at the school, officers took her into custody under the psychiatric, involuntary commitment section of your statutes." Madison paused, tipped his chin, and raised his eyebrows. "I hope you realize, we take this to the media, and every red-blooded mother on the planet will be throwing rocks at your glasshouse. I can hear the shouts. 'What loving mother wouldn't have reacted the same way?' I'm doing you a favor here. Giving you a chance to sweep this under the rug without it going public—no media. But if you don't, I assure you there'll be a press conference, and Jessica Johnson will become poster mom of the year. Didn't I hear you say you're running for office? Are you ready to trash the female vote?"

Jake made eye contact with the prosecutor. "Javi, you *really* want to take on Clarence Darrow?" He pointed to Phil Madison. "I don't think you do. But pay attention to what I have, confer with the chief, and we'll go from there."

By the top of the hour, after reviewing Jake's evidence, the state attorney gave in. All pending charges were dropped.

When Jake settled into the driver's seat of his Lexus, he telephoned Scarlett. "Jessica's free on all counts. That should relieve some of the pressure, but no word on finding the suspects. I'll let you give her the news."

"At least, there's *some* good news. Did you turn Jessica's computer from the storage unit over to Kirby?"

"He didn't show, but I gave it to Deke, along with the data Liz tracked down, using that genealogy site, regarding relatives of Jeb Thomas and the corresponding property records from the Internet. Thomas has family in Alabama and West Florida. However, before I let Deke have the computer, another email came in—a similar message to the first one. It said, 'She's gone forever. Your dumbass luck has run out.'"

"That woman is evil incarnate. God, I hope they find her soon."

"The Bureau techs will do a deep dive on the computer and the email account for any info they can find. The suspect likely used public computers, but when they trace the IP addresses, they'll have an idea of the location where the messages originated."

"This waiting is tedious. What if they can't find Xenia and the guy?"

"They'll find them. After you make the call to Jessica, why don't you try to reach your movers and have your furniture delivered tomorrow? Sabrina will be staying with me this weekend, and we can help you settle in."

"Good idea. I can move out of your apartment."

CHAPTER THIRTY

Saturday morning, Scarlett's doorbell rang at eight-fifteen. Through the viewer, she saw Jake and Sabrina standing in the hall. Glancing around the room, Scarlett spotted both Ebony and Casper perched on nearby boxes. "Give me a second to lock up the cats," she called out.

When she opened the door, Jake grinned. "Scarlett, you remember my daughter, Sabrina."

"Of course. The beautiful ballerina. Maybe I can come to one of your performances," Scarlett said to the young teen.

Sabrina broke into a big smile. "Dad can bring you to our *Nutcracker*."

"That would be nice." Scarlett glanced up at Jake, who wore a proud-father face. *Easy to see that he adores her.* Refocusing on Sabrina, Scarlett said, "Come on in. I hope your dad hasn't coerced you into helping me unpack all these boxes."

"No, ma'am, he didn't." She took a step inside, looking around. "But there was a tiny bit of bribery."

"Well, you guys feel free to leave anytime. I don't want to intrude on all your daughter-dad time." She glanced over at Jake. "As I recall, you said nine o'clock. I guess they forgot to teach you how to tell time at Yale."

Sabrina laughed.

He shrugged. "Did I say nine? Well, I guess I'm early." Holding out a bag, he said, "Brought some bagels and spreads, along with coffee, tea, and hot chocolate. Peace offering. Figured your pantry might be bare."

"And you'd be right. I guess I'll have to forgive you for showing up forty-five minutes early."

"He's always early. He wasn't supposed to pick me up until eight-thirty, but he was at Mom's way before eight. I was still asleep. Pissed off Hal."

Jake's face tensed with displeasure as he shot his daughter a hand signal meaning halt. "Whoa! Sabrina. Watch your mouth. That's my vocabulary, not yours."

"Sorry. Mom says it."

"Well, you don't."

After taking time to eat the bagels, the trio went to work empty-ing the containers. Jake did the lifting and moved pieces of furniture. Under Scarlett's direction, he hung mirrors and wall décor, while she and Sabrina put away clothing, dishes, and arranged accessories.

At noon, Jake stepped back, sizing up the painting he hung minutes before. I think that's straight. Wiping perspiration off his forehead, he said, "How about I make a lunch run?"

Sabrina's face lit up. "Tacos, please."

Scarlett smiled. "Tacos sound good to me as well."

"I guess I'm outnumbered. You comin', Ayita?"

"Ayita?" Scarlett said with a quizzical expression.

"Means 'first to dance' in Cherokee." He placed his hammer back into the tool chest on the floor. "My mother gave her the nickname when she began ballet classes. So what's the verdict, kiddo? Coming?"

Sabrina plopped down on the sofa. "No sir. Think I'll crash for a few minutes. I'm knackered."

Scarlett frowned, again reflecting confusion.

"Her ballet teacher is British," Jake said to Scarlett before turning toward Sabrina. "Have it your way. I'll be back in a flash."

Scarlett walked him to the door, locking it behind him. When she turned and started toward Sabrina, the teen said, "Are you and my dad dating?"

Taken aback, Scarlett rolled her eyes. "No. Absolutely not. Why would you think that? I'm working with your dad."

"Hal thinks you're dating."

"Does he?" *The Kirbys are talking about us?* "Do you have any idea why?"

"He says there's something different about Dad when you're around. Mom thinks it's a good idea. She says it's about time someone tamed him."

Not sure I like being the topic of conversation in the Kirby household. "Well, I don't think that will be me."

"Mom feels guilty. She and Hal cheated on Dad. They don't think I know, but I do."

What am I supposed to say to that?

"Dad didn't tell me. I figured it out. Can I go pet your cats?"

Oh, my gosh. Yes. Please go pet the cats. "Sure, honey. They're in the master bath. Ebony, the black one, is a little standoffish, but Casper loves attention. Don't let them out. They might slip through the exterior door and try to find their way back to Atlanta."

At four-thirty, the last box was empty. After gathering the trash, Jake took it to the dumpster, and then he and Sabrina went upstairs to his apartment to shower and change for dinner. Since both Scarlett and Sabrina confessed to exhaustion, the trio went to a nearby restaurant, ate, and made it back to the apartment before eight.

"Would you like to go with us on an adventure tomorrow?" Jake said to Scarlett as she unlocked the door to her apartment.

"I appreciate the offer, but you and Sabrina deserve time to yourselves, and I have to touch base with the family. I'll shop for groceries—maybe read a book for pleasure."

CHAPTER THIRTY-ONE

The cell rang several times before Jake woke and grabbed it. His clock read two forty-three. "What the—"

"Shepherd, you awake?"

"Hell no. What's up?" In a fog of bare consciousness, Jake could hardly read Weston on the ID line.

"We think we may have a location on the suspects. Kirby says if you want to be on site, you need to get your ass moving."

Jake shook his head to clear his mind and vision. "I'm on it. Where?"

"West Florida. It's not certain, but our intel confirmed Thomas has a grandmother with a house on a large, undeveloped piece of land. We're wheels up in an hour."

"I'll be there. Have to get Madison to charter."

"I'll text you details, but it looks like you'll need to fly into either Tallahassee or Panama City. But I expect we'll head to Tallahassee. There are two resident agencies there. I'll update you when I know more."

"Is there a plan?"

"So far, only to set up a command post. We've got multiple variables—whether they're actually there, who else is there, do they have the child, do we need to secure the area? Gotta go. I'll stay in touch."

As the call terminated, Jake's mind raced. Hitting Liz's number, he blinked several times, struggling to become completely alert while pulling on the jeans he left over a chair the night before.

"Jake. What is it?"

"Kirby's team may have the suspects within sight. I've got Sabrina here and need to get airborne ASAP. Can you cover—stay with her until Jackie can pick her up in the morning?"

"On my way."

"If you don't mind, give Jackie a call with the plan? She's up because Hal is heading out. I've got to get Phil to arrange a flight and wake Scarlett."

"No problem. You'll need me to look after the animals, and I assume Scarlett's going with you."

"She would put a hit out on me if I left her behind. You have a key to her place, don't you?"

"I do. I've got it all covered."

Thank God she's a former Fed and knows the ropes, Jake thought as he terminated the call. As he was about to tap Phil Madison's number, a text came in from Deke Weston.

Tallahassee. Jefferson Street office.

With the text app closed, Jake called Madison. As it rang, he went to the closet and jerked out the duffle bag he kept packed for sudden departures. When the call went to Madison's voice mail, Jake hung up and redialed. Madison answered on the third ring.

"Phil. I need a plane ASAP. Kirby's people think they have the client's sister and boyfriend scoped out in West Florida. Scarlett and I need to get to Tallahassee, and I'll need a car. Can you make it happen?"

"Ronald Reagan?"

"Yep."

"It could take three to four hours, but I'll stress the urgency. I'll text you details for the flight. Keep me posted, Jake."

After ending the call with the lawyer, Jake put a Keurig pod in the machine, grabbed a dog treat for Kai, and took off for Scarlett's apartment, dialing her number as he skipped down the stairs, barefoot and shirtless.

When she answered her cell, her voice was groggy. "Jake? What's wrong?"

"I'm at your door."

She sat up straight, threw her feet on the floor, and grabbed a robe off the foot of her bed. Nearly tripping over a cat as she rushed to the door, she made it in record time.

"What's wrong?" she said as she opened the door.

"Grab your gear; throw on jeans and comfortable shoes. We're on our way to Florida."

"Florida?"

"Kirby's got intel that the suspects are in what sounds like a rural area of the northwestern section. Madison is arranging a plane. I'm heading to the airport in no more than thirty minutes. Can you be ready?"

"Of course. Yes. I keep a bag packed as you instructed. What about Sabrina? The animals?"

"It's covered." He reached out and squeezed her upper arm. "This could be it, Harvard."

"Oh, my gosh."

"I'm going back for my stuff. Meet you here."

"Right."

"And don't forget your ID and electronics—phone, tablet."

She nodded.

Back in his apartment, Jake pulled on socks and comfortable boots, together with a dark green T-shirt, paired with a camouflage-print flannel shirt. After cooling his coffee with a bit of water, he gulped down half a cup and proceeded to address his weapons, ammunition, and electronics—Kai watching his every move. "Not this time, sport. You don't need to be in a possible line of fire." Jake's adrenalin rush went into overdrive as he strapped on his shoulder holster, his watch, and tucked a small pistol in his boot. "This is who I am. Yep. Who I am." He reached down and scratched the shepherd behind his ears.

When everything was ready for departure, Jake stood in front of Sabrina's door for several seconds, debating whether to wake her to tell her he was leaving. *No. No way do I have time to explain the urgency involved. Liz can give her chapter and verse, and Jackie will know the story with Hal leaving.* He put a palm on the door in a meaningful gesture.

Within seconds, he reached the second floor to find Scarlett dressed, her bag on the carpet next to her. Speaking in a low voice out of respect for neighbors, he said, "I'm impressed, Harvard. I didn't know a female could move that fast."

"Yeah. Well, you underestimate me a lot. But I admit, I've got butterflies playing football in my stomach. Do you think they've really found Xenia and Thomas?"

"Odds are good. No way Kirby's gonna leave the comfort of home in the middle of the night on a whim. Hey, I think I hear Liz." He grabbed Scarlett's bag and started down the stairs with Scarlett trailing.

Halfway down, they met Liz Glover. "You are a saint, madam. There'll be a bonus in your next check."

"All in a day's work."

"You have keys to both apartments, right?"

She held up a lanyard with two keys. "Right here. You guys be safe and bring that little girl back to her mom."

Scarlett nodded.

"Now go. God be with you."

The faint purring of the Lexus motor was the only sound heard during most of the drive to the Ronald Reagan Airport. When they reached the parking area, Jake stowed his weapons in his bag.

"I haven't flown private. Do we still go through security?" Scarlett asked.

He nodded as his phone pinged with a new message giving him the specifics for the flight. "Looks like we're ready to rock and roll," he said, slipping the phone into his pocket. "Just hope we aren't delayed by problems with the plane, pilot, flight plan, or clearance."

Access to refreshments was scarce at four a.m., but Scarlett noticed a drink machine close to the waiting area. "Want anything from the machine? Soda? Water?"

"I'm good for now. There should be drinks, coffee, tea, alcohol on the plane."

"I don't think I need alcohol. Or maybe I do. I'm nervous, Jake. What if Faith isn't found? They may have done something with her."

"Think positive. Nothing to be gained otherwise."

Silence dominated during their wait. At five after five, they got the call to board the plane. When the pilot welcomed them aboard, he apologized for the delay. "I live on the other side of DC. Probably should move closer if I continue flying out of here."

"We're good. You got here earlier than promised. How long will the flight to Florida take?" Jake asked.

"Two hours, give or take. It's under a thousand miles."

"That's what I thought."

"Please help yourself to anything in the kitchen. I'll apologize again for no flight attendant, but we were told the trip was urgent. It could have cost at least another half-hour to bring someone on board with us. But I'll give you a tour of the plane."

Jake held a hand up. "That's not necessary. We'll find the kitchen. Let's get airborne."

"As you wish." The pilot's expression indicated a trace of apprehension in response to Jake's curt declaration.

Once in the air, Jake said to Scarlett from a luxury seat facing hers, "Try to get a nap. There's no way to know when you'll have another opportunity. Want a blanket?"

"That would be nice."

He stood, walked down the length of the aircraft, and opened several cabinet doors until he found pillows and blankets. Armed with both, he returned, handed Scarlett her share, and took his seat, immediately tucking a pillow under his head and closing his eyes. He wasn't drowsy but did not want to talk. *I know she has questions, but I just can't make conversation right now.*

At six-forty, the wheels touched down with a bump that woke both Jake and Scarlett. He threw off the blanket but waited until the plane reached a stop to unbuckle his seat belt. "Ready, Harvard?"

She took a deep breath, sighed, and twisted her head around to loosen stiffness in her neck. "Ready." Touching fingertips, first to her forehead, she made the sign of the cross. "Please let us find that child, and please let her be okay."

Jake stood, patted her on the shoulder, and headed back to the restroom.

CHAPTER THIRTY-TWO

Jake and Scarlett reached the FBI Resident Agency in an F-150 Ford pickup he had rented. When Scarlett questioned him at the airport as to why a truck, he said, "Might need to blend in. You don't show up in the rural South in a fancy car unless you want to be a magnet for suspicion. I'll need to dirty this one up a bit. Maybe put on a sticker or two."

As they entered the conference room, one of the men looked at Jake, stood, and said, "Damn. We can all go home now. Sherlock Holmes is in the house."

"You sure you can find the way home without a guide dog?" Jake said, his somber expression erased by a broad grin as he extended his hand to greet Clive Rollins. "What are you doing in Florida?"

"Transfer and a bump up."

"So, this is your house?"

"You might say." Rollins turned toward the table where Hal Kirby, Deke Weston, and Jarrod Bush were sitting. "You guys didn't tell me it was Shepherd coming."

"We didn't want you to lock the door," Deke Weston said.

"Good point. He and his dog ran all over us in North Carolina a while back."

"That's Shepherd all right," Weston said, grinning.

"And this is?" Rollins said, gesturing toward Scarlett.

"Scarlett Kavanagh. I'm breaking her in on the job," Jake said. "But don't underestimate her. She comes with over a decade of litigation experience and a law degree from Harvard."

"And very attractive. Nice to meet you, Ms. Kavanagh."

"What have we got?" Jake said as the three took seats around the table. "Any new developments?"

"Aside from a tip the suspects may be in this area, we have this," Kirby said as he held up folded papers.

"And that is?"

"Tell him, Deke."

"Arrest warrants, buddy. Your hunch was right. The suspects were in a stolen vehicle. A Toyota 4-Runner, matching the description of the one caught on camera near the school, turned up abandoned at a cheap motel about two miles from your client's apartment. Although police failed to make an immediate connection, fortunately for us, they have a top-notch forensics team. Since we had a flag out on the DNA of the suspects, the samples collected from the vehicle produced a hit on both Thomas and Arnold, plus Faith Johnson. Turns out the SUV disappeared from a home in North Carolina the day before the abduction."

Upon hearing Weston's revelation, Scarlett's eyes lit up as she squeezed her fingers into fists and covered her smile with one.

Jake broke out in a huge grin. "Damn! So, this is no pickup for questioning?"

"Nope. It's a full-blown warrant for arrest on charges of Federal Kidnapping and Federal Motor Theft for a start. Only glitch now is finding them."

"What's the status?"

"Right now, unknown. We've got information they may be on a large tract of rural acreage, but we're handicapped by the size of the property and the position of the old house. It sits slap dab in the middle of a huge clearing, surrounded by dense woods. No way to get close enough for a visual without arousing suspicion."

"What was the source of the lead? And any evidence they're inside?"

"Our source was an undercover working inside the hub of the gang," Kirby said. "All he gave us is the word circulating in the crew saying Thomas planned to dock at his grandparents' house and get back to the business of leading the Florida chapter. The UC was afraid to press for further details. It was Liz who gave us the location from her dossier on Thomas's relatives." He tapped a finger on the table. "As to who might be in there, the grandfather died about a year ago. Whether the grandmother is there is unknown. We basically know nothing for certain, and I'm not keen on knocking on a door where we don't know what's on the other side. We were just discussing plans for gathering intel."

"Wouldn't a scout to quiz the locals—service station attendants, convenience stores—be logical?" Jake said. "In that type of community, everyone knows everyone."

Rollins shook his head. "ASAC Kirby and I were brainstorming right before you arrived, trying to decide who to send on a scouting mission."

"I think we can agree one of us should go," said Kirby. "The local police are known in the area and not likely to evoke spontaneity from the neighbors."

"So, you think you're going to send a Brooks Brothers suit with a Madison Avenue haircut to obtain information from a good ole boy?" Jake said. "Good luck with that plan."

"Give me a break, Shepherd. We planned to dress him for the part."

"Hell, Kirby, which one of you can pull that off on short notice? Where are you from? Philadelphia?"

"Pittsburg."

"Same difference. City boy. Yankee speech. And, Deke, I know you're from Chicago. Where's the kid from? Not that you need to send in a newbie." He turned toward Bush. "No offense. We all started in the same place." Turning back to Kirby, he said, "Even Rollins hasn't lost his Boston clip, despite his time in Carolina. I'm the one you need."

"Shepherd, I told you, when I agreed to let you in on this, you aren't going to take over."

218 · JUDITH ERWIN

Jake turned to Deke Weston. "See if you can crack his anti-Shepherd mindset. I'm the logical choice for the job." He did a scan down his clothing and stretched out a leg to show his boots. "I'm dressed for success." Finger combing his hair, he said, "Even have the right style and speak the language. All I need is a couple of fake tattoos. Think you can help with that, Rollins?"

"I think it can be arranged."

As the discussion progressed, a new man, with an official nametag hanging from a lanyard around his neck, entered the room, handing Clive Rollins three files. But he did not attempt to interrupt the conversation. Rollins motioned for him to take a seat. Scanning the folders, Rollins said, "Looks like we have dossiers on the suspects, including data from Jacksonville on the murder case."

"From all I gathered, we are looking at a class A felon," Jake said. "A guy who probably doesn't mind bloodshed—plus a mentally unstable female. The sooner you guys take them down, the better. There's a child still missing, hopefully still healthy."

"What are you driving?" Weston asked Jake.

"An F-150. Just needs a little mud on the wheels, a few empty beer cans in the back, and a long gun—shotgun or rifle—propped up in front. Rent a Car or whoever I got it from might not like us attaching a gunrack."

With a tip of his head, Weston said, "Jake's right, Hal. He's the man for the job. Hell, he might get lucky and find a female clerk he can charm with his cowboy charisma. Don't you agree, Rollins?"

Jake shot his former partner a dubious look while Scarlett covered her mouth to hide a grin.

Before Rollins could respond, the newcomer said, "Who the hell is this guy?"

"Jake Shepherd, private investigator," Rollins said.

A frown creased the man's forehead as he pulled his chin back in a show of disbelief.

"He's former HRT, Marty. Fellows, this is Special Agent Martin Shaughnessy."

Appearing distracted, Hal Kirby tipped his head to acknowledge Shaughnessy but said, "Discussion done. I concede. Shepherd goes fishing. Assuming he learns the suspects are likely in that building, what else are we dealing with in terms of the area, Rollins?"

"Typical rural. Farms surrounding the property. A marshy creek on one side feeding into a murky pond. From the intel we've gathered, most of the land is thick with scrubs, pine trees, probably a healthy share of snakes and gators. A long, narrow dirt road leads to the cleared area in the center—a *big* area, making getting close to the two-story house undetected difficult. There's a barn at the back of the clearing and an old mobile home to the left. At some point in time, the land was likely farmed."

"Do we know if there are any vehicles on the premises?"

"Only way to know would be to do a flyover or send someone in."

Kirby shook his head. "I don't like going in with no idea of how many we might be facing. Is there any way to be sure we don't have any innocent travelers stumbling by or any of his gang coming to visit?"

"That could be a problem. Good thing is there's only one egress-ingress, a two-lane county road. There's no way to come through on the backside short of being Tarzan or Cheeta. If we try to put up roadblocks, it will likely alert the occupants to something going down. I've considered staging a fake MVA, but it would only work going one way. No way to get away with two."

Scarlett had been silently sitting next to Jake but spoke up. "I don't mean to intrude." She looked around at Jake as all the men turned their attention to her. Jake nodded.

"What if you blocked the road because there was a dangerous animal loose that needed to be captured? Maybe a bear, rabid dog, raccoon. You should be able to block both ends that way?"

Jake smiled as Deke Weston spoke. "That might work. Could get our people on the property to scope out how many we might be dealing with."

"Good idea," Rollins said. "I'll call in FWC to make the blockade and search look legit."

"FWC?" Scarlett said.

"Fish and Wildlife Conservation," Rollins said. "Game wardens—fully authorized law enforcement officers. Better call in the county animal control agency as well but keep them on the perimeter for show. They're not trained for this type of confrontation."

"Have the local cops been notified we have an operation in progress?" Kirby said.

"I'll take care of it right now," said Rollins. "To clarify, we don't want them on board to start. Right?"

"Right," Kirby said. "Ask that they remain on standby, prepared for a call for assistance once we know if the suspects are present."

Now, all we need to know is *if* we have suspects to go after," said Weston.

"Suspects and the child," said Jake.

"Why not use a drone?" Bush asked.

Jake and the Feds all looked at him.

"You've got to be a city boy," Rollins said. "In a rural area like we have, if either suspect happens to catch sight of a drone, it would put them on red alert."

Kirby rubbed an eye, gave his head a shake, and slapped the table as he stood. "Game on, gentlemen—and Ms. Kavanagh."

"She rides with you until I complete the mission," Jake said.

Kirby gave him a perplexed expression. "You want her with me?"

"Yeah. I know you'll enjoy chatting."

"And you know Kirby's vehicle is the safest in the posse," Weston said to Jake.

"Is it?" Jake said. "Good to know." He turned toward Kirby. "I'll rendezvous with you about a mile from the target zone, assuming you have subjects to serve the warrants on. Don't lose the warrants."

Kirby gave him a look of disgust as Jake continued, "I'll scout the area for a viable meeting point as I drive."

"There's a church about four miles from the target," Rollins said, "but with it being Sunday, we'd better not attempt to use their lot. However, there's a school about five hundred feet behind the church. It's down a narrow road on the west side."

"We'll keep our distance behind Jake," Kirby said. "Rollins, can you set him up with communication equipment as soon as he gets the body art? Bush, you and Shaughnessy dress up the truck."

Jake raised a finger for attention. "And I need a vest for Scarlett. I only have one."

Kirby nodded and made a sweeping motion around the room with one arm to indicate the assembled group. "And for the record, don't feel a need to consume the beer to empty the cans you're going to fill Shepherd's truck with."

They all laughed.

CHAPTER THIRTY-THREE

While Jake went to have the tattoos applied, Scarlett waited in the FBI conference room, feeling like a fur coat in the tropics. Everyone had a job and moved to get ready for the operation. An incoming text from Jessica pinged on her phone, causing her to jerk.

> *Have you heard anything? Please call me. My mom, Colleen,*
> *is here. We are so scared. If anything has happened to Faith, I*
> *don't want to live.*

Scarlett stared at the words for several seconds, her tense nerves causing tears to build. *This is unbearable. We've got to find Faith.*

On the way to the airport, Jake had made it clear no one should alert Jessica to what was happening.

"No need to raise her hopes, only to have them dashed if it turns out to be a false lead," he had said.

"Ready, Ms. Kavanagh?" Hal Kirby stood in the doorway.

Startled, Scarlett jumped. "Yes. Of course."

Noticing Scarlett wipe her eyes, Kirby said, "Are you okay?"

Scarlett cleared her throat. "I'm fine. I just had a text from Ms. Johnson. This is destroying her."

"We're putting our complete efforts behind this operation. Maybe we'll get lucky."

"I'm praying you will. And please call me Scarlett. I feel odd enough without the formality."

"You've got it. Likewise, I'm Hal. Looks like we have a kind of social as well as professional relationship."

She gave a slight smile, nodding. *I wasn't aware we had a relationship.*

"We're pulling out in about ten minutes. Jake is leaving now."

Scarlett nodded. "I'm ready."

"Is there anything you'd like before we leave—something to eat, drink, restroom break? There's no way to estimate how long we may be out there."

"Probably the latter. Where are the restrooms? Do you know?"

When they reached Kirby's vehicle, Scarlett was surprised to see a blue, four-door Camry. *FBI car or rental?*

Bush opened the passenger door, but Weston moved past, toward a large van stopped in the center of the parking garage, its motor running. Watching Weston climb aboard the pewter-colored vehicle, Scarlett felt a pang of disappointment. *I would rather be riding with him than Kirby. What the heck were you thinking, Jake? I don't want to converse with your former boss, husband-in-law, or whatever he is.*

Another FBI agent, unknown to Scarlett, entered the van as well, while Rollins and Shaughnessy got into a black SUV nearby. All the men wore protective vests, emblazoned with the letters FBI, and all were armed. A wave of exhilaration coursed through Scarlett's body, causing the hair on her arms to stand as Kirby held the left rear door open for her.

"I'm not showing a lack of respect by having you sit in the back. It's a shade safer, should trouble arise," he said.

The vest Kirby had Scarlett put on before they left the office felt awkward, much like she felt in general. *I do not want to be treated like a piece of fragile crystal.* She lamented missing an opportunity to speak with Jake before he took off. *Why did he want me with Kirby? Deke, or even that guy Rollins, would have been more comfortable.* As she settled into her place, she noticed the expression on Bush's face. *This is your first rodeo too, and you have to sit next to your boss. At least I don't have that pressure.*

Kirby cranked the motor but made no attempt to put the vehicle in drive. As Scarlett stared out the window at the side of the parking garage, her heart pounded. When the black SUV drove past, Kirby put the car in drive and pulled out behind it. Although she couldn't see it, Scarlett heard what she assumed to be the van behind them.

It took the small entourage thirty minutes to clear the city of Tallahassee. During the drive, no one in the car spoke. Glancing from driver to passenger, Scarlett thought how both fit the stereotypical image of an FBI agent. Natural confidence described Kirby. In contrast, Bush broadcasted effort not yet ripe. *How long has he been out of the academy? Jake doesn't fit the suit and tie profile of a typical agent.*

A few minutes on the open road, Kirby broke the silence. "Have you found a place to live in DC?"

With the question coming out of the blue, Scarlett wasn't sure whom he meant to answer. When Bush did not, she said, "Are you talking to me?"

"Yeah. I was wondering if you've found a place in the District."

Jake isn't the only one fishing. "I have. Arlington actually. I leased an apartment in Jake's building." *No secret there. Sabrina is sure to give them chapter and verse.*

"Nice place."

Interesting comment. *I doubt you've ever been inside Jake's apartment.*

"Looks like we are here. Rollins is turning."

CHAPTER THIRTY-FOUR

Jake stepped out of the truck onto a gravel surface. A sign on the flat-roofed, rectangular building read, "GAS & GROCERIES."

Glancing up at the sign and back at the store, Jake thought, *Bet there's not many groceries in this place.* Posters, including one for Florida's Lotto, obscured visibility into the store. *Feeling lucky today. Maybe I should buy a few lottery tickets.* Two gas pumps stood sentinel behind him; a large, white metal box with vertical lettering spelling out ice was at the end of the building with an older model Corolla parked behind it. *Pretty good chance I'm dealing with only one clerk, probably female, considering the car. Guys around here probably drive trucks.*

He wore a cheap, wide-brimmed bucket hat with a flat top, purchased in a hurry at a Tallahassee Walmart. Jake had cut off the chin strap. It wasn't his trademark cowboy hat, but cocked to one side, it mimicked the look. The rolled-up sleeves of his camouflage shirt provided a glimpse of the fake tattoos—one a nude woman, another the word "Mama," and the third, a dagger, all chosen by Deke Weston. Jake drew the line when his former partner suggested adding a couple of teardrops to his face.

"Hell, no. Not even fake ones."

"Come on, Shepherd, you wouldn't be committing fraud. I know you've filled at least two body bags—one this year and one when we took down that psycho bomber back in the day."

"Not moments I want to remember or memorialize even in fake ink."

As he pushed open the door with one hand, he glanced down at his watch. *Nearly three o'clock. Still a good bit of day left.*

A skinny girl with a waist-length ponytail stood behind the counter as Jake entered. He purposely avoided eye contact but could feel her sizing him up. *Gotta take this slow. Not sure what's on her mind? Don't want to spook her.* After looking around the interior for a few seconds, he turned to the cashier. "Hey, hon, you got a men's room?"

She smiled and pointed to the left rear of the store.

After taking the amount of time he estimated credible for the pit-stop, he emerged and began pilfering through the snacks. Spotting a container of boiled peanuts, he said, "There's something I haven't had in a while." The girl smiled again as he scooped a generous portion into a small plastic bag provided.

After wandering around the tight area for three or four minutes, adding potato chips and jerky to his stash of purchases, he called out to the girl, "You got any aspirin?"

She reached to a display behind her and held up a small packet. "Sure do, mister."

With his hands full, Jake walked to the counter and dropped his bounty. "Mind if I leave these here for a second?"

"Not a problem." She added a packet of the analgesic and flashed him a grin with a coy expression.

I'm in, he thought as he turned to go for a six-pack. *Looks like she's alone.*

Returning to the counter, Jake put down the beer and reached in his pocket for his wallet.

"Where you from," the girl asked.

"Oklahoma," Jake said. "You a native?"

"I am."

"You wouldn't know a dude by the name of Jeb Thomas, would you?"

The cell phone in her pocket rang. She jerked it out, looked at the ID, and turned it on. "Yeah, Ma. Can I call you back?" Sliding it back in her pocket, she said, "Sorry. She worries about me when I'm in the store alone. Where was I? Oh, yes, Jeb. He stays at the family place a couple of miles up the road, sometimes. How'd you know him? You a member of that gang I heard he rides with?"

"Nope. I'm a solo act. We met a while back, and he said to look him up if I ever got to this neck of the woods. I'm headed to Louisiana and thought I'd give it a try. Seen him lately?"

She tipped her head to the side. "That place you knew Jeb. It wouldn't have been Raiford, would it?"

Jake grinned. "Now aren't you the smart one."

"What's your name?"

Could she be thinking of warning him someone is asking questions? "Jake."

"Jake what?" She squinted one eye.

"Jake Jones."

"That sounds fake."

"It is."

She burst out laughing. "Now who's the smart one? You gotta wife, Jake Jones?"

I'm back in. "Not anymore."

"Oh. She wouldn't wait."

"Something like that."

"How long you gonna be around?" The register pinged as she rang up each item.

"Depends."

"Depends on what?" She stopped checking out his purchases and made eye contact.

Jake stared at her for several seconds. She began to fidget. "I guess it depends on whether Jeb's around and what else there is to do in this burg."

"Well, I can tell you Jeb's at the old place. Been there since Thursday, I think. Got some woman with him, but she ain't of the sociable kind. The two of them waltzed in here like they owned the place. Hadn't seen Jeb but once or twice since his vacation in the pen." She blinked. "But if you hang around, I might could find something for you to do."

Dodging the inuendo, Jake said, "That must have been the one his sister hooked him up with." He began to peel off a fifty-dollar bill, with the young woman paying attention to the thick stack in his wallet. The money, furnished by Rollins, served as another prop in the operation. "I think she has a kid. Was a kid with them?"

"Naw. I didn't see no kid." Her face tensed. "You ain't the kid's daddy, are you?"

This gal's smarter than she looks. "Don't think so since I never met her. Just heard Jeb carry on about what a good—you know."

The clerk relaxed and handed him his change. "I didn't check them out. The woman being so—whatever. They coulda had a kid in the van."

They're driving a van now. Jake gave her a seductive once over as he said, "So, if I stay around, what time do you get off?"

A noticeable flush covered her face. "My daddy takes over at seven."

"I'll need an address and phone number. No name needed. I'll just call you Angie 'cause you look like an angel." *Careful, Shepherd. Don't overplay your hand.* "Sure you wanna spend time with an ex-con?" He gave his hat a slight tip forward.

"I can tell by lookin' at you—you didn't do nothin' too bad." She picked up a pen and small pad and began writing. "Maybe they busted you for selling a little weed?"

He smiled as she handed him the slip of paper. "You are a smart one." He tucked the note in his wallet and removed another fifty-dollar bill. "Here, babe. Give me ten quick picks and keep the change."

CHAPTER THIRTY-FIVE

After wrapping up the purchase and giving the cashier a wink, he left the store. Back in the truck several minutes later, he drove west toward the subject property. Clicking on the FBI's radio, he contacted Kirby. "It's a go. Thomas and Arnold are known to be in the area as of Thursday, driving a van. No intel on the child. I wasn't comfortable doubling back as it might create suspicion on the mark, so you'll have to move forward to set up the command post. I'll radio when I see a rendezvous spot. Have the search teams move in and secure the property."

When Jake spotted a deserted building with a parking area about a mile and a half from the target, he pulled off and exited the vehicle. Within five minutes, the FBI vehicles arrived.

"We shouldn't all hang out here for long. Never know who may drive by and send out word on social media or whatever vine the locals use," Jake said as Kirby, Rollins, and Weston approached him.

"I'll send the van ahead, Hal," Weston said. "It's the most conspicuous."

"Good idea," said Kirby. "Bush and Shaughnessy can go with it. That'll cut down on the population."

"Well, don't think you're incognito with Glocks on your hips and wearing bulletproof vests screaming FBI on the back," Jake said.

Weston smiled. "Jake's gotta point."

"Taken," Kirby said. "Everyone better get back in the cars until the FWC arrives."

"Shouldn't be long," Rollins said. "Once they establish the blockades, we should be good to go."

"When I pull out, the rest of you follow. Weston, tell the agent driving the van. What's his name?"

"McCormick," Rollins said.

"Tell McCormick to pass the private road to the subject's house and pull off as if taking a rest."

Jake broke away from the group and walked over to Kirby's car. As Scarlett rolled down her window, he said, "You okay, Harvard?"

"I am."

"How about joining me in the truck?"

She lifted the doorhandle before he finished the question. "I thought you'd never ask." As she exited the Camry, two vehicles approached—a pickup truck and a sedan. Both were white with streaks of green and had emergency light strips across the roof. Embedded in the trim was an emblem bearing a gold star and the letters FWC.

As he watched the vehicles pull off the road, Jake said, "Some of the Fish and Wildlife guys are here."

Rollins immediately greeted the uniformed officer exiting the sedan with a handshake and escorted him over to Hal Kirby. After a brief exchange, the FWC vehicles drove away.

"Kirby's getting ready to leave. Let's move," Jake said. "Once those guys block the road, we're good to go."

Once in the truck, Scarlett said to Jake as he cranked the engine, "Do you have any idea what is going to happen?"

"I can guess. The first order of business is to get as much information as possible on how many and who might be on the premises. Best way to know is through ground observation by the FWC guys. I suspect more are coming—maybe from the opposite direction. They'll be looking for how many vehicles are present on the property, running any plate numbers, and making note of anything else they observe—sight or sound."

"Will the team do a forced entry into the house?"

"No. Not likely. There are three options on the table, which response of the suspects will dictate. They can surrender, come out shooting, or hole up. Once everyone is in position, someone, probably Kirby or Weston, will get on a bullhorn, identify themselves, announce to the occupants they have arrest warrants, and demand they come out—hands in the air without weapons."

"If they don't?"

"They won't. You can bank on that. Jeb Thomas is not interested to going back to prison. But the ball is in his court at that point. I bet the coward will get on the phone and try to call for help."

"Would his gang members come?"

"Not likely. That would be war, which they don't want with the FBI. They make a move like that, and six hundred agents will appear—plus local backup from the state and county if needed. If you think it's not nice to fool with Mother Nature, it's pretty fatal to fool with the FBI."

"How do you see it ending?"

"Not good. Kirby's primary concern will be to avoid harm to the child if she's in there. Whether they can subdue Thomas without violence is anyone's guess. If he stays holed up, Kirby will likely put out a call for a hostage negotiator, maybe a tactical team. He's probably already put them on alert, since we've a better idea the perps are in the area."

Ten minutes later, with both sides of the county road blocked, the players convened at the entry point to the subject property, waiting for a reconnaissance report. While Jake joined the Federal agents, Scarlett remained in the truck. *This is for real. I should be scared, but what I feel is more like stage fright—waiting in the wings for my entrance.* Her phone pinged and she looked down to see another text from Jessica. Not knowing what to say to the terrified mother, she wanted to ignore the message—not even read it. *That's not fair to her.*

Her hand trembling, Scarlett opened the text.

Please call me, Scarlett. Please. Why aren't you talking to me?

After dropping the cell into her lap, she covered her mouth with both hands, trying to think how to respond. Poor woman. She's out there with her gut tied in knots. What can I tell her? Can I put it off until this is finished? Scarlett let her chin drop as though bowing her head and rubbed her forehead. After several seconds, she picked up the phone and typed.

> *I'm so sorry, Jessica. I haven't meant to ignore you, but Jake*
> *has me doing a lot of research on Jeb Thomas's relatives.*
> *If I hear any news about Faith, I will let you know*
> *immediately.*

Staring at the screen, she reread the message three times before hitting send. *It's true—sort of.* Before she could put the cell away, it pinged again. *Jessica?* Checking the ID, she saw it was from Liz.

> *Any news? Tell Jake that Jackie picked up Sabrina, and all is*
> *well up here. I'm sure he's pretty tied up.*

Relieved to see the message was from Liz, she immediately responded.

> *Nothing to report so far. Waiting.*

After sliding the phone into her jeans pocket, she rolled down her window and scanned the vehicles assembled around the dirt drive. With the county road blocked, law-enforcement drivers made it a parking lot. An additional FWC vehicle, plus a county sheriff's car, which had happened on the scene, added to the mix of FBI convey-ances and the truck she occupied. The cluster of law enforcement stood at the base of the drive, along with Jake. While the conversation looked low-key, Kirby suddenly held up a hand for silence with his radio to his ear. After a few seconds, appearing elated, he lowered the device, spoke to the group, and all disbursed.

Scarlett sucked in a gulp of air. *Something's happened.*

When Jake reached the truck, he opened the passenger door. "You're going into the van."

"I don't understand. What's happened?"

"FWC spotted a family type van parked by the house. Running a trace on the plate, they discovered it was stolen in Georgia, Thursday a week ago. All evidence suggests Thomas and Arnold are in the house. There's only one other vehicle visible—an old Ford Escort registered to the grandmother. The safest place for you right now is in the Bureau van. Okay?"

She nodded and climbed out of the truck. Jake walked her to the door of the mobile communications station. Scarlett's stomach churned with a combination of excitement and apprehension. "Be careful, Jake."

He smiled. "I'm always careful. You stay put and cross your fingers." As he opened the door, he said to no one in particular, "Take care of her boys."

She wanted to watch him walk away but the only see-through glass was the windshield. Once she took a seat, the driver cranked the soundproof vehicle and turned it around, barely missing a roadside mailbox. Maneuvering the large conveyance deftly while in reverse, he trailed the small convoy along the narrow pathway. Even in the dim light of the van, Scarlett could tell it was well equipped for communication and observation. When they reached the assigned parking position, a tech agent, who had been sitting at a desk with various monitors and a computer, stood and exited carrying a bag. Scarlett remained seated, silent. *I wish I knew what was happening. I can't see or hear anything going on outside.*

The driver rose, stretched, and turned toward Scarlett. "I understand you're a private investigator, and your partner was one of us."

"It's more like I'm learning to be an investigator, and my *boss* is a former agent. I practiced law for over ten years."

"That's interesting. I'm Special Agent Roy McCormick." He thrust a hand forward.

Scarlett shook hands with him and said, "Nice to meet you. I'm Scarlett Kavanagh. Forgive me for asking, but what is happening?"

"Right now, they're all getting into position. John Reiner, the computer tech who just left, has gone to set up cameras and give the sound equipment to the chief."

"I assume you've been on a lot of operations of this type."

"A few. But each one is different."

"What will we know from here?"

"John will be in constant contact with Supervisory Agent Rollins, and he can hear much of what is happening on his headset and has the capability of switching to a speaker mode. You've probably guessed; this vehicle is soundproof."

"I knew it was different. I assume you backed in so exiting would be easier?"

"Exactly. Narrow road like this would clog a rapid exit, even though I'm pretty good at moving it in reverse."

"Do I really need to keep this vest on in here?"

He smiled. "Afraid you do. Think of it like a life preserver. Never know when the boat might capsize."

Nice guy. As McCormick returned to the driver's seat, Scarlett's phone pinged again. When she opened the message app, Jessica's text produced a photo of a pretty little girl staring into the camera, a happy smile on her face.

Tell Mr. Shepherd to please find her. I'm begging.

Ms. Lassiter says if anyone can find Faith, Mr. Shepherd can.

Scarlett covered her face, choking back her emotions. With the silence in the vehicle, McCormick heard Scarlett's gasp and turned to see her distress.

"Are you okay, Ms. Kavanagh?"

Hugging herself for a moment, she looked at him and then held up the phone. "Here is what this is all about. That photo is the little girl these people snatched. Grief and uncertainty are torturing her mother."

McCormick took the phone and studied the photo. "Pretty child. I can relate to what's going through her mother's head. I've got two daughters."

The tech returned as McCormick handed the cell back to Scarlett.

"All set." He took his place at the workstation, putting on a headset.

After what seemed like hours to Scarlett, Reiner raised a hand. "It's going down. Kirby just broadcast a demand to the occupants for the suspects to surrender."

Scarlett flinched, every muscle in her body sprung to attention. With her hands clasped together under her chin, she squeezed her eyes shut. *Please let them surrender. Please let us find Faith.*

No one spoke for several minutes.

"Has anything happened?" Scarlett couldn't stand the silence.

Reiner shook his head.

Several minutes more passed, and Reiner again held up a hand. "Second demand."

After another long pause, Reiner spoke into one of his radios. "ASAC Harold Kirby, Federal Bureau of Investigation to Captain Carson requesting helicopter backup on County Road—"

Scarlett's phone pinged, masking the remainder of Reiner's words. Glancing down, she saw it was a message from her sister, which she ignored. *Jake, tell me something. You could text.*

"Shots fired!"

Oh, my god. Jake?

CHAPTER THIRTY-SIX

At the edge of the clearing, directly in front of the Thomas house, the cluster of agents stood motionless for a few seconds.

"Who fired on the suspect?" Kirby called out.

"What the hell does that matter right now?" Jake said. "The bastard was shooting at us. The better question is, was he hit, and if so, what's the extent of the injury?"

"Tell Reiner to get on that film. He had a camera on the front of the house. I want to know exactly where a round or rounds penetrated if he was hit."

"I'm pretty sure there was a hit," Jake said.

"Did you fire on him?" Kirby said, a vicious look on his face.

"I think you know the answer to that question. If I had fired, he wouldn't have walked back in that house. Check my weapon if it makes you feel better."

"Hal," Weston said. "Reiner says it looks like he took one in the chest and one in the abdomen. Doubt he's feeling too good."

"Chances are he's down," Jake said. "But Arnold's still healthy, and no telling what her munitions stockpile might be."

"We need a line of communication. I'm sure she's got a phone or two. Give me the bullhorn."

With the amplifier, Kirby called out to the suspects. "Hello, in there. We know Thomas is hurt. It's time to establish communication. I'll give you my cell phone number. Call it and give me yours. Don't be stupid. You're outnumbered, and this isn't going to end well unless we work something out." After giving her the information, Kirby handed the amplifier back to Weston. "The ball is in their court."

"Looks like we need to call in a negotiator. I don't see anyone raising a white flag," Weston said. "What do you think, Jake?"

"Depends on how long that's going to take and how long the fuse inside that house will burn. Thomas dies, and Arnold may go off the grid."

"He's right," Rollins said. "From what I read in the files, she's not exactly stable."

"Rollins, pass the word down that no one fires unless I give the order. If this woman comes charging out of that house, I don't want her dead before we know what's happened to that child," Kirby said.

"If she does, I suggest Jake be the one to take a shot. He stands a better chance of disarming her without a fatal outcome," Weston said.

Rollins gave him a puzzled look, his brow furrowed.

Weston nodded toward Jake. "Shepherd was a sniper on the HRT. He puts a bullet wherever he wants it to go. He was born on a range with a semi-automatic in one hand and a rifle in the other."

Kirby started to speak, but the helicopter arrived, almost drowning out the ability to be heard. As it circled the house, Weston shouted, "Hal. Reiner says the copter pilot wants instructions."

"Tell him to make two passes, one low, but staying out of firing range, and then set down in the open field across the road. I want a show of power to those people."

After the aircraft completed the assignment, Jake said to Kirby, "Doesn't look like you're going to get a response to your proposal."

"I'll give it another try." He once again took the megaphone in hand. "Thomas, Ms. Arnold, I'm guessing you need medical attention. That's not going to happen if you don't communicate with me. I gave you my number. Use it. I want to help you."

Everyone stood silent as though afraid motion might jinx hope of a reply. When none came, Jake broke the silence. "Looks like you're going to have to move to plan B. Assuming you have a plan—"

Kirby's cell buzzed. But before he could speak after opening the line on speaker, a stream of profanity worthy of a saltiest sailor came screeching through, ending in, "You motherfuckers shot Jeb. He's bleeding."

"Ms. Arnold. We know Jeb may be seriously injured. You're going to need help."

"You aren't fuckin' gonna help us."

"What do you think is going to happen to Jeb if we don't?"

Silence.

"I repeat. You need help. Who is there with you besides Jeb?"

"None of your business." She hung up.

"That went well," Jake said. "I would say she's light-years from coming out of that building peacefully."

With sparks shooting from his eyes, Kirby turned toward Jake. "And what's your brilliant idea, Shepherd?"

Kirby's phone rang, silencing the group.

He glanced down and saw it was the same number. "Yes, Ms. Arnold. What can I do for you?"

"Jeb needs bandages, pain medicine, antibiotics. Can you bastards get that for him?"

"Of course, we can. It will take a little time. Are you sure you don't want us to transport him to a hospital? We've got a helicopter standing by."

"No. He's not going anywhere with you. You'll just let him die. I know your kind. You'd say it would save the taxpayer a dime or two."

"I'm sorry you believe that. It's not true. We would do our best to get him the medical care he needs."

"No. Not up for debate."

"Okay. Okay. I get it."

She hung up.

Jake clicked his head and sucked his teeth. "As I said. This is going well."

"What's the Shepherd solution?" Kirby said with an unmistakable expression of hostility.

"You need to get someone in there. Send her what she asks for—
but use a messenger who can negotiate with her. Gain her trust. Find
out if the child is in there."

"I hope you're not thinking that's you."

"I don't see a negotiator anywhere around."

Without warning, a female voice cut through the male voices. "*I'm
a negotiator.*"

....

CHAPTER THIRTY-SEVEN

Everyone's head turned as Scarlett rushed forward.

"Ms. Kavanagh, you need to be in the van. This is no place for you," Kirby said.

"Please. Listen to me. I heard what you were saying from a speaker in the van. I can go in; talk to Xenia. Find out whether Faith is in there."

"Are you out of your freaking mind?" Jake said. "Go back to the van. Bullets may come flying at any minute."

"He's right, Ms. Kavanagh. You're a lawyer. These are dangerous people."

"I'm also a mediator. And I'm a woman, a civilian, a twin—just like Xenia. She's not going to listen to any of you. Cops put her in jail. Men abused her in foster care—even her father abused her."

"This is too insane to even talk about," Jake said. "That woman is capable of murder."

Ignoring Jake, Kirby said, "You're a mediator?"

"I am."

"Official? Trained?"

"Yes. I'm a registered neutral in the State of Georgia and have over one hundred hours of training. I've presided over dozens and dozens of domestic mediations over the past six years with a high rate of resolution. I'm good."

"Oh, my god. I'm not hearing this," Jake said as he turned and walked a few paces before turning back. "You're not giving this any consideration are you, Kirby?"

"I'm listening."

"Hell will freeze over before I allow that to happen."

"It's not your call, Shepherd."

"The hell it's not. She works for me—not you."

"She's a free agent, and I'm in charge here."

Jake turned to Scarlett. "You're not doing this. End of discussion."

Scarlett reached in her pocket and drew out her phone. "Look at this photograph, Jake. Look at it." She held up the cell with the image of Faith. "Look at that precious little girl. I have to do it."

"No. Absolutely and unequivocally no."

"She's five years old. Think—what if it were Sabrina?"

"Oh, don't go there. Don't try to pull that one on me."

"I will go there. We have to save her."

Kirby and the others moved away to give Jake and Scarlett a modicum of privacy.

"Not you, Scarlett. *We*. We've got to save her. Trained professionals. I shouldn't have brought you along."

"I'm better trained at this than you are. You don't negotiate; you shoot. You said it yourself that night in the bar. 'I don't negotiate.'"

"It won't be me. Kirby will get an experienced pro out here."

"Not one that is close enough to this family to be willing to volunteer to go in there. And probably not a woman, much less a twin, and maybe not soon enough. This is my assignment. My name is written all over it."

"I'll never agree. If you do this, you no longer work for Shepherd and Associates—that is if you come out alive."

"Like Kirby said, 'that's not your call.' Saving Faith means more to me than working for you."

"Damn . . . damn . . . damn." He squinted, shaking his head. "Just how to do you think you're going to get through to this dangerous nutjob?"

"Jake, listen to me. Xenia is not stable. We know that. She's been planning her revenge for years. Right now, she needs medical supplies, but there are two other things she wants. First, punishing Jessica, but the second we can give her. We've got something she desperately

242 • JUDITH ERWIN

wants. You said, 'To get something, you have to have something to trade.' *Quid pro quo.* Remember?"

He squinted. "What do you have Xenia Arnold could want?"

"The possibility of finding her daughter."

"What?"

"I can promise her we can find her daughter. You heard all those people at the prison say she was obsessed. I've done that Jake. I've tracked down birth parents in my family law practice. I can recite chapter and verse to Xenia."

"She's not going to buy it. She knows she's going back to prison."

"She doesn't want to go back. I'll give you that, but I know she cares more about her child than going to prison. Trust me. She does. Besides, worst-case scenario, I buy some time, find out if Faith is in the house, and whether anyone else is there. I trust you and all these guys to cover me."

"No. This is not an episode of *Law and Order,* Scarlett. No director is going to say 'cut,' and everyone goes home safe and unharmed. Worst-case scenario is you become Arnold victim number whatever. You are out of your friggin' mind."

"I know that's what you think, but I can and will do this. You can't stop me."

He took a deep breath, looked away, and then back. "Hell. You're right. I can't." He looked toward Kirby with fire shooting from his eyes and then unfastened his vest. "Here. Swap with me."

Scarlett looked puzzled.

"You can't go in there with FBI on your back and convince Arnold you're there to help. Give me your wrist."

She pulled her hands closer to her body. "What are you going to do?"

"Give you my smartwatch. You're going to leave your phone. Hand it over. Arnold's smart. She would take it the minute you walk in. Think what you have stored on it. But before you go, call it from my watch, and keep the line open. We'll mute on this end. That way we can still hear you if something were to go wrong with whatever device Kirby's guy hooks you up with. Just a precautionary backup."

"Thank you."

"Listen to me, Scarlett." He softened his tone. "I'm sure you have negotiation skills, but this woman is as dangerous as a wounded tiger. When you're in there with her, stay calm, whatever is happening. Lose your composure, your confidence, and you *will* lose the battle. Engage her in eye contact and don't waiver. Do not let her seduce you into an argument, ignite your temper, or induce your fear. You must stay in control."

"If I feel I'm slipping, I'll think Jake."

He smiled. "Good girl. Think what an arrogant SOB I am."

"I know it's only been a short time, but you've taught me so much."

"Not near enough. But try to remember everything I've said."

He reached forward and took her hand. "Don't try to be a hero, Harvard. If it starts going south, give us a warning."

"How can I do that?"

"Weave a color into your conversation—whatever you can fit into the situation without alerting Arnold. Mention anything but red. If the situation moves to a crisis stage, do whatever you have to do to say red. Shout it out if necessary, and we'll breach the door."

"Any color for a warning?"

"Any color but red."

"Am I still fired?"

"Yes." He grabbed her shoulder and gave it a squeeze. "I'm not sure if I want to strangle you or hug you, but under the circumstances, I can't do either."

As Jake turned away from her, Kirby stepped forward to address Scarlett. "I'll attempt to get Arnold back on the phone. You're sure you want to do this, Ms. Kavanagh?"

"Absolutely."

Jake glared at Hal Kirby but said nothing.

Before making the call, Kirby turned to Rollins. "Have you got a trauma kit in your vehicle?"

"Yeah. But we might want to add a couple of extra Israeli bandages. FWC can probably help us there."

"Good. You take care of that, and Reiner can provide her with a communication device."

Scarlett waited beside the ASAC as he gave instructions while Jake crossed over to where Deke Weston stood, leaning against Kirby's car.

"We've got her back, Jake. We won't let anything happen to her."

"You can't guarantee that."

CHAPTER THIRTY-EIGHT

After Kirby finished issuing instructions, he turned to Scarlett. "You have a three-fold assignment. Do what you can to provide first aid to the wounded suspect, identify and locate all the occupants of the house, and negotiate with Arnold for surrender. I've alerted local law enforcement to standby as we may request tactical support."

"You mean a SWAT team?"

"Exactly. Right now, you're taking her a medical kit designed specifically for emergency injuries such as gunshots. That should get you in. Thomas must be in serious condition. Without proper care, he won't survive. Arnold's not likely to give on allowing us to move him in time to save him. The best you can do is try to make her see surrender is the best alternative. But be aware, if he doesn't make it, she could melt down. If you realize he *is* gone, try to delay her discovery."

"I understand." She started to walk away but stopped. "Something you may not have thought about. I'm still a lawyer. My counseling with her could create a legal relationship, making anything she says to me protected under the attorney-client privilege. I wouldn't be able to repeat anything she says to me unless it is made clear to her that I am not her legal counsel. Would it be possible for you to inform her I will *not* be representing her under any circumstances? I'll confirm it before I start the negotiation, but if I bring it up without a previous warning, it could impair my ability to gain her trust."

His eyebrows pinched together. "If I don't tell her you're a lawyer, how would she know?"

"She may have a computer. If she knows my name, she could Google me. But even if she doesn't, any subsequent defense lawyer who passed the bar would find out and use it to exclude my testimony in court, probably move to disbar me for violating the privilege. Even if she does not find out, I know."

He nodded. "Good point. Yes, I'll make sure she's informed. I have to admit you impress me. Jake's lucky to have you."

"He fired me."

"Really?" He gave her a dubious look. "That's bullshit. Jake's not that stupid. You just nicked his ego. Don't worry; he is angrier with me than he is with you. He'll cool off."

"You think so?"

"I know it. Jake and I may not be best friends, but we respect one another. If that weren't the case, he wouldn't be here right now."

When Scarlett returned to the FBI van, John Reiner set her up with a streaming camera in the form of a pendant.

"I understand Shepherd gave you a smartwatch as a backup."

"He did."

"Good idea. Keep this device facing out. We should be able to pick up the audio as well as video."

The vehicle's passenger door opened as Reiner finished adjusting the length of the silk-like cord holding the camera pendant. Shaughnessy reached in and handed McCormick a black MOLLE pack.

Delivering it to Scarlett, McCormick said, "Here's the trauma kit. It includes antiseptics, sterile gauze, chest seals, Celox granules, Israeli Emergency Bandages, and a jar of Vicks. Are you familiar with how to use all of these?"

Her eyes widened as panic set in. "No. I've never heard of some. What's the VapoRub for?"

"A little in or under your nose will mask offensive odors—help stifle nausea. Here, go through the kit. We'll give you a crash course on using the bandages. Don't freak out. It's pretty easy." He turned to the other agent. "Reiner, pull up a YouTube video on how to give emergency first-aid to a gunshot. Thomas is probably in shock and should be kept warm. Even if you know CPR, don't try to resuscitate him if he stops breathing. Probably would do no good and could expose you to who knows what."

Scarlett took a deep breath. "Please, give me a second to get my head focused. I want to make sure I understand and remember everything. There'll be no way to ask for help once I'm with Xenia."

After the first-aid lesson, Scarlett secured the bag and turned toward the exit.

"Good luck, and be safe," Reiner said. "We'll be monitoring you."

"Thanks." *I'd be lying if I said I'm not a little afraid—maybe a lot.*

When she stepped out of the van, she saw Jake, standing with Deke Weston, a somber expression on his face. *He's angry.* She took a deep breath and walked over to him.

"I know you're not happy with me, and I'm sorry we can't agree. But this is something I have to do."

"I'll leave you two alone," Weston said and walked away.

Jake looked her in the eye for a minute. "I *don't* agree with the risk you're taking, but I'm not angry. Let's just say my apprehension is in overdrive."

"I know what to do if I lose control of the situation, Jake. You taught me. I've been mentally replaying over and over everything you've told me."

He shook his head. "You know so little, Harvard. Two weeks? A couple of self-defense lessons? There's so much more. Give me your word you won't hesitate to use the code word at any sign she's going off the grid. We should be able to hear you but may not see her body language. Can I count on you to reach out?"

"Yes, you can. I promise."

He squeezed her arm and nodded while the muscles in his face relaxed, offering a look of resignation and compassion. "Stay calm. Stay in control."

After two or three seconds locked in eye contact with Jake, Scarlett broke away to begin her assignment. As she approached Kirby for final instructions, she silently repeated her new mantra. *I'll be fine. I can do this.*

"Ready?" he asked.

"Ready."

He took out his cell and made the call to Xenia Arnold. It went directly to voice mail. "The supplies you requested are here," Kirby said into the recorder.

"What now?" Scarlett said.

"We wait. If she doesn't respond, I'll make another attempt, possibly use the bullhorn."

Minutes passed, and Scarlett's tension increased. *Why doesn't she call?* Her hand holding the straps of the trauma pack grew clammy.

Just as Kirby was about to pick up the megaphone, his cell rang. Glancing at it, he said, "It's her. Hold tight."

"ASAC Kirby here. Ms. Arnold. We have the supplies you requested, plus some designed to give emergency aid to a gunshot wound. I'd like to send them in to you. The messenger is a female volunteer. I expect you to allow her safe passage and treat her with respect."

"Is she an EMT or a nurse?"

"No. I'm afraid not. She's an attorney, but she will *not* be representing you or giving you legal advice. She's coming to help you take care of Jeb."

The phone remained silent. After several seconds, Arnold said, "Send her. No funny business."

"You've got it. Take note—she is unarmed." He nodded to Scarlett.

Before she began the walk across the clearing, Scarlett took one final glance back at Jake. He gave her a tip of his chin and pointed to his wrist. He's right. *This woman could kill me, or Jeb could kill me if he's not as seriously injured as they believe. Stay calm. Stay in control.* She gave him a thumbs-up and made the call to her cell.

As twilight dimmed the sky, Scarlett could feel rocks through the thin leather soles of her loafers with each step she took. Her acuity intensified. The smell of the dirt beneath her feet filled her nostrils; a slight breeze chilled her exposed skin, and a deafening silence ran contra to the drone of previous conversation between the lawmen surrounding the area. *In a march toward potential death, one becomes exceedingly aware of life.* She estimated the distance from the edge of the clearing to the house to be roughly forty to fifty yards. *Half the length of a football field.*

When Scarlett reached the house, three wooden steps led to the porch. As she was about to mount the first one, she saw blood in the daylight that remained. *Oh, my god. This is real. What did you expect? They shot him.* The trail of blood led to the door, some of it smeared by the dragging of a foot. She stepped gingerly, hoping to avoid contaminating her shoes or the scene. As she approached the door, a wave of doubt swept through her body. *Was Jake right? Am I in over my head?* For an instant, she ached for his strength and protection. *Confidence. Control. Calm.* She raised her hand to knock, but it flew open before she made contact.

CHAPTER THIRTY-NINE

"Xenia?" *She's Jessica's twin for sure but hard. Her skin looks like leather with lines on her face Jessica doesn't have. That long, stringy hair needs a good shampoo.*

"Who the fuck did you think would be here?" The woman held a semi-automatic with one hand and extended the other toward the kit. "Give me the stuff and get lost."

"I can't do that. We need to talk. But first, we need to attend to Jeb."

"I don't need you. You're no doctor or anything."

"Yes, you do. Right now, I'm the only one here to help with Jeb and the only one standing between you and about twenty lawmen with a lot of guns and more cops on the way. This is a war you can't win, but I can help you." Scarlett's words came at rapid-fire speed, not allowing Xenia a chance to interrupt. "Xenia, I can also give you something you want more than anything. Let me in so we can talk. What can it hurt? You've got the gun. And at the very least, I can help you with Jeb. Do you know how to stop his bleeding—how to use an Israeli Emergency Bandage?"

"What the fuck are you talking about?"

"I didn't think so. It's a unique first aid bandage designed to help stop a hemorrhage. Do you want to take a chance on not applying it correctly?"

Xenia glared at Scarlett. "Who the hell are you?"

"My name is Scarlett Kavanagh. ASAC Kirby told you I'm a lawyer, but I'm not here as a lawyer, and I can't represent you. I'm here because I'm also a mediator. I do not work for any law enforcement agency, and I didn't have to do this. I volunteered."

"Why? Why would you volunteer to come in here?"

I've got to get into the house. Almost pushing Xenia aside, Scarlett crossed the threshold, and when the woman did nothing to stop her, she walked into the hall. To the right was a living room where Jeb Thomas lay on a plump, fake-leather couch, inconsistent with the age and style of the house. Blood-soaked towels covered the ex-con's chest and abdomen. *Is he dead?*

"I think I understand you, Xenia. We have something in common."

"I didn't say you could come in, bitch."

Scarlett ignored her, looking around for signs of Faith.

"And we ain't got nothin' in common. Look at you. Designer jeans, I bet. And that watch. That's one of those smartwatches, isn't it?"

This is not good. Stay calm. Distract her before she becomes more curious about the watch. "As a matter of fact, these are warehouse jeans—less than twenty dollars, and the watch is a knock-off." *Is there such a thing as a knock-off for these watches?* "But I'm a twin, like you."

Xenia stiffened, staring straight into Scarlett's eyes. "So what? That's got nothin' to do with me."

"I believe it does. Like you, I know what it's like to have a twin betray you. Believe me. I know the anger you feel."

"What did yours do?"

"Slept with my fiancé, got pregnant, and married him. I was planning a wedding, and they were—you know."

"Shit." Xenia frowned and cocked her head slightly. "Families suck. But that's nothin' compared to—." She stopped abruptly and glared at Scarlett. "Why am I telling you anything? I don't even know who you are."

"You don't have to tell me. I know your story. You blame your twin for the years you spent in prison. She drove away, leaving you to get caught when your boyfriend robbed that convenience store."

Another layer of anger rose on Xenia's face. "How do you know that?"

"The FBI knows everything, Xenia. They probably know the last time you took a shower and whether you like your eggs fried or scrambled. You had a baby in prison—a precious little girl. I can help you find her."

"Shit." She shook her head. "How could you do that? Who are you?"

"I told you. I'm Scarlett Kavanagh. I'm a family law attorney. We do things like that. I've done it in a dozen cases. I cannot and will not be your lawyer, but I will use my research skills and contacts to help you find your daughter. Can you please point that gun somewhere else and let me help with Jeb? After we do what we can for him, we can talk. I want to help you. I know what a hard life you've had."

Xenia appeared to freeze in place.

I've got her attention. I can do this.

The two women stood face to face like rigid pawns on a chessboard. Xenia took her time responding. "I'm not saying I believe you. But why would you do that? You probably charge big money for somethin' like that."

"I'm not looking for a fee. I'm looking for something else."

"I knew there was a catch."

"No catch. I just want to know where Faith Johnson is. Is she here?"

Hostility again flashed across Xenia's face. "You're a fuckin' cop."

"I'm not a cop. Do I really look like a cop to you?"

"Cops don't always look like cops."

"Where's Faith, Xenia? I'll help you find your little girl if you help me find Faith."

"I have no fuckin' idea. I don't know nothing about a Faith. I don't know what you're talking about."

"You're lying, Xenia. The FBI has rock-solid evidence that you and Jeb took your sister's child. Where is she? Is she upstairs?"

"I told you, I don't know what you're talking about. I haven't seen my asshole of a sister in ten years. I don't know anything about her having a kid."

"Look, we can't argue about it now. Let's do what we can for Jeb." Scarlett forced herself to walk over to the couch. *I can do this.* "He's lost a lot of blood. You should let the FBI come in with medics and transport him to a hospital. They've got a helicopter across the road. You don't want him to die, do you?"

"No!" Xenia shouted. "He's not going to die. That's not happening. Give me that bag."

"You're making a mistake." Scarlett set the MOLLE on a table at the end of the couch where the ex-con lay, eyes closed, his shallow breathing barely moving his chest. She leaned slightly over him. "Jeb, can you hear me?"

Scarlett waited, but no response came from the man. "He appears to be in a coma." She took an Israeli bandage out of the kit, handed it to Xenia, and turned back to the injured suspect. "Check it out."

Xenia's eyes grew large as Scarlett took out the needed supplies and opened the vacuum-sealed package of an identical bandage.

As she turned the package in all directions, Xenia said, "It don't look special. Looks like an Ace Bandage."

"Well, it's not. Look closer." Scarlett held up the wrapping. "See where it says, 'hemorrhage control'? EMTs and military medics use these. It's Jeb's best chance."

"I don't know. What's that handle-looking thing?"

"That's how we apply pressure on his wounds to stop the bleeding. We need a blanket to wrap him in. He's probably in shock. Can you get one for me?"

Xenia gave Scarlett a look. "Don't think I'm going to fall for that. You want me to leave the room so you can do somethin' to Jeb. Maybe let some of those bastard cops in."

Scarlett's head snapped around. "Do you want Jeb to live?" *Whoa, Scarlett. Keep calm.* "Don't be foolish, Xenia. I'm not a doctor, but I can tell you, if we don't get the bleeding stopped, he *is* going to die."

"Maybe he'd rather die than go back to Raiford."

"Maybe he wouldn't."

For several seconds, the two women glared at one another.

"Who else is here, Xenia? Is there anyone who can help us?"

"No one."

"No offense, but I don't believe you. I hear someone upstairs on the left side of the house. Is it Faith?"

"You're hearing's off. There's no one here but me and Jeb."

"Have it your way. I repeat, if you don't work with me, Jeb hasn't got a chance. If you're worried I'm trying to trick you, ask yourself why I would have risked my life to come in here. You're holding a gun." While talking, she slipped her hands into a pair of surgical gloves from the kit.

Xenia had stripped away Jeb's shirt, and when Scarlett lifted the bloody towels from his bare chest, the sight of two bullet holes repulsed her while the rusty odor of blood nauseated her. His blood-streaked tattoo art reminded Scarlett of desecrated graffiti. *I can do this.* She dug the jar of Vicks VapoRub out of the bag, and using her uncontaminated hand, dabbed a little under her nose to avert the nausea. "We need to put these bloody towels in a garbage bag. Get me some clean towels when you get the blanket."

"All right. But you're coming with me, and don't try anything." Xenia waved the Smith and Wesson at Scarlett.

Thank God, she's giving in. This man is barely alive. "Fine." *It doesn't take a medical degree to see he's not going to make it.*

Performing the procedure, she learned only an hour before, and explaining to Xenia the purpose of each step, Scarlett treated both wounds. Xenia provided little help but did assist in lifting him when Scarlett wrapped the Israeli Bandage around his body. Xenia refused to abandon her weapon, cramming it inside the waistband of her jeans while helping.

As she stared down at the unconscious man, Scarlett assessed the situation. *He's still alive but won't be without qualified treatment.*

Scarlett peeled the gloves from her hands and dropped them into the garbage bag containing the bloody towels. "I've done all I can for Jeb, Xenia. It's not going to keep him alive. You need to think really hard about signing his death warrant. He needs competent doctors. Don't answer me now. Think about it for a few minutes. I need to use the restroom."

"No way."

"What do you think I'm going to do? Climb out a window?"

"I don't trust you."

"The only restroom I've had access to in the last four or five hours was a semi-private one in a van with two strange men. I'm still human. Don't torture me. I've done nothing but try to help you."

"The only bathroom is upstairs. This ain't no modern house."

"That's fine." Scarlett walked to the staircase and started up. Xenia followed. As they grew closer to the second floor, the shuffling sound Scarlett heard earlier became more pronounced. *I'd better pretend to ignore it until I use the restroom.* Glancing around the hall, she noted four doors. All closed. The bathroom occupied the center spot at the head of the stairs—its door open. *Someone is definitely in the room on the left.* Once inside, she closed the door and eased it locked. Although the room appeared clean, articles of clothing were hanging over the shower rod and towel bars, presumably drying.

When relieved, Scarlett turned on the water and flushed the toilet simultaneously. With her back to the entry, she spoke barely above a whisper into the watch. "Someone is in the left, back corner room." Taking a deep breath, Scarlett hoped Xenia had not heard her over the rush of water.

As she exited, her hands still wet because of the lack of a towel, the expression on Xenia's face caught her attention. *She looks different. There's a crazed, wild look in her eyes. Did she hear me?*

"You're up to something."

Scarlett steadied herself. "Exactly what do you think I could be up to?"

"You're figuring out a way to turn me in—have those bastards come get me."

"Xenia, if the FBI wanted to come for you, they would come. They don't need any help from me. There are at least seven agents and a former agent out there, plus I don't know how many law enforcement officers from the state. Coming through that door would be simple."

"Get back downstairs."

"Is there some reason you don't want me up here?"

"Shut up."

Scarlett took another deep breath and walked down the steps. Xenia kept the gun aimed at her back. *I think she's losing it. Reality may be clicking in.*

When they reached the lower floor, Scarlett turned to face her nemesis. "I told you earlier I can try to find your little girl. Did you give her a name?"

"Shut up. You can't do that."

"Do you have a better option? I'm telling you. I have found birth mothers and adopted children. No. I won't lie to you. I can't guarantee I can find her, but I have a good chance. We know who took her. There are records."

"You gonna give her back to me?"

"I can't do that. I can't even promise you'll get to see her. But there's a chance if I find her, you'll at least know something—her name. And I can probably get photos of her. What have you got now?"

"You're trying to trick me."

Scarlett glanced around the area, wanting to check on Jeb without being obvious. The glimpse she caught unnerved her. *He looks dead.*

"Be smart, Xenia. End this peacefully while you can. I'll vouch for your cooperation. Let the authorities come in and get Jeb. Save his life and yours."

"They ain't gonna kill me as long as I've got you. They'll have to shoot through you, and I'm thinkin' they ain't gonna do that."

"Where's Jeb's grandmother, Xenia?"

"What difference does it make?"

"I was just wondering. You said no one else is here, but this is her house, isn't it?"

"Sorta. It's also Jeb's. She's not his grandmother. His grandmother is dead. She's the second wife."

"Where is she?"

"Gone."

"Gone where?"

"None of your business. To a sister's, I think."

"Please consider surrendering."

"Never." She fired the gun.

Scarlett jumped. "I get it. It's dark outside. The sky is really black."

CHAPTER FORTY

"Arnold fired," Jake said. "I'm going in."

"Stand down, Shepherd. You don't make the calls."

Jake glared at Kirby. "Arnold fired a shot, and Scarlett sent us a code word. You've got to let me go in." He turned toward the other agents nearby. "Rollins, let me see the images of that house."

"You're not the one to do it," Kirby said as Rollins handed Jake the photos. "You're personally invested, Shepherd."

"The hell I'm not the right one. Look at this picture. There's a roof running over the front porch and windows to the second floor right there. I can fast rope in, gain entry through one of those windows, and neutralize Arnold."

"Right. Just like in the movies. As I recall, the last time you tried to neutralize an assailant holding Ms. Kavanagh hostage, he left in a body bag. If this woman dies and that child is not in the house, we have no hope of finding her."

"Damn you, Kirby. You saw the video on that shoot. I had no choice. Get over yourself. How many years was I an HRT operative?"

"The better question is how many years *ago* were you an operative? You're not the man for the job, Shepherd. When was the last time you made a fast rope descent? Ten, fifteen years ago. You haven't seen thirty in how long?"

"Stop effing around, Kirby. I'm the best resource you have. If you keep twiddling your thumbs and something happens to Scarlett, it's on you. You sent her in against my protests. Arnold just fired a round, and you know the hardest trigger pull is the first one." Jake clenched his hands, his jaw firmly set, as he glared at Hal Kirby. "If Arnold kills her, who's going to do the notifications? You? Get me to that helicopter before it's too late. If I fuck it up, then you have me to blame."

"Ms. Kavanagh is wearing a vest."

"Yeah? So was my dad, and I still had to go to his funeral. Who else have you got? Deke? Rollins? What's his name? No. I'm the only one with hostage rescue history—tactical training. I keep myself in shape—maybe not sliding out of helicopters, but I am the one who has done it."

"I'm betting some officer out here has military experience and can make the descent."

"No one has worked with Scarlett. She'll know what to do if I go in."

"I let you do this, Shepherd, and you fuck it up, the six o'clock news will lead with, 'Two killed in botched FBI incident when supervisor sends in his wife's ex-husband to rescue girlfriend.'"

"What's more important to you? Doing your job or headlines? I won't botch it, and you know it."

Kirby looked over to Deke Weston.

"He's right, Hal. He's the only one with that kind of experience, and we don't have time to call out a SWAT team."

"He's got personal feelings for the hostage."

"He's also a rock-solid pro. If he says he can do it, I believe he can. Admit it, Hal. Jake's as good as he thinks he is."

With a grin directed toward Weston, Jake said, "We're wasting time. I'm probably the only one who can shoot straight enough to disarm the woman without killing her. Your only other alternative is to breach the door, and you know how high the risks are there. This woman is not going to give up. Her boyfriend is probably dead, and Scarlett knows it. When Arnold figures it out, she will blow."

Kirby made eye contact with Weston, who nodded. He then turned to Rollins, who did the same.

"What do you need?"

"I'll need a radio. Somebody check with the copter pilot and be sure he has the equipment to drop me. He should. He's likely done

260 · JUDITH ERWIN

this type of mission. I'll need cover. Arnold is aware of the helicopter and won't suspect it's doing anything but surveillance. But I'll need a distraction when I land. You guys need to light up the area with flashbangs, stun grenades, fireworks, whatever. Make it the Fourth of July."

"You sure you want us to do that? There's a risk it could spook Arnold into thinking she's under attack—put Kavanagh at risk. I could get her on the phone or use the bullhorn to distract her," Kirby said.

"Too much uncertainty with either one. No way to be sure she'll answer or that talking with her will cover me. I get ambushed, and everyone loses. As long as she doesn't hear gunfire, I'm thinking she won't go off the chart. Begin taking it down as soon as you see me gain entry."

"Your call. What else do you need?"

"Earplugs, heavy gloves for the descent, a flashlight, a length of about fifty feet of nylon cord, half-inch should do it, two sets of cuffs, and a pair of athletic type, rubber-soled shoes—size eleven or close to it. Boots are not good on the rope, for tiptoeing across the roof, or navigating the interior unheard."

"Can you wear eleven and a half?" Rollins asked. "I've got a pair of tactical boots in my car for hikes through rough terrain. I'm sure you know the type."

"Yeah. Those will work. While I'm getting there, Kirby, you need to engage Arnold if possible. Ask her if there's anything else she needs. Just keep her talking as long as you can."

"What if there's someone in the room you break into?"

"If so, they've managed to stay quiet since Scarlett's been in. She's given us the heads-up that the back, left corner room may have an occupant." He reached into his shirt pocket and removed Scarlett's cell. "Hold on to this, Deke, and try to stay awake. I know it's been a long day."

"We've got your back, buddy. Go get her."

CHAPTER FORTY-ONE

As the helicopter hovered over the old house, the sky erupted in a blaze of flashing light and deafening sound from the explosive devices. A cloud of smoke rose over the clearing and obscured visibility. Without a glitch, Jake slid down a rope from the helicopter, landing on the porch roof. After disengaging the tether, he crept across the roof and removed a screen from the far-left sash window. When it didn't give upon an attempt to raise it, he used a glass cutter with a suction cup to gain access to the latch. Gaining entry, he discarded the heavy gloves and slipped on a latex pair. Cautiously navigating the empty bedroom, weapon drawn, he aimed the beam of his flashlight toward the floor while the noise and light outside faded. When he reached the door to the hall, he eased it open and could hear Xenia Arnold's agitated but indiscernible rants. *She's off her game—exceedingly dangerous.*

Gently closing the door behind him as he exited, he slithered into the hall, extinguishing the beam and relying on the ambient light from below. Spotting the room suspected of having an occupant, he proceeded to the door, looped a lasso of nylon cord over the knob, pulled it tight, tied the thin rope to the knob of the parallel bedroom, and cut the excess. Once the doors were secured, he repeated the procedure with the two rooms on the opposite side of the hall and began a descent to the first floor, weapon again drawn. The lower he moved, the more distinct Arnold's words became. He could tell the two women were in the room to his left.

"He's dead. It's your fault. You let him die," she shrieked. "You lied to me. Maybe you poisoned him. You said you would help him." A phone rang, but Xenia ignored it. "What's going on out there? Are they going to break down the door?"

262 · JUDITH ERWIN

"I have no idea what's going on," Scarlett said. "Xenia, I begged you to let the FBI take Jeb to a hospital. I did all I could. You need to consider giving yourself up before it's too late. As long as you're alive, there's a chance you may someday see your daughter."

"Bullshit. If they storm this house, you'll be the first to die."

Jake could clearly hear Scarlett's voice from his crouched position even though her tone was lower than Xenia's. *This is good. Arnold's back is to me.* He stood and eased to the bottom of the stairs. When he rounded the corner, Scarlett immediately caught sight of him. He nodded, and she dropped to the floor as he fired his Glock.

Caught off guard, Xenia froze.

"That was your warning. Drop the gun, Xenia. It's over."

She made no move.

"Make one wrong move, and my next shot is going to hurt. Scarlett, move out of her line of fire."

Jake's eye did not leave Xenia, his finger on the trigger, ready to pull if her arm made the slightest move in the wrong direction.

As Scarlett crept to the side of the room, to Jake's surprise, Xenia's hands rose above her head, but she held onto the gun. *She's not suicidal.* He quickly advanced and snatched Xenia's gun with his left hand while his right jabbed the muzzle of his weapon against her back. After thrusting her Smith and Wesson into the waist of his jeans, he holstered his gun, grabbed Xenia's hands, and cuffed them behind her back.

"Any other weapons I should know about?" he asked, as he ran his hands down her sides, back, and legs.

"No, damn you. How'd you get in? She let you in."

Scarlett had scrambled to her feet. "How did you get in, Jake?"

"Magic. You okay, Harvard?"

"I am now."

Jake looked over to the sofa where Jeb Thomas lay. "Is he dead?"

"I'm pretty sure he is," Scarlett said.

"Are you the one that killed him?" Xenia shrieked.

FAITH LOST • 263

"No, ma'am. I'm not."

"You're FBI. I saw it on your vest."

"Nope. It's a loaner." He turned to the microphone clipped to his collar. "Did you hear that, Kirby? One suspect neutralized; the other presumably deceased. However, there are signs of life in the house. So, send in your boys to do a sweep."

"I'm going upstairs to see if Faith is there," Scarlett said.

He held an arm out to block her. "Whoa, Harvard. We don't know if there's friend or foe behind that door. Let Kirby's people take over. If she's there, we'll have her out in minutes."

Xenia spat at Scarlett, who jumped back to avoid the contact. "I told you. I don't know anything about a kid."

Scarlett gave her a dirty look.

"Open the front door, Harvard. No sense in overzealous agents kicking it in."

Scarlett hardly had it open when the lights of FBI vehicles blinded her as they skid to a stop in front of the house, and the team swarmed in.

"Upstairs, left rear. I secured the door," Jake said as Shaughnessy came through the entry, followed by Bush. "You might keep your eyes peeled for additional weapons. My guess is either this one, or one you find in a search of this place, is going to be a ballistic match for the shot that killed Jerome Powell in Jacksonville."

As Deke Weston entered, followed by Hal Kirby, he approached Xenia, holding two documents in front of her to read. "Xenia Arnold, you're under arrest for the Federal Kidnapping of Faith Johnson, and for Federal Motor Theft, and for transporting a stolen vehicle across state lines. I suspect there'll be more to come. You have the right to remain silent. Anything you say may be used against you in a court of law. You have the right to an attorney."

Xenia spat at Weston, hitting his vest. He just shook his head.

"If you cannot afford an attorney, one will be appointed for you." Shaking the document held in his left hand, Weston said, "If you read

264 • JUDITH ERWIN

closely, you'll see this one is a search warrant for this property." He folded the documents and stuck them in the waistband of her jeans. He turned to Jake, "Thanks, buddy. I'm going to enjoy the steak dinner Kirby's going to buy."

"What was the wager?"

"That you could pull this off with everyone left standing."

"Thanks for the support. Without it, I'm not sure he would have given in." Jake nodded in the direction of Hal Kirby.

Kirby stood to the side, listening and shaking his head. "Yeah, Weston said you hear better than an elephant and move like a cat." He reached out and shook Jake's hand. "Congratulations. Job well done." He turned toward Scarlett. "Both of you."

From upstairs, they could hear the agents shout "clear" with each room. Rollins stood at the base of the staircase.

When Shaughnessy reached the room noise had emanated from, he shouted. "Have someone in the back, left corner."

"Faith?" Scarlett said and quickly moved to the foot of the stairs next to Rollins.

"Child or adult?" Rollins called out.

"Adult. Female. Bound and gagged."

Scarlett's face fell as she turned back toward Jake and the Feds. "It's not Faith."

"Told you," Xenia said from the chair Jake had forcefully guided her to.

"So, where is the child?" Jake said, conveying a high degree of hostility with his tone and the expression on his face.

"I don't know nothin' about a kid."

"Well, we don't buy that, Ms. Arnold. We have your DNA, the child's DNA, and his"—Kirby tipped his head toward the couch where the body of Thomas lay—"DNA in the vehicle you used when you took the child from her school. Make it easy on yourself. Tell us where she is."

"I ain't telling you scrum bags shit. I don't know where any kid is."

Scarlett's face contorted in a stern grimace.

Reiner and McCormick entered the house and approached Kirby, with Reiner extending a stack of evidence bags to him. "Thought you might need these."

Kirby took them and passed one to Jake. "Unless you like having that S and W stuck down your pants, drop it in this. And for once, we don't need to bag your Glock. I assume that hole near the ceiling is your artwork, or is it Ms. Arnold's?"

Jake grinned. "Mine. I saw a spider but missed."

"Right. If you saw a spider, he'd be dead on the floor."

From the chair, Xenia lifted her feet and stomped them on the floor.

"Something you want, Ms. Arnold?" Kirby said.

"I've got to pee, you mother fucker."

"Then, I'd say you have a problem unless you want to do it with the door open. Because you're not going anywhere by yourself."

"That's cruel and unusual punishment," she shouted.

"Is it?" Kirby said.

"You want me to pee in the back of your fuckin' police car?"

"Reiner, go out to your van and check with FWC for a female agent on site who can accompany Ms. Arnold on a mercy mission."

"Why can't she?" Arnold nodded toward Scarlett.

"She's not an armed law enforcement officer. As I told you, she's a volunteer. Her job is done."

A few seconds later, Reiner came back through the front door. "Kirby, there's a female deputy sheriff on the way."

CHAPTER FORTY-TWO

By the time Jake and Scarlett neared Tallahassee after leaving the crime scene, her phone read eleven-fifteen. "Can this still be the same day you woke me to make the trip down here?" she said to Jake as they neared Tallahassee.

"It's been a long one."

"How are we going to tell Jessica we found Xenia but still do not know what has happened to Faith?"

"Want me to have Brenda and Sonny tell her?"

Scarlett took a deep breath and sighed. "That would be cowardly. Jessica is looking to us to find Faith. I have to tell her. Maybe I could wait until we get back."

"No reason to upset her tonight. We'll be in DC tomorrow evening. At least we won't be sharing a ride with Kirby. He's flying out early."

"What about Deke and the other agent?"

"They'll be staying to escort Arnold to DC."

"That will take an extradition process, right?"

"Yep. But the Feds will move it through in a hurry. Kirby had the Assistant U.S. Attorney on speed dial."

"Are Weston and Bush going to interrogate Xenia before they take her to DC?"

"You heard her screaming for a lawyer. Wasn't that covered in Crim Law 101 at Harvard?"

She nodded with her eyes focused on the dash. "But what about Faith? Can't they? Of course, they can't. You're right. They can't do anything with Xenia until she has a lawyer. Jake, we've got to do something to find that child." She put both hands to her face, rubbing her temples. "Surely they didn't hurt that precious little girl. How terrified she must be, wherever she is."

"We all hope she's okay. Deke and Bush are going to interview the step-grandmother tomorrow. She was too overwrought tonight."

"After being bound and gagged for hours because she wanted to kick them out, can you blame her?"

"She's lucky they didn't kill her. Pretty sure Deke will let us observe. Nothing we can do tonight."

"How many guns did they find in the search?"

"Three. For Xenia's sake, the Smith and Wesson she had on you better not have been the one that killed Powell."

He made a turn into a hotel drive. "Looks like this is the hotel Rollins set us all up with. I'm ready to eat and crash. I hope the food he ordered is here."

"I'm not hungry, but a shower and a comfortable bed sound wonderful. I hope I can sleep without replaying images of Thomas bleeding and Xenia pointing that gun at me."

"Welcome to the world of things you can never unsee, Harvard. Sure you want to work in this business?"

"I thought you fired me."

"That's right. I did."

When they reached the front desk of the hotel, Kirby, Weston, and Bush were about to head for the elevator. Weston held up a hand to Jake. "The clerk has your food. See you guys tomorrow."

Jake nodded, raised his hand to acknowledge the information, and then took out his wallet.

"May I help you, sir?" the desk clerk said.

"Shepherd, Jacob. I'm part of that group you just checked in."

"Oh, yes. I have your reservation, and is that Ms. Kavanagh?"

"It is."

"Will that be one room or two?"

"Two, adjoining, please."

"I'm sorry, sir. We do not have any adjoining rooms left tonight."

"Well, that's a problem." Jake turned to Scarlett. "One okay, Harvard?"

She took a second, glancing down at the floor and then toward the elevator where the three agents were entering. "One. Being alone tonight could be—just take one with two beds."

After Jake palmed the room key and grabbed the take-out order, they proceeded to the elevator. As she pushed the call button, Scarlett said, "The one room. Don't get the wrong idea, Shepherd. It's just that—"

Jake broke out in a seductive grin. "No need for explanations, Harvard. I get it. We're not a couple—at least not on Sunday. But since you no longer work for me, your barrier for a relationship is gone."

She snapped her head around to make eye contact. "And please explain to me why I would ever consider a relationship with someone who fired me?"

"That's an explanation you don't want to hear. The elevator's here."

Monday morning, Scarlett was up first and coming out of the shower when Jake swung his feet off the only unmade bed.

"This is a first. Jake Shepherd sleeps in until—what time is it? Six-fifteen?"

"Much as I hate to admit it, age is catching up. Sliding out of that bird, I pulled something. But I'll work it out. Soon as I take a shower, we'll head down to the restaurant for breakfast."

"No workout today?"

"Nope. No workout. I'll double down tomorrow."

As they entered the hallway, twenty minutes later, they ran into Deke Weston. His eyes lit up as a smug smile crossed his face. "Sleep well, guys?"

Scarlett took a deep breath and cut her eyes toward Jake.

"Like a log," he said. "What time are you heading out to interview the witness?"

"Probably around ten. Kirby's plane takes off a little before eight. You guys going down to breakfast?"

"We are. Probably see you there. I want to check the truck first."

"We'll get a table large enough for all of us," Weston said.

Jake gave a thumbs-up. "Just what I've been hoping for. Breakfast with my husband-in-law."

"You spent all day yesterday with him. Think you can make it through another hour?"

"As long as you don't seat me next to him, I'll survive. See you there."

As Weston walked toward the elevator, Jake and Scarlett moved in the opposite direction to take the stairs down to the side of the building where he parked the night before.

"That was great," Scarlett said.

"It was? How so?"

"We might as well have taken an ad in *The New York Times*. Shepherd and Kavanagh found in a hotel room together."

"Deke isn't going to tell anyone."

"What do you mean he's not going to tell anyone? Did you see the look on his face?"

"Yep. But Deke knows my daughter lives with Kirby, and his feelings toward Kirby are not a whole lot better than mine. He won't say anything."

When they reached the six-seat, round table in the restaurant, Kirby sat between Bush and Weston. Scarlett and Jake took chairs that positioned Scarlett directly across from Kirby and Jake between her and Bush.

"Good morning. Quite a day we had yesterday," Kirby said.

Scarlett smiled, and Jake said, "Good one to put in the rearview mirror."

"You both did outstanding jobs. I admit; I was impressed. You make a good team."

"We're not a team. Remember? Jake fired me."

Kirby shook his head. "You mean he hasn't retracted that dumbass statement yet?"

"Not yet."

"I'll tell you what. If he doesn't give you the job back, come see me. The Bureau could use an agent with your skills."

"But I didn't accomplish what I set out to. Xenia never surrendered."

"You accomplished a lot more. You pinned down who was in the house and where. Don't underestimate that."

"And aren't you up to your old tricks?" Jake said. "But this time, you're out of your league with Scarlett. I hereby, publicly, officially, and unequivocally retract my termination of Scarlett's employment. She is back on my payroll."

Weston struggled to keep from laughing aloud while Bush's eyes cut back and forth with a look of discomfort.

Jake turned to Scarlett. "You never believed you were fired, did you?"

She scrunched her face and then raised a hand, wiggling it in the maybe gesture. "You're not exactly predictable."

Weston gave up and released a belly laugh. "She's got you pegged, Shepherd."

Scarlett's face took on a serious look as her eyebrows pinched together, forming wrinkles, and all traces of a smile disappeared. "I've got to ask you all. What are the chances of finding Faith alive?"

No one answered.

After a pregnant pause, Kirby said, "Weston. What's your take?"

The seasoned agent gave a slight shake of his head. "It's not looking good. When we didn't find her with the abductors, it stands to reason she may have been eliminated. Not easy to hide a living five-year-old. What do you think, Jake? You're the one with ESP."

"I prefer not to think about it until every rock is turned. But if I were giving odds, I think we've got a thirty percent chance of finding her—finding her alive, more like twenty."

"Really, Jake?" Scarlett said. "That math comes out to eighty percent she's likely dead."

"Sorry, Harvard. I don't like it any better than you do. The mom has touched my covert soft spot, but statistics are not in our favor."

"But you're good at what you do. You solve cases."

"I solve cases, but I don't control the actions of bad guys."

"I agree with them, Scarlett," Kirby said. "Maybe even less optimistic. I see a ten percent chance for our hoped-for resolution, and I see another possibility. We may never find her. There are way too many cases where that has happened. But it doesn't mean we're giving up. We're going to continue full force until all leads are exhausted. But right now, it looks like the buffet table is set up, and I'm starved."

After breakfast, Kirby left to catch his flight back to Washington while the rest returned to their rooms.

At nine-thirty, Jake and Scarlett drove back to the FBI Resident Agency to observe the interview of Irene Thomas, Jeb's step-grand-mother, and for Jake to turn in the FBI money he used at the convenience store and the rifle used as a prop in the truck. When he handed the cash and receipts over to Rollins to check in, he reached in his wallet a second time and took out a ten-dollar bill. "Add this. I bought lottery tickets from the gal at the store. Who knows? One might score, and I would hate to turn the windfall over to the DOJ."

Rollins chuckled. "I think you used up your weekly allocation of luck when you fast roped out of that copter."

"Think again, my friend." Jake pointed an index finger at Rollins. "That was not luck. That was sheer skill."

"Damn, Shepherd. Your ability is only exceeded by your ego."
Scarlett laughed.

"Don't knock it. It gets me through the tough times. You might try it." He thrust a hand forward to shake Rollins's. "Always a pleasure working with you."

CHAPTER FORTY-THREE

As Jake and Scarlett sat in a corner of the waiting area for their board-ing gate at the Tallahassee airport, she checked her phone. "I've got a message from Jessica." She looked over toward Jake, who was read-ing the current edition of *The New York Times*. "I don't want to open it."

"You can wait. We'll be boarding soon and should make it to Reagan by five-thirty. Should give us enough time to freshen up at the apartments, have a quick dinner, and run by the safe house afterward."

"I dread it. How do I tell her we don't know any more about where Faith may be? At least she has Colleen with her." She paused as if thinking. "It just registered with me. Jessica doesn't need the safe house and security with Xenia in custody and Jeb dead."

"I'll be releasing Brenda and Sonny tonight."

"But Jessica doesn't want to go back to her apartment without Faith."

"We can't take care of everything, Harvard. I don't know the terms of the rental arrangement on the house, but it's probably paid for a month. She can finish out that time and then figure out what to do if Faith isn't found."

"I thought Irene Thomas would be of more help, but she didn't seem to know anything. Did you take away anything from the interview?"

"Very little. There was certainly no love lost between her and Jeb. She did say he was capable of murder, but she wasn't sure he would kill a child. However, there are many ways to kill a child indirectly."

"Indirectly? What do you mean? How?"

"Take a young child into dense woods and leave her. Tie her up in an abandoned building in an isolated area with no food or water. Things like that."

Scarlett looked at him without speaking as if processing the horror of his explanation. Just as she started to comment, an airline agent announced the boarding of their flight over the intercom.

By the time Scarlett and Jake reached the safe house, it was nearly eight o'clock. He had called Ted McKay before they left for dinner and explained the situation, asking if the engineer would be willing to visit if Jessica wanted him. McKay enthusiastically agreed. Scarlett chose not to contact Jessica, relying instead on Jake's giving notice of their intended visit to the security team with a recommendation Jessica not be told in advance.

When Jake knocked on the door, Sonny Lassiter answered. The two shook hands as Jessica sprang to meet them. It did not require Jake's keen ability to read people to recognize the panic on her face.

"You look serious. No. No. She's not—"

"Hold on, Jessica. We don't have good news, but we don't have bad news either," Jake said.

"Have you found her?"

Jake shook his head. "I'll let Scarlett explain."

Colleen Powell stood behind her daughter with an expression equally as concerned.

"Let's sit down," Scarlett said and moved forward to escort Jessica to the sofa in the living room.

"Tell me, Scarlett. Please, tell me," Jessica said as Colleen looked on, tears welling in her eyes.

Scarlett took Jessica's hands in hers once they were both settled. "The FBI located your sister and her boyfriend. They were in a house in a rural area of North Florida. When they attempted to serve arrest warrants, the boyfriend came out shooting. He was shot by law enforcement and died a few hours later. Your sister held the authorities off for about five hours before they were able to arrest her. But Faith was not in the house. We don't know where Faith is."

Jessica's chin quivered, and tears flooded her cheeks.

"Could someone else have taken her?" Colleen asked.

Jake spoke up. "The FBI was able to obtain forensic evidence putting Faith in a vehicle with Xenia and Jeb Thomas—not far from Jessica's apartment. They are sure Xenia was the one who tricked the school into releasing Faith to her custody."

Jessica dropped her face into her hands, her entire body shaking. "I'll never see her again. They'll never find her. She could be any-where, maybe—no, I can't say it. I can't believe it. She never did anything to deserve this."

"You never did anything to deserve it either," Colleen said.

"Jessica," Scarlett said. "Ted McKay is waiting to hear from us. He wants to come over, but it's up to you."

"I thought Mr. Shepherd said he couldn't."

"The threat's over," Jake said. "Your sister is in custody. She can't hurt you."

Jessica's head slowly moved up and down in agreement. "I would like to see him."

Jake made the call, and within minutes, Ted McKay arrived at the safe house.

"How did you get here so fast?" Jessica said as he walked in. "Shepherd gave me the address earlier, and I've been at a coffee shop a couple of blocks away hoping to hear. What has happened?"

Jessica stood and crossed the room. McKay took her in his arms as Jake gave him a thumbnail picture of the current status. When Jake finished, McKay said, "Pull out every stop you have. Bill me. Do whatever you have to do to find Faith."

"We're already doing just that," Jake said.

"Look. I know money talks. Fortunately, I can afford it. Spend whatever is necessary. Pay the sister if you have to."

"Mr. McKay. Ted. I think you know trying to bribe the sister won't work. We're doing everything possible. There's a good team working the case for the FBI, and they've included me in the process. Scarlett and I will be meeting with them again, when the full team returns, to go over the evidence collected at the Florida house and from the vehicle the couple was using. We all hope something turns up that will point us in the direction of where they took Faith."

"How did you dispel the FBI theory Jessica was involved in Faith's disappearance?" McKay asked.

"That's a long story. They would have gotten there eventually. I just put the process on fast forward."

"Have they questioned the sister? What does she say?"

"There, we have a problem. She's not talking. The process to extradite her to Maryland is underway and should happen quickly. When she arrives, and a defense attorney is appointed, the Bureau will take another stab at breaking her silence. But be prepared; pushing Xenia off the Fifth Amendment perch may not happen."

"And if she doesn't talk?" McKay said.

"I'm pretty sure we can count on that. Obviously, we have our work cut out. The canvas we're working on includes anywhere the abductors could have traveled within the time frame. Since they don't operate like regular citizens with bank accounts, standard cell phones, credit cards, Social Security numbers, even driver's licenses, it could take time. But I've got an idea or two. It'll take the combined efforts of the Feds, but I'm not giving up by a long shot."

Scarlett looked at him quizzically. "You haven't mentioned that to me."

"I haven't because it had not thoroughly jelled. You and I will talk it through with Kirby and Weston. I'm pretty sure Kirby will go along with me. We've covered all we can cover tonight. How about we go home and get a good night's rest? It's been a long thirty-six hours."

"Will you keep me informed with what you find?" Jessica asked, wiping tears from her cheeks.

"Don't expect instant results. Be patient. We'll let you know when we have something definite, but I'm not going to get your hopes up until I know something concrete. Your emotions don't need the rollercoaster ride."

"Jessica," Sonny Lassiter said, "I think Brenda has told you, but I'll confirm it. If anyone can find your little girl, it'll be Jake. I've known him a long time. He's not only smart and intuitive; he is also as tenacious as John Walsh about bringing about justice."

Jake smiled. "Thanks, Lassiter." He turned back to Jessica. "Sonny and Brenda will be leaving tonight. You and your mother can stay a couple of weeks if you like. I spoke to Phil Madison earlier, and he said the rent is paid for a month. Your decision."

CHAPTER FORTY-FOUR

Tuesday morning, Jake knocked on the door of Scarlett's apartment at seven-thirty. When the door opened, and he saw she was dressed and ready to go, it took him by surprise. "I thought you might like to stay home and finish getting settled in."

"I'm settled." She reached down and gave Kai a pat on the head.

"And you don't want to be left out if something breaks in the case. Right?"

"I decline to answer on the—"

He chuckled. "Yeah, yeah. Come on. Let's go before traffic gets worse."

Once in the Lexus, Scarlett asked while buckling her seatbelt, "What's the plan you mentioned last night?"

"I'd rather wait to talk about it until we're with Kirby's team."

"You are infuriating. I work with you. Don't you think you should share information with me?"

"And I will. It's not classified. I'd just rather put the pieces together when I know what all was confiscated in the search. We left before they finished. Remember?"

"Good morning," Liz said as Scarlett, Jake, and Kai entered the office. "You made the headlines."

"We did?" Scarlett said.

"You did." Liz held up a copy of the morning paper so Scarlett could see the headline.

After Liz handed her the periodical, Scarlett began reading the article aloud with Jake looking over her shoulder. "'FBI Assistant

Special Agent in Charge, Harold Kirby announced the arrest of Xenia Arnold and shooting death of her paramour, Jeb Mayfield Thomas, in North Florida on Sunday. The couple was wanted for the kidnapping of five-year-old Faith Johnson from her Silver Spring school two weeks ago. At this time, the child is still missing, and the search continues.'"

As Scarlett read further, the article mentioned the help she and Jake provided to the FBI.

"Well, that's a first," Jake said. "Bet Kirby would never have mentioned me if Scarlett hadn't been involved."

Liz laughed. "Don't knock it. Should get us some business. By the way, Lila called it to my attention about fifteen minutes ago. I hadn't even opened the paper."

Scarlett looked at Jake. "Is that the insurance executive?"

"Only Lila I know."

"She wanted to know who Scarlett is," Liz said, her eyebrows raised forming a mischievous expression.

"Did she now? And you told her?"

"I said she is a new investigator with the agency."

Jake nodded while Scarlett cut her eyes back and forth between the two.

"And her response?" he asked.

"She said, 'Business must be good.' Moving on. You've got a stack of phone messages to address on your desk, and your inbox is bursting at the seams. Do you have time today to review them and separate those I can handle for you?"

"Yep. There's nothing we can do on the Johnson case until we meet with Kirby. I hope that'll be tomorrow."

Scarlett spent most of the day screening requests for services and doing intakes on those fitting Jake's criteria. However, as instructed, she informed those she considered appropriate that Jake would have the final say on acceptance. Some she set up for office interviews and some for telephone consultations.

Jake remained in his office, working on files. At four-thirty, Liz buzzed him and said Deke Weston was on the line. A couple of minutes later, he appeared at Scarlett's door. "Arnold is in DC. They will be interrogating her as soon as an attorney is assigned, which could be anytime. Close up what you're doing, and we'll head over to the Field Office."

A wave of exhilaration flowed through Scarlett, despite Jake's pessimism about Xenia Arnold revealing any worthwhile information, much less a confession. *I can't help hoping.* She gathered up her purse, tablet, and jacket and then met Jake at Liz's desk.

"Liz is giving Kai a ride home. Better let her feed your cats. No way to know how late we'll be."

"Do you mind?" Scarlett said.

"Of course not. One of you call me if anything exciting surfaces."

Jake gave her a thumbs-up.

Thirty minutes later, they sat in the conference room of the FBI Field Office, waiting for word on the Arnold interrogation and for the agents to bring them new information.

Deke Weston arrived first, shook hands with Jake, greeted Scarlett, and took a seat at the table.

"How was the ride with Ms. Arnold?"

"Colorful, to say the least. If we weren't Federal Agents, and she had not been handcuffed, we'd probably been thrown off the plane. That one is hell on wheels with a mouth that makes me blush. I hear Kirby gave you some press."

"A shock, for sure."

"I think he had a King David moment when you came out of the helicopter. He realized if you missed the roof, you could easily be in the crosshairs of Arnold's weapon, which could look dicey, considering who his wife happens to be."

"Yeah, but our dirty little triangle is yesterday's news."

"Don't underestimate the court of public opinion, plus he would have to face your daughter. By the way, a computer and three disposable phones were found in the search. The computer wasn't password protected and appears to have belonged to the Powell family."

"Was anything found that would show where the suspects traveled?"

"The van was a pigpen. The evidence crew bagged all the trash as well as trash found in the house. Rollins is having it packaged and sent up here for us to sort. The electronics and weapons came with me. Our lab is running the ballistics." Weston glanced through the glass entry. "Here comes Kirby and Fran Silverstein."

"Shepherd, Ms. Kavanagh," Kirby said as he passed by Jake and Scarlett on his way to the head of the table. "You remember Agent Silverstein."

Jake and Scarlett nodded as the analyst took a seat on the opposite side of the table, a chair separating her from Weston.

"Is the newbie coming?" Jake asked.

"No. He's doing paperwork. Weston can fill him in. Let's get down to it. While ballistics hasn't given us a report yet, Weston probably told you we have a computer that is definitely the one taken from the Powell house during the home invasion. Certainly puts a bow on adding that felony to Ms. Arnold's growing list of charges. Whether she pulled the trigger or not in the death of Powell, she's got a problem."

"Weston said three phones turned up. Has any data been lifted?"

"Silverstein, want to tell Shepherd where we are with that?"

"So far, the one Xenia Arnold used on Sunday has little stored information. We're tracking the numbers she called and those she received, but there's not much. It looks like she primarily communicated with Thomas. The other two appear to be his and contain a significant amount of data—texts messages in and out, plus voice mail—we haven't found email accounts yet."

"Have you traced where they were purchased and when?" Jake asked.

"It's in the works."

"I suspect they tossed a few disposables, but maybe you can pick up locations from the past two weeks. I know we're looking for that needle, but even though they did not use traditional accounts, with a little luck, we might be able to trace their route," Jake said.

"What's your idea on that, Shepherd?"

"If the trash yields any evidence of places they may have been, that will be great. But it appears they played musical chairs with vehicles. That suggests they were frequently stealing new transportation."

"So?"

"I don't think Jeb was that slick a car thief. Armed robbery and drug deals are more his style. He might pull off one or two, but without experience in that department, he would risk getting caught. Also, from what we've seen, they used specific vehicles—vans and SUVs. I suspect that's because they avoided motels as much as possible. Probably didn't even stay in the Silver Spring one—just used the parking lot. No motels to pay or risk leaving a trail on surveillance cameras."

"So, what are you saying Thomas did? Order stolen cars on Amazon?"

"The gangland equivalent. He communicated ahead to gang members with his order. With the reach of that gang, it should have been easy to acquire whatever he requested. In order to do that, he likely used one of those phones."

Scarlett stared at Jake as he spoke, occasionally glancing toward Kirby to check his reaction.

"Trace where and when the calls or texts were sent, and you should be able to build a map of their journey," Jake said. "Jeb never used his phone to contact anyone we would be checking, so he was not concerned about trying to dispose of it. He probably believed it would never pop up on anyone's radar."

"Damn, Shepherd. I like your theory," said Weston.

"I agree it would narrow the search," Kirby said, twirling a pen between his fingers, "but we'd still be looking at a lot of ground to cover with no knowledge of where they left the little girl."

Jake nodded. "True. But they abandoned every vehicle. There should be one in most every location where a fresh one was stolen. While you may or may not track where they went for the next vehicle by Jeb's phone records, you can most likely check where they had been by the stolen ones left behind. You have the last one. Work back from there. Also, pair up the calls with police records for thefts of Thomas's vehicles-of-choice and put out BOLOs for all of those matching the description—even if they've been returned to owners. Have them retained in custody, pending forensic examination. We've already seen that Thomas and Arnold were not diligent in cleaning up what they left behind with the exception of a crime scene."

"I think you've got your assignment, Silverstein," Kirby said. "Keep me up with everything your team finds."

"Yes, sir."

"And you'll brief me?" Jake said.

"Weston will keep you in the loop." With that, Hal Kirby stood. "That should cover it for today. I'll push all our people. Too much time has slipped through our hands since that child went missing."

As the conference room door closed behind Kirby and Silverstein, Jake glanced toward Deke Weston, eyebrows raised. "Back to the old Kirby we know and can't love. Putting the fence up between us."

"Don't you prefer it that way?"

"Affirmative. Give me a call if you interrogate Arnold."

"Good thing she can't hire Madison."

"Even if he wasn't representing her sister, Xenia doesn't fit his client profile. He prefers a *pro bono* client to be innocent."

"Sounds like someone else I know."

Wednesday and most of Thursday passed with only a failed interrogation attempt made of Xenia. As expected, she asserted the Fifth
Amendment on every question presented. Shortly before lunch on
Thursday, the ballistic report came in with a finding that a second
semi-automatic Smith and Wesson matched the bullet that killed Jerome Powell.

"The State Attorney in Florida will have a challenge building a
murder case against Arnold," Jake said to Scarlett when he received
the report from Deke Weston. "I doubt if she will accept a plea.
Putting that gun in her hand will be difficult. Deke said the prints and
DNA on the murder weapon belonged to Thomas."

"He probably killed Jessica's father. I don't think Xenia is the
tough cookie she wants to be," Scarlett said. "Should I tell Jessica?"

Jake looked at her. "You don't think Arnold is a hardass?"

"I think she bluffs some of that steel exterior. She gave up when
you had her pinned in a corner. At the end of the day, she didn't want
to die. Didn't that surprise you a little?"

"I suppose it did. Sure made an easier end to the standoff. As for
Jessica, you can tell her any of this. Just don't go into the process we
hope will pinpoint where Faith may be."

"She deserves to hear something from us."

He walked into the break room with Scarlett following. "She will
in time. Want a soda?"

"Thank you, but I'll wait until our lunch arrives. Is there anything
else I can tell Jessica? This waiting is tedious for me. I can only imagine what it is for her. Silence from all of us has to be unbearable."

"We're doing the best we can. If you give her too much hope, bad news will come harder. If you show pessimism—well, you know how that would affect her."

"Colleen is entitled to know about Jeb Thomas and the murder weapon."

"She is. I'm sure Jacksonville will let her know."

Kai started for the reception area with a muffled growl.

"Food must be here," Jake said. "Easy, boy."

At one-forty, Jake's cell pinged. Liz had excused herself, and Scarlett was about to return to her office. Glancing down at the screen, Jake said, "It's Weston." He opened the call. "What's up? You're on speaker. Scarlett's with me."

"That's fine. Something has come up we thought you'd want to know."

"Don't keep me in suspense."

"We received notice about an hour ago that some hikers in Tennessee discovered what appears to be the remains of a female child of the approximate age and description, taking into account decomposition, of our missing girl."

Jake's face went from relaxed to serious in seconds. Scarlett curled her lips with shock and anguish covering hers.

"I'm assuming this is preliminary with nothing to prove the identification."

"Right. We just thought we'd give you a heads-up. Because of the decomposition, it's going to take a DNA analysis to come up with a positive."

"Any idea as to time of death?" Jake asked.

"Only a preliminary. The ME estimated at least two weeks, which unfortunately puts it within our time frame."

"What about your tracking of the suspects? Any sign they were in Tennessee?"

"Not yet. Since we don't have a positive ID, nor evidence putting the suspects in proximity, we're not notifying the mother at this point. We'll leave it up to you and Madison to make that call."

"Keep me posted."

"Ten-four."

"Damn," Jake said as he clicked off the call and glanced over toward Scarlett.

She had sat back down at the table and dropped her face into her hands.

From his end of the table, he could see Scarlett's phone lying on the surface in front of her. He stood and walked over. "You okay, Harvard?" Looking down, he saw Faith's image on the screen. "Scarlett, we don't know it's Faith."

She sniffled, shaking her head. "All of you said there's hardly any chance she's still alive. It isn't fair. She was just a little girl—so innocent."

He turned the phone over, took her hand, and pulled her up, encompassing her with his arms. "We don't know she's dead."

"Eighty percent. That's what you said. Kirby said even less."

"Forget what we said. There is still hope."

"What good was everything we did if she's dead?"

Liz appeared in the doorway. Jake looked up and saw her. "They found remains of a child, possibly matching the description of Faith Johnson."

Compassion filled the former FBI analyst's eyes. "I'm so sorry. But do I understand they have not made a positive ID?"

"Right."

Scarlett pulled away from Jake's embrace, went to the sink, and wet a paper towel. Dabbing her eyes, she said, "Even if it's not Faith, it's somebody's little girl. Some despicable, evil monster took her life and destroyed the lives of those who love her."

"She's right. But let's continue to pray it's not Faith," Liz said.

Still standing over the sink, facing the wall, Scarlett said, "I won't be able to tell Jessica. I just won't."

Jake walked over and put his hands on her shoulders while Liz watched. "You won't have to. The notification will be Kirby's responsibility if it happens. We'll be there, and we'll make sure McKay and her priest are too." He turned her around and gently brushed a stray lock of hair from her forehead. "Put it out of your mind for now. There's no use in tormenting yourself when we don't know." He pulled her close.

"I'm sorry I'm such a weakling."

Jake chuckled. "You're no weakling, Harvard. What you did in Florida? Ninety-nine percent of the population wouldn't have the guts to do. I get it. You're a compassionate soul. No need to apologize."

She pulled back. "Thanks. I'm fine now. We'll wait."

On Friday morning, Scarlett and Jake drove to the FBI Field Office again to meet with the team. When they arrived, Kirby, Weston, Bush, and Silverstein were settled around the conference table.

"Have a seat, Jake—Ms. Kavanagh." Kirby motioned toward two empty chairs.

"Any new developments?" Jake said.

"We've made some progress on tracking the stolen vehicles Thomas and Arnold used. However, Tennessee is dragging their feet on the DNA of the murdered child."

Scarlett exhaled a sigh of relief.

"So, what's the progress?" Jake asked.

"We found on the van, confiscated in Florida, that Thomas used the GPS. He either didn't know those devices store data or never considered our finding and connecting them. Following that info, we had the local police check the vehicle abandoned up here after they picked up our missing child. The same. He had used the GPS to travel from North Carolina to Silver Spring. Now, all we need is the vehicle they drove away from Maryland in and hope it has a GPS."

"It hasn't turned up?" Jake said.

"Not yet. With the number of cars in the greater DC area and the number of car thefts, it may take some time."

"How far up the chain have you managed to go, and have they found the child's DNA in any other vehicle?"

"Not as far as I would like. None of the child's DNA in the last vehicle."

"Where in Georgia was that last one stolen?"

"Rome."

"That's in the northwest part of the state," Jake said. He looked down at his phone. They didn't drive directly back to Florida. The route from Maryland to Tallahassee begins midway down the east side and cuts diagonally southwest to Florida. Nowhere near Rome. They were coming from somewhere else."

"Also," Deke Weston said, "it doesn't take four days to travel from here to Georgia."

"What about a timeline?" Jake said. "Silver Spring to Tallahassee looks like a one-day trip—thirteen to fourteen hours. They didn't hit North Georgia for four days. I don't see them sightseeing or visiting friends."

"They obviously went somewhere to discard the child, hopefully not her body," said Kirby.

"We've got to figure out where. It must have been west of here, given the route home."

A knock came at the door. "Sorry to interrupt." The staff member looked at Hal Kirby. "I thought you'd want to know. A call just came in from Detroit PD. They recovered a van that may be one you're looking for."

"Bingo," said Weston.

"Get them on the phone," Kirby said, "and transfer the call in here."

The room went eerily quiet as they all waited for the phone to ring. When it did, Kirby answered, putting it on speaker.

"ASAC Harold Kirby here. Whom am I speaking to?"

"Detective Carol Beech, Detroit PD. I believe we may have a vehicle fitting the description of one you're looking for."

"Tell me what you have?"

"It's a Honda Odyssey. According to the license plate, it was stolen from Washington, DC two weeks ago Sunday."

"Have you done a forensic sweep of it?"

"Not yet. They're working on it now. It was roughed up a bit—local vandalism. Pretty much stripped."

"How about a GPS?"

"Let me check. I know the tires, battery, and contents, if there were any, are gone. May I put you on hold?"

"Do it."

As they waited for an answer, the room remained quiet. Although only five minutes passed, Scarlett felt like it was an hour before the Detective came back on the line.

"ASAC Kirby?"

"Yes. Right here."

"There is a navigation system in the vehicle, and it appears undamaged. I'm guessing you want data from it, but I don't have anyone in the station with that ability at the moment. I will call in a tech and send you a report. Will we need to remove the device for evidentiary purposes?"

"Yes, to all your queries. I'll have my people secure a warrant for the device. I appreciate your cooperation in this matter."

"I'm very happy to assist. I understand this involves a missing child of tender years."

"Correct. So, you understand time is of the essence. Also, we would like a report on any DNA captured by your evidence recovery people. We'll be in touch." Terminating the call, Kirby turned toward Jake. "Getting closer, Shepherd. Getting closer."

"Too bad we don't know when the vehicle reached Detroit, but maybe the report will show where it had been. The child's DNA should be in that van. The question is . . . would it be in the next set of stolen wheels? I believe this info answers the question about why the last van was stolen in Rome, Georgia. Look at this map of driving directions from Detroit to Tallahassee. Takes you very close to Rome." Jake held up his phone, followed by Silverstein holding up her tablet with the same map."

Kirby closed the leather portfolio on the table in front of him. "Unless someone has questions or more to add, I think we'll stop here and reconvene this afternoon. Maybe by that time, we'll have more data from Detroit." He looked down at his watch. "Say two-thirty. Anyone have a problem with that?"

Everyone present shook their heads.

"Good. Bush, take care of the warrant for that GPS."

Jake and Scarlett were back in the FBI conference room at two-fifteen. Weston, Kirby, Bush, and Silverstein walked in at two twenty-five.

"Bad news. Data on the Detroit vehicle's GIS had been erased. They're sending it, and we'll have our techs see if there's any possibility of recovering data, but it'll take time."

"I don't believe the body found in Tennessee is Faith," Jake said.

"That's interesting," Kirby said. "Care to share what you base your theory on?"

"Decomp. As I understand, the ME set approximate time of death for the Monday of the abduction. We've pretty well established Thomas and Arnold weren't in Tennessee until several days later. They would not likely transport the child's corpse that far before dumping it. We know they were in Detroit. What better place to dump a body than Lake Erie?"

Deke Weston nodded. "Jake's got something there. Of course, the DNA results will prove or disprove his theory."

"Question is: Where were the suspects between Maryland and Michigan? If it wasn't part of a route, why would they travel to Michigan?"

"It's on the Canadian border," Silverstein said.

"Exactly," Jake said. "What would stall a search more than transporting the child across a border? Have any bulletins gone out to Canada?"

"Not yet. Nor have they gone out to Mexico or Europe," Kirby said.

"Wait a minute," Scarlett said, her eyes lighting up. "When I was in the Thomas bathroom, there was some laundry hanging on the shower rod as if the items had been washed and hung to dry."

Jake looked at her quizzically.

"What does that suggest to you, Ms. Kavanagh?" Kirby asked.

"I was under a lot of stress at the time and trying to get a message to you, but something about one of the tee shirts resonated with me. Like it was familiar. Is there any way to get a photo of it? Did they take any of Xenia's clothes out of the house?"

"I'm still not following you, Ms. Kavanagh."

"Hold on. Let me text my sister." Scarlett took her phone from an outside pocket on her purse and sent Grace Burton a text while the group watched.

"Kirby," Jake said. "Reach out to Rollins and ask if they took clothing from the house."

Kirby gave him a puzzled look.

"If Scarlett thinks it is important, I'm going along with her. What did the shirt look like?"

"It was tan or pale yellow. There was a black dog and a rabbit. The caption read 'Canadian Hare of the Dog.'"

Without a word, Deke Weston took out his phone and made a call to Clive Rollins before Kirby could respond.

"This is Special Agent Deacon Weston, DC Field Office. Put me through to Rollins ASAP." The group turned their focus to Weston.

"Hey, Rollins. What's the status of Arnold's clothing and personal items left in the Thomas house?" His eyebrows went up. "Fantastic. Have someone dig out a tee shirt that was hanging in the bathroom. Hold on. I'll let Ms. Kavanagh describe what we're looking for." He held the phone out to Scarlett.

"The shirt is light yellowish-brown and has a black dog walking a white rabbit with a caption that says, 'Canadian Hare of Dog.'"

Pulling the phone back, Weston said, "Got that? Good. I'll hold. If you find it, text me a photo."

Scarlett's phone pinged. Glancing down, she said, "Here. Look at these. These are the tee shirts my sister's family brought back from their vacation to Canada a year ago. The second one is like the one I saw in the bathroom."

"And," Kirby said.

"Are you asleep at the wheel, Kirby?" Jake said. "This connects Arnold to Canada. Where in Canada did your family buy the shirts? Do you know?"

"Toronto. Look at the shirt. It has 'Toronto' written over the artwork."

"Bingo. Somebody with a tablet handy pull up a map," Jake said. "Run directions from Toronto to Tallahassee. I'm betting you'll slide right through Detroit."

"He's right," Silverstein said. "Look." She held up her iPad.

Without waiting to hear from Rollins, Kirby buzzed his assistant and instructed him to get someone up the chain of command at the Toronto Police Service on the line. Within three minutes, Kirby received notice a Deputy Chief was on the line.

"Chief, this Hal Kirby, Assistant Special Agent in Charge at the FBI Field Office in Washington, DC. We need your help. We have a missing five-year-old child, abducted from her school in Maryland nineteen days ago. We identified the abductors, arrested one, and the other was killed in the course of the arrest. However, the suspect in custody refuses to talk, and the child is still missing. Today, it has come to our attention that the suspects likely visited your area shortly after the abduction. Can you check your files for any possible matches and, if none, alert other agencies in Ontario as to our search?" He nodded to the group.

As Kirby spoke, Weston's phone pinged. Motioning to Scarlett to share her photos, he compared them with ones just received from Rollins. Nodding, he mouthed, "It's a match," and held the two phones up for Kirby to see.

"Great!" Kirby said into the phone. "I knew we could count on your cooperation. No. Unfortunately, we have no info pinpointing where they may have stayed or otherwise conducted business in your area, other than the purchase of a souvenir tee shirt. Thank you for your help. I'll have my assistant forward you a description and photos of the child."

As he hung up, he turned to Bush, "Go tell Charlie to take care of sending the images and description forthwith." Turning back to the group, he said, "Who the hell would have thought a tee shirt might lead us to that little girl?"

"Take your clues where you find them," Jake said. "If it's okay with you, we'll hang around in case you hear back from Canada."

"As you please."

CHAPTER FORTY-SIX

The afternoon drug on as Jake and Scarlett killed time, hoping Kirby's phone would ring with news. At four-thirty, they took a brief break for Jake to get a cup of coffee. As they sat down in a coffee shop, Scarlett said, "I want to hear, and I don't want to hear."

"Afraid it will be bad news?"

"Exactly. I guess it could be one of three answers. They have Faith, and she's fine; they don't have any information; or—you know the or."

"What do you want me to say? Whatever the answer, we have to deal with it." As he was about to take a sip of coffee, his phone pinged, indicating an incoming text.

You'll want to get back up here.

Kirby's on the phone with Toronto.

"Let's go." He took one more gulp of the coffee as he stood, almost spilling it. "Kirby's gotten a call."

When they reached the elevator, Jake punched the "UP" button. When it didn't respond immediately, he hammered it. The ride up seemed endless to Scarlett. Neither spoke as if afraid to jinx the news they would receive.

Once on Kirby's floor, they rushed through the pool of desks to Kirby's office. Deke stood by the door. As Kirby hung up, Scarlett held her breath.

"They may have our girl."

Jake jerked forward. "Damn. Alive?"

Kirby gave a thumbs-up.

"Are they sure?"

Scarlett felt tears flooding her face.

"No. But it looks good. A Children's Aid Society in Toronto has a little girl in custody, matching Faith Johnson's description and the photos we sent. The child was found wandering alone in a large Toronto shopping mall the day after Faith was abducted. They are recommending we bring the mother for a positive ID. Think you all can handle it?"

"Hell, yes. We can handle it."

"Is there any possibility that it's not Faith?" Scarlett asked. "I can't think of anything worse than for Jessica to have her hopes up."

Hal Kirby nodded. "I agree, but I think the odds are in her favor. They are emailing photos."

"Maybe Ted McKay can arrange a private plane," Scarlett said.

"If he hesitates, I'm sure Phil will spring for one more."

"Weston can either go with you, if you charter, or fly on the government dime and meet you there. He will be collecting evidence on behalf of the Bureau to be used in Arnold's case. While I'm sure you could do the same, Shepherd, occasionally, it's better if we do our job."

"How are you handling the official notification?"

"Deke and I will go on behalf of the Bureau. We'll meet you and Scarlett. By the way, where is Ms. Johnson?"

Jake smiled, picked up a pad from Kirby's desk, and wrote down the address.

"What about Ted McKay?" Scarlett asked. "I know he would want to be there with Jessica."

"I'll call him," Jake said.

"He'll want to know what's going on, and it will give us a chance to ask him about a charter," she said. "Oh, but we can't tell him before Jessica finds out."

"Don't worry about that. Jake can handle it. By now, you should know he's the master of avoidance," Weston said.

She laughed. "You're right."

An hour later, the two vehicles pulled into the drive of the safe house behind Ted McKay's Jaguar. After the quartette exited, Kirby led the procession to the front door. When McKay answered, Jessica stood behind him, a terrified expression on her face.

"May we come in?" Kirby said.

The veins in McKay's forehead popped from the tension in his facial muscles.

"We are not the bearers of bad news. So please relax," Kirby said.

Scarlett walked over to Jessica, a slight smile on her face, glancing over to the archway to the dining room where Colleen Powell stood.

"We have reason to believe Faith is in Canada, Toronto, in the care of a Children's Aid Society," Kirby said. He opened his portfolio and withdrew three photographs. "Look at these and tell me if you believe this is Faith."

Jessica's hand shook as she took the photos; her other hand covered her mouth. When she smiled, a collective sigh of relief went around the room as all faces lit up.

Jessica's pupils dilated as she sucked in a breath and then said, "Yes. Yes. That's Faith. Oh, my god. That's Faith."

Chills brought the hair on Scarlett's arms erect as Jessica turned and hugged her, the happy mother's tears soaking Scarlett's blouse.

"Thank you. Thank you all. It's Faith. She's alive. Thank you, God. How can I bring her home?"

Colleen stepped forward, looked at the photos, and wrapped her arms around Jessica's shoulders.

"Yes, Agent Kirby. What is the procedure? How does Jessica get Faith home?" McKay said.

"An official identification will have to be made. The Toronto police recommend that Ms. Johnson fly to Toronto with any documentation proving Faith is her child. If a private flight can be arranged, Agent Weston, Shepherd, and Ms. Kavanagh would like to accompany her."

"I can take care of that. I'm calling my secretary." He pulled a cell out of his pocket. "She'll set it up immediately."

It was after eleven p.m. when the group arrived at their Toronto destination. Faith was curled up asleep on the couch of a private office while a social worker sat nearby. Weston provided officials with documentation while Jessica stood paralyzed in the doorway, staring at her child, tears flowing down her face. When the social worker realized who Jessica was, she gently nudged Faith, who simply stretched but did not open her eyes.

"Faith? Your mom is here," the woman said.

Suddenly the child's head popped up. When she saw Jessica, she screamed, "Mommy!" and flew to Jessica. "You're not dead."

Standing several feet behind Jessica, tears again came to Scarlett's eyes, and without awareness, she reached for Jake's hand. McKay, who had a hand on Colleen Powell's shoulder, was noticeably moved by the scene. As Scarlett looked at Jake, she could tell the scene affected him as well.

Weston had not accompanied them to the office but remained with officials to collect all information available on the circumstances surrounding their finding Faith.

After several minutes of emotional hugging. Jessica said to Faith, "Why did you think I was dead, baby?"

"That lady said you were. She said you were in an accident, and she had to take me where they were nice to orphans. What's an orphan?"

"A little boy or girl who doesn't have a mommy or a daddy. But who was the lady who told you I was dead?"

"I don't know. The man called her Zee like the last letter of the ABCs. She looked like you, but she didn't smell like you."

"And she told you I was dead?"

"Un-huh. She said I couldn't tell anyone my real name, or they would send me back to a terrible place where orphans are treated bad."

Scarlett looked at Jake. "So that's how she kept that child from telling the authorities who she was."

"Young children believe what adults tell them," he said.

"Why, Jake? Why would Xenia take that child and abandon her in a shopping mall?"

"She's a nut case. I'm guessing she wanted to put Jessica's child in the same position her child had been in. It could have been worse—not that there was anything acceptable about what she did. But those remains in Tennessee aren't Faith."

"Oh, my gosh. How right you are."

On the flight back to Washington, Faith slept, her head in her mother's lap. Jessica stayed awake, staring at her daughter while McKay nodded on and off.

Although exhausted, Scarlett found she could not sleep. The exhilaration of the outcome had her nervous system stimulated. In contrast, Jake slept without a problem.

CHAPTER FORTY-SEVEN

When they finally arrived at the apartment building, despite telling herself she would not, Scarlett allowed Jake to spend what remained of the night in her apartment. Even though the emotions of the last day were positive, having him around stabilized her.

On Saturday morning, Jake resumed his routine of going to the gym—although later than usual. While he was gone, Scarlett got up, tended to the cats, and dressed. When he returned to her apartment after his workout and a shower in his apartment, he said, "Let's celebrate with a lavish brunch. I'm starved."

"You're on."

He reached into his pocket and pulled out his wallet. "Need to check my cash to see if I should stop at an ATM." When he opened it, he noticed the lottery tickets purchased in Florida. "Well, look here. I forgot all about these. Got them at that convenience store down south. Want to check and see how much I won?"

"Yeah. Right. Give them to me. Maybe you won enough to redo the office."

He made a face. "What's wrong with the office?"

"Oh, nothing. Nothing a small fortune and a designer with good taste couldn't fix."

"And you wonder why I won't make you a partner?"

While they talked, Scarlett pulled up the Florida Lotto website on her phone. In short order, she said, "Oh, my gosh. You actually won— not the big jackpot. But you've got all but one of the numbers."

"Let me see that." He studied the phone and the winning ticket for a minute. "Damn. Glad I reimbursed the Bureau. What can I do with twenty-five hundred dollars?"

Scarlett snatched the ticket. "I know exactly what we can do with it."

"We? Did I miss something?"

"Let's go. We're going shopping after we eat."

"Where are we doing this shopping?"

"You'll see. It was already on my agenda for today, but you can go half with me with part of your windfall."

"And what are you going to let me do with the rest?"

"Buy your daughter something special."

"Damn. You're as bossy as a wife."

"So, aren't you glad we're not married?"

"More like glad you're not my business partner."

"I will be. You just don't know it yet."

After breakfast, Scarlett used the GPS on her phone to direct Jake to the place she wanted to shop. After she made her purchase, she called Jessica and told her they were dropping by.

"I hope you know what you're doing, Harvard."

"I do."

When Jessica opened the door, Faith stood behind her, along with Colleen. Jessica took one look at what Scarlett held and said, "Oh no. Is that?"

"This is a welcome home gift for Faith." Scarlett extended the fluffy calico kitten toward Faith, who jumped up and down for a second and then gently took the little ball of fur in her arms.

"Is it mine? Really mine?"

"She's all yours."

"Can I keep her, Mommy? Please."

Jessica's chin trembled. "You can keep her, angel." She looked back at Scarlett. "Thank you. Thank you so much." She then hugged Scarlett.

"Jake paid half."

Jessica turned and hugged him as well. "Can you come in? Have a cup of coffee?"

Scarlett smiled. "No. That would be nice, but we have to get to work."

"But it's Saturday."

"Really? Shepherd, did you realize it's Saturday? Aren't we supposed to be off?"

"Not when there's work to be done." He slapped his free hand down on her shoulder. "You're a PI now. No banker's hours."

Scarlett gave him a dirty look while Jessica laughed.

"I don't think I've heard you laugh since we met," Scarlett said.

Jessica smiled. "I wasn't me. But I want to have you and Mr. Shepherd over for dinner soon, if you'll come."

"Of course, we will, but we've got to go now." Scarlett smiled at Faith, who was cradling the kitten and rubbing its fat tummy. Jake reached around Scarlett and dropped a shopping bag with cat supplies on the floor.

"Faith, you need to thank Ms. Kavanagh and Mr. Shepherd."

"Thank you. I love her so much. Thank you."

Scarlett leaned forward toward the happy child and said, "We'll be coming to see you dance in your next recital. Jake's daughter dances at the same studio you do."

As they drove away, Jake said, "I meant to tell you. We're singing at the bar tonight."

"What? No way. I'm not singing. You are."

"You didn't read the fine print in your employment agreement. There's a clause, which says, and I quote, 'At the boss's discretion you sing with him at the bar.' Sorry, Harvard, it goes with the territory."

She slapped his shoulder. "We don't have an employment agreement."

"Careful. I'm driving. And please tell me how two lawyers don't have a formal, legal agreement?"

"Because we don't, and I will not be on the stage with you, Shepherd. I'll be in the audience, applauding you, but not on the stage."

"We'll see." He gave her one of his eye-twinkling, sexy smiles.

She took a deep breath and pushed her hair back with both hands. "What a difference a week makes."

"Indeed, it does. Indeed, it does."

"Maybe I made a mistake, concentrating on my career and not having a child. Even though I've been around both of my sisters with their children, I don't think I've ever fully realized what it's like to be a mother. I almost wish I could have a baby before it's too late."

He reached over and patted her leg. "Hold that thought, Harvard. After we perform tonight, I'll give you some help with that project."

ABOUT THE AUTHOR

JUDITH ERWIN is the award-winning author of eight books, including the Shadow of Dance Series, three standalone novels, and Books 1 and 2 of the Shepherd & Associates Series. She won an FAPA gold medal for *The Studio*, which was also a finalist in the international Reader's Favorite Contest. Her romantic novel, *Shadow of Doubt* was a Royal Palm Literary Awards finalist. A retired attorney and freelance writer, her work has been published in numerous periodicals. A native of Atlanta, Georgia, she lives and writes in North Florida.

Learn more about Judith Erwin and subscribe to her newsletter to receive notice of new releases, giveaways, discounts, recipes, and more at

www.juditherwinofficialwebsite.com

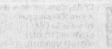

CPSIA information can be obtained
at www.ICGtesting.com
Printed in the USA
LVHW040717141121
703161LV00004B/23